NOEL Forgotten

Nicole Y Hanson

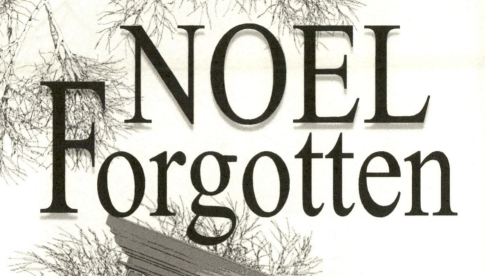

NOEL
Forgotten

Nicole Y Hanson

Content Warning

Please be aware this book contains content, scenes, and references that may be triggering for some readers.

Abduction, alcohol consumption, assault, blood, cheating, death, drugging, drug overdose (only mentioned, no graphic details), foul language, hospitalization, hostage situations, mind-control, manipulation, murder, needles, orphan, physical violence, self-harm, suicide (referenced, no graphic details), sexual harassment, stalking, terminal illness, torture, weapon violence.

For Owen

May you always remember it's never too late to follow
your dreams as long as you are patient enough
to put in the work.

"Remembering everything is not the only solution. Perhaps, forgetfulness can make us live in peace too."

—Mwanandeke Kindembo

1. Escape

The jump into the hole isn't far, and I free-fall before my bare feet splash through icy, shallow water. Its sudden shock, the sensation of landing on pins, shoots its way through my feet and up my legs. A tremor forms at the base of my skull, almost a tickle, until it reverberates into an immense shiver creeping down my neck and spine. I gasp, filling my lungs with frigid air that coats my insides with a burning frost.

Moonlight illuminates me as the dislodged snowflakes trickle down onto my shoulder-length blond hair. My loose, thin gown does nothing to shield me from the bone-chilling February night, and the darkness cloaks everything beyond the white puffs of my breath.

The trek ahead should be impossible, given the circumstances. But the impossible doesn't frighten me. It fuels me, igniting the deep pits of my soul, the parts that have gone dark long ago because of what I had to become, because of what I have lost.

As I rush forward, I drag a palm against the cold, damp concrete wall, hoping there aren't obstacles along the way. The pin-prick-sized hole at my temple throbs with every step. I can still feel the coolness spreading, working its way through my brain, down my spine, through my veins. How long until it takes over and I'm no longer me?

Don't stop.

Keep moving.

Keep fighting.

The blueprints demarcated an exit. I've memorized every inch of this place. Every window, every door, every air duct, every sewer. Beyond that? I don't know. But it led me to this sewer tunnel. There's no telling how long it stretches before stepping into the outside world. I need to escape before they notice I'm missing. My guess is I only have minutes to spare.

I keep jogging. Getting hypothermia is not part of the plan. But as my pulse quickens, the throb on the soft spot of my head heightens, matching its rhythm. The tunnel is silent except for the echoing splashes. Silence is good; they haven't noticed my absence yet.

Sharp tingling shoots up my feet as the water numbs my toes. The tunnel turns right, and ahead is a faint light—not light—moonlight. My heart hammers in my chest. I try to run and falter from involuntary trembling. Every inch of my aching body is telling me to stop, but my willpower is too strong to surrender.

Abandoning all sense, I jog at a steady pace, getting closer with each step. I draw nearer, and a glint of light catches my eye. My knees give out from beneath me when I realize a chain-link barrier stands in the way of my freedom.

"No." I crawl toward the barrier. Panic sets in as I grasp the cold metal and mutter, "No, no, no. This can't be happening."

NOEL Forgotten

Shouting in the distance tells me I'm out of time. I pull myself up and rush my hands over the edges to find any give in the barrier. I've come too far to get caught. A siren wails across the grounds and echoes through the tunnel. My quivering hands slide along the edges, finding a weak spot. I link my fingers through the holes, unable to close them completely, as if they're frozen open. I pull with all my strength—it barely gives. Heart throbbing, teeth chattering, and panic rising, I close my eyes and take a deep breath, willing my body to calm itself.

"I can't go back. I can't go back," I whisper, thinking of the pain, torture, and mind control. I focus on the rage rising deep inside. Rage for twenty-two years of manipulation.

It gives me the focus I need. Heat ignites within my arms as I activate my strength enhancement. NOEL shouldn't have made me strong if they didn't want me to escape. I wrench at the barrier again. It bends and curls inward. The opening is narrow, but I can't waste any more time. I wedge my body through. It takes all my willpower not to scream out as the sharp metal slices deep into my right bicep, followed by a gush of warm liquid. I fall onto my hands and knees and land on the snow-covered ground.

Smears of red stain the snow. Hastily, I rip a strip from the bottom of my gown, wrap it twice around my arm, and tighten it with my teeth. Lightheadedness rushes my head as I stand. Is it from the exertion? From the cold? From the blood loss? Or is it from the serum coursing through my body? Shaking off the feeling, I look back at the large brick building that took away my freedom. Next time I see it, I hope it's crumbling to the ground.

I sprint toward the thicket and hide behind it. Even then, I do not slow despite my blurred vision. Dead branches scrape my exposed arms and legs, but it doesn't hurt, and I realize it's because I'm going numb. Soon, I won't be able to continue. But I must until I make it to safety, until there's no fight left to give.

Shouting pursues me, and flashing lights follow in the distance. I veer to the right to throw them off, but the heavy footsteps keep a steady pace behind me. NOEL made us fast, but speed training was never my strong suit, and running barefoot is no match for the person in traction boots.

A hard force hits my face from the side, lifting me off my feet, and I roll several yards away until my back crashes against the base of a tree. A large silhouette of a man stalks forward as burning gasps struggle to escape me.

I dig around, hoping to find something hard or sharp to hit the figure with, but the only thing is snow and more snow. *Damn.*

The tall burly soldier in black stalks toward me. His ski mask hides the man underneath. Once upon a time, we might have been friends. Once upon a time, he might have been kind. Then NOEL erased his mind and turned him into a killer. Now his void eyes stare at me. No hint of a soul. No chance to show me mercy.

I should be afraid to be captured, beaten, or killed, since that's what they do when you try to escape. They frighten us with their threats—something I didn't realize until my teenage years. Until then, I went with anything they said because it was the only thing I'd ever known. Then they made me smarter, and I knew I had to get out, to escape and see what's beyond the building, beyond the wall, beyond the grasp of NOEL's hold. Little did I know, leaving would never be an option, and trying to escape is suicide.

The soldier closes the distance, and I stand with bare fists up. I will fight with everything I have in me, even if it kills me, because NOEL trained me to fight.

The rest of the world disappears as I focus on the target. Adrenaline courses through me, diminishing the pain, dizziness, and fatigue.

He swings, which I dodge by ducking away. He groans when his fist connects with the tree. I throw a hook at his rib, and he hunches over with a grunt. In one stride, I get behind him and drive my foot to the back of his knee, and he crashes to the ground on all fours.

There's no time for hesitation. I leap onto his back, wrap an arm around his neck, and squeeze with all my might. He struggles against me, flailing his arms around. Grabbing at my arm, he digs a finger into the fresh slash. I yelp, loosening my grip, and it's enough for him to flip me over onto my back.

He wobbles as he stands and gasps. His slow movements are my advantage. I swing my leg around, tripping him. I lunge toward him as he falls, and I pin him to the ground. With my fist, I strike his face once . . . twice . . . three times. His head jerks from side to side. Blood sprays from his nose as I deliver blow after blow. His eyes close and body goes limp, but I keep striking without a clear thought of when I will stop. Maybe until his last breath. Maybe not even then.

A close range of shouts pull me from my manic attack. Flashes of light are within my sight. I search his body for a weapon but come up empty. I should have guessed they'd be unarmed. If Dr. Sheffield wanted me dead, she would have done it three days ago, when she captured me last.

Trees pass in a blur. Shouts recede, and the siren has stopped. Direction and time has abandoned me, and I don't know if I've been running for minutes or hours, but I cannot stop despite my numb feet and burning lungs. I must find somewhere to hide.

Fatigue sets in, and each stride feels forced, like I'm fighting against the current. I chance a glance behind me and see no one following. I turn back ahead, but my foot catches in a log, and I plunge forward. It's as if the world suddenly opened up and swallowed me whole, sending me to the pits of hell. If only I were that lucky. Hell sounds like a vacation compared to where I've been.

I land with a thud, then roll hard and fast down into the ditch. Snow burns my flesh. Fallen sticks tear at my gown and skin. The world swirls in my vision, and I cannot stop, no matter how much I claw at the earth. I tumble and scrape down for what feels like forever.

Each roll sends a wave of shock through me, expelling my breath with each rotation, preventing me from screaming in pain. I roll, thump after thump, and with them, three cracks snap. Once in my ribs, another in my leg, and another to the back of my skull—then I'm still.

I'm no longer falling, yet the snow-covered branches, the moon, and the stars swirl above. The drive to push forward is strong but impossible to do with my injuries. But the impossible fuels me. This can't be the end.

I press into the earth, but the pressure is excruciating and forces me back down. My breathing comes in shallow bursts. Blood saturates the makeshift bandage, dripping down my arm and off my fingertips. Black dots seep into my sight. I'm at the edge of consciousness. The world fades away. Today, the impossible wins.

Is this how it feels to die? I should be scared and defeated, but I'm calm and comfortable. The cold now feels warm, the pain receding. I'm numb, inside and out. If this is the end, then I welcome it with open arms. I gather the only strength I have left to say my last words, although I know no one will hear them.

"I'm sorry I failed," I whisper as the world fades into darkness.

2. United Hospital Center

BEEP—BEEP—BEEP.

I open my eyes to brightness, and I squeeze them shut. Unwavering beeps fill the room. When I open my eyes again, the blurriness makes it difficult to see anything but blobs of colors. I blink until the room comes into focus, but nothing looks familiar.

A woman stands at my bedside, scribbling on a clipboard. The source of the beeping comes from my heart monitor. An IV drip protrudes from the vein in my arm. Something terrible has happened, but I can't remember my name, what happened to me, or how I got here. The thought is unnerving, and the beeps quicken.

My first instinct is to pull out the IV. I reach for it and groan as a sharp pain radiates through my body. A sudden turn from the woman in light-blue scrubs freezes me in place.

"You're awake," she screeches, dropping the clipboard. "Don't move. It'll only make things worse."

222222

I sit up, and dizziness washes over me. I close my eyes and breathe to fight the urge to rest.

"Whoa, whoa." She raises her free hand, palm forward. "You need to relax. We're going to take good care of you. You're safe now." She retrieves a phone from her pocket. "Jane Doe in forty-three eleven is awake." Setting the phone aside, she reaches for a pink cup with a straw. "Here. Drink this. You must be parched."

"Wha . . ." My voice cracks, barely a whisper. I clear my throat. "What is it?"

My voice is unrecognizable, hoarse, and quiet.

"Water, dear," the nurse says. "It's just water."

She holds the straw to my lips. Hesitantly, I sip. Cool water quenches the burn at the back of my throat. I suck in more.

"Not too fast." She pulls the cup away, sets it on a nearby table, then focuses on her clipboard.

I try to make sense of my surroundings. My leg is in a cast, and I have a bandage on my arm. Windows to my left display the night sky with the city lights below. Aside from the nurse, I'm alone in the room. To my right is an open door, and a woman wearing a white coat and a stethoscope around her neck enters.

"You gave us quite a scare. My name is Dr. White. I'm the physician who treated you when you arrived. Do you know where you are?"

It's obvious to me where I am.

"A hospital."

"You are at United Hospital Center in Bridgeport, West Virginia."

My eyes wander over my injuries once more. "What happened to me?"

Her forehead creases slightly. "We're not sure. A paramedic found you unconscious near the ER doors three nights ago." She pauses, looking at me with a raised brow. My face remains impassive. "You lost a lot of blood and had several injuries that needed attention. We didn't think you'd survive the first night." Her tone is professional, but concern lines her eyes.

She waits again and looks at me for any sign that I might explain what happened. I can't. None of this sounds familiar. My face remains catatonic.

Dr. White cocks her head and furrows her brows. "You wore a gown like this. You didn't have identification on you. Can you tell me your name?"

I know Jane Doe isn't my real name. It should be a simple question to answer, but it's not for me.

"I can't remember." Dr. White's eyes widen, and she glances sideways at the nurse. "I can't remember anything," I say matter-of-factly.

I find the situation annoying, even though a normal reaction would be to panic.

"It's typical to experience memory loss after a traumatic event. For now, you need to rest." She instructs the nurse of my follow-up care and exits the room.

The nurse regards me for a moment. "You can call me Nurse Olivia. Can I get you anything right now?" I shake my head. "All right. I'll be back in an hour to check on you. If you need anything, press the Call button on the bed."

I close my eyes to recall some scrap of a memory. Something, anything. But all I know is this room. It's a strange feeling not remembering a single moment, yet I remember words, numbers, and colors. If asked, I could recite all fifty states and their capitols, then take it a step further and spout out the countries in South America. But I can't recall how I learned these things. Not knowing should frighten me, but it doesn't, and that's equally refreshing and disturbing.

The next day, Dr. White arrives after breakfast. "Along with minor cuts and bruises, you have a fractured fibula, two cracked ribs, a collapsed lung, and needed eight stitches in your arm. There's also slight frostbite on your fingers and toes. They should heal nicely. However, I'm concerned about the laceration on your head. I believe it's the cause of your memory loss. Hopefully, it's only temporary." Dr. White removes her glasses. "There is one more thing. A police officer needs a statement."

"How can I give a statement if I can't remember my name?"

My words come out annoyed.

Dr. White holds up a hand to stop me. "For now, he only needs your picture and description."

I clutch the bedsheets and stare out the window. The sun beats down, melting the icicles, and I breathe to the sound of the drips before muttering, "I don't even know what I look like."

Dr. White regards me for a moment before opening a drawer and producing a handheld mirror for me. As I stare at my reflection, a part of me hoped seeing myself would jog my memory, but the girl staring back is a stranger. Paper-thin cuts line my forehead and cheeks. A greenish-blue bruise tints my jaw. Deep sea-green eyes—like the color when the sun hits the water just right, reflecting a hint of yellow—stare back at me, revealing pain and loss.

I hand the mirror back to Dr. White. "Thank you."

Dr. White waves at the middle-aged, balding officer, who doesn't bother to look up from his phone as he enters. He taps away at the screen. His heavy breathing makes me think he doesn't want to be here anymore than I do.

Without so much of a warning, he holds the phone in my direction, snaps a picture, then shoves the phone into his pocket.

He and Dr. White converse about other hospitals in the area. She asks him if any patients are missing, and he reassures her everyone's accounted for. Dr. White tells him the details of my description, and he jots the information on a notepad. I'm sure he'll have no problem finding out who I am. How many missing twenty-two-year-old, blond-haired, green-eyed, white females who are five three and one hundred thirty-five pounds can there be? There can't be that many. Right?

As Dr. White tells him the details, he only looks at her. Never once does he acknowledge my existence. Is that who I am now? Nobody? I don't have a name. No one knows who I am. So, are they going to treat me as if I'm no one? As if I don't matter?

"I think I have everything I need." He turns to walk away.

"Excuse me, Officer?" I ask before he leaves. "What happens now?"

"Now, we put your information out there and hope someone recognizes you." He leaves the room before I can ask any more questions.

My grip unclenches the sheets I didn't realize I had been holding. I inhale a long breath and close my eyes.

Dr. White approaches my bedside. She listens to my heart with a stethoscope, then types on a laptop. "I also arranged for a psychologist to help you with the trauma you endured."

"Is it still trauma if I can't remember it?"

"Yes." She closes the laptop. "He might help you get your memories back."

"When is he coming?"

"Day after tomorrow. I think you've had enough excitement for today. You still need your rest." She glares and points, and I roll my eyes.

***

Two days later, scans and blood tests fill the morning. Most of the pain has subsided, aside from my ribs. I still wince whenever I stretch. I've just settled into my bed when Dr. White enters.

"Let's see if your test results are in, shall we?"

Nurse Olivia walks into the room, distracting me. A custodian enters behind her, pushing a cart of cleaning supplies. He keeps his head lowered, as if he doesn't want to be noticed. The hem of his blue jumpsuit is above his ankles. He's tall and muscular—not the typical physique of a custodian—and I wonder if they didn't have a jumpsuit to fit him.

"The bathroom is behind the door, and the garbage is in the corner," Nurse Olivia instructs.

Remaining silent, he empties the garbage. She rolls her eyes and stands next to Dr. White. I keep my attention on the custodian who doesn't look over or speak. The last custodian was older and friendlier. He greeted me with a smile and told me about his wife and kids. This one is younger but quiet. If only I could see his face, I might sense something from him. Does he have kind eyes, or is he the type of man I should steer clear of?

"Everything is healing as it should be," Dr. White assures me, pulling me from the distraction of the custodian. "In fact, better than it should be." She scrolls through the results on her laptop. "Blood work came back normal. Your vitals are great, and your head injury is almost healed. No bleeding or swelling."

My hands clench into fists. "Then, why can't I remember anything?"

The words come out more aggressively than I mean them to.

Dr. White lowers her gaze. "I know it's frustrating, but this is a good sign. It means there's nothing wrong with your brain, only the memories. They may come back."

"May?" I shake my head. "Does that mean I may never remember?"

Dr. White leans forward on the bed. "I don't want to lie to you. It's hard to say if you'll get your memories back. If there were an injury, it would explain the memory loss. Without the injury, it's hard to say why you have amnesia."

I close my eyes and take a deep breath. I thought I would wake up one day, and my memories would flood back. Without these memories, I'm an unfinished puzzle with a piece missing.

"There's still hope," Dr. White assures me. "The psychologist will be in shortly. Your amnesia isn't from anything medical but may be from something emotional."

"Like I repressed it all or something?"

"Possibly. You were in terrible shape when we found you. Something traumatic happened. He can help." Dr. White gives my hand a small squeeze, then she and Nurse Olivia exits.

It's as if I'm grieving the loss of myself. Stage one is denial. I can check that one off the list. Which takes me to stage two—anger. It burns inside of me. What I want to do is punch something, but I'm bedbound.

I grab the closest thing to me and hurl it across the room with a growl. The custodian exits the bathroom as the cup slams against the wall, splashing water onto his undersized jumpsuit. It doesn't startle him. Instead, he picks it up and wipes the water with a towel.

"Oh my gosh." Heat rushes to my cheeks, and I cover my mouth with my hand. "I'm so sorry. I didn't know you were still here."

"Don't worry about it," he mumbles, keeping his head down while he cleans the mess.

"Thank you!"

I hope he'll turn my way so I can catch a glimpse, but he doesn't. He only touches the brim of his hat and nods as he leaves.

A moment later, a man stands in the doorway, knocks twice, and asks in a gentle voice, "May I come in?"

He has a full head of neatly groomed dark brown hair. It makes him appear younger than he is. The only hints that he's middle-aged are the silver flecks framing his ears, the crease across his forehead, and the crow's feet of wrinkles protruding from the outer corner of his eyes. Evident signs of his life, full of worry, full of laughter.

He strides to my bed. "I'm Dr. Wagner, a psychologist. It's nice to meet you." He holds his hand out, and I shake it. Dr. Wagner sits in a chair and puts on a pair of square-framed glasses. He opens a leather-bound notebook, clicks the end of a pen, then scribbles away at the paper. "I've read your chart. You are one tough gal."

"Sure, I guess."

"I understand you don't remember your name."

"I can't remember anything before I woke up."

"Is there a name you want to use?"

No one has asked me that question. It wasn't something I had considered. This is my chance to be anyone I want, but I can only think of one name.

"Jane."

"Jane?" His head cocks to the side, and he stares momentarily. "I like it. It suits you." The pen touches the paper once again, but this time, I see what's written—my new name in all caps at the top of the page. "All right, Jane. Tell me how you're feeling."

"Better, I guess." He nods, waiting with raised eyebrows, and I realize he doesn't mean physically. "I threw a cup at the wall a few minutes ago," I mumble.

"How come?"

"I was angry."

"What angered you?"

I look away and shake my head. "Dr. White says my brain is fine. Which means the amnesia has nothing to do with my head injury."

"I can understand why that would anger you. My job is to help you cope with all of this."

Dr. Wagner encourages me to recall every emotion I've had since I woke up. Through it all, he keeps eye contact. When it's his turn to speak, he talks to me like I'm a real person and doesn't treat me like the cop did—like I'm fragile or unimportant. He treats me as his equal.

"Jane"—Dr. Wagner flips a page in his notebook—"I know you said you can't remember, but do you remember anything at all? A certain sound or smell? Any small detail?"

"I've tried to remember, but it's all blank."

"Let's try something different. Tell me every detail of your first memory."

I recite every detail I can remember about that first day, from the beeps of the monitor to the conversation with Dr. White. Dr. Wagner writes in his notebook as I tell him what I heard, what I smelled, what I saw, every small detail.

He looks up from his notebook. "You did great. That was *very* detailed. I think it's safe to say you have no problem with your current memory. I'll have to run more tests to confirm, but I think you have a photographic memory."

I laugh but stop when he doesn't laugh with me. "What . . . no . . . I can't . . . I mean . . ." I look at my hands, then the wall, then the door. Finally, I look back at Dr. Wagner, and his face shows only patience. "How can I have amnesia with a photographic memory?"

"The brain is a miraculous thing."

"So miraculous I'll get the rest back?"

He sighs. "I don't know, but I'll try. We'll need to talk about anything and everything. Nothing is off the table. One small thing can trigger a memory. If you're willing to keep me as your psychologist, I will do everything in my power to help you remember."

"I have a choice?"

"Of course you do. You can choose someone different or no one at all. This is your life. You get to choose whether or not you want to remember."

I don't want to make the wrong choice. Do I want to remember and relive whatever terrible thing happened to me? Or do I want to move on and be someone else? A strain of a feeling hasn't gone away, no matter how hard I try to suppress it. A strain so small, yet it consumes me, one I need to know, that I need to remember.

I sit up a little straighter. The cast pins the blanket to the bed, dragging it away from my body. "I want you to help me remember."

He smiles. "Then, I will." He stands and stretches out his hand. "It was nice to meet you, Jane. I'll come back tomorrow, and we can talk more."

I shake his hand before he leaves. It's the first time someone's addressed me as a person. Such a minor detail yet so significant. I'm not merely a patient occupying a hospital bed. I'm a person with thoughts, feelings, and a past. A past Dr. Wagner wants to help me remember.

***

Days turn into weeks. Snow melts, and buds form on the trees. I insist everyone calls me Jane. They remove my cast after five weeks and require me to take physical therapy three times a week. It only takes three sessions for me to walk without assistance, but they want me to continue to build strength.

Dr. Wagner visits almost every day. He tells me it's necessary to work through the trauma. I still can't remember, but he's hopeful.

Once the tests and therapy are over, I'm left to spend the day as I please, roaming the halls and visiting the shops. It's thrilling, the things I hear and see when there's not much else to do. I hear stories of people's personal lives. I see the joy from births or the sorrow from deaths. I laugh, smile, and cry with these strangers, but I resent them because I'm merely a spectator yearning for those experiences and emotions. To have someone here holding my hand and telling me everything's going to be okay.

I stare out the room's window. Buds have bloomed, and the grass is a little greener. Trees have sprouted leaves that sway with the wind. I press my cheek to the glass, imagining the breeze against my face. When Dr. White enters my room, I break away.

"I have some good news. You get to go home tomorrow."

My shoulders slump forward. "I don't have a home to go to."

"I know this is hard, but I have better news." A hint of excitement elevates her voice. "Someone heard your story. They paid for six months of rent for a house here in Bridgeport. Fully furnished, and the fridge is stocked. It's nothing fancy, but it's somewhere."

"Who would do that?" I ask, bewildered.

"It was an anonymous donor. And the members of the church donated women's clothing for you as well. Now you can wear these instead of scrubs." She sets a bag on the bed. "You will need to continue your weekly PT sessions for your leg, and Dr. Wagner wants to continue meeting twice a week at his office."

Unable to speak, I nod to confirm I understand. She hands me a folder with informational papers and a key to my house.

I knew I would have had to leave eventually, but I imagined it happening far in the future. Now that it's here, I'm mixed with emotions. After tossing the papers onto the bed, I pace the room, but the sudden racing in my chest forces me to lie down. This room always felt big, but as I look out the window, I realize how small it really is. There's more beyond these four walls and the gift shop and the other rooms. An entire world is out there, and I don't know how to live in it. Pulling the blankets over my head, I breathe in gasps.

Minutes later, my heart slows to a normal rate. Then tingles spread throughout my body. I throw off the covers and reach into the bag. I put on the new clothes, and I smile. As I look out the window, the world doesn't seem so big anymore, and hope swells inside of me. I will no longer be a spectator of other's lives. I'll get to live it for myself. There's an adventure out there waiting for me, and I plan to find it.

THREE MONTHS
LATER

3. Secret Ninja Skills

Aloud rattling on my bedside table wakes me from a deep sleep. I feel around for the source of the noise, knocking over a glass cup of water. The cup lands with a clunk, and I brace for its shatter. To my relief, it doesn't come. I blindly feel around until my fingers land on the pulse of a vibrating cell phone. The screen's brightness makes me close my eyes. I swipe my thumb across the glass and hold the phone to my ear.

"Hello?" I answer groggily.

"Where the hell are you?"

The urgency in Trish's tone jolts me awake.

"Shit! I overslept. I'll be there in ten minutes."

I leap out of bed and shuffle around my bedroom, slipping on a puddle of water, then landing on my butt with a loud thud. Grunting in frustration, I stand, go to my closet, and yank my work uniform off the hanger. I dress quickly and run to the bathroom to freshen up.

Last night's makeup stains my face. Smeared lipstick and mascara streaks make it look like I was trying to imitate The Joker. Dried black tears run down my cheeks—which reminds me I spent the non-better half of last night hugging the toilet. The taste of old vomit and tequila makes me gag.

I stare at myself in the mirror, wondering how I got to this point. I've done nothing special since I've lived here because I've accepted that's who I am now. I'm just a plain Jane from Bridgeport, acting as anyone my age does. It's a constant repeat of the same thing over and over. Go to work at the country club. Go to Chubb's bar. Dance a little, drink too much, puke—lather, rinse, repeat.

Then there are the boring times I don't go out, and I'll sit on my porch, reading a book, drinking a cup of tea. My mood is either a twenty-two-year-old party animal or a fifty-year-old widow—there's no in-between.

I leave my face a blank canvas. The white toothpaste turns pink as I forcefully brush my teeth, trying to get the rancid taste out of my mouth. The tumbleweed of knots in my hair makes it impossible to comb through, so I toss it into a messy bun atop my head. Grabbing my phone and purse, I sprint toward the front door.

The disadvantage of not having an identity means I can't get a license. The summer weather makes walking to work bearable, but time is not on my side. A Lyft will take too long to get to my house, so I dash to the Bridgeport Country Club.

I pant as I enter. My shirt clings to my back, courtesy of the humid summer. Trish stands in the kitchen doorway, wearing an identical uniform, and waves me over to her. Her light-brown skin, high cheekbones, and long, curly black hair causes the nearby golfer to stare in her direction. She has that effect on most men, especially the one she went home with last night.

Trish lets out a high-pitched whistle. "That was a close one. How did you get here so fast?"

"I ran." I lean against the bar rail, clutching my side.

Trish crinkles her nose. "You smell like tequila." She leans in and takes a whiff, then leans back. "And vomit."

"Oh, really? You don't say." I roll my eyes. "Remind me never to do tequila shots with you again."

Trish is the only reason I have any sense of sanity left. She befriended me when no one else tried. Doctors saw me as strong and brave, but since I've been out in the real world, people avoid me. For the first month, people would have hushed conversations about me, calling me awkward. As much as I wanted to tell them off, it was best to stay quiet to avoid conflict. It's hard fitting in with others when I have nothing in common with them. Being surrounded by people every day, trying to socialize when I don't understand their lingo, is something else entirely. As much as I want to be seen, in hopes someone will know who I truly am, I am small and invisible. Dr. Wagner says it's culture shock. It would have consumed me if it wasn't for Trish. She makes me feel normal. The alcohol helps, too, helps me to feel something or nothing at all.

Trish hands me a water, and the condensation is refreshing in my sweaty palm. Its coolness flowing down my throat is only a fleeting moment of joy. I toss the bottle in the recycling bin, then tie the apron around my waist. Before I join Trish in the restaurant, I put on a fake smile to pretend I love serving food and drinks to golfers.

***

"That was the longest shift of my life," I say to Trish as we leave.

She pulls her sunglasses to the tip of her nose and looks me in the eye. "Only because you're hungover." She pushes the frames back in place. "A Garfield's burger and a beer will help with that."

"Can't. I have an appointment with Dr. Wagner."

"Hasn't it been long enough? When will the therapy sessions end?"

I roll my eyes and scuff my shoe against the sidewalk. "Probably never."

Lately, I dread going to therapy because it's like I'm falling down a never-ending tunnel, and my memories are at the bottom, which doesn't exist. Every time, Dr. Wagner hopes he'll trigger a memory, but I leave more hopeless.

***

Sitting on a hard chair, I bounce my knee and cross my arms, rubbing my thumb across the raised line on my bicep. Sometimes, feeling the scar calms me. Other times, it's like having a reminder, even if I don't know how it got there. A picture may be worth a thousand words, but my scar is worth a lifetime of memories I'll never get back. But, sometimes, I find peace with that.

Maybe the past is overrated anyway. It couldn't have been that great if no one has come to find me by now. Whoever—if anyone—knows me proves I'm obviously not worth the trouble to find.

A nurse in scrubs enters the lobby. "Jane Doe?" She looks back at the chart with confusion. I think I hear her say "Is this a joke?" but her lips don't move.

I don't recognize her as one of the usual nurses. She must not be familiar with my case.

"That's me." I stand, raising my hand.

"Right." Her cheeks flush pink. "Of course. Dr. Wagner will see you now."

As I enter the open door, Dr. Wagner sits at his desk, fingers hastily tapping at the keyboard. I clear my throat to make my presence known. His eyes peer above black square-framed glasses.

"Jane." He smiles. "I only need one more second. Please, have a seat."

I make my way into the room and sit where I usually do, on the gray sofa.

Moments later, he closes the laptop and sits on the recliner opposite of me. He opens his brown leather-bound notebook and clicks his pen, signaling the start of our session. "Any change in memory since our last visit?"

He always begins with the same question. My answer is always the same.

"Nope."

He sighs. "I'm afraid you may never regain your memories."

I nod in agreement. It doesn't bother me anymore. Two months ago, when the cops stopped following up on my case, I gave up on my memories. No reports in West Virginia of a missing person match my exact description. To the outside world, I'm a ghost. I'm only able to get into bars because my estimated age of twenty-two is public knowledge to the whole town.

"I don't want to give up yet." Dr. Wagner closes his notebook and leans forward in his chair. "Would you be willing to try hypnosis?"

My eyes widen in shock. He must be joking.

"Are you serious?"

"Yes. I am." He holds his hands out in defeat. "I don't know what else to do. It may be your only chance to remember something."

I lean forward at the idea, but I'm not all in. "Is it dangerous?"

"You may experience some discomfort and emotional distraught."

"I don't know." I wrap my arms around myself and lean back onto the couch.

He raises a hand as if to stop my train of thought. "If you change your mind, just say the word." He opens his notebook again and leans back in the chair.

I tell him about work and my wild nights with Trish. He doesn't judge but also looks disapproving of my moderate indulgences. As usual, I leave, feeling hopeless, but the thought of hypnosis hovers in the back of my mind. The thought it might work gives me a sliver of hope.

***

Trish sways to the beat around my bedroom, cocktail in hand. My head bobs with each bump of the bass, causing me to pause between strokes of eyeshadow.

"Hurry up," she shouts as she dances. "We have to get there early if we want a table."

"I'm almost done." I fasten the last strap of my wedged sandal and quickly give myself a once-over in the mirror. My top is too low, and my shorts are too short, but it's modest compared to what other girls wear.

I run a hand through the blond waves that fall past my shoulders. Two weeks ago, I decided on a fresh hairdo for my new identity. I made it all the way to the salon before deciding against it. My description is out there with shoulder-length blond hair, and I thought if I changed it, it would be harder for someone to recognize me.

"All right, let's go," I say.

As we wait outside for a Lyft, Trish surveys the dark empty road, shivering, despite the heat.

"It's kind of creepy out here at night," she says.

I look both ways down the street. "It's not that bad."

"There are literally two houses. Yours and the one across the street." She strains her neck toward the neighbor's house. "Does anyone live there?"

Only one light shines through the second-floor window. Curtains are drawn, but no shadows sway behind. "Yeah. I think so."

Her eyes widen. "You still haven't met your *only* neighbor?"

"Yeah, so?"

"This is Bridgeport. Everyone knows their neighbors."

I shrug. "It's probably an old quiet person who wants their privacy."

"All the more reason to be neighborly," she says matter-of-factly.

It's a quick ride to our favorite bar, Chubb's. Muffled booms echo from the outside. The line is long, but the bouncer lets us in ahead of everyone else—an advantage for being regulars. Groans and complaints come from the people in line.

We enter, and the bass pulsates through my body. I bounce to the beat, letting the music flow through me. We claim an empty table and order our drinks—two Vodka Cranberries.

Trish raises her glass. "To a night I won't remember."

I clink my glass against hers. "With a friend I won't forget."

We each take a sip.

Every night we go out, we start our first drink with the same toast. It's more of an inside joke against my amnesia. Trish is the perfect friend for my situation after her childhood of neglectful parents. Like me, she also has no one else.

"There are a couple of fine guys over there." Trish gives the men a flirtatious stare and winks. One man licks his lips, rubbing his palms together. She turns her attention back to me, ignoring the exchange. It's her tactic to get the guy to approach her. If they don't, they're not worth her time.

She finishes her drink and waves the server over. We order another round and head to the dance floor. Vibrations from the bass radiate through my feet. The effects of the alcohol emerge, tingling in my veins, and I know tonight is the night I drink to feel *something* rather than nothing. We move and bounce to the rhythm of the music until our throats are dry and hair clings to the back of our necks. We retreat to our table to catch our breath and order another round.

After the server sets down our drinks, the two men Trish had her eye on earlier strut toward our table. Trish notices and winks at me. "Works every time."

"I'm Mark," the dark-haired man says. "And this is Julian."

"I'm Trish, and this is Jane," Trish replies without missing a beat.

"Is it okay if we join you?"

"Sure. Have a seat."

Mark sits next to Trish. She hides it well, but I know she's elated. I can't deny his attractiveness. Tanned skin, slicked-back dark hair, brown eyes, and a wide, beaming smile. His defined chest and the top of his abs shine through his unbuttoned silk shirt. The appearance gives off a cocky vibe, like he thinks he's better than everyone in the room. Exactly the type of guy Trish goes for, but she'll hear no judgment from me.

Julian is about the same height, but he's more handsome than Mark. Unlike Mark's ensemble, he's casually dressed. I can tell he works out by the way his shirt hugs his body. I bite my lip at his short, intentionally messy dirty-blond hair. It's hard not to notice his defined jawline with slight stubble.

Julian walks to my side of the table. His hazel eyes meet mine, making my heart flutter, before he quickly looks away. He sits next to me—leaving a comfortable distance between us—with perfect posture. I give him a small smile, and he stares ahead.

Trish and Mark whisper in each other's ears while Julian and I sit in awkward silence.

Trish's beauty and outgoing nature attracts men all the time. She'll talk to them for hours as I sit on the sidelines. It doesn't bother me because I've never found a man enticing enough to pursue. But now one's sitting next to me, handsome as can be, and I don't know what to say.

The server approaches our table. "Anyone want another round?"

I raise my glass and eagerly say, "Please," hoping another drink will calm my nerves. Trish shoots a wide-eyed glare at me, then excuses us to use the restroom.

We stand in front of the mirror, applying more lipstick.

"What's wrong? Why are you just sitting there?" she asks.

"I'm not as social as you." I lean my forehead against the mirror, and when I pull away, a smudge of dried sweat remains. "I don't know how to flirt and make small talk."

Trish places her hands on my shoulders. "Just try. He seems nice. You might like him."

We return to the table, and Mark continues to flirt with Trish. Julian scoots toward the wall, letting me sit on the edge. We watch Mark and Trish flirt, and it's as if we're nonexistent to them. I rub my scar to calm myself.

Julian says something to me, but I can't hear him over the music.

"What?" I yell.

"I said, are you having fun?"

Right as he shouts, the music fades to a softer song. Others look in our direction, and I cower.

"Yeah. Definitely."

I try to sound sincere but end up sounding bored.

"Maybe you'd have more fun if you tried to relax. Or are you worried about something?" Mark raises his eyebrows, as if he's accusing me of something.

"Excuse me?"

"All I'm saying is you need to relax. Might help if you smiled more."

He flashes a smile, but it's not a genuine one or to show he's joking. It's a mocking smile as if to show me how it's done.

Normally, I avoid conflict as much as possible, but Mark's statement aggravates me. I take a deep breath to calm myself, but it doesn't work. Fuck avoiding conflict.

"If you want me to smile, then maybe you should be funny." I give him a wry smile.

"Wow! Okay." He laughs it off. "Let's order you another drink to loosen you up."

Another drink, really? As if a drink could put me in a good mood.

Mark turns his attention to Trish, but she leans away, scowling.

"What I need is none of your fucking business." My hands ball into fists.

Mark leans back in his seat with an amused smirk and studies me. His smirk, his demeanor, and his cocky attitude snaps something within me. Something that's been hiding deep in my core, screaming to shout back. Confidence and courage surge through me, and I don't break eye contact. If he wants a challenge, he has one.

"I'm sorry." He stands with his hands up and steps toward me. "I didn't mean to offend you." He rests his hand on top of mine.

I glance at his hand, then back at him. The gesture shows he's apologetic. The grin says otherwise.

The plain Jane in me is telling me to recoil, but someone else is trying to fight to the surface.

I give Mark a challenging stare. "Don't touch me."

Mark squeezes my hand and smiles when I wince. He leans in closer and drops his voice. "You better watch your bitch mouth before something bad happens to you again. Not like anyone would come looking for you anyway. Or else they would have found you already. Isn't that right?"

"Mark, give it a rest."

Julian's voice is stern but cautious.

Mark's grin widens as he drags his hand away without breaking eye contact. Like a wolf claiming his dominance. I look at Trish's wide eyes.

Tears fight to rise to the surface at his last statement.

"I think I've had enough." I stand and face the table. "Trish, I'm going home."

When I turn, Julian shouts, "Mark, don't!" Mark's large hand clamps onto my shoulder.

Blood rushes through me. Mark's muffled voice is hard to understand because I'm deaf with fury. My body reacts before I have time to think. Grabbing his hand, I twist it behind his back, causing his knees to buckle and his body to lie on the table. I hold pressure and pin him facedown.

Trish and Julian jump out of their seats. Trish is against the wall, and Julian starts toward us.

"I said, don't fucking touch me, asshole."

My words come out in a growl. If he wants a show of dominance, I can win.

"Okay, okay . . . Ow!" he whimpers. "I'm sorry. I'm sorry."

Julian is at my side now, arms raised in caution. I shoot him a glare and release Mark. The music has stopped, and a crowd gathers around, phones raised in our direction. Heat rushes to my cheeks, and I run toward the entrance before slamming through the door into the humid night. I hunch over, gasping the hot air.

I can't comprehend what happened. How did I do that so effortlessly? I didn't have to think about what to do, but my body knew exactly how to do it.

Trish rushes through the door. "What the hell was that?"

I still can't wrap my head around what unfolded.

Adrenaline pumps through my veins as I pace the sidewalk. "I'm sorry. I know you were into him."

"What?" She looks at me, puzzled. "Fuck that guy. I don't care about that." She waves, as if she's swatting at a fly. "How did you do that? You were like Jessica Jones back there."

I swerve out of the way for a group of passersby. "I don't know. I just snapped. His vibe rubbed me the wrong way."

She smiles with her hands on her hips. "That was pretty impressive."

I hadn't realized I was worried she would be mad at me for crippling her crush.

I exhale a long breath. "It was, wasn't it?"

"He's at least six inches taller and double your weight. I bet he's in the bathroom right now, cleaning the shit out of his pants."

We both laugh.

We're halfway down the road when Julian calls my name. He stands in the middle of the sidewalk, looking in the opposite direction. Something in me wants to go to him, to explain my behavior. Or ask him to give me a second chance, a do-over. Another part of me wonders if he's like his friend, a misogynistic creep.

"Come on, let's go home." Trish pulls my arm, and I turn away from him.

We walk for several blocks before we hail a Lyft. Trish discovers a viral video of the altercation—whatever that means.

I only use my phone to order Lyfts, order food, or contact Trish—one out of the two numbers in my phone. The other is Dr. Wagner's office.

We laugh and replay the video. Trish brags like a proud mother to the driver. Grateful, I smile, knowing someone cares for me as much as I do them.

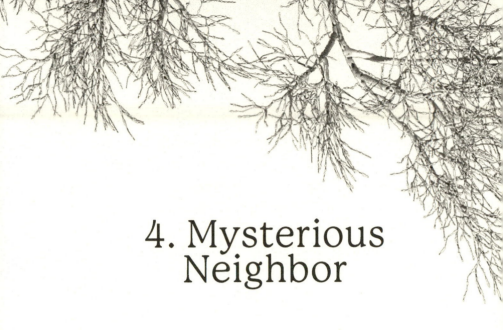

4. Mysterious Neighbor

Sundays are my favorite. It's the one day without responsibilities. No work, no therapy. I'm free to spend the day as I please. Sometimes, I spend the day cleaning the house. Other times, I do nothing but lie there and stare at the ceiling. But today, the clouds are gathering, and I rush to fill the kettle. I will spend the day watching the rain splatter against the ground and splash back up. Watch it form patterns from the droplets rippling outward in the puddles.

When the kettle whistles, I grab my tea and my book and curl up on the bench under the porch awning. I cup my mug with both hands, sipping slowly on the tea. I close my eyes and relish the constant tapping of water against the earth, letting it wash away my worries. The downpour pitter-patters against the awning, drowning the noises of the outside world. It's as if time stops and nothing else matters except this moment.

Winds howl through, indicating the rain will turn into a storm. I love the cooling winds before a storm and how it can turn the hottest day into the coolest. But it's the relief from the chill I enjoy the most.

Lightning flashes, illuminating the sky, and a roar of thunder immediately follows. Thunderstorms don't scare me, but they're not my favorite, either. Thunderstorms jolt an odd feeling in the pit of my stomach. It gives me focus and determination, like I can accomplish anything, but then quickly turns into despair, like something is going to go wrong. Maybe I feel this way because of something that happened in my past life. It's almost like déjà vu. Like I was in a thunderstorm to accomplish a task with such focus and determination, but then it all went sideways, and I lost all hope.

The rain continues, the wind rushes through, and more lightning pierces the sky. It's days like these when rumbling thunder mixed with the downpour's hum either clears my mind or runs it. I either think about nothing at all or everything at once. Today's the latter.

A jagged streak of lightning shoots from beyond my neighbor's property, and I no longer have the clarity to read. But I hold the book and shift between skimming the pages and glancing at my neighbor's house.

Trish found it strange that I've never met them, and now I can't stop thinking about it. Who lives there? What do they look like? What do they do all day? I've never given much thought about them until recently.

I stare at the two-story house with an opaque mirror-tinted front window. While other windows have the curtains drawn, a light shines from inside the upper-story window, but I can't see anything beyond the curtain. A black Nissan Altima rests in the driveway. Sometimes, the driveway is empty when I come home, but the car always returns shortly after.

A stack of wood lay against the side of the house, neatly lined and chopped into small logs. Next to it are larger logs waiting to be chopped, with an ax lodged into the top, unchanged since I've moved in. I never see smoke coming out of the chimney or the firepit on the side of the house being used.

Lightning strikes again, thunder follows moments later. The rain lightens to a steady drizzle, and the wind subsides. Light from my neighbor's window turns off, and I stare, hoping to catch a glimpse of the mystery person, but I see nothing. It's eating at me. Part of me wants to go into the rain, cross the street, and knock on their door. I could simply introduce myself and do the neighborly thing Trish talked about, but it would be weird now since it's already been three months, and they haven't been neighborly either.

I could think of another excuse to go there. I could act like I need help with the circuit breaker or ask to borrow a cup of sugar. But, for all I know, they could be an ax murderer. The thought sends a chill through me, and I hurry into the house, lock the door, and draw the curtains closed.

***

Early Monday morning breakfast shifts at the country club are my least favorite, mainly because I don't like to wake before the sunrise. Trish and I are the only two servers, which means double duty, serving tables and managing the bar.

Trish and I stay in a rhythm of taking orders, delivering food, and pouring drinks. Sweat beads on my forehead from the nonstop shuffle. I don't mind it. Hustling keeps me focused on only the task at hand. Everything else disappears, and it's easier for me to forget that I can't remember my past.

Just when I think it may never stop, the tables clear out, signaling the end of the breakfast rush. We sit with blank stares, counting the minutes, until the end of our shift.

Trish absentmindedly spins a fork on the table. "Sometimes, I wish I was like Jane."

I give her a sideways glance. "Why would you wish that?"

She stops and sits up straight. "Huh?"

"Why do you wish you were like me?"

Trish furrows her eyebrows. "I didn't think I said that out loud." She shakes her head quickly. "I really need to get more sleep," she mumbles. "I just meant . . . you make it look so easy serving tables. I sometimes wish I had a photographic memory." She slaps the table, and I jump in my seat. "You know, I forgot to bring drinks to three different tables today." Her face juts forward as she holds up three fingers. "Three." She drags the word out. "I was running around, trying to make sure I got the food out in time that it completely slipped my mind." Slumping back, she spins the fork again. "If I was like you, that wouldn't have happened."

I can't relate to her frustration. I've never forgotten to bring anything to a table or have had to write a single order. When I'm serving tables, it's like my brain can categorize tasks based on priority and timing so I can do my job efficiently.

When I rest a reassuring hand on top of hers, she stops spinning the fork again. "Don't sweat it. It was an unusually busy morning."

She glances at the clock on the wall. "We only have forty-five minutes left. One of us needs to stay behind the bar while the other does the dishes. Rock, paper, scissors for it?"

"I did the dishes last time." I raise an eyebrow at her.

In defeat, she sighs deeply, then sulks to the kitchen.

I lean on the bar, zoned out from exhaustion, when a throat clearing brings me back to the present. "Sorry!" I whip around, embarrassed that I wasn't paying attention. "What can I get for you?"

Julian stands before me, avoiding my gaze.

I freeze, holding my breath. What is he doing at my work? When I see the golfing glove on his hand and the bag of clubs resting against the counter, I relax.

"Hello again." His voice is shaky, and his cheeks turn red. "I'm sorry about the other night. Mark's an idiot."

The reminder of Mark infuriates me, but Julian was kind to me. I can at least return the kindness.

"Julian, right?" I snap my fingers and point at him.

The gesture feels wrong and awkward. Heat rushes to my face, and I hope he doesn't notice. I quickly cross my arms, rubbing the scar.

"That's me."

"Is your friend okay?"

Not that I care, but it seems like the right thing to ask. Part of me hopes I had broken his arm to remind him how not to treat women.

"Oh, he's not my friend." Julian shakes his head and holds his hands up. "I moved here a week ago and decided to check out the town. Mark was just . . . there." He rests his elbow on the bar and leans forward. "For the record, I'm impressed with your ninja skills." He winks, and I suppress a giggle. "Where did you learn to do that? Do you take martial arts, Krav Maga, or something?"

"Um . . ." I realize telling him I have amnesia could be off-putting. "It's a long story." Seeming to accept this answer, he nods. "Did you want something to drink?" I add as an afterthought, momentarily forgetting he's here for a reason.

"Yes, please. I'll take a Bud Light." I hand him the beer. "Thanks. Maybe I'll see you around." He smiles and leaves.

Trish turns the corner, drying her hands on a towel. "Was that the guy from the bar?" I nod as she makes her way to my side. "Weird. What did he want?"

"A beer."

"Not to drink, moron." She rolls her eyes. "What did he say to you?"

"Apparently, him and Mark aren't friends, and he's impressed with my ninja skills."

"He seems nice." She smiles. "You should go out with him."

"Because he's nice?"

I don't hide my sarcasm.

"Yes. And because he's hot." She raises her index finger in the air. "Most importantly, he won't do anything stupid because he knows you can kick his ass."

"I don't know. He seems quiet."

"I think he deserves the benefit of the doubt."

Our shift ends, and we walk out together, as we always do. I give Trish a hug and wave to her as she heads toward the parking lot.

A parked black Nissan Altima catches my eye, making me suck in a quick breath. Nonchalantly, I peer across the lot, but the car is empty. Glancing around, I hope they'll emerge, but no one's in sight. I scurry back inside and look around, but I recognize everyone in the restaurant. I swear under my breath and turn toward the door, then crash into Julian's chest.

"Oh my gosh," I say. "I'm so sorry."

He smiles. "I thought you left."

"I did . . . Hey, what kind of car do you drive?"

"Honda Civic." He squints. "Why?"

I settle for a lie so he won't think I'm weird. "Someone left their headlights on but don't worry, it's not your car." My eyes linger on his lips a moment longer. "Anyway, I should go." I hurry away before I make things more awkward.

I rush through the door and stop dead in my tracks. The car is gone, nowhere in sight. Shaking my head, I second-guess if I even saw it at all. I don't dwell on the thought and head home.

As I turn onto my block, the Nissan Altima is parked in the neighbor's driveway. I sit on my porch for hours, hoping to catch a glimpse. Only when my hunger becomes too much do I retreat indoors.

The aroma of a microwavable Salisbury steak TV dinner fills the air. Steam rolls out from the container, swirling its way up.

As I blow on a hearty slice of meat and mashed potatoes, a car engine roars to life. I drop the fork and dart to the living room window. My neighbor's car reverses out of the driveway and drives down the road.

I curse under my breath. It almost feels like they knew I was watching them and left the first chance they got.

Later that night, I sit on my porch bench, enjoying the calmness of the night and the fresh air in my lungs, waiting for my neighbor to come home. Under the small porch light, I sip my tea while I lose myself in the story of a book.

A flash from headlights snaps me back to reality. Glancing at my phone to see the time, I discover it's almost three in the morning. The car pulls into the driveway, and the mystery person exits the driver's side, but it's too dark to make out many details.

Their hoodie makes it hard to see their body shape, but they look too tall and broad to be female. The person strides up the porch steps.

Who are you, mysterious neighbor?

He turns his head my way, and I'm paralyzed with shock because I swear I can hear him whisper "What?" but that can't be. He's too far away. It must be my mind playing tricks after the tiring day.

I can't see his face, but I know he sees me since I'm exposed to the porch light. Trish's advice about being neighborly comes to mind, and the only thing I can do in the middle of the night is wave. He hesitates before he waves back, then pauses when he reaches the front door to look back at me again. He looks like he's going to say something, but he shakes his head and enters the house.

5. Circle of Doors

My energy is different while I wait to see Dr. Wagner. Usually, I'm filled with hopeless dread, but hopeful expectation assumes that position.

The receptionist tells me he's ready to see me, and I rush to his office.

"Good evening, Dr. Wagner."

"Good evening, Jane. Have a seat."

We both take our usual spots.

I planned to ease the hypnosis talk into the conversation. Instead, I blurt, "I want to try hypnosis." I take a deep breath to calm my nerves. "Today, if possible."

He eyes me cautiously. "I have to say, I'm surprised. After our last session, I didn't think you would consider it. First, let's talk."

I nod and relax into the couch.

"I have to ask . . . have you experienced any changes in your memory?"

"No." I shake my head. "Well, maybe. I don't know exactly."

"That's okay. Regaining memories can be disorienting. Tell me what happened."

I retell the events of the night with Mark. Dr. Wagner remains quiet, although I can tell he wants to comment by the way he rubs his chin.

"I know it's not a memory per se, but I don't know any woman that could do what I did without training."

He leans back in his chair and crosses his arms. "You were full of adrenaline. It could've been luck."

I lean forward, shaking my head again. "No! You don't understand. It was precise and articulated. It wasn't luck. I knew exactly where to grab his hand, which way to twist, and how much pressure to put."

"I suppose it could be muscle memory. It's possible you could've had self-defense training."

"I think it means I was a badass in my former life."

I can't hide my smirk.

"Knowing you, I wouldn't doubt it for a second."

All this time, I've been a plain Jane. A girl who waits tables and spends her free time alone on her porch or drinking herself into oblivion. I never thought of myself as special, but there's a chance I was someone braver in my former life. Someone who knew how to fight.

"So? Can we try hypnosis?"

Dr. Wagner retrieves a pendulum from the bookshelf and places it on the table. "I want to warn you what could happen if we're successful. Remembering might be traumatic."

"I understand the risks. I want to do it anyway."

Dr. Wagner gently tells me to relax and clear my mind. I keep my breathing steady. My eyes follow the pendulum ball left, right, left, right. I concentrate on the clicks, and, eventually, my body feels weightless. Darkness creeps into my peripherals like I'm looking through binoculars.

Slowly, the darkness spreads inward, like I'm looking through a tunnel with the pendulum at the center. The clicks are steady, like the second hand of a clock. Darkness envelops the background, leaving a floating pendulum in its wake. The clicks get slower, and the pendulum fades until I'm left in complete darkness.

I see nothing as I look around. It's as if I'm floating in a sea of black when I look down. A door appears to my right. Another to my left. One by one, dozens of doors appear, encircling me. Moving along the ring, I study their various shapes and sizes, each one a unique design. I stop at one I recognize—a wooden door with an aluminum frame and a rectangular window above the handle. I rest my hand on the knob, take a deep breath, and open it.

A bright light blinds me. Instinctively, I squint and shield my eyes with my arm as I step through. I lower my arm and blink to adjust my sight.

It's me, lying in a hospital bed the day I woke up and became Jane. The first day I remember. The earliest memory I have.

Looking at myself from the outside makes me feel uneasy. She reaches for the IV and hunches over in pain. I wince when the ache runs through me, as if it's happening in the present. My once-broken leg gives out, and I collapse. Pain from every broken bone, every cut, every sore muscle of the past bursts within me.

I crawl back into the darkness. The pain vanishes as quickly as the open door does, leaving an empty space where it once stood. Once again, I circle the doors, hoping one will draw me in. I stop in front of a white door. A square window frames the top half. It's frosted over, but I'm drawn to it by some force, like a magnet.

The room builds itself as I enter. The wall frames and windows pop into existence, then the ceiling and the floor. All around me, rows of small desks appear, all facing a bigger desk. It's a classroom. Children are sporadically seated at the desks, ages varying. Younger ones, who appear to be around seven, sit in the front, and the older ones, who appear to be around ten, sit in the back. Each child wears navy slacks and a white collared shirt.

A boy and a girl with dark-brown hair step through an open door. Although they look frightened, they hold hands. The teacher welcomes them and tells them to sit in the empty seats.

I follow them to the back, and the kids snicker at them for holding hands. The boy lets the girl pick her seat, then walks toward an open one on the opposite side of the room. Another kid sticks his foot out and trips him. He tries to right himself but accidentally bumps into a stocky boy's desk. He keeps his head down as he apologizes and takes his seat.

In the desk next to him is a girl with a blond ponytail and green eyes, and I realize that girl is me, about eight. She flips through a textbook and writes in a notebook, oblivious that her seat mate has been tripped. The stocky boy sits in front of her, and he faces the new boy.

"Are you sad you can't sit next to your girlfriend?" he teases.

The new boy keeps his head down. "She's my little sister."

His voice is quiet but protective.

"You and your sister should know that I run things around here. Don't get on my bad side, or you'll be sorry."

My younger self stops writing to look at him. Her demeanor is calm, but her voice is serious.

"Zeke?"

"Yeah?"

She looks him dead in the eye as if to challenge him. "If you touch either of them, I will break your fingers."

Her tone is casual but threatening.

I'm disturbed children behaved this way. I feel what she's feeling, and I know she means every word.

What kind of child was I?

Zeke's face goes white, and he quickly turns away. She turns to the new boy and gives him a soft smile. "Don't worry. As long as I'm around, you and your sister are safe."

Parts of the room disappear. I shuffle backward toward the open door, worried I'll be stuck in here forever if I don't escape before it collapses. Before the last desk disappears, I step into the darkness and watch as the door vanishes before my eyes.

Everything I've been searching for is in this abyss. All the answers I need are in front of me. I want to see it all. I want to explore every door.

I roam the circle of doors, looking for one that attracts me. One is all metal, with no windows or doorknobs. Despite not feeling the magnetic pull toward it, I'm intrigued. I try to push it open, but it doesn't budge. On the door is a metal plate, engraved with random numbers without a pattern: 152211419.

I curve the edges again, trying to find a door that calls to me. As I turn, something wobbles beneath my feet. Gravity seems to push me downward, and I can't step forward, glued in place.

Below me is a sewer drain, but it seems out of place among the doors. I don't remember it being there before. Cool air hits my face when I bend down to look. I stick my fingers in the holes and lift the cover. Although it's not real, it's heavy beneath my grip. Looking through, I only see black. With no visible ladder or rope, I know I must jump.

I'm nervous, but down there is an answer my subconscious wants me to see. I sit on the edge, dangling my feet, then inch my way down until I'm hanging by my fingers. My feet don't reach the bottom, but I have to let go.

I fall for a second, then land with a splash. My knees bend from the impact, and my hands catch my fall. The cold takes my breath away, and I shiver. My lungs burn when I inhale, and my breaths come out in foggy puffs. In front of me, my past self brushes the wall with her hand to guide her, and I follow.

I feel her fear of being caught and the urgency to escape. Each step she takes feels like walking on pins. My temple throbs as if it has a heartbeat, and coolness spreads throughout my veins. She turns, then tries to run but falters. I know what she's thinking and feel what she's feeling. She's freezing and tired and wants to give up, but the urge to keep going overpowers her physical state. Ahead is a circle of moonlight, and something catches my eye. We both fall to our knees when we see the barrier. Panic rises inside of me because it's her panic.

She crawls beside me as we make our way to the end, whispering "No" but I scream it. She tugs and pulls, but the barrier won't move. Far-off shouts bounce off the walls, and I try to help her pull on the chain-link barrier, but my hands go straight through.

Stopping, she closes her eyes and breathes. Warmth spreads throughout my arms, filling me with a sense of sudden strength. She yanks on the barrier again, and as it bends, I'm transported to the outside of the tunnel and watch her squeeze through. I grab at my right bicep. The raised scar burns beneath my touch. She doesn't make a sound, but I scream in agony and fall. She fashions a bandage around her arm, then runs for the trees.

"Wait!" I scream. I run after her, but the scene fades. "Wait!"

When the scene disappears, the only thing in front of me is Dr. Wagner.

"What happened?" I ask frantically.

"I pulled you out."

His skin looks gray.

Forcing myself to my feet, I ball my hands into fists at my side. "Why?"

"You were screaming, and I was worried."

His dismay breaks me out of my anger, and I sit again. "Take me back in." I place my palms on the table and lean forward. "I need to see what happens."

Dr. Wagner shakes his head. "I can't do that, Jane."

"But I need to know what happened. It could answer so many questions." My voice cracks in desperation.

His face grows soft and compassionate as he looks at his watch. "Our time is up for today. We can try again another time."

I know he says this to console me, but doubt creeps into his words.

He doesn't want to do it again. He couldn't see what I saw, only my reactions. I try to put myself in his shoes to see what he was seeing. My fear and my pain as I screamed.

It must have been frightening to see me like that, and I understand why he pulled me out. But he won't want to see that again, so I will need to convince him.

***

The next day at work, Trish and I begin our shift washing dishes. She hands me a plate, and I scrub it on autopilot. Yesterday's session with Dr. Wagner has left me exhausted. Being hypnotized was mentally draining, but last night, I kept replaying the memories. Analyzing every detail. Trying to see if there was something I didn't pay attention to. The more I thought about it, the more my head hurt, and the splitting headache prevented me from sleeping.

Those memories are part of me now. I remember physically being there, not just watching it through my hypnotic projection. But now I remember things the hypnosis didn't reveal to me. The smell of chalk in the classroom and the book I was reading, *The Art of War* by Niccolò Machiavelli. But there are still gaps.

When I told Zeke I would break his fingers, I meant it, and I know I would have done it. Why would I—at eight— be so violent? Why was an eight-year-old reading a book about war strategies? Who are the kids I was defending?

When I was in the tunnel, I remember the urgency to escape but not why or from who. I remember what I felt, seen, and heard, but it makes no sense without the history behind it.

"Hello? Earth to Jane." Trish waves in front of my face. "You've been washing that plate for five minutes."

"Sorry." I pass her the dish. "I'm exhausted. I couldn't sleep last night, and now I have this major headache."

She squints. "What's going on?"

"I was thinking about yesterday's therapy session."

I don't want to reveal everything to her yet without knowing enough, but, thankfully, she doesn't pry.

I grab another dish from the sink and scrub it with a soap-infused sponge, then pass it to Trish. Trish rinses the suds and stacks the dishes in the rack to dry.

"I saw Julian today."

Her tone is casual, but the way her eyebrows raise gives off a different vibe. She's up to something.

"Okay, and?"

"He was asking about you."

"What about me? What did you say?"

"Relax. He asked if you were working today." She seems unfazed by my demeanor. "I think you should go talk to him. Ask him out for a drink. You know"—she nudges her shoulder against mine—"get to know him."

She must sense my hesitancy because she drops the subject, but her expression implies she doesn't want to.

The lunch rush is slower than usual. I wipe the tables with a small towel and notice movement out of the corner of my eye. I turn to greet the new guest, and Julian stands before me.

"Jane." He smiles. "I hoped I would see you today."

"Julian . . . Hi. Were you golfing today?"

"Yes. Perfect wind for it, you know?" I nod, not knowing what the wind has to do with golfing. "Okay, well . . ." He shoves his hands in his pockets and avoids my gaze. "I wanted to say hi before I left. I'll see you around."

He turns and leaves, and I'm reminded of Trish's words. I swear under my breath and go after him.

"Julian?"

He stops and faces me, my cue to say something, but I stand there like an idiot.

My heart races, and my cheeks blush. I've never felt this nervous before, and I've probably ruined any chance of him agreeing.

"Would you want to grab a drink with me sometime?" I blurt.

He squints and cocks his head. "What was that?" He steps toward me.

I take a deep breath and clear my throat. "I was wondering if you would be interested in having a drink with me sometime."

My tone sounds too formal, as if I'm inviting him to a business meeting. I want to turn and run, but I try to stand there with confidence, waiting for the rejection.

He looks like he's trying to find the words to let me down nicely. Then he smirks. "Tomorrow night. The Gathering Place. Nine o'clock." He leaves, and I stand there in shock.

Trish approaches and pulls me out of a daze.

"I think I have a date tomorrow night with Julian. We're having drinks," I breathe.

"Really?" She bounces with her hands clasped together. "This is exciting. What are you going to wear?"

I tug at my apron, then at my collar. My mouth goes dry, and I can't find the words to speak.

Trish puts a hand on my shoulder. "Hey. It's just drinks. You have nothing to worry about. I'll come over and help you get ready."

I sigh with relief and give her a grateful smile.

6. First-Date Jitters

T rish reaches into my closet for another outfit. Clothes are scattered across the floor and bed, making it look like a tornado has come through. My anxiety about tonight's date turns into annoyance after outfit four. By outfit nine, I'm completely frustrated. After she hands me the tenth outfit, I yank it with a grunt.

"I should cancel." I throw my hands up in defeat.

"No, you shouldn't." Trish closes the closet door.

I groan and study the ensemble. It's not as flashy as the others; the rest were full of sequins or revealed way too much skin. Outfits I wear when Trish and I go dancing and want all the attention. Though, all the attention is always on Trish and never on the girl with no identity. But tonight, someone will notice me, and wearing flashy or revealing clothing is not the impression I want to make on a first date.

I close the door to the bathroom and study the simple but fashionable outfit once more.

I put on the off-the-shoulder rose-colored bodysuit and the black high-waisted jeans that flatter the curves of my hips. My frustration disappears when I accent it with black heels. Trish's eyes light up when I enter the room. I twirl so she can get the full effect.

"That's it. That's the one." She clasps her hand over her heart. "Now we have to accessorize and fix your hair and makeup." She plops me in a chair and gets to work. "Subtle and natural." She presses the brush to a nude-colored eyeshadow. Afterward, I stand back as she studies me from head to toe. "You look absolutely beautiful, Jane."

Her voice is full of adoration.

"I couldn't have done this without you."

"You're right." After blowing on her fingernails, she checks her phone. "Your ride should be here in a few minutes. Remember to have fun and be safe." She blows me a kiss before the door clicks behind her.

I take a last look at Trish's masterpiece in the mirror. Subtle and natural, yet I've never felt more beautiful. My eyes pop with the black mascara, complemented by the soft brown shade on my eyelids. A subtle pink outlines my cheekbones, matching the gloss on my lips. I ruffle my hair, then head for the door, lock it behind me, and wait outside for the car.

From my phone, I track the car traveling to my house, and it shows it took a wrong turn, delaying my pickup by five minutes. One disadvantage of living on a lonely street.

"Damn it." I stomp in frustration.

I pace in front of my house. "Hi, Julian, it's so nice to see you again," I say to myself. "No, that's too formal . . . Hey, good-looking . . . No, that's creepy. I guess I could just say hi, but then I sound shy."

Headlights illuminate the street.

"About time."

Lights leave a soft glow on my neighbor's porch, and I see someone sitting there. Heat rushes to my cheeks as I wonder if he saw me shuffling and talking to myself.

The car stops, and I rush to the backseat, hoping to get off the block as fast as possible.

The ride is short to The Gathering Place, but I wish it was longer. My heart flutters with nerves. I reach for the door handle but quickly pull away.

Am I ready to date? Or is this a mistake?

The driver let's out an impatient sigh, so I take a deep breath and open the car door.

I follow the hostess to a booth where Julian waits. He looks in my direction, and I wave to him. I mentally kick myself for the reaction. He smiles and stands to greet me. The sight of him takes my breath away. His snug black tee defines his biceps, and the khaki shorts show off his muscular calves.

"You made it after all." He smiles. "I got worried you were standing me up."

"Sorry I'm late. The driver got lost picking me up."

We take a seat on opposite sides of the booth, the worn leather creaking under our weight. Murmurs of conversations surround us while servers zoom past with trays of food. The smell of fried food drifts through the air, making me realize I should have had something more substantial than a PB&J sandwich for dinner.

Julian smiles. "No worries. The wait was worth it."

A wave of warmth washes over me that takes away my hunger. I shy away with flushed cheeks.

"You look stunning," he breathes, a hint of shyness in his tone.

"Thank you. You look great, too."

My eyes trail over his face. He has shaved since I last saw him, and his bare chin reveals a dimple I had missed before.

A server arrives with two pints of beer.

"I already ordered drinks. Is beer okay?" He slides the glass over to me.

"Beer is perfect." I take a sip. "You mentioned you recently moved to Bridgeport, right?" It's the first thing I think of to break the silence.

"Yeah. Just over a week ago. A job opportunity opened up that I couldn't refuse."

"Where did you live before?" My fingertips drum on the table.

"Not far. A small town on the Maryland, West Virginia border. About an hour-and-a-half drive from here."

"What kind of work do you do?"

"Boring insurance stuff." His eyes shift to my fidgeting fingers, then back to my face. I reach for my glass and sip. He chuckles. "See? You're already bored."

I laugh. "I assure you I'm not bored. Just a little nervous." I clasp my fingers together, resting them on the table, willing myself to relax. It doesn't help. I slide my left hand up to my right bicep, feeling the raised line.

Julian glances at my arm, then back at me. "Can I let you in on a little secret?" He leans in closer, and I do the same. "I am too," he whispers. I grin and drop my hands to my lap. "Tell me something about you."

My hand drifts up to my arm again. I had been too focused on what to wear and how to greet him that I didn't prepare what to divulge about myself.

People already see me as an outcast. To them, I'm a puzzle, and my puzzle piece doesn't fit in with theirs. I don't want Julian to see me that way. I want him to see *me*.

He must sense my hesitancy because he shakes his head. "You don't have to tell me anything if it makes you uncomfortable." He reaches for my hand but pulls away before making contact. "I can keep talking about insurance."

"No, it's not that." I run a hand through my hair as I attempt to stall. "It's a weird story about my past. People look at me differently once they know." I look away to avoid his pity.

"The same story of how you became a ninja?" He flings a karate chop, and I laugh. "Then, don't tell me about your past. Tell me about your present."

His quick wit is refreshing, and it puts me at ease.

"You already know I work at the country club and that I'm a secret ninja on the side."

We laugh.

He asks me about Trish. I tell him how we met and how we spend our time together. He tells me he has always wanted to try golfing, which is why he joined the country club. His jokes make my stomach hurt from laughing. When the night gets late, Julian waits outside with me until my ride arrives.

"I had a great time."

His smile is soft and genuine.

"So did I," I say.

"When's your next day off?"

"Sunday."

"Perfect. I think I will teach you how to play golf." I respond with raised eyebrows. "Don't worry. It's miniature golf. That is, if you're interested."

His tone is confident, as if I won't reject the offer.

"Miniature golf sounds fun. I'm in."

Despite the butterflies in my stomach, I keep a casual tone. The Lyft car pulls to the curb, and I point with my thumb. "This is me."

"May I be a gentleman and kiss your hand before you leave?"

Smirking, I hold out my wrist. He clasps his fingers around mine, soft yet masculine, sending a flutter in my stomach. His lips brush across my knuckles. Butterflies intensify, and I wish the driver wasn't waiting for me so I could prolong his hand in mine, his lips on my skin. My mind wanders to what his lips would feel like against mine.

"Good night, Jane." His eyes are still locked on me, and he doesn't remove his hand.

"Good night, Julian." With my free hand, I lace my fingers around his wrist and move in, the sound of my heartbeat in my ears. I'm ready to take a chance and lean in for a kiss, but the blaring honk of the Lyft driver evaporates my boldness.

He drags his hand away, leaving a small piece of paper in my palm. I hold on to it and get into the car. Julian waves to me as the car drives away.

Once out of sight, I open the tiny folded paper to find his number written on it, and I smile at the smooth, clever gesture. I only have to read it once to have it be a permanent part of my brain, but I still enter it into my phone, typing his name with a heart emoji at the end.

For a while, I stare at the name, wondering if I should call and tell him how much of a great time I had. Tell him I didn't want it to end. Maybe be promiscuous like Trish and invite him over for a late-night drink. Instead, I look out the window and replay the perfect date in my head.

It's nearly midnight when the driver arrives at my house. My elation keeps me from going inside and to sleep. I sit on the padded porch bench, absorbing the fresh air of the summer night, to extend the day. I watch the taillights turn away, leaving only the moonlight to see by. Stars are visible under the clear sky, and I admire them until headlights come into view. Did I leave something in the car? I inspect the contents inside my purse, and everything appears to be there. I look up and notice it's not the same car as the Lyft.

It's a black Nissan Altima.

Tonight, I'm not exposed under the porch light, so he shouldn't notice my presence. I remain as still as can be, hoping he doesn't see me, hoping I can see him.

He exits the car, but the darkness obstructs my vision, and I can only make out his silhouette. Faintly, I hear him talking. I assume he's on the phone from the upward bend of the elbow. He's too far away to distinguish the conversation. He raises his voice, and I hear his last sentence as he reaches his door.

"I said I have it handled. Now, leave me alone!" He slams the door behind him.

His words were full of anger, yet I wasn't frightened. I detected a hint of anguish behind them, as if he received horrible news and the person on the other end was trying to console him.

I've heard that anguish and anger before in the hospital, when people lost loved ones. But it wasn't I-want-to-punch-something anger. Their screams and sobs escaped them, as if they were shattered. As if their universe was turned upside down, and they're angry because of their helplessness.

That's how my neighbor sounded. Angry about something he has no control over.

There's this pull in me to cross the street to see if he's okay, to see if he needs anything. But I know my words of kindness will bring him no comfort because I'm just a stranger who lives across the street.

I still think it's odd that, in the three months I've lived here, I haven't once seen him or thought about his existence. Now I've seen my cryptic neighbor twice in a week. I can't decide if it's because I still don't know what he looks like or because he has stayed invisible for three months. Either way, I suspect he prefers his privacy. Although I should keep my distance, the urge to find out more about this mysterious neighbor intensifies. Would he have reacted differently if he knew I was here watching him?

Quietly, I enter my house as stealthily as possible to avoid exposing myself for spying. I feel my way around in the blackness, only turning on the bathroom light for sight. Its sudden brightness reminds me of the doors in hypnosis, and everything I've been through the past week crushes into me. I lean against the wall and sink to the ground. What are the meanings behind my newfound memories? What's up with the mysterious neighbor I haven't seen until now? I had a terrific time with Julian, but how long should I wait to call him? With all these thoughts running through my head, I know it will be another sleepless night.

7. Trip and Fall

Physical therapy for my leg ended two weeks after I left the hospital. They made me promise I would keep working on building strength. My leg feels great, but I run once a week, like I promised I would.

My favorite playlist blasts through the earbuds while I stretch, then I jog three miles to a local park that has a paved oval trail. I pace myself to not overdo it before I get there.

I concentrate on even strides and steady breathing, lap after lap. I'm halfway through my routine when the music stops, and I slow the pace to check my phone. As I suspected, it's dead. Shoving the headphones in my pocket, I keep going with nothing to drown out the outside noise.

The hustle and bustle distracts my tunneled focus from the path. Children play on the playground with their parents close by. Teenagers on the court play basketball, and contrary to my previous oblivion, I'm not the only runner. Two women in their thirties speed walk, engaged in conversation. Two middle-school boys take turns timing the other. Four other solo runners all run at different speeds.

I fixate on the surrounding people, and without the earbuds in my ears, it's as if I can hear all the conversations going on at once. The hum of voices boom in my head, and I have to stop on the side of the trail. I press my ears with my hands, but it doesn't dim the noise. The droning heightens the pressure in my skull. I let out a groan, and all I hear are the birds chirping and the basketball bouncing. I look around, and everyone is going about their day. Meanwhile, my head feels like it's about to explode.

I take a deep breath before continuing, trying to block everyone else out, but my attention draws to a solo runner. A tall man, sprinting, passing everyone. He's as oblivious as I was. His focus is only on the trail in front of him. He wears black basketball shorts, a gray cut-off tank darkened by sweat, and a black baseball hat. Veins protrude from the muscles in his arms, and I can't help but wonder what it would feel like to be wrapped within his embrace.

He runs in the opposite direction from me and will cross my path any moment. I should look elsewhere, but I can't force myself to look away. As he approaches, I stare, trying to see the face under the hat. We lock eyes after he shifts his focus to me. Mine widen because I wasn't expecting him to notice me. He diverts his gaze for only a second, then back at me again. Shaking his head, he slows to a jog, then looks down.

As he passes, I trip over my feet and fall forward. I reach out to brace the descent, except the gravel never comes. A firm hand pulls me backward and rights me onto my feet. I stand, transfixed, trying to process why I'm not lying across the pavement.

"Are you okay?" asks a deep, raspy, out-of-breath voice.

The man holds onto my arm. My flushed cheeks from exertion hide my embarrassment. I partly wish he would have kept running and didn't look back to see me trip. Another part of me is grateful I won't have scraped hands and knees.

"Uh . . ." He towers over me by a foot. Dark-brown hair sticks out beneath his hat, which matches the short manly scruff that covers his chin. His blue eyes look at me with concern, and he has a small white scar through his left eyebrow, leaving a bald line. "Yes. I'm fine. Thank you!"

"Good." He releases my arm. His concerned expression turns into irritation. "You might want to tie your shoe before you start running again."

I look at my untied shoelace, then turn my attention back ahead to thank him, but he is already several yards away, sprinting, focused only on the path. Mortified, I tie my shoe quickly and sprint away, not slowing until the park is several blocks behind me.

***

Trish lies on my bed, twisting a Rubik's cube, listening as I tell her about my embarrassing encounter in the park.

"I'm sure it wasn't that bad." She spins one blue row to match another.

"Are you kidding? It was horrible. It was embarrassing enough he caught me looking at him like a weirdo, but then I trip over my shoelace. I wanted to crawl into a hole and die."

She sits upright, abandoning her concentration on the cube. "Next time you go on your run, make sure to tuck in your laces." She tosses the Rubik's cube to me, and I catch it. "And try not to stare at handsome men."

"I never said he was handsome." I shift my focus to the cube, absentmindedly twisting the rows.

"You described him *in detail* and tripped over your shoe when you saw him. It's implied. Your actions spoke for themselves."

"I don't like you right now." I stick out my tongue at her.

"You love me." She tosses her hair back with her hand. "Enough about the hot guy in the park. Give me the deets about Julian." She lies on her stomach with her chin on her hands.

I set the puzzle on the bedside table and tell her about my date with Julian. She gushes and awes over the adorable details.

"At the end, he kissed my hand and slipped me a note with his number on it."

Trish pouts, holding her hand to her heart. "That is the sweetest thing I ever heard. Have you called him yet?"

"Not yet. I didn't want to do it too soon."

"Don't wait too long, or someone else might grab him up." She grabs the solved cube from off the table. "How did you do that so fast? I've been working on this thing for weeks, and you did it in two minutes."

I stare at the completed cube but hadn't been paying attention to it. I don't know how to explain how I did it, so I shrug.

She shakes her head, as if she's not as surprised as I am. "Anyway, I gotta go. I'll see you at work." She exits the room but quickly comes back in, pointing a finger at me. "It's Friday, so make sure you're early." She turns before she can see me roll my eyes. "Call him," she shouts from the living room. A second later, the front door closes.

I pace around my room, phone in hand, and draft a message.

> *Hey!!! It's Jane . . . How are you??*

I examine my message, then wipe it.

> *Hey! It's Jane. Slick move, slipping me your number.*

I delete it again.

> *Hey! It's Jane. Now you have my number. Do with it what you will . . .*

My finger hovers over the Send button. I close my eyes and press down. My heart hammers in my chest as I stare at the appearing bubble with three blinking dots.

> *Julian: There she is. I was worried I blew it and wouldn't hear from you.*
>
> *Me: Not at all. Just busy and lost track of time.*
>
> *Julian: I understand. We still on for mini-golf Sunday?*
>
> *Me: Absolutely! I need to know where I'm going and what time to be there?*
>
> *Julian: I'll pick you up at noon. We can grab lunch then play. What's your address?*
>
> *Me: 121 Farnum Dr.*
>
> *Julian: Perfect! I'll see you on Sunday.*

8. Hearing Things

F riday nights at the country club are always busy. I hustle along, waiting on tables, not letting the bustle ruin my cheerful mood. A table of four sits in my section. I recognize the two men as regular golfers, yet they've never come into the dining hall to eat. Their wives sit next to them, and the stench of overpriced perfume wafts through the air. The wife to the right wears bright red lipstick that stands out dramatically against her fair complexion. The dozen bangles around the other wife's wrist jingle with the slightest movement.

With a fake smile, I greet them, but all four stare at their menus, not acknowledging me. For a second, I stand there in silence, then clear my throat to get their attention.

"Can I start you off with drinks?" I ask.

The wife with bangles glances in my direction, raises her eyebrows, and looks back at her menu. "I'll come back when you're ready." As I turn away, she blurts she'll have a Vodka Tonic.

Then, all at once, the other three tell me they will have a gin martini, a bourbon Manhattan, and a tall summer ale. I glance back, and they're all still engrossed in their menus, so I don't acknowledge them.

A few minutes later, I return with their drinks. As I lay them on the table, I'm confronted with confused faces.

"We didn't order these," says red-lipstick wife.

"Yes, you did."

The man to my left grabs the beer out and gulps half of it. "This is exactly what I wanted." He raises the half-full glass and demands a toast from the rest of the table.

They clink their glasses, and the man who started the toast tells me his meal order. I listen to every word, memorizing all the modifiers he wants to his meal, trying to tune out the disgusted stares from the wives.

After the last order, I turn and take one step before the wife with bangles says, "I can't believe they let her work here." I whip my head around to look at her.

Both men are engaged in conversation as the wives stare blankly at them. Neither of the women are talking, but I continue to hear them say, "There's something weird about that girl, and I don't want her anywhere near my town." She glances at me and squints.

I look away and rush to the kitchen.

Trish is traying up an order when I enter, out of breath.

"Whoa! You okay?" she asks. Her mouth is clearly moving, so I know she's talking to me.

"Yeah." I force a smile. "Just busy."

She nods and shoulders the tray.

I avoid the table as much as possible. Not my usual style of serving, but the fact I heard her say that has me on edge, even though I've heard roughly the same thing many times over the months I've been here. The words and the voice were hers, but when I heard it, her mouth wasn't moving, and no one reacted to her statement. Did I make the whole scenario up in my head? I push the uneasiness aside and continue with the rest of my shift. It's easier to do once the table of four clears out.

A few hours into my shift, I'm at a terminal, typing in an order, but Trish is reciting one of her table's orders in my ear. I try to tune it out, but her voice is getting louder.

"Can you shut up for a minute? I'm trying to concentrate on my order." I turn my head to the side, but no one is there. As I glance around the room, I see Trish on the opposite side of the restaurant, plugging in an order on a different terminal.

My palms clam up, and my heart quickens. I scurry out of the dining room, through the kitchen, and to the back walk-in cooler, where I close myself inside. Coolness rushes over my prickly neck.

Breathe.

You're not going crazy.

Breathe.

You're not hearing voices.

Breathe.

Everything is fine.

Breathe.

With each deep breath, my heart begins to steady itself.

The last table leaves right before closing time. Trish and I rush around, cleaning tables and stacking chairs.

"You okay?" she asks.

I look at her but don't answer. After the night I had, I can't trust that she said anything because I might be hearing things again.

She raises her eyebrows. Her lips move as she says, "Jane? You okay?"

Rubbing the back of my neck, working the tension away, I wait for my heart rate to slow before answering. "Yeah. I had a bad night."

She wipes a table, and I stack the chairs. "Would it make it better if Julian showed up with a rose?"

I scoff. "Like that's going to happen."

"Hmm." She shrugs. "You never know." Smirking, she shifts her gaze beyond me. I turn and see Julian waiting by the door with a single pink rose in hand. "Go." She nods in his direction. "I can finish up."

I stroll toward him, and he meets me halfway. "Sorry, sir. We're closed. You'll have to come back tomorrow."

"That's a shame. I'm starving."

"In that case, I recommend Garfield's down the road. They have great burgers."

"Ah. I've heard that, but . . ." He leans in and lowers his voice. "I hear the service here is better."

"That's true, but it could still be enjoyable with the right company."

"Then, I better find someone to accompany me."

"Have anyone in mind?"

"Perhaps. I'll have to see if she's free." He holds up a finger, then retrieves his phone from his pocket and taps at the screen. My phone dings in my pocket.

Julian: Dinner tonight?

I suppress a smile and type.

Me: Sure.

He reads the message on his screen and looks at me with a smile. "Look at that. She's available." I laugh, then he hands me the flower and holds out his hand. "Shall we?"

I put my hand in his, and we go on our way.

Garfield's is packed when we arrive, and I'm sure we'll be added to the wait list. Julian and I stand at the entrance. The hostess seems overwhelmed by the crowd of people. She shuffles around and calls out names of parties. She barely looks at us when we approach. "The wait is about an hour," she says apologetically.

Julian leans toward the hostess, his eyes flicking to her nametag. "Marcy?" She looks at him. "That's a pretty name." She blushes and smiles. "An hour is a long time to wait for me and my girl over here." He tilts his head toward me, but she doesn't take her eyes off Julian. "Can't you move us to the top of the list? Please?"

The hostess blinks rapidly before she stares at Julian in a haze. A second later, she snaps out of the haze, smiles, and nods. "Yes. I can do that."

Julian flashes a beaming smile. "Great."

We take our seats, and Julian glances over the menu. I stare at him, and he shifts his eyes to me. "Why are you looking at me like that?"

"I can't believe she moved us to the top of the list just because you asked."

"I can be pretty persuasive."

I raise my eyebrows. "Or she has the hots for you."

Smiling, he sets the menu aside, then leans in close. "I wouldn't have noticed because you're the only woman I want to look at."

My cheeks heat as Julian studies me, outlining my features with his eyes. I wish I had taken a moment to freshen up before heading out. I can only imagine what I look like after working a busy shift. Hair a mess, face shining with sweat, but he looks at me as if I'm the most beautiful girl in the room. I pretend to study the décor, but when I look at him, he's still staring in wonder.

The attention is suddenly too much, and my hand slithers up my arm, finding the raised scar. My voice is heavy in my throat when I ask, "Besides golfing, what else do you do for fun?"

"Not much. My work is time-consuming. What about you?"

"I like to read."

He rests his clasped hands on the table. "What do you read?"

"Anything and everything. Preferably fantasy."

"Why fantasy?"

I shrug. "It helps me escape from reality."

"What are you escaping from?" His tone is light and curious.

"I wish I knew." I laugh and brush it off as if it's nothing.

Before, I read to escape the past I couldn't remember. But thanks to hypnosis, I know I was escaping someone or something, and the books I read don't seem that far off from reality anymore.

My present reality is that I'm stuck in a town without an identity, and I can't escape, even if I wanted to. Without a license, traveling is not an option, but then again, I wouldn't know where I'd want to go.

I set my elbows on the table and lean toward Julian. "If you could go anywhere in the world, where would you go?"

Julian's eyes widen. He's silent and furrows his brow, as if he's deep in thought, then smiles. "This is going to sound weird, but I'd go to Disney World."

His answer is a delightful surprise. I place my hand in his. "Why Disney World?"

He clears his throat. "I went once as a kid. It was the best time of my life. I was four, and my parents wanted to take a family vacation before I started preschool. I remember being so excited to meet Mickey Mouse. We went to all the shows, and I met all the characters. The last night, we watched fireworks. It was almost like a dream."

"Did you and your family take lots of vacations?"

He looks at the floor and clears his throat. "No."

"How come?"

He doesn't look up when he slides his hand out of mine. "Because my parents died."

My heart sinks, and I cover my mouth with my hand. "I'm so sorry. I didn't know."

Julian's head snaps up, eyes wide as if I startled him, then squints. "Sorry about what?"

"Your parents."

He stares at me. "I didn't say anything about my parents."

Heat rushes to my cheeks as my heart pounds in my chest.

This can't be happening again. Am I going crazy?

"I'm sorry," I blurt. "I thought I heard you say your parents died."

He reaches across the table and grabs my hand. "They did, but I . . . " He shakes his head. "Maybe I didn't realize I said it out loud." After clearing his throat, he smiles. "Anyway . . . Let's continue. Where would you go?"

Hesitating, I wonder if the night is ruined, but Julian stares at me, unfazed. I exhale and shrug. "I don't know. I know nothing outside of Bridgeport."

"You must have some idea where you would go."

"Where do I start?" I think back to the books I've read with settings in places all around the world and some not even part of this world. "I want to see the ocean and the mountains and the northern lights. I want to fly in a plane and stare out the window at the clouds below. Or take a cruise and watch the waves ripple behind me." Julian's eyes twinkle when he sees my excitement, and I breathe the first relaxed breath of the night and smile widely. "I want to see the entire world."

As we eat, we talk about the different places worth visiting, prioritizing the cuisine, sights, and weather. The top three are the places any tourist would go—Paris, London, and Rome. Then we talk about how we would travel and where we would stay. The supplies we would need if we hiked the Appalachian Trail. All the while, the hypothetical travel plans include "we," as if he and I would do it together. My heart swells at the thought, and I can't imagine traveling with anyone else.

After dinner, Julian drives me home and escorts me to the front door. I turn to him, making no move to get my keys yet. "Thank you for dinner."

"The pleasure was all mine." I wait for him to lean in for a kiss. "Good night." He turns away, leaving me disappointed.

"That's it?" A hollow laugh escapes me. "You're just going to say good night and leave?" He stops midway to his car and looks genuinely confused. "We had a great first date. Then you show up to my work with a rose, being cute and funny, asking me out on a second date, which I thought went pretty well." I rest my hands on my hips. "Now you're going to leave without giving me a kiss good night?"

He smirks, then ambles up the porch steps, and stops a foot away. "My apologies." He gently takes my left hand

and presses his lips to my knuckles. Without letting go, he peers at me. "Better?"

Slowly, I shake my head.

He leans in closer and traces my face with his eyes. He rests his palms on the sides of my face and kisses my forehead. "How's that?"

I giggle and shake my head again.

He tilts my head to the side and kisses me on the cheek, then looks at me for approval. His gaze sears into me, and butterflies flutter in my stomach.

"You're getting closer."

My voice is a heavy whisper in my throat.

He steps closer, leaving only inches between us. Heat radiates off his body as he leans his face close to mine. He traces his thumb along my forehead, down my cheek, then across my jaw. The sensation ignites tingles throughout my body. My breath hitches, and I close my eyes. His hand stops at the nape of my neck, and I almost burst with anticipation. Just when I can't hold back any longer, he leans in and places a soft, innocent kiss on my lips. A shock of desire clenches in my stomach, but it only lasts a moment before he pulls away.

When I open my eyes, he's looking at me. The want in his eyes matches my desire. Kissing him deeper, I clutch the front of his shirt to bring him closer to me. He grabs the back of my shirt and pulls me closer until I'm pressed into him. Lips upon lips, smooth as silk. When his tongue sweeps along my bottom lip, a fire ignites within me.

At the sound of a car engine, we pull apart, panting. Beaming headlights illuminate the road, and the car pulls into my neighbor's driveway. I mentally curse my neighbor for his timing.

"I should probably go." Julian kisses me again, swiftly, then hurries to his car. I wave to him as he drives off.

As soon as Julian turns off my block, my neighbor exits the car and slams the door as if annoyed, then strides across his lawn and onto the porch. Although he's only a shadow, I glare at him, hoping he can feel the burn from my gaze. I stomp into my house and slam the door as hard as I can.

9. Bar Nights

The atmosphere at Chubb's is the same every Saturday—loud music that pulsates through our veins, flashing lights, and sweaty bodies grinding on each other. We barely get through the door before Trish wants to start the night by taking tequila shots. My stomach churns at the thought. Instead, I settle for whiskey. After our usual toast, we slam three shots in a row, then order a beer to take with us on the dance floor. We weave through the crowd, occasionally bumping into others.

Trish dances seductively, prowling for the guy of the night. I bounce alongside her, generously sipping my drink, hoping to avoid attention. One song rolls into the next, and the beer glides down without effort.

"I'm going to grab another beer. Want one?" I shout over the music.

She nods and continues to dance.

I order two more beers and make my way back to Trish on the dance floor. She dances with a good-looking man, moving together in perfect rhythm. I lean against a metal post and watch them. Their bodies intertwine and flow as if choreographed. I'm not the only one mesmerized by their fluid movements; an astonished crowd gathers around.

They embrace as the song nears the end. He lowers her into a dip on the last drawn note. Holding that position, they stare deeply into each other's eyes. The crowd erupts into applause. He spins her, steps back, and joins in on the clapping. Trish pretends to be bashful, but she loves the attention.

She spots me, grabs the guy's hand, and leads him over to me.

I put my hand on Trish's arm. "Wow! That was amazing. I didn't know you could move like that."

"I had a great partner. Jane, this is Miguel." She gestures to the man. "Miguel, this is my best friend, Jane."

Another song comes on, and Trish grabs my free hand. "Come dance with us."

"Oh, no. I could never dance like that. There's an open table over there. I'll sit and watch."

"I don't want you to be alone. I'll come sit with you."

"I'll be fine. You go have fun."

"Are you sure?"

"Yes. Now, go."

As I sit at the empty table, watching Trish and Miguel dance, my purse rumbles from the vibration of my phone. My heart flutters when I see Julian's name next to the text icon.

Julian: I couldn't wait until tomorrow to talk to you again. How's your night going?

Me: It's alright. I just got to see an amazing dance between Trish and some guy. How's your night?

Julian: Obviously not as entertaining as yours. I'm catching up on some work.

Me: Didn't want to go out on a Saturday night?

Julian: I didn't have plans. But I don't want to keep you from your friend. Have fun. I'll see you tomorrow.

I don't want to stop talking to him.

Me: You're not keeping me from her. She's still dancing. I'm sitting at a table drinking alone.

Julian: Where are you?

Me: Chubb's.

Julian: I should call and tell them to warn all the guys to be on their best behavior.

Me: Lol. So far, so good. I don't think I'll need to use my ninja skills tonight.

Five minutes go by without a response. My once-full drink is half gone. I fidget in my seat, staring at a blank screen. Swearing under my breath, I shove the phone into my purse, gulp the last swig, then head to the bar. After two more shots of whiskey in my system and a full beer in hand, I finally go back to the table.

Before I can sit, my phone vibrates in my purse. I desperately reach for it. Three dots appear on the screen, then disappear. They appear again, then disappear. What does he want to say?

Julian: I bet you look amazing tonight.

Not the response I was expecting, but I welcome it. The alcohol gives me the liquid courage to play around with him.

Me: Absolutely. I guess you'll have to use your imagination.

Julian: I am, and it's running wild.

I smirk. I like playful Julian. Or maybe it's because I'm drunk. Either way, I want to keep this going.

Me: Care to enlighten me?

Julian: Well . . . if you're wearing anything remotely close to what you were wearing the first night I met you, then I know there isn't a set of eyes that aren't looking at you.

The compliment makes me smile.

Me: If I remember correctly, you barely looked at me, so how would you know?

Julian: I had to look away to keep myself from undressing you with my eyes.

My mouth falls open, and my heart races. He's always been such a gentleman, but this side of Julian is sexy. Fingers hovering over the letters, I stare at the screen but can't seem to find a flirty response. Trish would know exactly what to say.

I hold my breath as three more dots appear on the screen.

Julian: I was wrong. You look more amazing than I could have imagined.

My eyebrows scrunch, and I blink quickly, thinking I read it wrong. After reading it again, I confirmed I read it correctly the first time. I hesitate to respond, then his message pops onto the screen.

Julian: Look up, Gorgeous.

I look up, and Julian is leaning against one of the metal posts, grinning at me. With my mouth agape, I stare at him. My heart flutters when he struts over to me.

"May I join you?" he asks.

I grab his hand and pull him next to me. "I thought you were working?"

"I was. But I wouldn't be able to sleep tonight knowing you spent a Saturday night drinking alone while your friend has fun." He raises a beer bottle, and I clink mine against his.

Trish and Miguel stumble over to the table after the song ends, holding hands and laughing. They're out of breath, and droplets glisten on their face and neck. Trish kisses him, oblivious to mine and Julian's presence. Like she can't get close enough to him, she strokes his hair, his chest, and his back.

Julian and I chuckle, then I loudly clear my throat. Trish pulls away, ogling Miguel, before turning her attention to us.

Her eyes widen, and she smiles. "Julian! You're here," she slurs.

She introduces Julian to Miguel, then excuses us to use the restroom. My head rushes when I stand, and I grab the table to steady myself. Each stride intensifies the tingling in my body and my dizzy vision. I'm more drunk than I realized.

Trish takes the stall next to me. "Isn't Miguel amazing?" she shouts from her stall, the syllables dragging.

"Mm-hmm."

"I think I'm going to do the dirty with Miguel tonight."

"Should I do the dirty with Julian?"

"Do you want to?"

"I don't know."

Thinking of his comment about undressing me with his eyes, I bite my lip, wondering what his hands would feel like over my body as he caresses my arms, my hips, my . . .

The toilet flushes, and the faucet turns on. I follow a moment later with flushed cheeks.

Trish washes her hands next to me. "I think we're going to leave in a minute. Do you want me to wait with you until you get a Lyft?" We dry our hands with a paper towel.

"No. I'll be okay. I'm with Julian." She hugs me, pinning my arms beneath hers.

Unable to hug her back, I stand immobile until she lets go.

We return to the table where Julian and Miguel are talking. Trish steals Miguel's attention by kissing him on the neck. She tilts her head toward the door, and his eyes widen in understanding. They bid us a good night and go on their way. I watch them leave, and a hiccup escapes, then another one. Julian takes my hand in his.

"How about I drive you home?"

"Oh"—hiccup—"kay."

He takes my hand and leads me toward the door. I stumble over my feet, but Julian wraps an arm around my waist to steady me, then asks the bartender for a to-go cup of water.

Once we're both buckled in the car, Julian hands me the water. "Drink this."

Putting my lips to the straw, I sip at first, then guzzle more. The cool liquid sooths my burning throat.

"I'm glad you came tonight," I say between sips.

"Me too. I hope you remember that in the morning." He chuckles and turns at an intersection.

Streetlamps shine through the windshield as we pass rows of houses.

"I will. I have a photographic memory. It's ingrained in my brain." I snort and breathe in the cherry air freshener hanging from the rearview mirror. "That rhymes."

He chortles. "You're funny when you're drunk."

"HA! I know, right." I take another long draw of water.

"Drunk or sober, you're still beautiful."

I lean my head against the window. A blast of cool air from the vent hits me in the face. "Aww! Such a gentleman, Mister . . . I don't know your last name."

Julian stares straight ahead, watching the oncoming cars pass, before he makes a left turn. "It's Thomas. To be fair. I don't know yours either."

"Jane Doe." I should stop there but drunk me doesn't get the memo. "My name's not actually Jane Doe, but I can't remember my real name."

He keeps his head forward but glances sideways at me, grabbing my hand, giving it a slight squeeze.

"Why not? It's okay. You can tell me."

Despite my earlier reservations, I have an urge to tell him.

"I was in an accident about five months ago. I woke up with amnesia. Jane Doe is the only name I know."

Silence fills the space except for the gurgling as I drink the last of the water.

Julian places the cup in the cup holder, then strokes my knuckles with his thumb.

"Is that the story you were avoiding telling me?"

"Yes."

"I'm glad you told me." He peers at me and grins.

Julian pulls into my driveway and laces his fingers with mine as he guides me up the steps. I shuffle in my purse and pull out my keys, fumbling to insert it into the lock. His large hands wrap around mine.

"Allow me."

He unlocks the door and opens it. I trip over the threshold, but Julian catches me. He holds on to my hips, guiding me through the door. I feel around for the light switch and flick it on, and the brightness momentarily blinds me. Without letting me go, he closes and locks the door behind him.

"Which way is your bedroom?"

I point to the hallway, and we enter the dark room. He leads me to the bed and guides me to sit, then kneels to take off my heels. When his fingers brush my ankles, it sends a chill through my spine. The shoes come off, and my feet stretch automatically.

"Do your feet hurt?"

"Yes. Wearing heels is painful."

His touch works its way to the arch of my foot. I let out a small moan. He massages each foot for a few minutes. "Better?"

"Mm-hmm."

It's hard to see him in the darkness, but I can tell he's still kneeling.

I stand, and he jumps up, holding his arms out as if I'm going to fall.

"What are you doing?"

"I was going to turn on the light," I whisper.

He rests his hands on my shoulders, guiding me back down, but when he moves away, I stand again and squint when he turns on the light.

"You should be sitting," he says with a defeated sigh.

"I need pajamas. I'm not sleeping in this."

"Oh. Right." He gulps. "I can get them for you. Where are they?"

I point to the dresser in the corner. "Second drawer down. Blue shorts, white tank. To the right."

I study him as he glides to the dresser. The tightness in his pants perfectly outlines the crevices of his butt. As he walks back to me, my eyes flow over his body, wondering what it looks like underneath the clothes.

"I think you can take it from here." He turns away, and I grab onto his arm.

"Wait."

He stops and turns to me.

My eyes wander over every feature on his face, his hazel eyes, square jawline, freshly shaved so the dimple on his chin shows. They work their way up to his parted lips as I remember how smooth they felt against mine.

His heart drums beneath my palms. I slide my hands to his shoulders, then up his neck and through his hair. He watches me intently and licks his lips.

"What are you doing?" he breathes.

"Waiting for you to kiss me."

He inhales deeply, then wraps his arms around me, resting them on the small of my back. He kisses me, long and soft. I pull him closer, transforming the kiss into something more. His hands slide up my back and through my hair as he moves the kisses to my neck. My heart quickens, and my breath hitches.

I wasn't sure if I wanted this so soon, but now that it's happening, I'm ready.

In one fluid motion, I pull off his shirt and let my eyes drift over his defined abs, up to his chest, then to his face as he eyes me warily.

"You're drunk," he says.

"And?" I fumble at his belt, but he grabs my hands.

"You're not in the right mindset for this."

Stung by his words, I step back. "Don't you want me?"

He takes a cautious step toward me, wipes the hair from my face, and stares into my eyes. "Of course I do. But not when you're inebriated and can't give me your full consent. I want you fully sound and willing." He places a soft kiss on my forehead, then grabs his shirt and turns away.

I sit on the bed. Before he reaches the door, I say, "Please stay with me."

He hesitates with his hand on the doorframe. "Get dressed. Then I'll stay."

With his back still to me, I dress and get into bed. "All done."

The light flicks off, and he crawls into bed next to me. I lie on his chest as he holds me and strokes my hair, lulling me to sleep.

10. Miniature Golf

I wake to the smell of bacon and eggs. Sitting at the edge of the bed, I stretch my arms, then follow the delicious smell. Julian stands shirtless at the stove. I lean over the counter, marveling over the way his pants hang low on his hips. He grabs a piece of bacon and tastes it. As he licks his finger, he moans. He turns around, sees me watching him, and freezes.

"Good morning." I smile.

"Good morning. Hope you're hungry."

"Famished."

He saunters over to me. "Good." Grabbing my face with both hands, he kisses me. Bacon grease coats his lips and transfers to mine. "Because breakfast is almost ready."

I lick the saltiness from my lips. "Smells delicious."

Before he turns back to the food, the doorbell rings. We look at each other, confused.

"Expecting company?"

I shake my head. The doorbell chimes again, and I open the door to Trish looking like she just rolled out of bed.

She's barefoot, hair disheveled, and I'm pretty sure her shirt is on inside out.

"Thank God you're home. I thought you might have gone on a run." She pushes her way into the living room.

"Are you okay?" I pull on her arm and eye her from head to toe.

She smiles and winks. "I'm better than okay." I exhale and drop my grip. "I left my car here yesterday. My keys are on your counter. By the way, there's another car in your driveway."

She steps into the kitchen and stops. An enormous grin crosses her face. "Well, what do we have here?" She looks at me with raised eyebrows. "I take it he didn't come over shirtless just to make you breakfast."

"Good morning, Trish. Do you want to stay for breakfast?" Julian asks as he flips an egg.

"She was just leaving." I give her a stare that could set her hair on fire.

She snaps up her keys and leans into me for a hug, whispering into my ear, "You better call me later with details." Pulling away, she heads toward the door. "Bye, guys. Don't do anything I wouldn't do." She chuckles as she slams the door behind her.

I join Julian in the kitchen where he's buttering toast. He prepares two plates and pours two glasses of orange juice. I breathe in the scent before picking up a piece of toast and dunk the corner into the yolk of the over-easy egg. The sweet and saltiness of the thick gooey yolk mixed with the butter of the toast explodes my taste buds, making my mouth water. My eyes close before I switch to the perfectly crispy and salty bacon.

Julian gazes intently at me. "Is it good?"

"Mmm! Delicious."

When I finish eating every bite, Julian clears the table. He turns on the faucet and squirts dish soap onto a sponge.

"You cooked breakfast. You don't have to do the dishes, too," I tell him.

"It's no problem at all."

"Then, I'm going to help. This is my house, after all."

He doesn't argue, only smiles and hands me a soapy dish to rinse. Only the sound of clinking dishes and running water breaks the deafening silence. It builds to the rising tension. One of us needs to break it before it consumes us.

"You missed a spot," I say.

He stops washing and examines the plate in his hand. "Where?"

"Right here." I scoop a handful of tiny iridescent bubbles and wipe them across his cheek.

When he inhales sharply, I suppress a giggle. With a mischievous grin, he grabs the spray nozzle from the sink and triggers a quick burst of water at me. I scream in surprise while instinctively holding my hands up to cover my face. It does nothing to block the water. I throw a handful of soapy water at him, and he retaliates with more spurts of water from the nozzle. We erupt into a water fight, laughing and blindly trying to spray the other.

"Okay. Okay," I laugh, holding up my hands. "I surrender."

Stopping, he returns the nozzle. Soap bubbles drip from his shaggy, dirty-blond hair and down his chest. He grabs a dry towel and dabs the water on the counter, then wrings it out in the sink. His biceps flex from the twisting, and I bite my lip. Julian watches me watch him, looking at me with an intense hunger.

In one stride, his lips are on mine, hands running through my wet hair. Without stopping, he cups my thighs and lifts me onto the island counter. He kisses my neck, and I exhale a small moan. He abruptly pulls away, leaving me breathless and confused.

"Why did you stop?" I pant, digging my fingers into the counter.

"Because I was getting too carried away."

"I'm failing to see the problem."

"I don't want to pressure you in to doing something you don't want to do."

"I want this. I want you."

His hesitancy makes me wonder if he's waiting for me to initiate the first move. I rest my hands at the nape of his neck, lean in, and place a slow, deep kiss on his lips.

***

An hour later, we both lie on the bed in a daze from our second round of morning festivities. My head rests on his bare chest, his arms around me, thumb slowly rubbing back and forth on my arm. Keeping my eyes closed, I feel like I could fall asleep, but Julian shifts his weight, pulling me from relaxation.

"I have to go so I can get ready for our date." He gives me a swift kiss, gets out of bed, and gathers his clothes from the floor.

Watching him dress, I revel over the way his shoulders ripple when he pulls on his pants.

"I'll be back at noon." He blows me a kiss and heads on his way.

At noon, the doorbell rings. When I open the door, Julian pulls the aviator-style sunglasses to the edge of his nose, peers above the rim, and whistles.

"You look amazing," he breathes.

I do a curtsey in my light-pink-and-white polka dot dress. "As do you."

"Ready to go?" He holds out his hand for me.

I place my hand in his as he escorts me to the car. He gives me a quick kiss on the lips before he opens the door for me. Moments later, we are headed for our destination.

"What are we having for lunch?"

He smirks. "It's a surprise."

A short while later, Julian exits the highway and turns onto a side road leading to an open meadow. He parks the car and, like a gentleman, opens the door for me. I step out, and he places his hands on my shoulders.

"Wait here," he says and heads for the trunk. "Close your eyes." I obey and wait. A few seconds later, the trunk door slams closed. "Okay. You can open now."

I open my eyes to Julian holding a wicker basket. "Surprise." His voice cracks. I look at the basket, then at him. He eyes me warily. "Is this okay? Or would you prefer a restaurant?"

I grab the basket. "Are you kidding?" I give him a peck on his cheek. "This is perfect."

Hand in hand, we stroll through the meadow and stop by a patch of wildflowers. Julian removes a thin blanket and lays it on the grass. We take a seat, and I close my eyes, breathing in the fresh summer air with the fragrance of earthy trees and sweet flowers. The breeze feels refreshing against the warm sun.

When I open my eyes, Julian is staring at me. "Why are you looking at me like that?"

"Because I adore you, and I'm trying to figure you out. What were you doing just now?"

"I was appreciating the moment. I think people don't do that enough. I've noticed people often take things for granted and forget to appreciate the little things and what truly matters."

He rubs the grass and picks up a white-and-yellow flower. "Which is what?"

"To enjoy life and the time you have left."

Julian smiles and tucks my hair behind my ear. "I find you truly remarkable." After placing the flower behind my ear, his hand lingers on the side of my face.

"How so?"

"You were in an accident and lost your memories. Yet, you stay optimistic." He brings my hand to his lips. "Others would let it get to them, but you didn't." He brushes my knuckles with his lips before placing a kiss. "You amaze me more every day."

I hesitate to respond.

I had worried telling him about my amnesia would scare him away, that he would treat me as others had, like someone who doesn't fit into their world. That's not the case at all. Now, as I stare into his eyes, there's no pity or shame or disgust in them. When he looks at me, he sees me for who I am today. And that person is someone he adores.

He wraps his arm around my shoulder as I relax into him.

"I was in the hospital for six weeks. I didn't know who I was, and no one came to visit me. The only thing to do was watch the lives of other people. And I saw people wishing they would have done things differently before it was too late." I pause, and he gently squeezes my arm. "I should've died. It's a miracle I survived at all. I can't control the past. I can't bring my memories back. What I can do is make the best out of my second chance. When my time comes—hopefully a long time from now—I want to be able to look back at my life and die smiling rather than wishing I did things differently."

He clears his throat and pulls me tighter to him. He's quiet, probably at a loss for words.

Sitting up, I grab his hand. "Will you take a moment to appreciate this beautiful day with me?"

Closing my eyes, I breathe in through my nose. I peek with one eye and see him doing the same. Holding his hand to my lips, I plant a long, gentle kiss on his knuckles.

He smiles and opens his eyes.

"You know what would make this day better?" I ask.

"What's that?"

"If you showed me what else you have in that basket."

"Right." He shakes his head as if he's forgotten about our picnic. He opens the basket and takes out a bowl of mixed fruit, a plate of bite-sized sandwiches cut into triangles, a small tray of cheese and crackers, and two water bottles.

"Bon appétit!"

His French accent is terrible.

***

On the first miniature golf hole, Julian offers to go first. He lines his ball up, concentrates on the hole, closes an eye, and holds up his club, measuring the angles. The club meets the ball, jolting it forward, and it lands directly into the hole.

Thinking it should be easy to do the same, I place my ball. It springs forward and lands nowhere near the hole.

"It's okay," he says. "You keep trying until you get it in. Go ahead, take another shot."

I concentrate harder on the ball and hit it again. It slides right over the hole, dangling a few inches away.

"You only need to tap it," he says. "Don't put any force over it."

I barely tap it, and it finally goes in. "I did it!"

He cheers and claps for me.

We move on to the next hole, and he gets another hole in one, while I take another three tries to get it in. Each hole is more difficult than the previous, and every time, Julian gets a hole in one, and I take several tries.

The tenth hole has a small tunnel that snakes to a lower level. Julian takes his shot. It goes through the tunnel and onto the lower level but doesn't make it in the hole. Internally, I'm relieved he will need to take another shot. He lines up the second shot, and it smoothly goes in.

On my turn, I hit my ball with a hefty swing, hoping to make it through. It misses the tunnel, hitting the edge, and bounces back to me.

"How do you make it look so easy?" I drop the ball onto the fake grass. "This is impossible."

"Relax and breathe." He demonstrates how to inhale through the nose and exhale through the mouth.

It seems silly, but I follow his instructions.

"Look where the tunnel is and line your ball to that." I do as he says. "Good. Now take your stance." I stand on the side of the ball and line my club. "Your stance is wrong. Here, let me show you." I expect him to demonstrate with his own club. Instead, he sets his club aside and stands behind me. "Your feet are too close. Spread them out more." I widen my stance.

He steps closer, pressing against me. "Your hips are all wrong," he whispers against my ear as he grabs my hips, pulling me closer to him.

His touch reminds me of this morning, and my breath hitches. Glancing at him, I raise an eyebrow. His lips ghost along my jaw, and I squirm.

Just as I'm about to kiss him, he says, "Eye on the ball." He directs my chin forward, and I let out a frustrated sigh.

"How am I supposed to concentrate when you're trying to seduce me?"

He chuckles but doesn't back away. "Relax your shoulders. You're too tense."

His voice is husky, and he places his hands on my shoulders. His thumb strokes the back of my neck, giving me goose bumps. He slides them down my arms, springing shivers down my neck, then rests them over mine.

"Now, inhale and hold it." I do as he says, although every part of me wants to react differently. "Exhale."

As I exhale, he uses his grip on me to guide the club to the ball. We remain in the same position as we watch it roll into the tunnel.

My jaw drops. He releases me, and we walk to the lower level. My ball teeters at the edge of the hole. We watch in anticipation until it finally drops in.

I scream and jump into Julian's arms, kissing him quick on the lips. "I can't believe I did it."

We continue with the last eight holes, and I use Julian's techniques to improve my game.

***

Julian pulls into my driveway and leads me to the porch.

I turn to face him. "Thank you for a wonderful afternoon."

99

"No," he murmurs, pushing a strand of hair behind my ear. "Thank you."

He leans closer and kisses me. I wrap my arms around him and press myself against his chest. His body pins mine against the door, hands thrusting through my hair, lips trailing down my neck.

Unlocking the door, I hurriedly pull him inside. Julian slams the door behind him and scoops me up, kissing me while carrying me to the bedroom.

***

We lay in the bed, and I'm comforted by the soft feel of the sheets against my skin, and even more by Julian's fingers caressing my hair. Soft sunlight streams in through the window, bathing the room in a gentle warmth. We've been lying this way for hours, neither one with the energy to move. With my fingertips, I trace his chest, his shoulder, and down his arm. A small raised scar lies on the inside of his bicep.

"I have a scar on my bicep, too," I say, as I run my finger along his scar. It's half the size of mine, but his is still red, as if he got it recently. "How did you get yours?"

"I was abducted by aliens, and they put a tracker in my arm."

Giggling, I playfully swat at him. "I'm serious."

Laughing, he kisses my knuckles. "I don't remember, exactly. It was a drunken night, celebrating my new job."

"Party got a bit wild, huh?"

"You could say that."

"Can I ask you a personal question?"

"Mm-hmm."

"What were you like growing up?"

He stiffens beneath me. "Why do you want to know?"

"Just wondering, since I can't remember my childhood."

He takes a deep breath. "I didn't have a lot of friends growing up. Other kids thought I was weird, so they picked on me. The older I got, the worse the bullying did. I was the scrawny kid with a lot of acne. Perfect ammunition for bullies. By the time I was a teenager, I was so angry that I shut everyone out. I worked out a lot to relieve some of the aggression. After the acne cleared, and I wasn't weak anymore, it was too late to make friends. They already hated me, so I let them."

"I'm sorry. That sounds terrible."

He kisses the top of my head and pulls the sheets over my shoulders without disturbing our stance. "It was, but it's all in the past." He's silent for a moment, then asks, "Do you remember anything from before?"

"Yes."

His chest hardens beneath me, and he holds his breath. "What do you remember?"

I shrug, and the sheet falls off my shoulders. "I only remember because my therapist put me under hypnosis."

"What did you see?" he blurts.

I think back to my newfound memories, and I'm not sure if I'm ready to share them. I haven't told Trish, and she's my best friend.

"Tell me."

"I was a kid. Probably eight. I threatened some kid that I would break his fingers."

The truth comes out before I have time to think. It's as if I'm in a daze. I didn't want to tell him, but for some reason, I did.

"Then what?"

Feeling drawn to tell him more, to tell him about my accident, I know, deep down, I don't want to. The memory is mine, and I don't want to share. Fighting the urge to speak nauseates me. I breathe through it, and within seconds, it vanishes.

"Jane? Then what happened?"

Pulling the sheets back over my shoulders, I push out the strong urge to tell him. "Then nothing. That's it," I lie.

"Are you sure that's all you remember?"

"Mm-hmm." I lean over and place a quick kiss on his lips.

His phone rings, and he grumbles. He jumps out of bed and retrieves it from his shorts on the floor.

"Shit!" he says as he looks at the screen. "Hello? . . . I'm on my way." He ends the call abruptly and dresses in a rush. "I'm sorry, but I have to go. I'm late for an appointment with a client." I sit up, holding the edge of the sheet over my breasts, as he leans in and places a peck on my forehead. "I'll talk to you later."

With that, he leaves.

Growling in my stomach forces me out of bed. I reach into my purse for my phone and notice it's almost seven, which explains my hunger. I drape a robe around my naked body and head to the kitchen. The fridge and the cupboards are nearly empty. Nothing I have will make a substantial meal. Without another thought, I pick up the phone and text Trish.

Me: Dinner tonight?

Trish: I'm having dinner with Miguel, then we're going to the park to watch the fireworks. Do you want to join us?

I forgot it was the Fourth of July. That's exactly like Trish to think of me before herself and her date, but I won't impose, no matter how much I want to see the fireworks.

Me: Absolutely not. I will get something delivered. Enjoy your date. Love you!

Trish: Love you too! Oh, and BTW, why didn't you tell me your neighbor is a total babe?

Me: What are you talking about? I told you I've never seen him.

Trish: He was outside chopping wood this morning. I saw him when I picked up my keys.

Me: Hmm . . . I haven't seen him yet, so I'll take your word for it.

Trish: Miguel's here. TTYL.

Waiting for the delivery driver to arrive with my burger and fries, I sit on the porch and read a book.

Occasionally, I look over at the neighbor's house. I find it odd that I have never seen him except for late at night. He's home because his car is in the driveway, but the curtains are drawn, and as always, the mirrored front window offers no leeway for a visual inside. How is it I've never seen him but Trish has? What does he do all day and night?

The car pulling into my driveway interrupts my thoughts. The delivery driver hands me my food, and I eat on the porch, waiting for nightfall, hoping to see fireworks. Any thoughts on the mystery neighbor will have to wait.

11. Attacker

The sun peeks over the horizon, and the temperature is in the low seventies. I stand on my porch in my light-purple sports bra and black running shorts, stretching my legs as my mind races with terrible thoughts because Julian never responded to my texts last night. Maybe he was busy and forgot, but I can only think about worst-case scenarios.

Trying to clear my mind, I jog the usual three miles to the park. The park comes into view, and I head straight for the paved trail. Not a person's in sight. The park seems bigger without the bodies to occupy the space, and the emptiness is peaceful.

I'm on my third lap when I feel like someone is watching me. Nonchalantly, I take out my earbuds and put them in my pocket. Nothing seems out of the ordinary as I scan ahead. I continue running but keep a close eye on my surroundings.

Once I round the curve, running footsteps thud from somewhere in the distance. It's likely another early morning runner, but paranoia seeps in. I chance a glance behind me and see a man running about half the track back, and he quickens his pace. Thrusting forward at a full sprint, I push myself to go faster, but the distant tapping against the concrete increases. When I look again, a chill runs through me.

It's Mark from the bar, and he looks angry, vengeful. I was lucky last time to catch him off guard, but I don't expect for that to happen again.

There is no one in sight I can run to. My breaths are becoming more labored. I'm almost at my limit, but I push myself to go faster.

"You stupid bitch!" he yells after me. "You're going to fucking pay for what you've done!"

He's closing the distance, and I don't know how much longer I can keep running. Sweat drips down my back, and my legs burn with each stride. Fingertips brush my back, as if he were trying to grab me but fell short.

I need to think of the best exit strategy, but the entrance to the road is on the other end of the track.

He catches up and hits me hard on my head, knocking me off my feet. I fall and roll several feet away. My exposed arms and legs burn from scraping the gravel. Bitter, metallic-tasting blood fills my mouth. In an instant, rage replaces my fear.

Mark stands above me, and I'm exposed. If I try to rise, he'll only knock me back down. He stares at me with hatred. I return the glare.

He kneels and grabs a fistful of my hair, pulling down, yanking my gaze to look up at him. "You fucked up my wrist." He pushes me away before I can get a swing in, and I land facedown on the pavement.

Turning my head, I spit blood onto his shoe. "You deserve everything that happened to you, you piece of shit," I snarl between gritted teeth.

He rears his foot back, and I do my best to protect myself from the blow, but he kicks me right in the ribs, knocking the wind out of me. I wrap my arms around my midsection and try to take in a deep breath, but he presses his knee into my stomach, then pins my arms to the ground.

He leans in and whispers in my ear, "I should've killed you that night, but there were too many witnesses. I'm supposed to bring you in alive, but . . ." He stands, and I inhale a ragged breath before he stomps on my stomach. "I'll just beat you to death and call it collateral damage. They'll understand."

Unaware of what he's talking about, I have no time to analyze his words because he rears his foot back again. I curl into a ball, but before he can kick me, a voice yells, "Hey!"

Mark freezes mid-kick, as if his body can no longer move. It's all the time I need to react. I grab his outstretched foot with both hands. Heat tingles its way from my fingertips and through my arms. A heat I only remember feeling once during hypnosis. Without hesitating, I twist his foot. His leg bends with a *crack*, and he falls, howling in pain.

His pained screams give me pleasure and a rush of adrenaline. I swing my foot around and kick him in the face. Another crack sounds, followed by blood gushing from his nose. I rush behind him and wrap him in a headlock. He claws at my arms, but I don't let go. I can feel him struggle to breathe beneath my grip.

"Hey!" the voice shouts again. "Stop!" I'm so focused on Mark I barely see the man run in front of us with raised arms. "Stop. You're going to kill him."

"He deserves it," I growl.

His voice is calm, but I hear desperation underneath. "I'm sure he does, but you're not a killer."

"You don't know me." I tighten my grip, and Mark's struggle falters.

"Maybe not, but if you kill him, that will be on your conscience."

Through my eyelashes, I peer at the man with the familiar dark hair and a scar on his eyebrow.

His blue eyes plead for me to let go.

"Please."

Releasing Mark, I crawl several steps back. His limp body falls to the ground. My body shakes with shock as I wonder what I've done.

The man checks Mark's pulse. "He's alive." He breathes a sigh of relief. As if approaching a wild dog, he approaches me with raised hands. "Hey, are you okay?"

I stare at my trembling hands. My eyes water, blurring my vision. "I . . . I almost . . . ki-killed him."

"But you didn't. You're safe now." He kneels to my eye level, his awareness full of worry. "You're bleeding. Where does it hurt?"

I shake my head. "It doesn't."

"You're in shock. You probably can't feel it yet. I need to look and make sure you don't have any serious injuries." He leans closer, and I jerk away. "Sorry. I didn't mean to scare you. I won't touch you. I just need a closer look. Is that okay?" I'm wary of him, but he seems sincere. I nod, and he inches closer but keeps a comfortable distance. "You have scrapes on your arms and legs." His eyes wander over my body. "Your lip's busted. Looks like you'll have a black eye by morning. Can you stand?"

I stand, and sharp pain radiates from my left ankle to my leg, so I put all my weight on my right foot.

"Is your ankle bothering you?"

"It's only twisted. I'm fine," I say.

"Do you know him? Do you know why he did this to you?"

"Yes . . . no . . . I mean . . ." After inhaling deeply, I double over. Mark's last words and the memory of hypnosis replay in my head. "I only met him once, but now I think he knows me from before." The stranger cocks his head and looks at me, confused. "Never mind," I add quickly, realizing he has no idea what I mean.

"We need to call the police."

Panic rises, and I hobble backward. "They're going to arrest me."

"No, they won't. I witnessed enough. He attacked you, and you acted in self-defense. Plus, we want to call while he's still unconscious."

Taking his phone out of his pocket, he walks out of earshot, then returns a moment later.

"They'll need statements from us. We should wait on the bench over there, away from him." He scowls at Mark before turning his attention back to me.

I limp toward the bench. With outstretched arms, the stranger leans toward me as if to help me walk. He backs away when I shoot him a glare.

Adrenaline has worn off, accentuating the extent of my injuries. It hurts to take a deep breath, and my lip throbs. I sit on the bench, but he doesn't sit next to me.

An ambulance and the police arrive promptly. Paramedics immediately go to Mark and assess his injuries. They take him away on a stretcher while the police approach us. A male officer talks with the blue-eyed man next to the police car.

I stay on the bench while a female officer approaches me. I give her a quick rundown of the events, omitting the part where I was going to kill Mark.

She writes my statement in a notebook. "And what involvement did the man over there have?"

"He tried to stop the attack, but he was too far away. His shouts distracted Mark, and I was able to defend myself against him." I touch my lip and wince.

"Okay. Wait here while I consult with my partner."

The officers compare statements. From their faces, it seems they believe the man had something to do with Mark's injuries. Our statements must align because they let the stranger go.

The woman officer sends a paramedic to look over my injuries. They clean out my wounds and dress them, then wrap my twisted ankle with a bandage. They tell me to stay off it for a few days. The corner of my bottom lip is split, but it doesn't need stitches. They say I'm lucky and clear me to go home. After the officers drive me home, I crawl into bed and call Trish.

"Hey, girl!" she answers.

I've been able to maintain my composure until now, but Trish's voice breaks something inside of me, and I can only sob.

"Jane? What's wrong?" Her voice is full of fear, and I'm still unable to speak. "Where are you?"

I open my mouth, but only sobs come out. A shaky breath momentarily calms me. "Home."

"I'm on my way." She ends the call, and I wail into my pillow, smearing blood and dirt on the pillowcase.

12. Alpha-Staking Claim

Trish barges through the front door, shouting my name. She rushes to my bedroom and freezes with her hands over her mouth. "Oh my gosh, Jane! What happened to you?"

I want to tell her everything but thinking about how I almost killed a man forces me into silence. Physically, I'm in pain, but it's more of a nuisance compared to the emotional distraught of the attack. It was a normal day, and I planned on doing normal things, not kill a man.

When I don't answer, Trish scoots her way under the covers. She holds me close and finger combs my hair while I cry until there are no more tears left, but I do not speak.

"Do you need anything? Food? Something to drink?"

It's then I realize the burning in my throat is from lack of saliva.

"Water."

My voice cracks on the word. I never thought speaking would take so much effort.

She leaves the room and comes back with a glass of water. I bring the cup to my mouth to gulp and recoil in pain. I had forgotten about my lip. Gently, I sip. Water drips down my chin and onto my shirt. Trish watches me with concern.

"Thanks," I say.

Trish takes the glass from me and sets it on the bedside table. "Jane, what happened to you?"

My mind and body have finally relaxed enough to speak, and I tell her everything, leaving out the parts where I almost killed Mark and that I think he knows me from before.

Those parts, I'm still in denial about.

"That piece of shit!" She jumps off the bed and paces the room. "He deserves so much worse. I'm so sorry this happened to you. You didn't deserve this. I'm staying over tonight to take care of you."

"Shit!" I exclaim. "We're supposed to work today."

"Neither of us are working today. I already got our shifts covered."

"You're the best. I don't know what I would do without you."

Trish orders Chinese for dinner. She doesn't leave my side until it arrives. She sets the containers on the dining table, and the aroma of chow mien and egg rolls fills the room. My stomach grumbles, and I want to devour it all, but I nibble slowly to avoid stinging my lip.

Trish watches me intently.

"How was your date with Miguel last night?" I ask to take the attention off me.

"It was nice. We should do a double date sometime."

"Yeah."

"Speaking of Julian . . ." She bites into her egg roll and swallows before she continues. "I'm surprised he's not here waiting on you hand and foot."

After twenty-four hours, I have yet to hear from him. I'm worried, but I don't want him to see me like this.

"Is there something you want to talk about?" she asks.

"He left in a hurry yesterday. Said he was late meeting a client. I haven't heard from him since, so I didn't call him." I stab the chow mien with my chopsticks.

"This is bullshit!" She slams the table with her palm.

"It's not that big of a deal. I'm sure I'll hear from him tomorrow."

"It is a big deal. One, he should've at least texted you good night *and* good morning. Two, his girlfriend got attacked by the guy he was with when he first met you. Where's your phone? I'm going to call him." She stalks around the kitchen, looking in all directions.

"No, you're not," I say sternly, hobbling after her.

"The hell I'm not." She finds my phone next to the toaster, then hurries away from me and taps at the screen.

"Trish, stop." I lean against the island separating us, relieving myself from baring weight on my feet. "I don't want him to know."

She looks at me. "Why not?"

"Because I don't want him to see me like this."

"Do you plan on not seeing him for weeks? Because that's how long it will take for your wounds to heal." She gestures toward my face.

She makes a fair point. I can't hide from him for weeks.

"I'll say I tripped on a run and wiped out. I mean, I *was* running and wiped out, so it's not a total lie."

She exhales. "Fine. I won't say anything to him." She sets the phone back on the counter.

"Thank you!"

"Although, I think he deserves to know," she adds quickly. "But I'll respect your wishes."

We walk back to the dining table, and we're halfway there when there's a knock at the door. We look at each other, puzzled.

"Who is it?" I whisper.

"I don't know. This is your house. Are you expecting company?" she whispers back.

"Of course not."

"What if it's Julian?"

"Then, get rid of him. Tell him I'm sick or something. Better yet, tell him I don't want to see him."

"See, I knew you were mad at him for not texting you."

"Maybe just a little."

Another knock.

"Go." I push her toward the door while I hide around the corner.

She opens it a crack and peers outward, then opens the door wider.

"Howdy, neighbor," she greets in a cheerful tone.

Neighbor? Does she mean *my* neighbor? What is he doing here?

"Hi? Is the woman who lives here home?" he asks tentatively in a deep voice.

"Um . . . yes, hold on." She closes the door. "Jane?" she whispers. I peek my head out and look at her with wide eyes. "Your neighbor is here."

"Yeah, thanks. I gathered that. Why is he here?"

"I don't know, but this is a perfect opportunity to finally meet the delicious mystery man from across the street."

"Perfect is not the best choice of words for this situation."

"Get your ass over here." She waves me over. "He might need to borrow a cup of sugar or something."

Huffing, I limp to the door.

Trish stands beside me as I open it. The man standing in front of me is the man who saved me from killing Mark.

"You?" I say forcefully.

"Me," he blurts.

"You're my neighbor?"

"It appears so."

"Wait. You two already know each other?" Trish interrupts. She places her hands on her hips and raises an eyebrow. "I thought you said you've never met him."

Her tone is accusatory.

"I haven't. Not really. He was there in the park today. I didn't know he was my neighbor."

"Oh. I see. On that note, I'm going to clean up the dinner mess. Holler if you need me." She pivots and leaves me alone with him.

He steps back as I hobble out onto the porch and close the door behind me.

"I know this looks weird," he says, running a hand through his messy hair. "Showing up on your doorstep and all, but I wanted to come by and check on you. See if you're doing okay."

"I'm fine. Thanks."

He nods. "Good. I'm glad." For a moment, neither of us speaks. He opens his mouth but shuts it and clears his throat. "Okay, then. I'll leave you to it." He turns and strides toward the stairs.

"Wait," I call. He stops and turns to face me. "How did you know I was your neighbor? It's just . . . we've never officially met. I didn't know what my neighbor looked like until now."

For a moment, he stares at me before answering. "You read on the porch under the light. I knew what you looked like."

That makes sense. I read out there all the time, and I did wave to him that one night.

"Did you know it was me the first time you saw me in the park?"

"The first time?" He furrows his brows.

"I tripped over my shoelace. You caught me before I could fall to the ground."

"Right." He snaps his fingers. "I thought you looked familiar." A moment of awkward silence settles between us. "It was nice to meet you. You know where to find me if you need anything." He turns away.

He steps off the bottom step when I call out, "I'm Jane, by the way."

It irritates me he didn't ask my name, and I let it show in my tone.

He turns his head my way to say, "Theo."

"Hey, Theo?"

He turns to me once again. "I'm glad you were there today. I don't want to imagine what would've happened if you weren't."

"Neither do I. Have a good night. Jane."

He says my name like he is trying it out for the first time and doesn't like the way it sounds. It sounds foreign when he says it.

Only after he crosses the walkway and advances into the street do I turn and go back into the house.

"You bitch," Trish jokes. "Did you have to close the door? I wanted to eavesdrop."

I giggle. "Sorry."

"Well?"

She's desperate for the details.

"He's a little odd. Seems antisocial. His name is Theo." I shrug.

"So what? You're odd and antisocial, too. And he's a twelve out of ten on the hot scale."

"Do you ever think about anything else?"

"No. Not really."

Trish and I sit on the couch and turn on a movie, but she's too interested in her phone. She doesn't look up from the screen when she asks, "What's Julian's last name?"

"Why?"

"I'm trying to stalk his socials to see what he's been up to."

I scoff. "Give it a rest."

She looks up, feigning innocence. "I'm just looking. I'm not going to message him."

I roll my eyes. "It's Thomas."

She taps her screen with her thumb, then uses her finger to scroll.

When her eyebrows furrow, I ask, "What is it?"

"I can't find him anywhere."

"Maybe he doesn't have socials." I shrug again.

She raises an eyebrow at me. "He's like, what, twenty-three? What twenty-three-year-old doesn't have any form of social media?"

"I don't have social media."

She rolls her eyes. "You have an excuse. Plus, you barely know how to order a Lyft."

I throw a pillow at her. "Yes, I do."

Trish giggles and throws the pillow back at me, abandoning her search on Julian and sitting back to watch the movie.

Every five minutes, she looks at me like I'm going to spontaneously combust or something. It's annoying, but I know she does it because she cares and worries about me.

She falls asleep thirty minutes into the movie, and I'm left alone with my thoughts. I keep checking my phone for any sign of Julian. When the unknown is too much to bear, I draft a text.

Me: Hey!

I receive a read receipt, so at least I know he's alive. He responds within seconds.

Julian: Hey there, gorgeous!

I'm relieved he responded but also furious I haven't heard from him all day. I told Trish I didn't want him to know what happened to me, but a part of me wishes he were here to hold me.

He better have a good excuse.

Me: Is everything okay?

Julian: Yes. Why?

Me: You said you would "Talk to me later." But you've been radio silent since you stormed off yesterday.

Julian: Are you mad at me?

Me: You bet your ass I am.

Julian: I'm sorry. I didn't want to "storm" off, but I told you I was late meeting a client.

His audacious, mocking tone irritates me.
I can play that game, too.

Me: No. I'm sorry. I didn't realize meetings with clients lasted 28 hrs.

Julian: Yup. You're mad.

Me: You think?

Julian: I'll make it up to you. I promise.

Me: Don't bother.

I receive a read receipt, but he doesn't respond. Then ten minutes go by without a response. I'm regretting my last text. My intensions were supposed to show him I was upset, not to end things with him.

Three loud bangs rattle the door, and Trish jolts awake.

"Jane? It's Julian," he yells.

"Shit!"

Trish sits up with one eye open. "What's Julian doing here?"

"I texted him. I was angry, and it kind of sounded like I was breaking up with him."

Three more bangs on the door. "Come on, Jane. Open the door!"

"What are you going to do?" she asks.

"I didn't think he would show up here. I can't let him see me like this."

"I got this," she says with confidence.

I lie on the couch, pulling a blanket over me. Trish opens the door only wide enough for him to see her face.

"Trish? Where's Jane?" he asks, desperation behind his words.

"She doesn't want to see you right now."

"Please? I need to talk to her. I need to know if she meant what she said."

"I think you should go. Call her tomorrow after you both sleep it off and calm down."

"Calm down?" he snarls, raising his voice. "I won't calm down until I talk to Jane."

It's nearly midnight, and his angry tone will only get louder if I don't talk to him. My sweatpants hide my leg wounds, but I need to hide my arms and lip. Limping, I grab a hoodie, put the hood over my head, and pull the strings. I look silly, but it helps. Hopefully, the darkness of the night conceals my face.

"Julian, you need to leave. Now," Trish demands.

I place a hand on her shoulder. "It's okay, I got it from here."

"I'm not going anywhere. He's drunk," she whispers to me.

"Julian," I say cautiously from the doorway.

"Jane?" His shoulders relax. "Baby, I'm so sorry. Please don't be mad at me." I step outside, grateful I forgot to turn on the porch light.

Trish stands right by my side.

"Why are you here?" I ask.

"Because you're mad at me, and I'm trying to make it up to you," he slurs.

His car is parked in the driveway, which infuriates me more.

"This is not the way to do it." He steps toward me, but I step backward. "Please don't." I hold up my hands to ward him off.

"I can't give my girlfriend a hug and kiss?" he snaps.

"Not like this. You're drunk. What's worse is that you drove here drunk."

"Fuck." He stomps and loses his balance, almost falling off the top step, but he catches the railing. "Why am I fucking everything up lately?"

Trish stomps to him and grabs his arm. "Enough!" She leads him down the steps. "Jane doesn't need this right now after the day she had."

He whips his arm away from her. "She had a bad day because her boyfriend didn't call her? There are worse things going on. Not receiving a phone call shouldn't be at the top of the list."

His voice is malicious.

"Had you called her in the first place, you would know that is not the case." She pushes him toward his car, and he stumbles backward.

"Don't—"

A door slams, and Theo sprints across the street. "Jane? What's the problem?" Stepping between Trish and Julian, he keeps his eyes trained on me.

Julian looks him up and down, snarling. "Who the fuck do you think you are?"

"I think you need to leave before you find out." Theo locks his gaze onto me.

"Okay, enough!" I shout, descending the stairs. Everyone looks my way. Trish retreats from the guys to my side. "Theo, thanks for everything, but this doesn't concern you."

"Yeah, *The-o*. This is between me and my *girlfriend*." His cadence sounds like he's marking his territory. He gives Theo an unsettling, mocking smirk.

"Who are you?" Theo asks Julian forcefully.

"Who are you?" Julian retorts.

"Theo, this is my boyfriend, Julian," I say. "He's drunk and upset that I'm mad at him. Julian, this is my neighbor, Theo."

"Of course he's your neighbor," Julian mumbles before turning to Theo. "You have some nerve being here."

"Julian, is it?" Theo turns and looks at Julian for the first time, anger writhing in his eyes. They stare at each other, like they're both wolves trying to stake their claim as the alpha. I find it quite disturbing. "I think Julius here needs to leave."

"It's Julian."

"I don't care," Theo says plainly, but his hands ball into fists at his sides. "You still need to leave."

"I'm not leaving."

"Jane?" Theo calls. "Do you want Jonah here to leave?"

I roll my eyes at his childish behavior.

"Seriously? It's Julian," Julian growls.

"Isn't that what I said?" Theo retorts. "Jane, it's up to you."

"He's drunk. He can't drive like this. He can stay here."

Theo's jaw clenches, and he rubs the back of his neck.

I don't know why he cares if Julian stays here. Besides the earlier event, he doesn't know me.

"Where were you earlier?" Theo asks Julian.

"Wouldn't you like to know?" Julian scoffs.

"You're right. I do. Because while your so-called girlfriend was being attacked, you were nowhere in sight. Thankfully, I was there before the worst-case scenario happened. Showing up here, acting aggressive, makes everything worse."

For the first time, Julian's aggressive demeanor fades, and fear replaces it. "What are you talking about? What attack?"

I didn't want Julian to know, but now that he does, I'm relieved.

Trish puts a concerned hand on mine, but I remove my hoodie, letting her know it's okay.

I limp over to Julian, and his gaze falls to my ankle. As I draw nearer, his eyes wander over the bandages covering my arms, his face filling with dread. He stares at my lip, and I'm almost certain half of my face is bruised. He reaches for my face, but I flinch away.

"Who did this to you?" he snarls.

I swallow hard and whisper, "Mark."

Julian's eyes darken, and his nostrils flare. "He's dead, right?" he growls as he turns to Theo. "Please tell me you killed that motherfucker?"

Theo shakes his head. "No. He's messed up pretty bad, though. Jane made sure of that."

"I don't understand."

"I'll explain later," I tell Julian.

"Are we all good now? Because I would like to go back to bed," Trish says.

I nod at her, and she goes back into the house.

"Come on, let's get inside." I motion for Julian, then direct my attention to Theo. "Thanks for everything, but we got it from here."

"You sure?" Theo asks, and I nod. "You know where to find me." He sneers at Julian, looking him up and down, before retreating across the street.

Julian follows me into the house, keeping distance, trying not to touch me. Trish is already fast asleep on the couch.

I lead us to the bedroom. He stops in the doorway, regarding me cautiously, before he enters and closes the door.

I get into bed, but Julian stands still, staring at nothing. "Are you coming to bed?"

"How?"

I don't have the energy to explain. Sighing, I pat the spot next to me. He sits at the edge, leaving plenty of space between us.

"I was running in the park this morning. Mark started chasing me. He hit me in the face, and I fell and rolled." I gauge his reaction. His face contorting with anguish, he closes his eyes. "While I was down, he kept kicking me and was saying things."

"What kind of things?"

"That he should've killed me the first time we met. Then something about how he's supposed to bring me in alive, and if I die, it will just be collateral damage."

Julian finally looks at me with a hint of something behind his eyes. Is it fear? Shock?

"Then Theo showed up, yelling for him to stop. It distracted him long enough for me to defend myself. I

126

broke his leg, then his nose." Pausing, I wonder if I should tell him the truth and finally say out loud what almost happened.

Will he think differently of me?

"I almost broke his neck," I say in a rush. Julian doesn't flinch or react, so I continue. "The thing that scares me is that I would have done it if Theo hadn't stopped me."

"Why did he stop you?"

"Probably so we wouldn't be having this conversation through glass."

He stares at the bed, quiet for several minutes.

"Say something," I whisper.

"I don't know what to say."

"Anything. What are you thinking? What are you feeling?"

"I should ask you those questions. Not the other way around." He turns his attention to me, and regret fills his eyes. I place my hand on top of his, and he inhales sharply. "Can you ever forgive me?"

"For tonight?" I ask. "Don't worry about it. It was a big misunderstanding. You were drunk. I antagonized you when I shouldn't have. You didn't know what happened to me, and you weren't supposed to find out like that. I honestly wasn't sure if I was going to tell you at all."

"Why wouldn't you tell me?"

"I didn't want you to see me like this. I didn't want you to know that the guy you were with when we first met was responsible."

When he doesn't respond, I crawl under the blankets. A moment later, Julian removes his shirt and shoes, then turns off the light and crawls into bed next to me. He doesn't kiss me or touch me.

Unsure if it's out of fear or courtesy or if he's still too drunk to process everything, I'm physically, mentally, and emotionally exhausted to analyze his pensiveness, so I close my eyes and fall asleep.

13. The Darkness Within

The bed is empty. I check my phone and see it's half past eleven and that I have two unread texts, one from Julian and one from Trish. I read Trish's first.

Trish: Hey! I didn't want to wake you this morning. I got your shifts covered for the rest of the week. Please rest and let me know if you need ANYTHING. Love you!

Me: Thanks Trish! You are the best. Talk to you soon. Love you!

I read Julian's next.

Julian: Good morning gorgeous! Sorry I had to leave you. I had important business at work that couldn't wait. I should be back this afternoon. Text me when you're up. Xo

Me: Hi! Just woke up. Going to take a hot bath.

His reply comes within seconds.

Julian: I'm leaving work in 30, and I'll be right over. Need me to bring you anything?

Me: Maybe some lunch?

Julian: Okay. See you soon. Xo

Getting out of bed, I bear full weight on both of my feet and wince. I limp to the bathroom, look in the mirror, and barely recognize my reflection. A purple bruise surrounds my right eye. The swelling on my lip has subsided, but that's also bruising.

I turn on the bath faucet and add Epsom salt to the water. It's going to sting but will clean out my wounds. Slowly, I peel off the bandages from my limbs. Cotton sticks to the dried blood, stinging with each tug. I remove the bandage around my ankle, and it's bruised but not swollen.

Standing naked in front of the full-length mirror, I assess the damage. I have several scrapes on my arms and legs. The largest of them on my outer thigh and shoulder, smaller ones on my knees and elbows and across my back. A sensitive, foot-sized bruise has spread across my ribs.

I step into the bath and wince as the salt seeps into the abrasions. With slow breaths, I ease my way to lie down, submerging myself. After a few minutes, the stinging subsides, and my muscles relax. I try moving my ankle under the water, the range of motion slight. I soak until the water turns cold, let it drain, then run the shower to wash my hair.

An hour later, Julian busies himself in the kitchen, wiping the counters and putting away the dishes as I finish my lunch. I throw away the empty container and lean against the counter with my arms crossed.

"You don't have to do that," I tell him.

"I want to," he says plainly. "How are you dealing with everything?"

"Okay, I guess. It's just . . ."

I tried not to think much about the attack, but after mentioning it, I'm worried about what might happen.

"It's just what?"

"I'm worried. What if Mark comes after me again? Or presses charges against me?"

Julian pauses mid-scrub, his grip tightening on the sponge. Suds seep out and drip into the sink. "You don't have to worry about that." He rinses off the dish and places it in the drying rack, then rests both palms on the counter. Without looking at me, he says, "I promise you'll never hear or see from Mark ever again."

"You don't know that for sure."

"Trust me. I do." He turns away to dry his hands on a towel.

If Mark is from my past, I can't trust he won't come after me again. Although I didn't get to see the full memory of my escape, I remember everything I felt at that moment. I was desperate to get away from something or someone. What if that someone was Mark? If he found me here, in Bridgeport, after all these months, he'll hunt me for the second time.

I place my hand on Julian's arm, and he turns to me. "There's something I need to tell you." Julian stiffens, but his demeanor softens. He nods for me to continue. "When I was under hypnosis, I had a memory of my accident. I was escaping from somewhere or someone. The things Mark said to me during the attack lead me to believe he's from my past. I think he will come after me again."

Julian grabs my hands, squeezes them slightly, and stares into my eyes. "I just made you a promise that you'll never hear or see from him again, and I intend to keep it. You don't have to worry about him anymore. I took care of it."

"How?"

He smiles. "Have I ever told you how persuasive I can be?"

My shoulders relax as I chuckle.

I've seen how persuasive he can be when he took me on our second date. I'm still not sure if it's enough to keep Mark away, but for today, I'm safe.

He kisses my forehead, then eyes me up and down. "Cute robe." He twirls the sash, eyes meeting mine, and he steps back before dropping it.

A moment of confliction dawns on his face. He wants to lean in for a kiss but doesn't. Thinking I'm fragile, he's afraid to make contact with me, like I'm going to break with the slightest touch.

I recognize the look all too well. It's exactly how I was treated in the hospital. The officer did it by ignoring me. Nurses would barely talk to me as they checked my vitals. I didn't like it then, and I certainly don't like it now.

Pursing my lips, I curl my hands into fists. "I'm not going to break," I say in a raised voice.

"I know." He shies away.

"Then, why won't you touch me?"

It comes out in a whisper, as if I'm desperate for physical touch.

"I don't want to hurt you," he whispers.

I understand where he's coming from, but I'm reminded of past feelings of rejection. Not wanting him to see the tears forming in my eyes, I go to my bedroom. I fling the robe off and put on a bra and underwear.

"Jane." Julian's voice draws near, and I quickly wipe the tears away. "Listen, I'm . . ." He freezes with his hand over his mouth as his eyes wander over my exposed body.

"Nope," I say, shaking a finger. "Don't do that. I need you to keep your composure. I don't want you to feel sorry for me." He closes his eyes and inhales deeply. "It's really not that bad. It looks worse than it feels."

He opens his eyes and seems to have gained his composure but turns away as I dress. "I want to tell you I'm sorry. What happened to you is eating at me, and I don't know how I'm supposed to act around you."

"You can act as you normally do. I'm still your girlfriend. You're allowed to touch me and kiss me."

"I know. I just need some time." He walks out of the room.

***

The Lyft driver drops me off at Dr. Wagner's office. I've been anxiously waiting for this session, hoping to undergo hypnosis again, but Dr. Wagner won't stand for it today, especially after yesterday's attack. He will want to spend the session talking about the attack and my feelings about it. He'll tell me it's necessary to work through the trauma and all that mumbo jumbo I don't want to hear about.

He's already waiting for me, sitting in his chair. His eyes land on my cut lip and black eye, then wander to my arms and legs. I wanted to wear pants and a long-sleeved shirt to hide the scrapes, but the summer heat made it unbearable. Now that I'm here, I wish I would have risked the heatstroke and put on the damned outfit.

His expression remains tranquil, I assume from years of experience. I imagine he has seen worse.

I take my seat on the couch and wait for him to ask his usual question to start the session.

Without looking away from my face, Dr. Wagner clicks the end of his pen against his notebook. "Any change in your memory?"

I raise an eyebrow. Given my appearance, I thought he'd want to dive right into what happened. Although I'm grateful he didn't, I'll now have to tell him I think I'm hearing voices so I can avoid the conversation about Mark altogether. Not that I want to bring up Mark at all, but I'll talk about anything else at this point.

I divert my eyes to the floor and grip the arm of the sofa. "I think I'm losing my mind. Or there's a delayed side effect from my head injury."

Dr. Wagner leans forward, resting his elbows on his knees. "Why do you think that?"

"I've been hearing . . . I don't know . . . things."

"Can you be more specific?"

"It's like voices in my head. Sometimes it's so loud that I can't understand. Then other times, I think someone is talking to me, but their lips aren't moving. And the other day at work, I heard Trish talking, but she was nowhere around me." I look up at him, and his eyes remain on me, but he's not looking at me like I'm losing my mind.

At first, he doesn't say anything, and I begin to regret telling him. Finally, he leans back in his chair and says, "I'm sure everything is fine. Sleep deprivation or dehydration can cause these types of symptoms. Just make sure you're drinking plenty of water and getting enough sleep."

He smiles and nods as if it's normal, but the crease forming between his eyebrows tells me something else. I sigh, as if I'm relieved, but I'm not fully convinced.

"Is there anything else you want to tell me?" Dr. Wagner asks.

I shake my head. "Nope."

He's silent as he looks at me with raised eyebrows, like he's waiting for me to finally explain my appearance. I fidget in my seat, looking around and tapping my thighs with my fingers.

"You're probably wondering what happened to my face," I say lightly, as if I'm telling him about the weather.

Dr. Wagner cocks his head as though I'm telling an interesting story. I wonder if it's a psychological tactic to get someone to talk.

"It's not that big of a deal. It looks worse than it is." I wave in dismissal. His expression remains the same. "I tripped while running yesterday. Fell pretty hard. No big deal."

He raises an eyebrow. His quiet stare is intimidating, and I can't keep up the act for the full hour if I'm going to convince him to put me under hypnosis again.

"Okay, fine." I throw my hands up in defeat. The quick motion sends a shock to my ribs, and I hold back a gasp. "Mark attacked me on my run yesterday morning. Happy now?"

"No, I'm not," he finally responds.

"I know what you're going to say."

"Please, by all means, enlighten me." He leans back into the recliner, crossing his leg, pen poised to the paper.

"You're going to tell me it's necessary to talk about the trauma in order to heal. Then you'll ask me a million questions I don't want to answer, like . . . What were you experiencing during the attack? How did the attack affect you afterward? How are you dealing with it now?"

"Why don't you want to answer those questions?"

"Because talking about it won't change the fact that it happened. And before you say anything"—he opens his mouth to interject, but I hold up a finger to stop him—"I know you're going to say I have to work through those feelings and emotions to move on and heal. The answer is no. I don't. I could recognize my feelings and emotions as they were happening. I processed them in a healthy way, and now I feel fine." I inhale and exhale deeply, not realizing I rambled with only one breath.

"Can you tell me how you were able to do that?" He seems intrigued.

"I knew I was nervous when he started chasing me, but I also knew I had to stay focused if I were to get away."

"But you didn't get away."

"Obviously," I say dryly. "There wasn't anywhere to go. I had to keep running until I reached the road or until he caught up to me. I felt his fist connect with my face, but it didn't hurt. The rolling across the pavement, however, stung like a bitch. Then he was standing over me, ready to attack, but I wasn't afraid. I was pissed." I stop and look at my hands gripping the edge of the couch, then relax them.

"Then what?"

"Then he kicked me. That hurt, which pissed me off more. I was waiting for an opportunity to defend myself. Then my neighbor showed up, yelling for Mark to stop. Mark hesitated, and that was my cue. I had a rush of adrenaline, then so much rage. I wanted to hurt him." Rage for Mark builds inside me.

"For revenge?"

His question throws me off guard. Yes, I wanted revenge, but it was more than that. Mark's words chilled me to my core. He could be from my past, and he wanted to kill me. But I don't want to tell Dr. Wagner. Not yet.

"No. For justice."

"Justice for you?" he asks.

I glance at the pendulum sitting on the bookshelf, and the memory of running through a tunnel, desperate to escape, floods back to me.

A brick wall surrounded a building. That's where I must have escaped from. But it was too large to only contain me. Who else is inside, desperate to get out? How many other people have suffered under Mark?

I steer my attention back to Dr. Wagner. "Justice for anyone he has caused pain to."

"Do you feel relieved, knowing you caused him pain?"

Hesitating, I think back. A surge of adrenaline coursed through me when I hurt him. I enjoyed causing him pain. My adrenaline was mixed with wrath. Disdain so strong that I wanted him dead. But then I remember how shaken up I was when I realized I almost killed him. Only soulless monsters can take another person's life and not feel remorse.

I'd like to think that was the reason for my shock, that I let my rage overcome me, that I almost did the unthinkable. But that's not what shocked me. I was stunned because I knew I wouldn't shed an ounce of remorse over his dead body. That I could carry on with my life like it never happened.

Does that make me the monster?

A chill creeps down my spine, raising goose bumps on my arms. I rub them away with my hands.

"Jane?" Dr. Wagner breaks into my thoughts.

"Hmm?"

"Did causing Mark pain give you a sense of relief?"

"No," I lie. "I was relieved knowing he couldn't attack me anymore, but I feel ashamed of how badly I hurt him," I say, thinking this is how a normal person should feel.

He appears to believe it, and I realize this was his plan all along. To understand what I'm feeling. I guess therapy works.

I understand now how the eight-year-old me was capable of such malice. She had a darkness in her. A malevolence that hid when Jane woke up.

Mark brought out that villain in me. I should suppress it, but I like the way it feels. My mind rolls over the possibilities of this new version of myself. Of hurting those responsible for my accident. I don't know who "they" are that Mark had mentioned, but I'm determined to find out and let the darkness fall upon them.

14. The Visitor

It's been five days since my attack. My lip has healed, and the bruises have faded to a pale yellow. Scrapes have shrunk, scabs have peeled off, and my ankle is as good as new, but Julian and Trish have been hovering over me nonstop, like I'm an infant needing to be waited on hand and foot. They're driving me insane, and I can't handle it much longer.

Sitting on the couch, I surf channels as Julian and Trish argue in the kitchen about what we should do for dinner. Trish thinks we should go to a restaurant because getting me out of the house will be good for me. Julian thinks we should order in because I'm not ready to be out in public yet. They talk about me as if I'm not in the next room and can hear everything they say. Neither one bothers to ask me what I want.

Quietly, I grab my purse, slip into flip-flops, and sneak out the front door. I run across the street, looking back to make sure they haven't spotted me, and knock on Theo's door.

He answers and looks at me warily.

"Can I hide here for a while?" I look behind me, then back at him.

He doesn't hesitate to step aside and let me in, taking another glance at my house before closing the door.

"Thank you!" I sigh, leaning against the door.

"No problem. It would be nice to know who you're hiding from in case they come looking for you."

"My boyfriend and best friend. They're treating me like a child, and I haven't been alone in five days." He nods. "Currently, they're arguing about whether we should go out or dine in and what situation is best for me."

"Well, what do *you* want to do for dinner?"

"Thank you," I shout, swinging my arm out wide, which bumps the table and jostles the ceramic dish of keys. The dish wobbles, causing the keys to clink within. I give Theo an apologetic smile, and he nods. "Apparently, asking me wasn't an option."

"If you're hungry, I have some food. Not much. I don't cook, but we could probably find something edible. Or we can get in my car and go somewhere."

"They're going to notice I'm gone soon. I just need a moment away."

"Suit yourself. Stay as long as you want." He leads me into the living room. "Welcome to my humble abode." He gestures to the living room.

Theo's place is simple. No TV, no décor on the walls, and the dining room comprises a foldable table with one chair. Everything is neatly in place, but the little furniture he has seems to clash. In the living room, two couches sit opposite of each other, with a coffee table between them. On top is a box, with wires jutting out in all directions.

I sink into the couch facing the window. The opaque mirror-tinted one that I see every time I relax on my front porch. But from inside, the view shows my house clearly. After we officially met, he had said he recognized me because I read out there. Is this how he saw me? While he sat in the comfort of his living room? Has he been secretly watching me?

Theo walks by and sits on the opposite couch. I wait for him to start a conversation so I can comment on how he has a *lovely* view. Instead, I'm distracted when he picks up the box from the table and messes with the wires.

"What's that?" I ask.

"An old radio," he says dryly.

I raise a hand to my cheeks. "Oh my gosh. I had no idea." Placing my other hand to my chest, I flash a wide smile and say, "Thank you for clarifying that for me."

He stops and peers at me. "Is that sarcasm?"

"Obviously." I roll my eyes and slink back into the couch. "What are you doing with the radio?"

"Trying to fix it."

"Why?"

"Why not?" he retorts.

I give up on the conversation. He clearly needs to work on his people skills. As he works on the radio, I sit in silence.

The quiet is peaceful, and I'm nearly asleep when my ringing phone startles my eyes open.

It bothers me Trish and Julian were so focused on arguing that they didn't notice my absence for thirty minutes. I know who it is without looking at the phone.

"Hello?" I answer, annoyed.

"Thank God," Julian breathes. "Where the hell are you?" he asks in a sterner tone.

"I left."

"Clearly. Where are you? I'm coming to get you."

I look over at Theo. If he's listening to my phone call, he hides it well by acting uninterested.

I lean my head back against the couch. "Don't worry. I'll be home in a few minutes." I end the call before he can respond. I stand and wrap my purse around my shoulder. "Thanks for letting me hide out for a while."

Theo doesn't look up. "Anytime."

***

When I open my front door, Trish and Julian are arguing about my absence.

"Enough!" I yell, slamming the door.

They both stop and look at me.

"Thank God you're okay. We were worried sick." Julian rushes toward me with open arms.

I hold my hands up to stop him. "I can't take it anymore. I'm not a child. I'm not broken. I don't have PTSD, and I don't need anyone to take care of me. I have said 'I'm fine' so many times it doesn't sound like a word anymore. I'm never alone. You don't let me do anything for myself. You argue about what's best for me but never bother to ask me what I want."

Julian and Trish exchange glances, then lower their heads in shame.

"You're right," Julian says.

"We're sorry," says Trish.

"Good because I'm starving."

"What would you like to do for dinner?" Julian asks.

"We can go out or order in. Whatever you want," Trish adds.

"I'm going to order a pizza, and the two of you can eat whatever you want, as long as it's not in this house." They look at each other, then look at me. "I'm kicking you out." I make my voice as firm as I can manage. "Both of you. I want to be left alone for a while. Please."

I sense their hesitancy, but, eventually, they agree. I open the door and usher them out.

Julian leans in to give me a quick kiss. "I'll call you later."

"No. I'll call you *tomorrow*."

I hope he gets the hint that I need at least the night without him.

Through the window, I watch them to make sure they drive away. As they do, I exhale a sigh of relief. The rumble in my stomach calls me away from the window and back into the comfort of my empty house. Not wasting any more time, I pick up the phone and place an order at the local pizza shop.

Twenty minutes later, the delivery driver hands me two boxes, one of the pizza, the other containing breadsticks. The delicious scent of cheese and oregano fills the kitchen. It's too much for just me, and hearing Theo say he doesn't have much food and doesn't cook didn't sit right with me.

Even though he's been invisible for months, he has really come through for me this past week. He saved me in the park, then came to my rescue when he thought Julian was a threat on my front lawn, then today—for letting me hide out. Food is one small way to repay his kindness.

Without another thought, I close the lid, pick up both boxes, and march across the street.

Theo answers, and his eyes rest on the pizza boxes, then he looks at me and raises an eyebrow.

"I thought you might be hungry." I smile.

He opens the door wider and steps aside. He moves the radio parts, and I set the pizza on the coffee table, opening the boxes. I grab a slice and sit on the couch. Theo does the same.

"What happened to your friends?" Theo takes a big bite.

"I kicked them out. I wanted to be left alone."

"I hate to break it to you, but you're still not alone."

"Touché. At least you don't treat me like I'm some fragile little girl."

"Why would I? You're the farthest thing from fragile."

I stop chewing for a second and look at him. "You think so?"

"Absolutely."

He takes another slice, and I look at him with questioning eyes, wanting him to elaborate.

He gets the hint.

He leans forward in his seat. "The way you were in the park. It was amazing the way you handled everything. You have some quick reflexes and killer moves. No pun intended." He smirks.

It's the first time I see him express emotion that's not serious. I smile in return, but he shakes off his smirk quickly, returning to his serious state.

We reach for another slice of pizza at the same time, and our fingers touch, sending a shock through my hand. We retract, and he gestures for me to go first. I get my piece, then he reaches for his. He guides the slice to his mouth and freezes as the doorbell rings.

"Are your friends looking for you?"

"They shouldn't be. I told them to leave me alone for the night."

He goes to the door and looks out the peephole, swears under his breath, then opens the door barely enough to look out.

"What are you doing here?" He growls.

"I told you I was coming."

The man's voice is low but friendly.

"I told you to give me a week."

"Well, I'm here now. Let me in." The man pushes the door open and steps inside.

He's shorter than Theo and has light-brown hair. When he sees me, he stops in his tracks.

"A—"

"A girl." Theo rushes to the man's side. "Yes, I have a girl in my living room." Forcing a tight-lipped smile, he shoves his hands in his pockets.

I've witnessed Theo being serious and amused, but this is the first time I've witnessed Theo flustered. I bite my lip to hide my amusement. Theo shares a stern look with his visitor, then turns his attention to me.

"This is my friend, Paul. Paul, this is Jane, *my neighbor.*"

"Of course she is," Paul says under his breath with an amused smirk. "It's nice to meet you. Jane, is it?" He steps closer to me with his hand out.

Nodding, I shake his hand.

"I didn't know you were expecting company. I can leave," I tell Theo.

"Nonsense." Paul clasps a hand onto Theo's shoulder. "I'm sure Theo here would want you to stay."

Theo clenches his jaw before forcing another tight-lipped smile at his friend. Paul flits his eyebrows up before sitting on the opposite couch. Theo sits next to me, resting his elbows on his knees. Paul grins, looking first at me, then at Theo. Theo clears his throat and shifts into his seat.

I gesture to the open boxes. "Pizza?"

Paul takes a slice. "So, how long have you two known each other?" He takes a big bite and leans back.

"Um . . . We officially met this week," I tell him.

"Ahh! Not wasting time, I see." He chuckles.

I realize now that he thinks Theo and I are dating.

"We're not . . ." I point between me and Theo. "We're not together. Just two neighbors sharing a pizza. I have a boyfriend."

Paul's smirk disappears. He glances at Theo before returning his attention to me. The exchange is odd.

"I'm sorry. I didn't mean to assume." He takes another bite. "How long have you lived across the street?"

"About three months," I say.

"Hmph." He shoves the last bite into his mouth and chews before continuing. "And you two only met this week?" He raises a brow. "That's interesting." Paul wipes his hands on his pants before picking up the old radio, fidgeting with the wires.

"It doesn't work," I say.

He chuckles and twists two wires together. The radio blares to life. "It does now."

Theo shoots him an evil-eyed stare and shakes his head. "Don't start."

His tone is threatening.

An awkward silence fills the room, and I think it has to do with me being here.

"It's getting late. I should go." I rise to leave.

146

Theo briskly stands. "Don't forget your pizza," he says, closing the lid and picking up the boxes. "I'll walk you home."

He carries the pizza as we walk across the street. "I'm sorry about Paul. He wasn't supposed to be here for a few more days."

His tone is agitated.

"It's fine." We reach my porch steps, and I turn to him. "Thanks for today, by the way."

"Anytime." He looks at me, and his face softens.

I stare into his deep blue eyes, searching for anything that will make him less of a mystery.

He clears his throat and diverts his eyes to the pizza boxes, holding them out to me. I take them from him, and he leaves without saying a word.

I put the leftover pizza in my fridge and turn on a movie, but I barely pay attention to it. Every so often, I look out the window at Theo's house, but there's never anything to see. Everything I'd seen from him before pointed to him being antisocial. Something was different about him tonight, though I can't place my finger on it. It could have been the moment he showed amusement or the split second he was tender toward me. Or it was how his demeanor changed once Paul arrived. One thing's for sure, something peculiar about him is drawing me in.

15. Betrayal

After a full day of being alone, I sit in the bathtub and let the hot water soak into my muscles. I hold my arms out to examine them. The remaining scabs are softening to where I'm able to peel them—fresh pink skin forms underneath. The scars will be faint, which I'm grateful for. One scar that will remain is the two-inch raised line on my bicep from the accident in my past life. At least now I know how it happened. I could see that much in my hypnotic state. There is so much more I need to know, like how this darkness grew inside of me. I haven't had to suppress it. It seems to only arise in certain situations, for which I'm thankful and equally dismayed.

The water cools, and I pull the plug, watching the water circle around the drain like a mini cyclone. The way it twirls sends me a familiar feeling, like déjà vu. Instead of soap swirling down the drain, I see stars circling in the sky.

I put on comfortable shorts, a tank top, throw my hair into a messy bun, then sit on my porch. There's a calmness before the sunset that I like to enjoy.

Phone in hand, I find Julian's name on my list of contacts. He's respected my boundaries all day, and I'm finally ready to call him.

A white car pulls into Theo's driveway. Theo and Paul exit the car with to-go containers in hand and look my way. I wave to them as I hit the Call button.

"Hey, Jane," Paul greets as they approach.

"One second." I hold up a finger, then point to the phone at my ear.

They continue to walk over in silence until they are at my porch steps.

"What?" Julian snaps after the fourth ring.

My face reacts before my words do. "Uh . . . hi to you, too," I retort.

"Jane?" A heavy sigh rings through the receiver. "Sorry. I thought you were someone else. You caught me at a bad time."

"Okay, I'll call you back later," I say shortly.

"No," he shouts through the receiver. "I'll be over in an hour. I have something important to tell you. Don't go anywhere. Stay inside and lock the doors."

I'm annoyed by the urgency in his tone.

"What? Why? What's going on?"

"I'll explain everything. Just do as I say."

The line goes dead before I can ask any more questions.

Theo leans against the railing. "What's going on?"

"Hell if I know. He's acting weird."

"Who's acting weird?" Paul asks.

"Julian. My boyfriend." I set the phone next to me but can't drag my eyes away from it.

Something about his tone and his words makes the hair on the back of my neck stick up.

"Weird how?" Paul's gaze sharpens.

"He told me to stay inside and lock the doors. Said he has something important to tell me, and he'll explain everything when he gets here. It seems urgent."

Paul nods to Theo, and without saying a word, jogs toward Theo's house. Theo looks at me.

"Does everyone know something I don't?" I ask.

"I don't know anything or what Joshua's talking about, but if he was adamant about you staying inside, I think you should listen." He turns away, and I rush into the house, locking the door behind me.

Through the window, I watch as Theo and Paul have a heated discussion on the side of his house. Paul uses a lot of hand gestures, while Theo nods. I wish I knew what they were saying. By the gestures, it looks like Paul is suggesting they get in the car and leave. Theo shakes his head and points my way. Paul raises his hands in defeat, then runs a hand through his hair. He points to Theo, then drops his hand and continues talking. Theo pinches the bridge of his nose, then talks again. Paul stares at him, then nods. Theo nods once, and they both go into the house.

Something funny is happening with these men, and they failed to include me in the joke.

I pace, watching the minutes tick by. My nerves are on edge, and I have an unpleasant feeling in the pit of my stomach.

Something doesn't feel right.

Julian arrives and knocks on the door. "Hey, it's me," he says through the door.

As soon as I unlock the door, he ushers in, closes the door quickly, and locks the deadbolt and chain. He looks out the window, then turns to me.

I tense, frightened, as I look at his messy hair, disheveled clothes, and sweat dripping off his forehead. "What's going on?"

"Nothing. Everything is going to be fine. Let's sit and talk."

His promise feels empty.

He leads me to the living room, and I sit on the couch, but he goes into the kitchen. Approaching me, he holds two glasses of water and hands one to me. On the other side of the coffee table, he stands, staring at the wall. His hand shakes, and the water almost spills out of the glass. After a few deep breaths, he drinks all the water in one gulp. I sip mine and set it on the coffee table in front of me.

"Julian," I say sternly, "why are you so skittish?"

He sets the glass on the table and sits next to me, making direct eye contact. "Stay calm," he says in a low, soothing voice, but I'm everything but calm.

"How am I supposed to stay calm when you're freaking me out?"

A brief look of confusion falls onto his face before fear replaces it, adding to my uneasiness.

"I need you to believe me when I say I never meant for any of this to happen." He looks away as if he's ashamed.

"What are you talking about?"

He jumps off the couch. "They're making me do it." He paces, rubbing his hands through his hair. "I said I don't want to."

My fingers dig into the couch cushion. "You're not making any sense."

Turning to me, he leans closer, hands in the air. "You don't understand!" I flinch. "I don't have a choice. I would take it all back if I could." He points toward the window.

"This is all his fault. He shouldn't be here. If he weren't here, we'd have more time."

He doesn't seem like he's in his right mind, like he might snap at any moment. I have to be cautious.

"Julian, please. I don't understand. Who are you talking about?"

He paces again. "I'm so stupid to think he wouldn't be here. That he wouldn't be close by. Of course I had to call it in. I didn't know that would mean a change of plans. But don't worry. I have another plan. It will all be better soon."

I don't know if he's talking to himself or to me.

I remain quiet, afraid to speak.

He stops pacing when he looks at the full cup of water. "I brought that water for you. Why aren't you drinking it?" he shouts.

"Okay." I hold up my hands. "I'm sorry." I grab the glass and take another sip.

He stares at me to drink more, and I take a big gulp, then set the glass on the table. He nods and paces again. Banging roars from outside. Julian stops pacing and looks toward the window.

"Shit! We're almost out of time," he says.

"What was that?" I move toward the window and push the curtain aside.

There's movement behind the windows at Theo's house. His front door hangs off the hinges. A loud crack follows a flash of light. A gunshot. I jump back, covering my mouth. *Theo . . .*

My vision blurs, and I feel dizzy. I hold on to the back of the couch to steady myself. After a second, I try to stand straight, but the room whirls around me.

Julian places a hand on my shoulder. "It's almost over."

He doesn't seem concerned. His eyes glass over, empty of emotion.

The room spins, and I realize now why he wanted me to drink the water. He put something in it.

"What did you do?"

I try to sound threatening, but my voice falters.

"I had no other choice. It will all be over soon." He tightens his grip on my arm to keep me from falling. "I promise this is for the best."

I whip my arm out of his hold, but as I take a step, my knees give out, and I fall to the floor, my legs paralyzed. Using the little strength I have left in my arms, I drag myself across the floor, but the feeling in my arms is fading fast. I manage to roll onto my back, and Julian stands over me.

"Why?" I want to shout, but it's barely a whisper.

My vision is fading away. Something about this feels familiar, like I've been here before. Every time I blink, a picture flashes in my head—the moon and stars circling in the sky and snow-covered tree branches. I force my eyes open, and Julian stands above me, reaching for something from his waistband. There's a glint of metal, then my vision disappears.

This is it, I think to myself. I trusted him too easily. He drugged me and is going to shoot me, and I have no fighting chance. How could I be so foolish?

Though fading fast, my hearing is the last to go. Everything sounds muffled, like I'm underwater. He said it would be over soon. I'm sure there are worse ways to die. At least I won't feel it.

The last thing I hear before death is a crash and a deep voice shouting, "Amelia!"

16. Kidnapped

My toes and fingers tingle. I'm alive? I try to wiggle them, but they barely twitch. Pinpricks move up my legs and down my arms. I'm too scared to open my eyes, but I'm somewhere dark. I concentrate on the sounds—wind and passing cars. My body bounces, and I think I'm in a moving vehicle. I chance a peek, and although my vision is still blurred, I can tell I'm lying in the backseat of a car. It's dark outside. The driver is the only other person in the car—a man wearing a baseball hat. It must be Julian. He drugged me and kidnapped me.

As to not alert my captor of my consciousness, I lie still. I look for any type of weapon to get away. The backseat is empty. I have only the clothes I'm wearing. With one hand, I reach for the drawstring on my shorts. I pull it out, inch by inch. I'll have to be quick with my movements.

To keep a good grip, I wrap the ends around my hands. In one quick motion, I sit up, wrap the string around his neck, and pull. He swerves to the shoulder, and the car slows. A thicket of trees line the side of the road, somewhere to run and hide in the dark. I don't hesitate to open the door and jump out before the car comes to a stop, then run into the woods and don't look back. The car door slams, and he coughs, but I stumble forward into the woods.

"Wait," he calls out in a hoarse voice.

Running footsteps close in from behind. I trudge through the woods, still sluggish from the drugs. I find a tree and hide behind it, unable to continue.

"Dammit," he says, close by. If I run, he'll see me. "Jane?" He pauses, but I don't hear him come closer. "Amelia?" he says tentatively.

Amelia? That was the last thing I heard before I lost consciousness. I risk peeking around the side of the tree. Even with his back to me, I know it's not Julian. His shoulders are too broad, his height too tall.

He looks out through the trees. "Where is she?" His voice is just a whisper, but I would recognize it anywhere. Then he turns in my direction. I relax against the tree before stepping out into the open.

"Theo?"

"Thank God," he breathes. "Come on, we have to get back on the road."

The urgency in his tone reminds me of Julian. They all knew something was happening, and I'm not sure if I can trust him. "I'm not going anywhere with you until you tell me what's going on."

"It's a long story, and we don't have time. I promise I'll explain on the way." He gestures for the car, and I stay put.

"What happened to Julian? Where's Paul?" I demand.

"I got to you just in time. I dealt with him."

"Did you kill him? Were those your gunshots I heard at your house?"

"Amelia, please. I will explain in the car."

I stomp and clench my hands. "Why do you keep calling me Amelia?"

"Because . . ." He sighs, stepping toward me. He stares, then whispers, "That is your real name."

His words take my breath away, and I stumble backward, then land with my back against a tree. He knows my real name? Then the thought hits me like a ton of bricks. How did I miss it before? The dark unruly hair and blue eyes. He was the new boy with his sister in my regained memory.

"How long?" I grip onto the tree as if it's the only thing keeping me from falling through the earth. "How long have you known me?"

He clears his throat. "Fourteen years."

I was right.

I push away from the tree to face him. "Why didn't you say something?" I ask through gritted teeth.

"Also a long story. The short version you didn't remember."

After striding toward him, I slam a weak fist into his chest. "You could've come forward. They've been trying to find out who I am for months." I ram another fist against his chest, but he doesn't even flinch. I stumble away, fighting the oncoming tears.

"That wasn't an option. It's—"

I hold up my hand. "Let me guess. A long story."

He steps toward me. "Right now, there are people coming after us that want us dead. We need to get back on the road and as far away as possible. I promise I will explain as much as I can. You can trust me."

He has only ever tried to help me. He saved me from Julian, after all. I consider what he told me about people coming to kill us, and now I know Mark was from my past.

Is he the one after me? I don't know, but I won't wait here to find out, either.

I follow him to the car, and he gets in, but I hesitate with my hand on the door. Can I trust him? I trusted Julian, and he betrayed me. How is this any different? I peer both ways down the road. I don't recognize where we are or which way is home. Even if I run, he'll catch me. Fifty feet into the woods, and exhaustion took over my legs. At least I'm not tied up like a prisoner. That must count for something. Right?

I get into the passenger seat and glance at my savior— or captor. He rubs his neck, and through the light of the streetlamp, I see a red line across his Adam's apple.

"Sorry about that." I point to his neck.

"Don't be. It's exactly what you should've done." He merges onto the road. "Word of advice. Next time, don't let go until they're unconscious or dead. Don't get me wrong, I'm glad you did because I mean you no harm, but you didn't know that."

We drive in silence for several minutes.

"I need answers," I urge.

"I don't know where to start."

"Start by telling me what happened back there."

"I'll try. You won't understand most of it because you can't remember."

Memories of hypnosis and Mark's words during my attack flash in my head.

"Try me."

He takes a deep breath. "When Paul and I heard you on the phone with Johnathon, we knew they were coming, so we were prepared. They ambushed us and tried to kill us, but Paul killed them first. I knew Jacob was either going to kill you or take you back to Noel."

"Julian." I roll my eyes. "Who's Noel?" Mark said "they" and so did Julian. Is Noel the "they" they were referring to?

"Not who, what. It stands for Noble Orphans Enhanced Legacy."

"What do they want with me?" I grip my seat as headlights shine through the side mirror.

Theo glances in his rearview mirror but doesn't seem alarmed. "They either want us back or dead. I don't want to find out which."

"Us? Like, you and me?"

"Yes, and the others."

"There are others?"

"Yes, our friends in Colorado. That's where we're going. Paul stayed behind to clean up, and he'll meet us there. The rest of us have remained invisible, so NOEL can't find us. You had a life in Bridgeport. Not as easy to disappear. People would notice and could file missing persons and then everyone we see along the way would report you. They'll be able to track us, and we don't want that. Paul knows how to make us disappear without causing suspicion."

It's a lot to wrap my head around. I know there's more to the story he can't explain right now. It would be helpful if I could remember something.

I adjust the seatbelt so I can turn toward Theo. "How did you know Julian was with NOEL?"

"I recognized him." His grip tightens on the steering wheel. "We were all in the same unit. We could never leave, so I didn't know if he had escaped like the rest of us. I've been following him since he arrived. Didn't think anything of it until you said you thought Mark was from your past. Then I knew Jameson was working for NOEL. Once he saw me at your house, it was only a matter of time before he alerted them. That's why Paul was there. I called him for backup."

"Mark was part of NOEL, too? They sent him after me, didn't they?"

Theo shakes his head. "I wasn't sure at first because I didn't recognize him, but there were a lot of us at NOEL. But when I was following Jasper, I saw them together sometimes. I think they were working together to get to you."

My stomach churns at the thought of Julian and Mark conspiring to get to me. Mark went for the kill, but Julian sweet-talked his way into my life. I choke back the rising bile and lean my head against the window. "This is a lot to take in." I sink deeper into the seat.

"I know. I'll give you a bit at a time. We'll stop somewhere soon and rest."

Theo drives in silence, and it feels like only minutes have gone by when he wakes me. We have stopped at a small motel.

Theo looks as exhausted as I feel. We enter the room, and I'm relieved to see two beds. He tells me he'll be right back and leaves.

The few minutes alone give me enough time to use the bathroom and splash cold water on my face. I pick which bed I want to sleep in and hurry under the covers. Theo returns with two backpacks, two bottles of water, and a handful of vending machine food. He hands me a cold water bottle, and I guzzle half of it. He secures the locks on the door, then draws the curtains closed, peering out of them every couple of minutes.

"Where are we?" I ask in a sleepy voice.

"Ohio."

"How long will it take to get to Colorado?"

"It's a full day's drive from Bridgeport. We only did four hours tonight. We'll need to stop several times to make sure we're not being followed. It'll probably take us another three days to get there."

I throw my head back against the pillow.

Three more days on the road is not something I want to be doing.

Finally, he steps away from the window and sits on the opposite bed. "I got some food if you're hungry. We'll get some proper food in the morning."

I'm too tired to eat, but I should. I settle for a bag of trail mix.

"What happened to me? My accident, that is. I was escaping NOEL, wasn't I?" Theo's face turns somber. "I remember." His expression turns hopeful. "Sort of. I went under hypnosis, and I remember walking through a tunnel. They fenced the exit off. That's how I got this." I point to my scar. "I ran toward the woods and then Dr. Wagner pulled me out, so that's all I got until . . ."

I pause as the memory of tonight flashes in my head, of Julian standing above me, while buzzes of a memory came to me every time I blinked.

"Until what?"

"Until tonight. When I thought I was dying. I had flashes of what I think are memories. It's like I was experiencing the same thing, so it triggered the memory. At least, I think that's why."

"Which was?"

Pulling a pillow into my lap, I hug it. "Lying there, not being able to move, waving in and out of consciousness, and thinking I was going to die. I think that was the same feeling when I escaped, but I saw the moon and stars spinning in the sky and snow-covered branches."

"You were in a ditch," he whispers. "I thought you were dead." Fingers digging into the blanket, he chokes on the last word, then clears his throat. "You were barely breathing. Your arm was soaked with blood and your leg was clearly broken. I drove you as far away as I could, but I was scared you were going to die. You woke up only for a moment and whispered, 'Bridgeport.' So, I took you there—even though I didn't want to—because that's practically right next door to NOEL."

"Let me guess. Small town in Maryland, close to the West Virginia border?" I lean backward, hitting my head on the headboard. I place the pillow behind me and look at Theo.

"Yeah." Theo narrows his eyes. "How did you know?"

"Because that's exactly where Julian said he was from." Rolling my eyes, I lie on the pillow.

I end the conversation there. Theo doesn't add anything, either. I close my eyes and will myself to recall anything from my past.

This journey would make a lot more sense if I knew what we were up against.

17. The Bet

I'm standing in complete darkness. Familiar doors appear one by one. I've been here before. Except, this time, I'm not under hypnosis. The only explanation is that I must be dreaming. I roam around the circle, waiting for a door to draw me in. Beyond the shadow of another door is an entrance to a cave. I take a deep breath and crouch through.

Faint moonlight illuminates the way. It smells like dirt and stone. I shiver from the cool, damp air. Flickering light from a small fire comes into focus, and five bodies appear around the flames.

I see myself first, who is standing next to Theo. To his left stands a man I have not seen before.

He has long curly hair. Light from the fire makes it look golden brown. Next to the man is Paul. He looks the same as the last time. Between me and Paul is a woman with dark-brown hair, identical to Theo's, the girl I saw holding his hand in the classroom—his sister.

"Tomorrow night is the night," Theo says. "It's our chance to finally take NOEL down for good."

Paul speaks next. "We only escaped a week ago. It's reckless to attack so soon."

Only a week ago? This can't be right. I saw my escape, and Theo confirmed that's when I ended up in the hospital.

"Amelia has gone over every detail. Her plan is solid. It should work," Theo says.

He looks at Amelia, and she nods. "It will work," she says. "It has to."

Theo's sister warms her hands by the fire. "It's too risky. We should go in hiding like the others did. Paul knows how to keep us invisible. We can run and never look back."

"They'll eventually find us," the long-haired man says.

"Then we keep moving."

"NOEL took my entire life away from me." Amelia steps closer to the fire, illuminating her features beneath the glow. She has an edge to her demeanor I don't recognize in myself. Her eyes are sharper, her posture confident. "I will be free, or I will die trying. But I'm certainly not running."

Even her tone sounds different from mine. Hers is crisper, harsher, and slightly more arrogant.

"I understand your reasons, Amy. I do. But I can't fight with you. I'm sorry."

She calls me Amy?

"What about you, Paul?" Theo asks.

"You know I go wherever she goes." Paul grabs Theo's sister's hand. "You'll have to count me out." He looks at Theo and directs his next comment only to him. "You understand." It wasn't a question. Theo nods. "We're leaving tonight. Put enough distance between us." Paul holds out his hand, and Theo shakes it.

"You take care of my sister," Theo says to him.

164

Theo's sister gives him a big hug and kisses him on the cheek. "I love you, big brother."

He hugs her back, nuzzling into her shoulder. "I love you, too."

She goes to Amelia, then grabs her hands, tears swimming in her eyes. "You fight and win, then come back to us. I need you as much as you need me. You're my best friend, always."

"Kat and Amy till the end." Amelia holds up a pinky.

Theo's sister laughs as tears fall down her cheeks. She intertwines her pinky with Amelia's. "Kat and Amy till the end."

Paul holds out his hand for Kat, and she takes it. Before they reach the cave opening, Kat turns around and adds, "You all better not die on me, or I'll be pissed."

Everyone laughs as they recede into the void.

Theo turns to the long-haired man. "What about you, Jackson?"

Jackson cracks his knuckles. "Let's go fuck some shit up."

Suddenly, the cave fades and transforms. Three of them run through the snow-covered forest. They duck behind a small hill, out of breath.

Theo holds a rifle and checks the magazine. After setting it aside, he blows in his hands, then rubs them together. Jackson tucks daggers into a band around his thigh. Amelia checks her watch and adjusts the timer.

"Thirty seconds," she says to Jackson. "You know what to do?" He nods, then a beeper rings from her watch. "Go!"

As Jackson runs out of sight, Amelia turns to Theo. "If this goes sideways, you know I can't go back."

"I know."

"I'm serious, Theo."

Lightning strikes, and a downpour erupts.

Why is there a thunderstorm in the middle of winter?

Amelia pushes away the wet strands of hair clinging to her cheeks. "I need you to promise me something."

Rumbling thunder rolls in, and lightning strikes again.

"Anything," Theo says.

"If I get captured, put a bullet between my eyes." Theo's face turns grim, and he shakes his head. Amelia clutches his shoulders. "I'm serious, Theo. I'd rather die than go back. Promise me."

I feel her determination. She means every word.

"Please don't make me. Anything but that," he pleads.

Lightning cracks, and thunder immediately follows.

Another beep from her watch rings. "I have to go now. Promise me." He doesn't answer. She shakes his shoulders and yells, "Promise me!"

"I promise," he blurts.

Amelia runs forward into the rain, and I follow, like an invisible tether is pulling me. She draws two knives out of her waistband I hadn't noticed before. She looks back at Theo, who is crouched behind the hill, rifle propped and ready to shoot.

A soldier in all black sprints toward her, and she doesn't have time to react, but the soldier flings sideways as if yanked backward by an invisible force. I feel her focus, rage, and determination. She knows exactly what she's doing.

Another soldier charges at her, wearing black metal armor and a black helmet shielding their face. She slices her at their stomach with the dagger, and the blade shatters. Jackson screams in the distance, and I feel her sudden panic.

Another scream from Jackson, and the rain suddenly halts, as if it was never raining. Amelia tries to fight off the attacker, but they stand unscathed.

Dozens more charge toward her as gunshots come from Theo's direction. Bullets hit the soldiers in the arms and legs but ricochet off them. He fires shot after shot, but the bullets don't penetrate the armor. Some soldiers fly—same as the one before—and land to the ground with a thud, but they immediately recover.

Two soldiers grab Amelia. She struggles to get free, but they're too strong. She closes her eyes in concentration, and heat rushes through my arms like they're on fire, but an intense amount of strength courses through me. Amelia's eyes shoot open, and she thrusts her hands outward, knocking the soldiers out of her grip.

Before they hit the ground, three more drag her back toward the opening in the wall. I feel her strength deplete, and the heat in my arms turn to ice.

"Do it," she yells. "Do it now."

She's yelling out to Theo to shoot her, but the shot never comes.

The rage and betrayal consuming her, I feel. I know what she's going to say next, so I yell it with her. "Do it, you coward. You promised. You fucking promised."

The attackers drag her as she fights. Her strength is gone, and her energy is nearly depleted, but she doesn't give up. She will fight until the end. She kicks, squirms, and screams as they slide her through the wall opening. When she makes it through, a bright light appears, then everything fades.

"Amelia," Theo shakes my shoulders. "Amelia, wake up."

"No! I won't go back." I swing my arms around.

Theo jumps back at my sudden movement. "Amelia, it's just a dream."

Sunlight shines through the motel window, and Theo is standing over my bed. I gasp. "Sorry. Did I hit you?"

"I'm fine."

Sitting up in bed, I rub my eyes and try to shake off the sleep. That dream was strange. It felt like a memory but in a warped nightmare way. I pinch the bridge of my nose as a headache creeps to the front of my eyes. I massage my temples, and Theo watches me with concern.

"What?" I snap.

"Are you okay?"

"I'm fine. It was only a bad dream."

He goes to the window, wearing fresh clothes. Scents of citrus and sage linger next to me where he was sitting. He's been up a while and had time to shower. "We should get going. It's already midafternoon," he says.

Looking at my dirty tank top and shorts I'll have to wear for the next three days, I think, *I wish I could at least shower. Clean clothes would be nice, too.* I sigh but don't dare say my thoughts out loud.

Theo turns to me with a curious look, his eyes wandering over my body. I furrow my brow in response. He shakes his head and crosses the room where the backpacks rest on a chair, then tosses one to me.

"I packed some of your things before we left. We'll leave in thirty minutes if you want to shower first." He returns to the window.

Clutching the backpack to my chest, I advance to the bathroom. I unzip the bag and take the items out— several socks, T-shirts, jean shorts, sweatpants, sneakers, a hairbrush, and clean underwear. Heat rushes to my cheeks when I realize he went through my underwear drawer. When I see the toothbrush and deodorant, I almost shout for joy.

I take the full thirty minutes to rid myself of the grime and make myself feel like a normal human being again. As I enter the room, Theo throws the strap of the backpack over his shoulder. His eyes shift over my body, starting at my legs, until he gets to my eyes, where they stay unwavering. "Ready?"

I nod and head for the door. "Do you want me to drive for a while?"

He laughs deeply. "Absolutely not."

"Why not?" I ask, offended.

Theo closes the motel door behind us and twirls the key ring around his finger before turning to me. "Because you never learned how to drive."

"How come?"

He shrugs as he walks to the car. "NOEL only taught a select few men how to drive."

I roll my eyes and hop into the passenger seat.

Theo eases onto the road and drives for a couple of miles before pulling into a diner parking lot. He chooses a booth close to the door next to a window. The doorbell dings as three young women walk through. They sit at a booth in the back corner, laughing and talking with each other.

One woman looks my way and stares at me a moment longer than necessary. I divert my eyes back to the menu, but when I look back at her, she's talking with her friends.

Various scents from the kitchen make my stomach growl and my mouth water. I read through all the choices, but it's too hard to choose because I want the crispiness of bacon but also the fluffiness of biscuits, along with the saltiness of hash browns. The server brings us water and says she will be back to take our order.

"What are you getting?" I ask playfully.

He doesn't look up from the menu. "I don't know yet. Hence the reason I'm reading the menu."

Scoffing, I say under my breath, "Always so serious."

I tap the straw on the table until it breaks through the paper. I hold the open end to my mouth and blow the wrapper at him, which hits him in the nose.

He jumps in surprise, and I giggle. "Really?" He smiles for the first time.

The server comes back, and Theo orders a club sandwich and fries. I order the big breakfast special that comes with three eggs, three different meats, hash browns, toast, and a side of biscuits and gravy.

Theo stares out the window, absentmindedly rolling the straw wrapper around his finger. It looks tiny in his hands. I bite my lip as I remember how strong they felt around my arm when he saved me from falling on my shoelace. Firm but gentle.

The server snaps me out of my daydream when she returns with our food.

Theo's eyes widen when she sets three plates in front of me. Smiling, I rub my hands together, ready to feast.

"There's no way you're eating all that."

"You bet I am."

"Okay, then. Let's bet on it." He sets both palms on the table and leans forward.

"It's an expression. Besides, you didn't pack my purse, so you will pay for this meal"—I point my fork to my plate—"and anything else we need along the way."

"We don't have to bet money." He raises his eyebrows, inviting me to play along.

I narrow my eyes at him. "Okay. If I eat all of this"—he lifts his chin in anticipation—"you teach me how to drive."

He scrunches his face and inhales through his teeth. "Fine." I do a small dance in my seat. "But if you don't eat it all, you have to tell me about your bad dream last night."

I fight the urge to smile, knowing I would have already told him about my dream if he had asked. "Deal."

Taking bite after bite, I dig into my food before I feel the effects of it.

I stare at my plate in agony. A half a biscuit, a piece of toast, and a thick slice of ham remains. My stomach feels like it is going to burst.

Theo had finished his food in ten minutes and is leaning back in the booth, smiling smugly.

"I told you you couldn't eat it all."

"I haven't stopped yet, have I?" I retort. I force another bite and chew slowly.

"You're going to make yourself sick." He scrunches his nose.

With a mouthful of food, I say, "If that's what it takes, then so be it."

"Why put yourself through this? To win a bet?"

Swallowing, I look at him. "It's not to win. It's so I can learn how to drive."

"You want to learn that badly?"

"Yes."

"Fine. I was going to teach you, anyway." He shrugs. "Please stop eating. Watching you is making me nauseous."

My fork and knife clatter on the plate when I drop them. "Seriously? You were going to teach me, anyway?"

"Mm-hmm."

I give him a deadpan stare. "You could've said that ten minutes ago, when I was full."

"Nah. This was way more fun."

He places cash on the table to cover the tab and tip, then stands and looks at me, tilting his head toward the door.

I squint at him. *I don't like you right now.*

The corner of his lip raises.

I sigh, then follow him to the door.

"You still lost the bet." He holds the door open for me to go first. I glare sideways at him as I pass. "You can tell me all about it later, when we stop for the night."

I step aside as an older couple approaches. Theo ushers them through the door. "I would have told you anyway, if you had asked."

"Wow!" He shakes his head. "We are terrible at making bets."

We walk through the parking lot, and I stop in front of the car and hold out my right hand. He looks at me like I did something crazy.

"Keys."

He laughs. "I'm not letting you drive on the main road without learning how to park first."

Huffing, I get into the passenger seat.

The woman who was staring at me in the restaurant rushes our way. "Wait!" she shouts.

Theo pauses outside the car as the woman approaches.

"You're her. Aren't you?" she asks me.

"Excuse me?" I ask.

"The girl from the bar. Here, look." She holds out her phone toward me, showing me a video of me disabling Mark. Theo shoots a concerned glare at me.

"Sorry. That's not me."

"Of course it is. You look just like her. You're a legend, standing up for yourself, empowering women." Without warning, the woman leans in close and snaps a picture. "This is going to look great on my feed." She then walks away.

"What just happened?" I ask Theo.

"Nothing good. We need to hurry up and get out of here before anyone else notices you."

Quickly, he gets into the car and pulls off onto the road. After several miles, I can't take the silence anymore.

"Can you tell me more about NOEL?"

Surely, if we talk about something else, we'll forget about the woman.

"What do you want to know?"

"What are they? What are they doing that is so bad that we needed to escape? How did we get there? You said it stands for Noble Orphans Enhanced Legacy. What does that mean?"

"Let's see . . ." He adjusts his hands on the steering wheel and checks his rearview mirror. "In a nutshell, NOEL is an organization that takes in orphans and does scientific experiments on them. Enhance is the term they use. They made us stronger, faster, and smarter. Each one has a unique skill and ability. They trained us in certain areas based on our skills and abilities."

"What are they enhancing and training us for?"

"Not sure exactly, but they train us like we're soldiers."

"You said you were there for fourteen years, but how long was I there?"

"I think since you were a baby. You never mentioned knowing anywhere else."

The thought makes me sad. Who were my parents and what happened to them? Being enhanced explains my photographic memory and my ability to fight. I felt the strength enhancement come through both in hypnosis and when I faced Mark.

"Do we all have photographic memories?" I ask.

"No. Just you. But you didn't get that from NOEL. You were born with it. You always finished your cognitive tests early and always scored one hundred percent. You would constantly remind us, word-for-word, what we had to do in training. Drove us all crazy." He laughs.

"It's still hard to believe I have amnesia with a photographic memory."

"Unless . . ." Theo checks his blind spot and switches lanes.

I wait for him to finish his thought, but he keeps on driving. "Unless what?"

With a furrowed brow, he shakes his head and murmurs, "Unless you were reconditioned. But that's impossible."

"What's reconditioned mean? Why is it impossible for me?"

"When NOEL can't control or manipulate someone, they send them for reconditioning. They inject them with a serum that we call the memory wipe." Theo pauses and clears his throat. "Everything that makes you who you are disappears. The eyes go blank when it happens. Like their soul leaves their body. They do it so they can recondition them into silent, obedient soldiers."

"And you think they did that to me?"

"I think they tried, but you escaped before they could. Like I said, once they inject it, there's nothing left. No human emotion whatsoever. You only know what they want you to know. As far as I know, it's irreversible."

"So, I didn't get the memory wipe?"

"The memory wipe works in seconds. You escaped, which means you still had your memories when you did. It wasn't until you woke up that you couldn't remember. So, the amnesia has to be from the head trauma. Right?"

"Your guess is as good as mine." I lean back into my seat.

I don't know how to tell him I think I got the memory wipe. During the hypnosis of my escape, I felt the prick in my temple and the serum coursing through my veins.

It's a lot to take in, but I understand why we needed to escape. The thought of what they are doing to these children, to me—being experimented on and forced to forget just by being human—makes my heart constrict.

We drive for two hours before we stop at a gas station. After Theo fills the tank, we go into the store and go our separate ways and pick food and drinks for the road ahead. Theo lays a prepaid cell phone along with our snacks on the counter. After he pays for everything, we head back to the car.

Once we're on the road, I ask, "What's the cell phone for?"

"To make phone calls," he replies dryly. I deadpan stare at him. He glances at me, and the corner of his lip twitches. "I need to call Paul."

"What happened to your cell phone?"

"Left it behind with yours. Once NOEL knew I was there, they would have tracked it. Can't let them know I survived the assassination attempt."

The drive continues in silence for several miles. I turn on the radio to help clear my head or help me think—I can't decide which. I flip through the stations until I find one that has music. Leaning back, I gaze out the window at the passing cars and trees, trying to digest everything I've learned.

There's still so much I don't understand. Why did Theo stay invisible from me knowing the dangers NOEL imposes? And why would NOEL recondition me if they were going to send Julian to kill me anyway?

A sudden swerve of the car snaps me out of my haze. My head whips at Theo. He shakes his head and rapidly blinks his eyes.

"Sorry," he says, straining to keep his eyes open, exhaustion clear.

"How much sleep did you get last night?"

"None, really. I was keeping watch."

Staring at the long stretch of road would put me to sleep, too, and I'm not the one who stayed up most of the night. "We need to stop somewhere so you can get some rest."

"We've only been on the road for four hours. I want to keep going at least until dark."

"We won't be going anywhere if you fall asleep at the wheel and kill us both."

He nods and pulls off at the next exit.

We pull into the first motel. It is like the first vacant, cheap, and an outside entrance for each room.

Theo throws his backpack onto a chair, then flops onto the bed. He's asleep almost instantly. I draw the curtains the same way he did the night before. I don't think we're being followed, but I peek out the window anyway. When I don't see anything suspicious, I retreat to the opposite bed.

NOEL Forgotten

Sounds roar through the room when I turn on the tv. Frantically, I hit the volume button to turn it down, then look at Theo, but he hasn't moved. I hop channels aimlessly, settling for a sitcom I've never heard of.

18. Pinned to the Ceiling

The sun finally sets, and I'm bored with television. My rumbling stomach reminds me I haven't eaten since lunch, and we left the snacks in the car. I assume his keys and wallet are in his pocket, so I'm out of luck. Since I won't be eating anything, I crawl into bed and try to turn my mind off, but Theo rustles in the bed, panting and talking in his sleep.

"I promise . . ." he mumbles. A few seconds later, he spouts, "Jackson! Watch out . . . Shit! They have Amelia . . . I'm almost out . . . Fuck!"

I can't let him sleep like this anymore.

"Theo?" I shout as I jump off my bed. I nudge his shoulder, but it doesn't wake him.

Sweat covers his forehead, and tears trickle down his face, eyes shifting under his lids. "I'm sorry. I'm so sorry I'm a coward."

I jump on top of him and shake his shoulders hard. "Theo, wake up!"

His eyes pop open as he thrusts his hands out.

I expect the force from his blow to stun me and knock me off the bed. Instead, I'm pinned to the ceiling, with nothing physically holding me there. It feels as if the surrounding air has condensed and hardened, holding me in place. I'm too shocked to scream or struggle. I look at the man below me, who's lying on the bed with his hands held in my direction.

"Amelia?" He comes to his senses. "Shit." He slowly lowers his hands, and with it, my body follows. He sits up and scoots back; my body lowers to the empty spot.

Finally, I'm in bed, sitting before him in complete and utter shock.

"What . . . the fuck . . . was that?" I run my hands through my hair, then down my arms.

I wasn't imagining it.

"Sorry," he mutters, cheeks flushing with shame. "I was having a bad dream, and you startled me."

"I meant the part where I was pinned to the ceiling by air."

It comes out in a rush, and I flail my arms toward me . . . toward him . . . toward the ceiling, then landing with both hands on the side of my head.

"Oh, that." He rubs the back of his neck. "I told you I have telekinesis."

I jut my chin out at him. "You certainly did not!" I look at the ceiling again and stretch out my arms, then slam them into the bed. "I have a photographic memory." My voice is getting louder and louder. "I would have remembered if you mentioned you had superpowers."

"We don't think of them as superpowers." He rolls his eyes.

"We?"

"Everyone from NOEL."

"We all have a superpower?"

"Again, they are not superpowers." He throws his hands up. "I told you we have abilities."

I'm quiet for a moment as I think back to our earlier conversation. "You didn't elaborate what abilities meant. Why haven't I seen you use it before?"

"It's not something I use all the time, but I used it in front of you a few times."

"What? When?" I scoot closer to him as if I'm a child interested in hearing a story.

Theo adjusts in his seat to face more toward me. He rests his hands on the bed, slightly rubbing the quilt. "How do you think your shoe got untied in the park?" He smirks.

"That was you?" My eyes widen.

"I panicked." He runs a hand through his hair. "I thought you remembered me." He looks away and grips the blanket. "I used it again to stop Mark. That's why he looked frozen mid-kick."

At the time, it didn't seem unnatural, but it makes sense now why he didn't move.

"What's mine?"

"Telepathy."

He states it as if it's obvious.

"I'm telepathic?" I ask incredulously, but then I perk up. "I'm telepathic. So, I wasn't going crazy?" Theo looks at me, baffled. I chuckle before I answer. "I thought I was hearing things. Well . . . I guess I was, but I'm supposed to."

Theo cocks his head. "You haven't been controlling it all along?"

181

"No. I wouldn't know how. Like I said, the few times I've heard people's thoughts, I thought I was going crazy."

"But you've projected your thoughts to me."

"I'm not following. What do you mean I projected my thoughts to you?"

"I don't know how to explain it." He looks up as if trying to figure it out. "The way you explained it to me is that you can make a direct connection between your brain and someone else's. Think of it like a radio. You have to be on a specific channel to hear what's playing. It's the same way with your ability. You need to find their channel, and you can hear their thoughts."

"I understand that. But what do you mean by projecting?"

"When we were teenagers, you wanted to expand on your telepathy. You thought, if you could reach someone's mind to read their thoughts, why couldn't you put your own thoughts in their head? You practiced with me." He runs his hand over the quilt, brushing the tips of my fingers.

Every part of me wants to reach out and wrap my hand in his, but he laughs and pulls his hand away. "I'll never forget the first time it worked. We were in combat training. I was fighting with Zeke, and the rest of the class was watching. You were there and said, in my head, 'He's going for the right jab.' Your voice in my head caught me off guard, and I froze. He punched me right in the eye. I still have the scar to prove it." He touches the scar above his left eyebrow. "I fell to the ground, but you didn't realize it worked, and you said, in my head, 'You dumbass. That was so obvious.' I looked at you with my good eye, smiling from ear to ear, and gave you a thumbs up. I thought, 'You did it. You finally did it.' And you heard me. You screamed with joy, and everyone thought you were cheering for Zeke."

Without a second thought, I place a finger on his eyebrow. "I wondered how you got that scar."

He doesn't flinch but closes his eyes as if enjoying my touch.

"I haven't thought about that day in a while."

I realize my finger is still on his eyebrow, and our faces are uncomfortably close. I jerk away as if it burned me. He clears his throat and scoots back.

"Anyway . . . you practiced your thought projection on me. Eventually, it was as easy as breathing for you."

"You think I did it without knowing? Like muscle memory?"

"Possibly. I also think, since you used it on me so much, you have a direct connection with my mind without knowing it."

"What did I project to you?"

"The first time was weeks ago."

"Weeks ago?" I say, bewildered.

"I came home late. You were on your porch, reading, and I heard you ask, 'Who are you, mysterious neighbor?' It freaked me out, and I looked at you and then you waved at me."

I remember that. It was the first encounter we had on that street. Now I know I wasn't going crazy when I heard him respond. The way he hesitated before entering his house makes sense now.

He continues. "You called my name after Paul shot the assassins. Then again, yesterday, when you said you wanted to shower and wear clean clothes."

I had wanted to say the words but hadn't. Now I understand the weird look he gave me.

"Then you did it again at lunch, when you said you didn't like me." He chuckles.

"Did I project my thoughts to other people to freak them out?"

"No. Only me. It was our little secret," he says with a hint of sadness.

"We were close friends, weren't we?"

He swallows. "Yeah. We were."

"I know I can't remember, but if it's any consolation, you're the best friend I have right now."

His smile turns into a genuine one.

I nudge his shoulder. "What were you dreaming about?"

He looks away. "It was nothing."

Bullshit!

He glances at me. "Were you trying to project that to me?"

"It worked?" I yelp.

I didn't have to concentrate to project to him. It was as he said—as easy as breathing. "So, what were you dreaming about?"

"I don't want to talk about it. Please drop it." He gets off the bed and goes to the window.

I concentrate on using my telepathy to hear his thoughts. I hear a soft *click*, and I know I've connected to his mind.

I can't tell her. She'll never forgive me. I'm such a coward.

I cut off the connection. By the way he was talking in his sleep and considering his thoughts, I know we had the same dream of me being captured. He thinks if I remember that night, I won't forgive him for not killing me. The old me, the one who remembers everything, might not have forgiven him, but if I've learned anything from my time being a plain Jane, it's that I can be kind.

When I approach him, I gently place my hand on his arm.

"I'm pretty sure we had the same dream. Except it wasn't just a dream, was it? It was a memory of you, me, and Jackson going back to NOEL to fight."

When I let go, he turns his body toward me. "You remember?"

I nod, and his jaw clenches.

He sits back onto the bed, putting his elbows on his knees and lacing his fingers. He keeps his head lowered, not meeting my eyes. "You almost died trying to escape. Now you have amnesia and are on the run. None of that would have happened if I kept my promise. I had one bullet left and a clear shot, but I couldn't pull the trigger. It's my fault that you're in this situation."

"You're right," I say matter-of-factly. Kneeling in front of him, I make eye contact and see he's trying to hold back tears. "If you had pulled that trigger, we wouldn't be having this conversation because I would be dead. You think I won't forgive you, but I do. I'm glad you broke your promise. I'm glad I'm alive, no matter how fucked up this is. Don't blame yourself. Blame NOEL."

After a moment, he nods, then opens the door.

"Where are you going?" I ask.

"I have to call Paul. I left the burner phone in the car." He leaves without looking back.

I peek out from the curtains. He takes the phone out of the bag and removes the packaging. He holds the phone to his ear and talks for a few minutes. When he exits the car, I run to the bed.

He enters the room without acknowledging my existence, grabs his backpack, and goes into the bathroom. The shower turns on.

Knowing I have a few minutes, I change into sweatpants and lie in bed. The shower turns off, and I pretend I'm sleeping to avoid the awkward tension.

As he exits the bathroom, he turns off the lights. The bed next to me squeaks as he lies in it.

I try to hear his thoughts, but those are silent as well. I tune in on the outside noises to drown the silence. Crickets chirp, cars pass, the occasional slam of another room door. Hearing anything—no matter how annoying—is better than being ignored. I hope the sounds will relax me enough to sleep. When I close my eyes, a bright light shines beneath my eyelids. A car door slams, and the hotel door bursts open.

19. Monsters In The Night

wo men in all black charge through, guns raised in our direction. I freeze, but Theo doesn't hesitate.

Guns whip out of their hands with a flick of Theo's wrist, then clatter several feet away. Theo charges at them and knocks one to the ground. They wrestle and roll over one another.

The other man charges toward me, and I kick him in the gut. He hunches over with a grunt, and I leap off the bed against the wall. There's no clear escape route. The man recovers quickly and stalks toward me. I shuffle backward, and my foot bumps against one of the fallen guns. The man rushes forward as I bend down to grab the gun.

As soon as my fingers wrap around the handle, he pins me against the wall, slamming my hand against it, trying to loosen my grip. I hold tight, and he wraps a hand around my neck, pressing deep into my windpipe. I gasp for air, and black dots swirl in my vision.

"Amelia," Theo calls out.

His telekinesis tries to pull me away from the attacker, but his arms are pinned, and the invisible tether disappears.

Tingling in my arms seeps in, and I lose my grip on the gun. It falls to the floor, but my attacker doesn't loosen his grip on my neck. I have seconds to act before I lose consciousness. I knee the man in the groin, and he immediately hunches over. With both hands, I grab his head and ram it into my knee over and over until he falls onto the bed. He lies motionless, blood seeping from his nose and mouth. My lungs expand with air, and the feeling returns in my arms. Adrenaline courses through me, and I know exactly what to do.

The attacker straddles Theo, using his knees to pin Theo's arms down. His hands are wrapped around Theo's throat. I grab the gun, rush to Theo, and ram the handle to the back of the attacker's head. He falls forward, unconscious. Theo pushes him away and stands, gasping for air.

"You okay?" I ask.

Theo leans on the bed, rubbing his neck, and coughs. "Yeah. Are you?"

My attacker stirs, and I point the gun in his direction, as if it has a mind of its own. The world around me fades, and my focus is only on the target in front of me. A target waiting to be eliminated. My finger wraps around the trigger, ready to press.

"Don't," Theo blurts as he places a hand on my raised arm.

"We can't let them live," I growl, but it's as if someone else is saying it.

"A gunshot will draw too much attention."

I barely register what he's saying, but something deep inside me knows he's right. Without thinking, I hand him the gun. He exhales in relief, but my mission is not complete until they're both dead. My attacker comes to his senses and rises to a sitting position. My body takes control, and in one quick motion, I twist his head to the side. The force snaps his neck with a crack. He tumbles off the bed and lands on the ground with a thud.

Theo gasps in horror.

"What the fuck, Amelia!" he shouts.

The other man stirs, and I don't have time for Theo's judgment. I leap over the dead body and snap the other's neck before Theo can protest.

"I can't believe you did that."

I shrug. "You said the gun was too loud."

Theo steps back, running a hand through his hair, wearing an expression of complete shock. I look down at the bodies, and it scares me how easy it was to kill them. What's more terrifying is that I don't feel bad about it. Darkness within has crept back to the surface. Is this who I was before? A killer?

Theo stares at the bodies.

Quietly, I sit on the edge of the bed and clasp my hands in my lap. "What do we do now?"

Theo continues to stare at the dead bodies, shaking his head in disbelief. "I don't . . . I don't know." He glances at me but quickly looks away. "I have to go." He heads for the door.

I jump off the bed and rush to him. "Where are you going?"

"I have to call Paul. I don't know what to do." He opens the door, but I pull onto his arm.

"You're leaving me here alone with them?"

"Jesus Christ, Amelia!" He yanks his arm out of my grip. "They're fucking dead. Are you afraid they're going to come back to life or something?" Huffing, he storms off.

I search the bodies for anything that might be useful but come up empty. No wallet, no phone, no sign of who they were or where they're from.

Of course I know where they're from. They were from NOEL, sent to kill us. How they found us is a mystery. Maybe it was the woman who took a photo of me. Theo was right to be paranoid.

When Theo returns, his face is grim. "We need to put them in the car they came in. I'll drive it miles away and leave it out of sight. Then I'll come back."

"I'll go with you."

"No," he growls. "You've done enough. I should be back before dawn and then we'll hit the road."

"I did this. I will be the one to clean it up," I demand.

He doesn't argue and lets me help him carry the bodies to the car. We lay them both in the trunk, side by side, and place a blanket over them.

Neither of us speaks as we drive into the country.

In the silence, the weight of what just happened sinks in. We were attacked by NOEL soldiers, and I killed them without a second thought. My instincts overpowered my rationalizations the same way they did with Mark.

Theo drives off the road and through an empty field. Tall grass will provide coverage of the car, so hopefully no one sees it. We hike two miles to the nearest town and call for a taxi to take us back to the motel.

The room is a wreck, and I shuffle around to tidy up, erasing the aftermath of the attack.

"Get some sleep," Theo says. "I got it from here."

Because I'm the reason we're in this mess, I want to argue, but as I bend over to pick up a pillow, I stumble and realize I'm too exhausted from the events.

Sitting on the bed, I turn to Theo. "Do you think someone will find them?"

"NOEL will cover their tracks. They'll send someone to retrieve the car and the bodies. We'll be long gone by then."

How long will it take them to notice? Hopefully long enough for us to get to safety. I can't take another attack.

I lie in bed and replay the scene over and over in my head. Could I have done things differently? Was there a better solution than killing them? My brain tells me no, but my gut tells me yes. This version of me has the capability of being ruthless, but the Jane in me is screaming at me to consider my humanity, disappointed in Amelia's actions. Jane would have found another way, and it would have been the best way.

Darkness keeps trying to pierce through, but I won't let it do it again. I thought I had to let Jane go, so I could be me again. But she is every part of me that is good. She brings light to the darkness, and I'm going to let her shine through.

20. Driving Lesson

On the road again, Theo avoids me and only speaks to me when necessary. I try to connect to his thoughts, hoping to hear why he's acting distant toward me, but I hear nothing.

After two hours, I can't handle the tension anymore.

"What is going on with you?"

I spit the words out in a rush.

"What do you mean?"

"You've barely said anything to me or looked at me since last night." He doesn't glance my way and tightens his grip on the steering wheel. "Like that. Are you mad because I killed those men?"

"No."

"Then, why are you avoiding me?"

"I'm not avoiding you," he murmurs.

"Yes, you are." I wait for him to respond or react in any type of way, but he doesn't.

He keeps his eyes on the road and one hand on the wheel. He doesn't want to talk, but I won't sit in silence all the way to Colorado.

"I'm sorry, but you know as well as I do we couldn't let them go."

"You're right." He sighs. "I'm sorry. I feel bad that you were the one to do it. It should've been me."

"It doesn't matter."

"Yes, it does. Because, once again, I couldn't commit."

"What are you talking about?"

"Nothing. I just wish . . ."

He doesn't finish his sentence, and I'm afraid if I speak, I'll yell.

What? What do you wish? I project, hoping my thought voice is less aggressive.

"That you could've remembered anything else but that night," he says with dejection. "Now you know how much of a coward I am. I couldn't kill the soldiers and couldn't kill . . ." He clears his throat.

He's referring to me. He couldn't kill me.

Something about that night has scarred him deeply, and I can't relate. Although I remember it now, it's not the same for him. To me, it's a distant memory. For him, he relives it every time he thinks about it. I don't press the conversation further.

He needs to work on it himself.

Theo pulls over into an abandoned parking lot and turns to me. "Time for your driving lesson." My eyes widen with excitement.

We exit the car and switch seats. My feet dangle far from the pedals. Theo leans in close to me and reaches between my legs, his arm resting on my thigh. I inhale at the sudden touch. Even when I realize he's just trying to pull the seat forward, I don't relax.

I breathe in his scent of sage and citrus as he adjusts my seat. His hand lingers on my knee, and my stomach clenches with desire. He turns toward me, our faces inches away, and the heat from his breath brushes my bottom lip, making my heart hammer.

"How's that? Can you reach?"

His voice is low and heavy.

Every part of me wants to lean in and place my lips against his, but I gulp and nod, unable to speak.

He fastens the seatbelt for me before he turns away, and I let out a long breath. The exchange was delightfully startling, and I'm embarrassed I wanted it to last longer. With a few breaths, I steady my racing heart.

Theo instructs me how to adjust my mirrors. I do as he says and place both hands on the wheel.

"Gently press the gas pedal. It's the one on your right." I press the pedal, and the car inches forward.

I get a rush of adrenaline and press the pedal harder, putting the car's speed to twenty miles per hour.

"In a minute, I want you to try braking. You'll take your right foot off the gas and use that foot to press the brake pedal on the left." I hit the brake pedal too hard, and we jerk forward from the sudden stop. "Oops. Sorry."

"It's okay. Ease into it. Try again."

I ease on the gas and move forward about fifty feet before I push down the brake again. We come to a slow and steady stop.

"Good. Now I want you to drive forward and try turning right. You'll need to let off the gas and brake slightly, not completely, when you turn."

I do as he says, but the car jerks as I hit between the brake and the gas. "Shit. Sorry." I white-knuckle the steering wheel.

"It's okay. Keep practicing. We have this entire lot. Take your time."

Driving forward, I attempt another turn. It's better than the first. I practice driving forward, then turning left and right. Eventually, the turns get smoother. I practice for an hour in the lot until Theo suggests I go on the road.

"Are you serious?"

"This road is pretty deserted. I think you'll be okay. Keep the speed limit so we don't get pulled over."

Theo explains the rules of the road while I drive on the highway. I listen to every word, knowing it will ingrain in my photographic memory. There's a peacefulness to driving I didn't know existed. I find it exhilarating.

For thirty minutes, I traverse on the deserted road without seeing another car. Then, right when I'm feeling comfortable, fields on both sides, Theo sees the deer first.

He slams his hands on the glove compartment and yells for me to stop. My inexperience causes a delay in my reaction. I slam on the brakes, but it's too late. We will hit the deer.

Theo's hand reaches out toward the dashboard. The deer levitates above us. He moves his hand, and the deer moves with it, landing safely on the side of the road.

"Are you okay?"

His voice is still panicked. My heart is racing.

"I think I'm done driving for today," I say breathlessly.

Theo gets out and opens my door, but I'm still paralyzed with shock. Still gripping the steering wheel, I stare straight ahead, as if that will save us from what almost happened.

"Amelia?" With a voice full of concern, he leans over and unbuckles my seatbelt, then guides me out of the car. "It's okay. We're okay."

At his words, I embrace him and burrow into his chest. I sense his hesitancy to hug me back. After a moment, he wraps one arm around my shoulders and guides me to the passenger side door. He helps me in and buckles my seatbelt, then returns to the driver's side. He drives, but we're silent for several minutes.

I replay the scenario in my head. Each time, it's more comedic, and I burst into laughter, startling Theo.

"I think you're in shock." His voice breaks with concern, but I'm laughing hysterically, barely able to catch my breath. "I don't know what's so funny."

I speak between laughs. "Do you . . . think . . . that deer thought . . . it could fly?"

"What?"

"The deer . . . It probably thought . . . it was flying."

Tears trickle down my cheeks from the uncontrollable laughter.

"That's why you're laughing?" He laughs, too, and then we're cracking up together.

Regaining composure, I let out a deep breath of relief. As I look out the window, we pass a road sign that reads, *KANSAS CITY – 47 MILES.*

"Can we stop in Kansas City for the night?" I ask.

"I wanted to drive farther than that."

"Please?"

"Why?"

"We've been driving or hiding in motels. I have too much energy to be sitting in a car. Can't we go out and have fun?"

He glances in the rearview mirror. "I'm not sure that's a good idea. What if we're being followed and they attack again?"

"You said we have a couple of days before they realize we got away. Plus, they won't attack if we're in public. Only for a few hours. Please?" I fold my hands and give him my best impression of pleading.

"I'll tell you what," he begins, and excitement rises inside of me, "we'll stop in Kansas City and get a motel. If I feel it's safe, we can venture out for two hours." He holds up two fingers.

"Yes!" I shout and pump my fist.

"But if another person recognizes you from that video, we hit the road."

An idea sparks in my head. Something I wanted to do weeks ago but didn't have the guts.

"I have an idea for that."

21. Kansas City

We arrive in Kansas City right before dusk. Theo chooses another cheap, rundown motel.

We sit on the beds and eat burgers and fries from a local fast-food place. I scarf down my food in minutes, eager to go out and recover a sliver of normalcy.

"So?" I crumble the wrapper and toss it in the trash, then look at Theo. "Can we go out?"

He sighs. "I guess we should be safe for a couple of hours. But, tomorrow, we drive the full ten hours until we're in Blue River."

"Deal." I jump off the bed and run to the bathroom with the plastic bag from the drugstore that I made Theo stop at on the way here.

He was reluctant to wait in the car but, eventually, yielded when I told him I had a surprise.

Forty-five minutes later, I stand at the bathroom sink, discarding hair clippings and wiping hair dye off the counter. I walk out of the bathroom and hold my breath as I look at Theo. My heart pounds in my chest as I anticipate his acknowledgment.

He lounges on the bed, but his jaw drops when he looks at me. I wait for him to say something. Instead, he strides over to me and runs his hand through my dark-brown bob.

"What did you do?"

Lowering my head, I flinch away. "I thought this would help so no one else recognizes me."

The room suddenly feels cold. I cross my arms and turn away.

Theo grabs onto my arm. He tilts my chin toward him, twirling my hair around his finger. "I like it."

"Yeah?"

He smiles. "Yeah. It looks good on you." He gazes at me a moment longer, and my heart quickens.

Though, this time, not in fear of what he thinks of my hair. His hand moves to my neck, and his face is only inches from mine. I'm, once again, holding my breath.

I'm about to lean into him when he pulls away and reaches into his back pocket for his wallet.

"You'll need this if you want to get into a bar."

I examine the plastic card he hands me. It has my picture on it but a different name.

"How did you get me a license?"

"I had Paul make you one." He shrugs. "Just in case."

I give him a grateful smile. I look at the license, memorizing the information. "Who's Mia Jones?"

Theo shrugs. "A made-up name."

"What's the name on yours?"

"Tyler Jones."

I raise an eyebrow and smirk. "Does that make us married?"

His cheeks redden, and he turns away. "Or siblings," he murmurs, and my heart immediately deflates.

I look back at the West Virginia license. Besides the fake name and address, the physical traits are correct. The signature even looks like I signed it. Then I notice the birthdate: August 22, 1999.

"Is this my real birthdate?"

"Yes."

The doctors had guessed my age correctly. I'm twenty-two.

"How old are you?"

"Twenty-four." I thought he had looked about ten in the classroom memory. "Ready to go?"

"Yes!" I shove the license into my back pocket, ready to have a couple of hours of fun amid all the chaos of the last few days.

Theo drives to a place called the Power and Light District. Music booms from across the street. We follow the crowd of people and enter the square.

A DJ rests in the center, with people dancing all around. Stairs lead to a second-floor balcony and club entrance. Lights and the beat course through me, and I think of Trish as I watch a group of women dance. She would love this.

A wave of sadness hits me knowing I may never see her again. I wish I could have at least said goodbye. I suppress the feeling. Tonight, I'm supposed to have fun, not wallow in the past.

I turn toward Theo. He gazes around, looking uncomfortable. I nod for him to follow me up the stairs to find a bar that's not so loud. We show our IDs and enter.

Upon entering, I realize how wrong I was. The staff's uniforms are swimsuits. The music is louder than the music in the square, and the dance floor is packed with bodies.

"One drink, and we'll find somewhere else to go," I yell, but I don't think he hears me.

A worker in a skimpy bikini walks by, and Theo's gaze follows her across the floor. His eyes widen, and I wonder if he enjoys what he sees.

I project my thoughts to him.

Oh my gosh! Are you gawking?

What? No.

He diverts his eyes to the floor, cheeks flushing red. His embarrassment makes me giggle.

In my head, his voice sounds the same as real life, as if he's speaking directly to me.

One drink, and we'll go somewhere else.

We approach the bar, and the busty bartender asks for our order. Theo looks at me to order first. I turn to the bartender. *Vodka Cranberry.*

Theo gapes at me. *You're supposed to tell her with your spoken words.*

I didn't realize I didn't speak it out loud.

Shaking his head, he stifles a chuckle and turns to the bartender. "The lady will have a vodka cranberry, and I'll take a Coors Light, please."

We go to an unoccupied corner and stand there awkwardly.

"Do you want to dance?" I try to shout over the noise.

"What?" He points to his ear and shakes his head.

A verbal conversation is impossible with this noise, so I project to him instead. *Do you want to dance?*

Oh, no. I can't dance.

Come on. I'll teach you.

I grab his hand and pull him to the dance floor. He stands still in front of me while I move my shoulders to the beat.

You have to move. Copy what I do.

He sways stiffly. I try to encourage him to loosen up by shaking his hands out. He bobs back and forth, offbeat to the music.

Relax. Feel the music and move with it. Like this.

Stepping closer to him, I hold on to his waist. He stiffens. I move, trying to get him to move with me. He's hesitant at first, then sways with me. Once he seems more comfortable, I move closer. The feeling of being close sends a tingle down my neck, and I'm reminded of the feeling between us when he adjusted my seat. Something inside of me craves closeness with him.

I wrap my arms around his neck. He gulps, and I wonder if he feels the pull as I do. He wraps an arm around my waist and finally loosens up and dances. We move together flawlessly. Our faces inch closer, and an intensity fills his eyes, matching mine. The song ends, and he backs away as if he can't get away from me fast enough.

"We had our one drink and a dance. Time to go somewhere else." He storms off the dance floor, leaving me standing there, breathless and alone.

He vanishes through the crowd. The sudden change in his mood confuses me. We were having fun, and I was almost certain he felt the same spark as I did. Maybe I read the signs wrong and crossed a line.

Amnesia prevents me from remembering our past relationship. He must have thought of me like a little sister, which would explain his desire to protect me and his discomfort with my touch. It would also explain his comment about our last name on the IDs, and I regret the married comment. But without remembering, I may never know, considering he doesn't exactly talk about his feelings.

Pushing my thoughts aside, I walk off the dance floor. I can't find Theo anywhere. The bar rail rests in the center of the building and may be my best chance to meet up with him. I stand there, hoping to spot him.

Theo. Where are you? If you can hear me, I'm by the bar.

Minutes tick by, and he doesn't show up. Out of the corner of my eye, a man approaches me. My shoulders relax, but when I turn, I see it's not Theo. The man next to me smiles, and I turn away, continuing to search for Theo.

"Hey there, beautiful! Can I buy you a drink?" he slurs.

"No, thanks."

"Come on. One drink." He clearly has had too much to drink already. Swaying, he uses a hand on the bar rail to steady himself.

"I said no." I continue to look out into the crowd.

Where the hell are you, Theo?

The man stumbles closer to me, and I back away. He rubs the back of my arm with his finger. "If you won't let me buy you a drink, the least you can do is dance with me."

I glance at the man's finger, then peer at him through my eyelashes. Rage courses through me as he reminds me of another man in a bar who thought he was entitled to touch me.

"I suggest you walk away before I break your hand," I growl.

"Mmm . . . You like it rough, don't you? I can play rough, too."

Just like Mark, he can't take the rejection.

I turn toward the drunk man, rearing my fist back. A large hand grabs my fist and spins me around. My back lands against a hard body, and big arms wrap around me.

"There you are. I've been looking all over for you," Theo says playfully. *Careful, we don't want to cause a scene.*

The other man, too drunk to notice I was going to hit him, sees me with Theo. He eyes Theo from head to toe, taking in the size difference, and stumbles away.

Theo unwraps his arms but keeps his hand in mine as he guides me toward the door in a hurry. I can tell he's angry. He holds on to my hand until we reach the other end of the square, then flicks my hand away as if my touch burns his skin.

"What were you thinking?" he snarls, quiet enough that only I can hear him.

His reaction surprises me, behavior of an adult chastising a child, and I step back, my anger rising. "What was I supposed to do? Stand there and let him harass me?"

"You could've walked away."

"To where? Where the hell were you? I was looking for you for ten minutes. I tried to tell you I was waiting by the bar. Did you not hear me?"

He takes a deep breath. "I needed air. I was out here."

"So, you left me there alone?"

"I'm sorry," he mutters, and I know he means it by the way guilt fills his eyes.

He wasn't acting out of anger but out of fear and guilt. He deserts me, and some drunk man makes a move on me. It wouldn't have happened if he hadn't left to get some air. My anger subsides, and now I feel guilty for making him uncomfortable that he felt he needed to get away.

"Forget it." I brush off. "Thankfully, you were there in time to stop me. No harm done. You promised me two hours of fun. We have one more hour to make the best of it."

"Fine. But no more dancing."

I trace an X over my heart.

His expression softens, and he smiles as if remembering something.

"What is it?" I ask.

"You used to do that when we were kids. I had forgotten until now."

I don't know why I did it. From what I remember, it's not something I have done before. I did it absentmindedly.

Theo leads the way to a piano bar, where two musicians are battling each other on the piano. It's a delightful change of pace with pleasant music, not drowning noise. We find an empty table to sit at, and a server takes our order. I request another Vodka Cranberry, and Theo asks for water. We listen to the soothing melodies of classical music and watch couples slow dance.

Theo leans over the table toward me and whispers, "This is the perfect setting to practice control of your ability. Try to hear them." He tilts his head toward the room.

"How?"

"Choose someone and try to tap in. Like finding a radio station."

I scan the room and land on an older gentleman who sits next to a woman I assume is his wife. I concentrate on tuning into his mind. *Is this song ever going to end?*

I gasp and look at Theo. "I did it."

He smiles. "Keep trying."

I concentrate on the gentleman's wife next. *I hope that cheating bastard is miserable being here. I can't wait to hit him with divorce papers.*

"Uh-oh!" I lean closer to Theo. "Trouble in paradise over there."

He chuckles. "What else do you hear?"

I settle on my next victim of mind invasion, the bartender, and commentate to Theo. "The bartender recites the recipes as she makes them. She can't remember if she added the rum. The guy in the corner over there"—I tilt my head in his direction—"only comes here because he has a crush on the bartender." I look at Theo and wiggle my eyebrows, and he chuckles.

I continue to scan the room and tell him what I hear. "She's thinking about work, but the guy she's with is thinking about sex . . . That guy is criticizing the pianist . . . That woman thinks he's great."

The guy thinking about sex's thoughts shout in my head, though I wasn't trying to listen to him. I look at him and squint in concentration. My expression is a mix of anger and disgust.

Theo notices and asks, "What's wrong?"

"He drugged her drink. That's why he was thinking about sex. He's impatiently waiting for her to take a sip."

"I'll take care of it." He sits up straighter and stares with focused determination. He lifts his fingers off the table and flicks them in the air. The drugged drink tips over and spills in the guy's lap.

My jaw drops, and I laugh.

The guy stands, irate. *Fuck! That was my only pill.*

The server brings him napkins. The guy yells at the server and charges toward the restroom.

Theo calls the server to us. "I saw that guy drug the drink he spilled. Can you warn the woman he's with? Probably should kick him out, too."

The server covers his mouth with his hand. "Oh my goodness. Yes, of course. Thank you for telling me." He hurries off and talks with the manager, who immediately tells the bouncer to go to the restroom.

A moment later, the bouncer escorts the guy out while the manager talks with the woman, and she looks horrified.

I listen to her thoughts.

Thank God I didn't take a drink.

"She didn't drink any of it. He must have just dropped it in," I reassure Theo.

"I don't know about you, but I think I've had enough excitement for one night."

I nod.

He stands first while I finish the remains of my drink. Standing, I glance back at the pianist. When I turn, Theo stares at me.

"On second thought . . ." He extends his hand. "How about one more dance before we go?"

"You said no more dancing. I even crossed my heart."

He smiles. "I know, but I want the night to end on a positive note."

When I place my hand in his, he leads me to the small dance floor, where a few couples are dancing.

Theo wraps an arm around my waist, and I place my hand on his shoulder, then he leads us in a twirl of circles. He's more relaxed with dancing this way—nice and slow. With each move, he sways us to the rhythm of the music, as if he has heard it before. It's the first time I have seen him relax and enjoy himself.

Despite the urge to move closer, I keep six inches between us. I don't want to make him uncomfortable again. The song ends and immediately rolls into another. This one is slower than the last. When he loosens his grip, I tighten mine.

"One more? Please?" I ask.

He pulls me closer to him and leads us into another dance. I lean in, closing the distance, our bodies touching. He doesn't tense, and I rest my head on his chest. The stable beat of his heart pounds beneath my ear. He's not uncomfortable this time. In fact, he seems at ease. We slowly sway, not caring that it's not to the rhythm.

22. Blue River

We check out of the motel at eight in the morning. Theo says the drive from Kansas City to Blue River is ten-and-a-half hours straight.

Theo drives, while I rest my head against the window, trying to sleep. I didn't get much last night after we got back to the motel.

My mind wouldn't stop turning. I keep trying to puzzle through Theo's mixed signals. One moment, he's distant and uncomfortable around me, then he's at ease, holding me close in a fluid dance.

I can't remember how our past friendship was, but I can't deny the spark when I'm around him. I wish I knew if he felt it, too. I pretend to be asleep and connect to his mind.

Maybe we shouldn't go. I don't know how they're going to react or what they'll say to Amelia. They could ruin everything, and she'll hate me. We could have more nights like last night if it were only her and me on the run. But then Kat would kill me.

I disconnect from his mind. I heard what I wanted to hear. He enjoyed being with me last night and wants more time with me. What does he mean someone might say something that would make me hate him? At this point,

I don't think it's possible for me to hate Theo. I clear my mind and let myself drift to sleep.

"Amelia?" Theo's calm voice wakes me.

"Hmm?" I grunt without opening my eyes.

"You've been asleep for four hours. You hungry yet?"

Opening my eyes, I nod. It feels as if I just drifted off to sleep. I sit upright in the seat and try to blink the exhaustion away.

***

Theo chooses a small diner for us to eat lunch. I stare at the menu in a daze, not reading the words. Without warning, a straw wrapper hits my nose, and I jump in my seat. As he chuckles, I glare at him and raise my chin, giving him a mischievous smile.

Without breaking eye contact, I slowly slide my water in front of me and take a long sip from the straw, but I do not swallow. I move the cup aside, rest my elbows on the table with my chin on top of my hands, and give him a close-lipped smile while projecting my thoughts.

You think that was funny, don't you?

It was quite amusing, yes.

So is this.

I spew a small stream of water at him, as if I'm a human fountain. He jerks back with a gasp. When I start to laugh, water dribbles out of the corner of my lips, and I have to clamp my hand over my mouth to keep it from spilling out. I swallow in time, and we both roar with laughter.

The server approaches, and Theo clears his throat while I look away, trying to regain composure. After the server takes our order, Theo holds out his hand to me. "Truce for the rest of this meal?"

"Truce," I say, shaking his hand.

As we eat, I tap into the minds of the people to practice my telepathy. The more I do it, the easier it becomes.

Theo gazes at me like a proud teacher when I relay what I hear.

As we walk back to the car, Theo says, "Catch." He tosses a ball of metal that clinks in the air.

I catch it flawlessly and look down to see the keys.

"You want me to drive?" I ask, panic-stricken. "Remember what happened last time?"

"Only for an hour or two. You'll be fine. I'll be awake the entire time, ready to"—he dramatically pushes his hand out in front of him and makes a whoosh sound—"if I need to." I giggle at his comical display. "Plus, you can't mess with me if you're concentrating on driving." Sticking his tongue out, he hops into the passenger seat.

I haven't seen the playful side of Theo often, and I wish he'd let loose more because we click better when he's not so uptight about everything.

I pull onto the road and drive with ease. Theo turns on the radio and occasionally dances in his seat.

"I thought you didn't like dancing?" I tease.

"I said I can't dance. I never said I didn't like it."

"If it's any consolation, I think you're a fine dancer."

"Not as good as you."

I smile at the compliment.

After almost three hours with no problems, I stop at a gas station. As I choose my drink, Theo calls my name.

He stands at a rotating rack of baseball hats, sifting through them before choosing one and placing it on his head. It's black with the letters *CO* embroidered in white on the front.

"What do you think?" he asks.

"It's . . ." I squint. It barely fits on his head. "A bit small."

"Hmph!" He takes the hat off, inspects it, then glances at me with a smirk before stepping closer. Gently, he places the hat on my head and sweeps my hair away from my face. He rests his hands on my shoulders and studies me.

My heart quickens, and I want to lean into him, but I remain cool and collected.

"So?" I pinch the brim of the hat and lift my chin toward him. "How do I look?"

"Perfect." He gazes at me.

Heat rushes to my cheeks, and I shy away, causing his hands to slide from my shoulders and down my arms. His eyes linger on me a moment longer before he walks away.

I wait while he fills the gas tank. As much as I want to keep driving, I don't feel comfortable pulling up to a house of strangers Theo considers our friends. After that nightmare, vivid memories have become a part of me, but I know nothing about them or remember our relationships. They may see me as a friend they're reconnecting with, but they are strangers to me.

We drive along the highway, listening to music, singing, and dancing in our seats with nothing but the open road ahead.

The scenery differs greatly from West Virginia. Lots of open, deserted land with beautiful golden grass begging for water. The sky seems larger here as it stretches for miles, and I can see every cloud in the sky. They take on shapes if I stare at them long enough. I feel in perfect harmony in this vast dry land. I wish we could stop and experience it longer.

There's a shift in energy the closer we get to Blue River. My heart flutters, and Theo's expression hardens, body tensing. I have a reason for my feelings, but if I'm to keep it together, I need Theo to be strong.

"Hey. What's wrong?"

"Nothing," he clips.

"Something's going on in that head of yours. Tell me. I'd rather not eavesdrop."

He sighs. "Nervous, I guess. I haven't seen them in five months. Kat's not happy with me for staying behind."

I grab his hand, giving it a small squeeze. "I'm sure it will all be okay."

He shrugs but doesn't move his hand away. I keep my hand on his for comfort until he's ready to let it go.

We enter Blue River right as the sun sets. The community is pleasant and quiet. Houses are enormous, with plenty of distance between neighbors. There's lots of coverage from blue spruce and pine trees. The landscape looks like a painting, with the jagged points of the mountains in the distance, mixed with the lively green of the trees against the orange-and-pink sky.

We turn onto a road that leads directly to the two-story, mahogany-colored house surrounded by woods. Three people emerge from the front door and wait on the wooden porch.

Theo parks the car and turns to me. "Ready?"

Taking deep breaths, I slowly open the door. Theo leads the way, but I stay a couple of steps behind, holding onto my right bicep. My heart thuds as I'm about to meet the friends I can't remember.

I notice Kat right away. She looks exactly like the dark-brown-haired girl from my dream, but there's something different about her eyes.

In the classroom memory, they were blue like Theo's, but they're almost gray, and her pupils are larger than normal. Other than that, she and Theo could pass for twins, except she looks a few years younger. She holds out her arms, and Theo embraces her.

"God, I've missed you," she breathes.

They break apart, and Theo turns to me. "This is my sister, Kat."

Kat forces a smile. "It's good to see you again, Amelia."

I notice she didn't call me Amy.

"The quiet one here is James." He gestures to a lanky man with neatly groomed, slicked-back black hair. He wears neatly pressed khakis and a button-up flannel.

James gives a small wave. His eyes seem to glow as he looks at me from head to toe, not only once, but twice.

I fold my arms across my chest and ajar my body away from him.

"And this ugly fucker is Zeke." Theo pretends to punch him in the gut, and Zeke flinches.

I wouldn't call Zeke ugly. He's not the type of guy I look for, but the girls in Bridgeport would swoon over him. He's freshly shaven with a buzzed head of light-brown hair. He's not as stocky as the boy from my hypnotic memory, but far more muscular. If I didn't know where he came from, I'd think he was a professional bodybuilder.

"I heard you have a mean right jab," I joke with Zeke.

"Hell yeah I do. I'd be happy to remind you by giving Theo a matching scar."

I deadpan stare at Zeke. "You could, but then I'd have to break your fingers."

Zeke's face falls, and I chuckle at his reaction, then notice no one is laughing. I scratch my head and clear my throat.

"It was a joke. Something I had said to Zeke before," I say, hoping to lighten the mood, but only Zeke breathes out a sigh of relief.

"Care to fill us in?" Kat sneers, folding her arms.

Theo looks shocked, and heat rushes to my cheeks.

"It was the first day you two arrived in class. Someone tripped Theo, so he bumped into Zeke. Zeke threatened him, so I threatened to break his fingers."

"I didn't tell you that story." Theo furrows his eyebrows.

I don't know why he seems bothered by it.

"I know," I say defensively. "I told you . . ." I halt.

The realization hits me. I never told Theo about that memory. I shared that information with only Julian. I try to recover. "I told you I went under hypnosis. That was the other memory I had."

Theo and Kat stare at me with skepticism.

Zeke chuckles. "Do you remember actually breaking my fingers?"

"No. Did I?" I ask, mortified.

"Only on one hand." He holds up a hand and wiggles his fingers like it's no big deal.

"Oh my gosh! I'm so sorry."

"I'm not. That's how I learned to be ambidextrous."

Kat rolls her eyes at Zeke and enters the house, with Zeke and James following.

Theo stares at me before finally motioning for me to go into the house.

You seem upset, I say.

Do I?

I'm sorry. I thought I told you.

Did you?

Yes.

Hmm . . . Funny.

What's funny? I ask.

Your photographic memory.

I don't know what that has to do with this.

You have a photographic memory. Therefore, you can specifically remember sharing that memory and with whom you shared it. Lying about it also makes your apology a lie.

Theo storms away, joining the others. I cut off the connection, not knowing how I'm going to rectify it.

We were getting along so well on our travels. I've never wished so much that I could turn back time to take back my snarky comment to Zeke. Better yet, turn back time and convince Theo to keep running with me and not go to Colorado.

I take a moment to compose myself before leaning against the kitchen doorframe where the others wait inside. The open-floor plan allows me to see the spacious kitchen, living room, and a stairway leading to the second floor, but I'm only marveling over the kitchen.

Marble countertops line two of the walls with a matching long island in the center that would put my tiny kitchen island to shame. A back door rests in the corner, next to a double-door refrigerator.

James and Zeke are sitting at the heads of the long rectangular dining table. James reads a book, while Zeke leans back in his chair, balancing on two of the legs. Kat busies herself by wiping the spotless island countertop, while Theo stands at the sink, hands resting at the edge and leaning forward with his head lowered.

I feel weirdly out of place, so I stay against the doorframe. Theo looks up and turns toward the room. He leans back to rest against the counter and folds his arms, then glances at everyone else.

"Is Paul back yet?" Theo asks.

Everyone stops what they're doing and glances at each other.

"He got in yesterday. He's in the garage trying to . . . fix something," Kat says. "You should go see if he needs help." Her eyes widen, as if she's trying to convey a message to Theo telepathically.

I don't know her ability, but I'm sure it's not the same as mine. Theo would have mentioned if it was. I connect to her mind, but all I hear is, *Oh boy, this should be fun.*

Theo squints at her. "Okay." He exits out the back door.

"Amelia, please have a seat."

Kat's tone is polite but forced.

Not wanting to be rude or awkward, I sit in the middle chair, facing Kat. Zeke leans forward, and the chair legs snap back to the ground. He places his elbows on the table and clasps his hands.

"So?" He directs at me. "What have you been doing for these past five months?"

I shrug. "Um . . . Normal things, like working and going out with friends."

"And you remember nothing?"

"Not until recently. I had a psychologist in Bridgeport who put me under hypnosis. I only had two memories during that time, then another in a dream on our way here."

219

"Let me get this straight." He holds a finger in the air. "Out of all the memories in your lifetime, you only remember three from before, and I was one of them?" He smirks. "You know what that means? I'm so awesome the memory wipe can't erase me from your mind." He wiggles his eyebrows at me.

"Zeke, that's enough," Kat interjects, annoyed. "Don't you have something better to do?"

"Not really."

"Well, go find something, or I will find something for you."

She sounds like a mother talking to a child. Taking her threat seriously, he walks out.

A moment later, James follows suit, leaving Kat and me alone.

She avoids looking at me, and I want to say something to make it less weird. Although I can't remember, I know we used to be best friends. It makes me miss Trish considerably more. Thankfully, we're not alone for long.

Theo and Paul walk back into the kitchen, huffing. Theo's face is red, his hands balled into fists.

Paul's flustered expression changes to a welcoming smile once he sees me. "It's good to see you again, Jane? . . . Amelia? . . . What should I call you?"

"Amelia is fine. It's my name, after all. I might as well get used to it."

The room is uncomfortable and quiet, but if I get up and leave, I wouldn't know where to go. Kat and Paul look around the room at everything and nothing. Theo leans against the fridge, staring at the ground, still avoiding me. Kat must feel the tension rising and breaks the silence first.

"I think I'm going to call it a night. There's some leftover takeout in the fridge if you're hungry." She marches over to Paul, grabs his hand, and pulls him with her. "Oh, I almost forgot." She turns to face Theo. "*Your* room is upstairs, first door on the right." With that, she and Paul leave.

I wait for Theo to acknowledge me, but he keeps staring at the ground.

"Theo," I say in a shaky voice, "please talk to me. I'm going crazy here."

He doesn't lift his head. "What is there to talk about?"

"Can you sit? Please."

He sits across from me without making eye contact. His clasped hands rest on the table.

"I'm sorry," I say. "Truly. I did not intend to lie. I panicked when I realized I didn't tell you about that memory."

"But you admit you told someone?" he snaps. "Who? Josiah?"

"Julian." I roll my eyes. "Yes, but I didn't give him the specifics. I didn't plan on telling him. Honestly, I don't know why I did. I didn't want to, but when he asked about it, I kept talking."

"Would you say you felt persuaded to tell him?"

I shrug. "I guess."

"That's because his ability is persuasion. He persuades people to do things they normally wouldn't do."

It never occurred to me to ask about the others' abilities, but I should have guessed Julian's the moment I found out we had them. How did I not put two and two together? The hostess at Garfield's, the urge to keep telling him information, and him joking about how "persuasive" he is.

A part of me misses what he and I had. I let him into my life, my home. I shared my mind, body, and soul with him, but everything was a lie. I haven't let myself feel the pain of his betrayal the whole way here. Now that I know the truth, my body reacts before my mind can catch up. The chair clatters to the floor as I stand, but I fall to my knees, hyperventilating.

"Shit!" Theo moves quickly. In seconds, he's on the floor next to me. I struggle to breathe and can't see through the tears.

"You need to sit." He places a hand on my back and guides me to sit. "Knees up and head between your legs." He rips the hat off my head and helps me get into the position. "Deep breaths. In and out."

After a few moments, I calm down. Theo continues to rub my back as I take deep breaths until I'm certain the tears are finished flowing.

"Better?" he asks.

"Yes and no."

"I'm sorry. I shouldn't have been a dick about it."

"I wasn't reacting that way because of you."

He lifts his head to look at me. "Then, why?"

I kneel in front of him. "I was overwhelmed learning about Julian's ability. I feel betrayed, manipulated and"—I swallow and choke out the last word—"violated."

He furrows his brow. "Violated?" He closes his eyes, and his face contorts as if in pain. "You didn't . . ." He exhales through his nose, then looks at me. "Please tell me you didn't sleep with him." Torment fills his eyes, and I look away, ashamed. "I should've killed him when I kicked your door in."

His words take my breath away, and I lean away, horrified. "He's still alive?"

"Hey . . ." Theo places a comforting hand on my shoulder. "You don't have to worry about him. Paul took care of it. He can't hurt you anymore." As he wraps his arm around me, I rest my head on his shoulder. "It's been a long day. We should get some sleep. You take the room. I'll sleep on the couch."

He helps me to my feet, then guides me up the stairs to the room. From the closet, he finds a spare blanket and takes one pillow off the bed.

"You heard Kat," I say. "This room is yours. You should sleep in it. I can take the couch."

"What kind of gentleman would I be if I let a lady sleep on the couch?" He mocks in an appalled tone. "It's fine. Get some sleep. I'll see you in the morning." With one small smile, he closes the door behind him.

It seems like a lifetime ago I was begging Trish and Julian to leave me alone, the relief liberating. Now I stand in the middle of a foreign room by myself, breathing in the scent of sage and citrus before it disappears.

I lie on the too-big queen-sized bed and stare at the empty space, where Theo's body would fit perfectly. Closing my eyes, I connect to Theo's mind but don't have the courage to ask him to come back. Instead, I break the connection and let the suffocating loneliness crush me.

23. Cliff Hanger

In the middle of the night, Kat's and Paul's faint voices wake me. I shimmy out of bed and tiptoe to the far wall, put my ear against it, and listen.

"How long are we going to let her stay here?" Kat says.

"It's Amelia. She can stay as long as she needs to," says Paul.

"That is not Amy."

"What are you talking about?"

"Think about it. She gets captured, only to escape three days later by herself and not get caught. Now she has amnesia. There's something fishy going on."

"What do you mean?"

"She walks, talks, and looks like Amelia, but she's different. I think NOEL reconditioned her to be this way to lure us out. They knew Theo wouldn't leave her. They sent Julian to make it look like she was in danger, so Theo would rescue her and lead her straight to us. I think this is all a trap."

A pause looms before Paul answers. "Shit, I didn't think of it that way."

"What do we do?" Kat asks.

"We'll talk with Theo in the morning. Make him understand the logic of it all."

"You know he will never abandon her."

"I know you don't want to hear it because he's your brother, but he needs to make his own choices."

"Not if it ends with him getting killed. I'd rather kill her and have him hate me the rest of my life as long as he's alive."

"She was your best friend. You wouldn't kill her."

"I would to save my brother and the rest of us."

"Let's hope it doesn't come down to that. We'll talk to Theo in the morning. For now, let's get some sleep."

Were they right? Was it NOEL's plan all along to use me to lead them to my friends? I will leave willingly to save them. The question is, will they let me go if they think I'm a spy? No. They will think I'm running back to NOEL to disclose their location. I don't know how to convince them I'm not a spy. Theo is the only one who will believe me. My only chance is to talk to him before they do.

I lie awake until nearly dawn. Right as the sun peeks above the horizon, I sneak out of the room and make my way to the kitchen for something to eat. I grab an apple from the fruit bowl and sit at the table. After a few bites, Theo walks in.

"Hey," he says, leaning against the doorframe and wiping his eyes.

"Hey back," I whisper. "How did you sleep?"

"Terrible." He stretches and cracks his neck. "You?"

"Same."

"I would give my left arm to sleep in a cheap motel bed again. My back is killing me."

"Hey, listen." I take another bite of the apple. "I offered to switch."

"Yeah, yeah." He waves to dismiss it as he drags his feet toward me before grabbing an apple from the bowl. Crunching apples break the silence.

He needs to know what I overheard, but I don't know how to tell him. He's my only chance if I'm to make it out of here alive.

"Would you like to go on a walk with me before the rest wake up?" I try to sound nonchalant, but my voice is heavy in my throat.

"Sure. Everything okay?" He eyes me skeptically.

"I think fresh air will help me process everything."

"All right. I'll get dressed. Meet you back here in ten?"

"That's perfect."

I toss the apple core in the trash, quickly freshen up, get dressed, then meet Theo at the front door.

We step out into the cool, damp air. The sun is halfway up the horizon, and the sky is mixed with shades of red, orange, and yellow.

We don't want to risk being seen by the neighbors, so we walk toward the forest. We step over fallen branches and duck under low-hung trees.

"I know it's a lot to take in, but these are your friends, too." Theo holds a tree branch back for me to pass through. "They need time to process. They remember the old Amelia."

"It doesn't change the fact that Kat sees me as a threat."

Theo halts. "What are you talking about?"

I pick up a twig and snap it in half before turning to him. "It doesn't matter. I need to leave now, before they wake up. Otherwise, they're going to kill me."

My voice cracks on the last part. I want to be strong and not let it get to me, but I'm terrified.

"You're not going anywhere," he says sternly. "You're safe here."

With his words, I see exactly what Kat meant. He won't let me go. My eyes fill with tears, blurring my vision. I must leave before it gets worse, not only for me, but for Theo.

"You don't see it. I'm not safe here. Kat thinks I'm a spy, and she wants to kill me."

"I'll convince them you're not."

"How?"

"I've practically followed your every move since you escaped. If you were a spy, I'd know."

Stumbling backward, I almost trip on a log. He's been following me? He didn't mention it before. I rest my hand on a tree. "What do you mean, you followed me?" I spit out in irritation.

He gives me a confused look, as if the information is not new. "I've been following you ever since I dropped you off at the hospital. I needed to make sure you were safe."

It was bad enough he was close by all along without coming forward, but discovering he has been there in the shadows the entire time strikes a nerve with me. "Following me where?" I snap.

He turns away, putting his hands in his pockets. He lightly kicks a pinecone. "Every time you left the house, I was close by." He faces me again. "Which is why you saw me running the day I untied your shoe. I tried to be inconspicuous, but then Julian showed up, and the Mark situation happened, and I knew I couldn't hide anymore."

"You've been stalking me for five months?"

"In a sense, yes."

I understand he feels the need to monitor me, but this crosses a line. All along, I couldn't remember who I was. He knew and lived across the street, never once making himself known. If he had come forward sooner, I might have remembered something. There's no denying the pull I feel toward him. If I had met him, I probably never would have dated Julian, and we could have avoided a life on the run.

"Why didn't you come forward sooner?" I shout with tears in my eyes.

"Because you didn't seem like you were in danger, so I stayed back."

Not in danger? I want to attack him for saying that. I was in danger with Mark and with Julian. Now I'm in danger from his sister, but he won't let me leave. Every second puts me more in danger.

Everything overcomes me like a crashing wave. I want to scream. I want to fight. I want to go back when everything was normal. If I'm to save myself, I need to get as far away as possible.

Tears flow down my cheeks, blurring my vision, but I don't care, and I run.

"Amelia?" Theo shouts. "Stop!"

Weaving through the trees, I almost trip on hidden stones, determined to lose him. Everyone has lied to me or wants to kill me. I hear Theo chasing me, and I push myself to run faster. I will run until my legs give out.

My hair whips my face, and I can barely see through the tears. I'm running blind. Theo's distant calls have an urgency to them that alerts my senses to listen. I swat the hair out of my face, the rising sun shining in my eyes. As I hold a hand up to block it, I'm immediately overcome

229

by fear. Before me is open air and no more land. I've run directly to the edge of a cliff, and it's too close for me to stop in time. I try to skid to a halt, but my feet slide over the edge, and I plummet to the earth below.

The only thing I can control is my screams. I can't control the gravity, which will force my body into the jagged rocks, ensuring a quick death.

Ironic, isn't it? I ran to escape death, only to meet the same fate. Twice now—once from NOEL and another from the people I'm supposed to trust.

Maybe this was my fate all along.

24. Flashes of the Past

As I'm hurtling through the air, rocks below me, fear coming up my throat like bile, the air suddenly seems to form a rope. The air rope catches me and flings me backward. Rocks below me recede, and I land with my back against a tree.

Theo stands in front of me, panting, arms wrapped around me in a tight embrace. His eyes, full of fear, rush over my face. Not loosening his grip, he slides his hand to my cheek and rests his forehead against mine as we pant in unison. His anguished deep blue eyes stare into mine.

"What . . . the hell . . . were you thinking?" he whispers between breaths.

Hearing him sends a jolt of recognition. This is real. I didn't die. The adrenaline to get away has disappeared, and I'm aware of how relieved I am to be alive yet terrified. Anger and fear clouded my judgment, and it almost cost me my life.

"I couldn't stop in time," I jabber.

The weight of everything crushes me, and gravity, once again, forces my body downward. My knees buckle, but Theo's grip keeps me from falling to the ground.

Tormented sobs escape me as I say, "I couldn't stop. I couldn't stop."

Theo scoops me into his arms, lowering us to sit, and cradles me in his lap. While I wail into his chest, he holds me and pats my head.

"Shh . . . it's okay. You're okay. Shh . . . Breathe, Amelia. Just breathe."

I start to calm. He lifts my chin with his finger, then gently sweeps my hair behind my ear. He wipes a tear from my cheek, then cups the side of my face and stares into my eyes.

"You scared the hell out of me." His voice is hushed, his eyes fearful. "I thought I lost you again. I can't lose you again." When his voice breaks at the end, he looks away.

I grab the sides of his face. "Hey . . . hey . . . I'm right here." I bring his face closer to me and look him in the eye. "Look at me. I'm okay. I'm right here. I'm sorry I scared you."

My eyes wander from his eyes to his lips, and I run a hand through his messy dark-brown hair.

He slides his hand to the back of my neck, causing my chin to lift and my eyes to close. I inhale his scent, mixed with earth and sweat, and part my lips.

Heat from his breath warms my bottom lip, and my heart flutters in my chest.

For days, tension has built between us—at least it has for me. We're inches apart, but it's not close enough. I stare into his eyes, searching for a sign. They reflect mine, full of desire and longing to be closer, and neither of us can hold back any longer.

Our lips collide in a deep, passionate kiss. Everything about it feels right and, somehow, familiar. In one motion, he flips me to straddle his lap. He runs his hands through my hair and down my back, pulling me closer to him. We are hungry for each other.

In an instant, flashes of memories come flooding back. Memories of Theo and me together as kids, playing chess. Then another flicker of our first kiss when I was fifteen, when we had snuck away to hide in a closet. It was quick and innocent, but it changed everything between us. Glints of us sneaking away to make out in closets or empty rooms to continue our secret love affair, and now I remember it's because NOEL forbids romantic relationships. Then a flash to our first time making love, slow and gentle. Then dozens more of our bodies intertwined again and again. The last flashback, a phrase between Theo and I from over the years. *I love you. I love you. I love you. I love you. I love you . . .*

The spark and pull I have felt for him transforms as the past feelings resurface. Feelings that have been trying to poke through the moment I saw him in the park. They aren't like my newfound memories—distant and known—but real and current.

The recollections only last a second, and I push Theo away with shock.

Worry fills his eyes.

"I'm sorry," he says, out of breath. "I shouldn't have—"

"I remember," I blurt.

"What do you remember?"

I smile and stroke his cheek. "I remember us. Just bits and pieces of moments we had. Now I understand the pain, worry, and fear you must have felt."

He pulls me in for another kiss. "It was so hard keeping it from you and not being able to feel your touch."

"I know. I'm here now, and I remember. You don't have to hold it back anymore." I kiss him softly and pull away before it progresses. "As much as I don't want this perfect moment to end, we need to talk about what's going on."

"Can't it wait?" he groans.

"Afraid not." I swing my leg off his lap.

Word-for-word, I tell him about what I overheard. He sits in silence, processing the new information.

He stands and chucks a rock off the cliff. "Fuck! She has completely lost her mind. She sounds crazy, right?"

"I don't remember being turned into a spy, but her concerns are valid and reasonable."

"I know for certain you are not a NOEL spy. I'll convince them."

"And if you can't?"

"Then, we run."

25. Interrogation

Theo and I stroll through the forest, reluctant to return. It's still early enough that our "friends" might still be asleep. A part of me wonders if I am the threat they think I am. Who knows what NOEL did to me in the three days between my capture and escape?

We enter the house hand in hand.

Zeke sits at the table, eating cereal. He glances at our hands and raises an eyebrow. "And what's going on here? Went out for some morning wood?" He smirks and wiggles his eyebrows.

"Shut up. We need to talk." Theo's voice is serious. "Where are the others?"

Zeke shrugs. "Still sleeping."

Theo charges up the stairs, skipping every other step. I sit at the table next to Zeke.

"How did you two become a thing?" Zeke asks.

"I remembered who he was to me." I smile, reaching into the box of cereal and eating a handful.

"About time," he exaggerates. "I felt the sexual tension between you two when you arrived, but Paul told us we weren't allowed to talk about it."

"Why would Paul say that?"

"Apparently, Theo called him the other day. Said to let everyone know to not mention his past relationship with you. He said he didn't want you to be with him just because you already were. He wanted you to make that choice on your own, with or without your memories."

Theo enters the room with a sleepy Kat, Paul, and James. Kat pours herself coffee and stares out the kitchen window at the trees lighting up from the rising sun. James and Paul take a seat at the table, eyes still half closed.

"Great," Theo starts. "Now that we're all here, we need to talk."

"I agree." Kat turns toward her brother. "But I think Amelia shouldn't be here." She looks in my direction. "No offense, but it's not like you would be useful to the conversation. You know? Amnesia and all."

She's full of spite.

"Amelia stays. This concerns her. I know what you and Paul were talking about last night." Theo slams his palm against the table. "Have you lost your mind? How could you think she's a spy?"

"Sorry to interrupt." Zeke holds up a finger. "But what are you talking about?"

Theo looks at Kat and raises his eyebrows. Kat purses her lips, then turns her attention to the table.

"I think NOEL reconditioned Amelia to be a spy. To lure us out and lead them straight to us. So, we need to do something about that, and she shouldn't be here to hear it."

"And I think you've lost it," Theo adds. "I was there in the hospital when she woke up. I pretended to be a custodian, so I could watch her while she healed. I bought her a house across the street from mine, so I would always be close by. *You* weren't there to see her live a normal life. I did. There is no way NOEL turned her into a spy. I would know if they did."

All this time, he was in the shadows. If I didn't remember how much he means to me, I'd rush out of the room in a rage. Instead, I listen to what everyone has to say.

"You, of all people, wouldn't see it," Kat yells as she slams her mug on the table, spilling coffee from the sides. "You're too emotionally involved that you are blind. You want her to be your Amelia so badly that you are delusional to the truth."

"You're wrong," he yells back. "You know what happens to someone after they're reconditioned. They no longer have a soul or are capable of human emotion. They can only try to mimic it. If you even took a moment to talk to her, you would know she is not a spy."

"Okay." Paul's voice is raised but calm. "Let's take a breath."

Theo and Kat glower at each other.

I hate that they're fighting because of me. They've finally reunited after five months, yet they haven't had the joyous reunion they deserve.

Kat sits next to Paul while Theo takes the seat next to me, palms flat on the table, fingertips pressing into the wood as if trying to break the surface.

"Good," Paul says. "Now, let's discuss this rationally."

"There's nothing else to discuss," Theo begins. "Raise your hand if you believe Amelia is not a spy." Theo raises his own hand.

He turns his attention to Zeke.

Zeke raises his hand a couple of inches off the table, but Kat shoots him a daring stare, and he recoils, muttering, "Sorry."

James raises his hand high in the air, causing everyone to whip their head in his direction.

Theo, pleased someone agrees with him, gives Kat a smug smile.

"I can say for sure she's not a spy," James says matter-of-factly. "One, if you haven't noticed, reconditioned soldiers don't talk, and she does. And two, I scanned her when she arrived."

"You did what?" Feeling exposed, I fold my arms across my chest.

"My ability is like X-ray vision, except I can see more than just bones. Basically, any machine in a hospital that takes internal pictures, I can do with my eyes. I scanned you when you arrived. I could see from the scan they didn't recondition you."

"How can you see that on a scan?" Paul asks.

"All the enhanced orphans have four genetic markers. One from each phase of the enhancements. Reconditioned soldiers have the same four markers, plus two others, along with the memory wipe coursing through their brain. Amelia got the memory wipe but doesn't have the extra two markers. Therefore, she couldn't have been reconditioned. However . . ." James directs his attention only to me. "It's puzzling how you can not only experience human emotions but also recall memories."

"So, my amnesia is from the memory wipe?"

"I believe so, but it seems to be wearing off."

"How is that possible?" Kat asks.

"It shouldn't be. Once one gets it, they can't feel happiness, sadness, or fear. They definitely wouldn't be able to recall any memories. As far as I know, it's permanent. With the right equipment and a small brain sample, I could study why it didn't work."

"Brain sample?" I ask, appalled. "You want to take a piece of my brain?"

"Only a small sample. You wouldn't feel it, and it won't harm you."

"Yeah, that's not going to happen."

James shrugs as if it's not a big deal. "Suit yourself."

Paul makes his way to the fridge. He grabs a bottle of water, then a banana out of the fruit bowl. He makes two slices of toast and wraps them in a paper towel.

"Theo and Zeke?" he calls. "Can you help me with that thing in the garage?"

Theo and Zeke nod and stand. Paul grabs the water, toast, and banana and walks out the door with Zeke. Theo stands behind me, gently squeezes my shoulders, and kisses the top of my head.

"I'll be back soon," he promises, then follows the others.

"If you don't mind, I'd like to take a shower," I say to Kat.

"Of course."

Kat leads us up the stairs and directs me to where I can find the towels. I smile at her and turn away, but her hand on my arm stops me.

"You can't remember," she says. "But it was a living hell at NOEL, and for the past five months, we were finally living in peace. Then you showed up, and I was scared it was all going to be taken away." I grip the towel tighter to my chest and nod. "But I was a bitch to you, and I'm sorry."

She doesn't wait for my acceptance before she leaves.

***

I walk into the kitchen, hair still damp, to find Zeke, Paul, and Theo talking in hushed voices. They stop when I enter. Zeke turns toward the sink, turns on the faucet, and washes his hands.

I lean against the kitchen island. "What's going on?"

I know they can hear the accusation in my tone.

"Nothing," they say in unison, an octave higher than usual.

I give Theo an accusing stare. He diverts his eyes to the floor, and a bead of sweat drips off his forehead.

Zeke turns off the faucet and dries his hands on a dish towel, then sets it aside, revealing bloody, split knuckles.

"Oh my gosh." I push away from the island. "Zeke, what happened to your hand?"

"Oh, um . . ." With a panicked look, he glances at Theo and Paul.

"He got mad and punched a wall."

I can tell Theo's lying.

"Really?" I ask, dryly.

They all nod. I squint and connect to Theo's mind.

He punched a wall. He punched a wall. He punched a wall.

Theo's mind is useless for information. I switch to Zeke's.

Don't think about Julian being in the garage. Julian is not in the garage.

"Julian's in the garage?" I shout, mixed with shock and fury.

"Fuck," Zeke says under his breath.

Theo and Paul give Zeke a death stare.

"What the fuck, Theo?" I rest my hands on my hips. "Explain. Now." Paul and Zeke try to sneak out of the room. "You two stay right where you are. This involves you, too." They stop in their tracks. I look back at Theo and raise my eyebrows.

He pinches the bridge of his nose. "After I rescued you back in Bridgeport, Paul captured Julian and was going to kill him. But he thought he'd be more useful if he kept him alive and brought him back here for questioning. There's too much we don't know, and he may have the answers."

"So, you're holding him captive in the garage, and what? Beating the truth out of him?"

"Well . . ." Zeke raises a loose fist, displaying his knuckles. "Trying to, at least. He won't talk."

"He hasn't said anything?" I ask.

Paul scoffs. "Nothing useful."

"He said he would talk if—" Zeke begins.

Theo punches him in the shoulder.

"If what?" I demand. They all remain quiet. I stare at Theo, waiting for him to tell me.

"He'll only talk to you," Paul blurts.

Theo shakes his head and runs his hands through his hair in annoyance.

A shiver runs down my spine. I don't know if I want to face Julian. A part of me never wants to see him again, but I know we need information, and facing him may be the only way to get it.

"Take me to him," I say as calmly as I can muster.

"No." Theo shakes his head. "You don't have to. We will get it out of him, eventually."

"You'll get nothing out of him if you beat him to death first. I can do this."

Theo's hesitant but agrees.

I follow them to the garage. We enter through the side door and pass over mounds of cabinets, tools, and boxes, heading to the far back.

Dust floats like a fog in front of the stream of sunlight shining through the dirt covered window, illuminating the cobwebs hanging in the corner. The air reeks of musk and stale motor oil.

Theo stands in front of me protectively, but I peek around his arm and see Julian on the floor tied to a pole.

His hands and feet are bound with ropes, and he has duct tape over his mouth. His clothes are dirty and torn. One eye is purple and swollen shut. Blood splatters speckle his face and shirt. The sight of him makes me feel queasy, and I choke back the rising bile. As much as I want him to pay for what he did to me, it's hard to see him being tortured.

Julian doesn't acknowledge our presence. Paul walks closer to him and kicks the bottom of his foot. "Hey. Wake up." Julian stirs but refuses to look at Paul. Paul rips the tape from his lips, and Julian winces. "Time to talk."

"I'm not telling you anything," Julian snarls.

Paul turns away and nods at me. I take a cautious step forward.

Theo places his hand on my arm. "You don't have to do this."

"I'll be okay."

I kneel beside Julian, leaving enough distance between us. He still hasn't noticed me. "Julian?" I whisper.

He whips his head in my direction and smiles. "Jane? You're really here." His eyes search me. "You changed your hair. I like it."

I resist the urge to thank him. Then he stares into my eyes, and his recent delectation vanishes.

"Are you okay? I've been so worried about you." He seems delirious, and I wonder how hard Zeke hit him.

"You know I'm not Jane. My name is Amelia."

I talk to him as if I'm talking to a small child.

"I know." He lowers his head. "But I liked it better when you were Jane."

"Julian, listen to me," I say calmly. "I need information that only you can give. Can you do that for me? Please?" Julian nods. "What was your mission with me in Bridgeport?"

"You shouldn't have been able to escape after the memory wipe. They were all scratching their heads and didn't know where you were. When they heard of a Jane Doe matching your description, I volunteered to see if it was you, and if you were with the others. When I reported you were alone and didn't remember, they told me to stay and keep watch until further notice. I was to report back if you showed any signs of remembering or contacted the others."

"Is that why you tricked me to date you? So you could get more information? That's what you do, right? Persuade people to do things."

I can't hide the agitation in my tone.

"What? That wasn't part of my mission. Us dating wasn't part of the plan."

"Then, why did you persuade me to ask you out or be in a relationship with you?"

Julian glares at Theo, then back at me. "I see where this is going. He's pinning me as the pervert."

I shake my head. "You used your power of persuasion on me for your own personal gain."

He scoffs. "Is that what you tell yourself to make you feel better? It's okay to admit you were falling for me. That you liked it when I had you on top of the kitchen island and naked in your bed."

"Okay, that's enough," Theo howls, then charges toward Julian.

"Theo, stop!" I shout at him, holding up a hand.

He stops, clenches his jaw, and balls his hands into fists.

"Did I hit a nerve, lover boy?" Julian mocks. "Does it bother you I made your girl come in ways you never will?"

Theo reacts before anyone can interject. His fist strikes Julian across the face. After rearing back, he strikes again. Julian's head jerks to the side as blood squirts from his mouth.

"Stop it!" I yell and grab Theo's fist. "If you can't handle what he says, then you need to leave." Julian spits blood and smiles with red teeth. More blood trickles from the side of his lip. Theo takes another step toward him, and I stand between them, glaring at Theo. "I'm serious. You need to leave." Theo's eyes remain on Julian as his nostrils flare, and he huffs in short spurts. "Zeke, get him out of here."

Zeke grabs Theo's arm, pulling him back. Theo resists, knocking over a pile of boxes in the process but, eventually, storms out of the garage.

I nod to Paul, and he leaves to give me privacy.

I turn my attention back to Julian. "That was stupid and childish. I know you used your ability on me. Why are you lying about it?"

"I didn't use it on you like you think. It wasn't for a date or sex. I would never use them like that."

"Then, when?"

"I only used it on you a few times to get you to tell me what you remember. Once after Chubb's and another after mini-golf. That's it. But somehow you broke the connection, and I couldn't get any more out of you."

"What do you mean, I broke the connection?"

"I don't know. It's as if you knew I was in your head, and you pushed me out. That's never happened to me before."

I recall both times telling him as if I was compelled to do so. But I also remember fighting it the second time, nauseous. No other time did I feel compelled to say or do anything. Is he telling the truth?

"Those are the only two times?" I ask.

"I tried again the last night in Bridgeport." His eyes dart away, as if he's ashamed. "I tried to persuade you to be calm. But it didn't work." He wipes the sweat from his cheek onto his shoulder, leaving dirt and blood on the sleeve. "I would never use it to make you do something you wouldn't normally do. I only needed information. Believe it or not, I'm not a bad guy." He shifts uncomfortably and winces when the ropes dig into his wrists.

I sit beside him again, and the dirt from the garage floor billows. "Says the guy who drugged me and tried to kill me."

"No. You have it wrong." He sighs. "Yes, I drugged you because I knew you wouldn't come with me willingly. But I wasn't going to kill you."

"I saw you reaching for a gun. I saw the metal."

"I was reaching for handcuffs."

"But you tried to have Theo killed. There were men at his house."

"I didn't do that. NOEL must have sent them."

"Let's say I believe you. Why were you trying to take me that night and not before?"

"It's a long story, so I hope you have time." When I nod, he continues. "The day before your run-in with Mark, I left your house suddenly because I got a call from Dr. Sheffield."

"Who's Dr. Sheffield?"

"The woman in charge of NOEL. She wanted to move in on you soon. I tried to convince her you weren't a threat. She told me they were taking me off the case. I was so mad about it, I got drunk at the bar. Then, I showed up at your house, and Theo came running to rescue you. Theo being there, changed everything. That next morning, I went back and told her Theo was there. She knew if they took me off the case, Theo would get suspicious and take you on the run, so she let me stay."

"But Mark was part of NOEL, wasn't he? He was going to kill me. Did Dr. Sheffield order that, too?"

"Mark went rogue. He was never supposed to come after you. Our orders were to observe until Dr. Sheffield said otherwise. She was very adamant that you were not to be harmed. When I told Dr. Sheffield what happened, she ordered me to take care of it."

"What does that mean?"

Julian squirms and looks away. "I made you a promise, remember?"

I don't say anything, but I remember his promise to me about Mark. *I'll never hear or see from him again.* I don't need him to say how he killed him, but my heart swells that he did it, then sinks after not knowing if it was for me or Dr. Sheffield.

I clear my throat, and Julian looks at me. "But what changed that last night? What did you mean by you didn't have a choice?"

He shakes his head. "Dr. Sheffield thought Theo was going to move in on you soon, so she ordered me to bring you in. I begged her to not make me do it, but she told me if I didn't bring you in, she'll send someone else for you. If I chose the latter, I knew she would recondition me for disobeying. That's what I meant by I didn't have a choice."

I can tell he's telling the truth. I look into his eyes and see the same Julian that I had feelings for. The kind, caring Julian who's happy being near me. Although he withheld the NOEL information from me, I can't deny I was falling for him, but my feelings for him don't matter anymore.

"Thank you. I think that's enough for now." I stand and turn.

"Amelia?" I stop and look back at him. "They're going to kill me, aren't they?" he asks, voice wavering.

"I won't let that happen."

"Then, what's going to happen to me?"

"I'll figure it out. And I'll make sure you're treated better. Do you need anything? Food? Water?"

"Paul gives me food and water so I don't die," he snaps.

"Give me an hour to talk with them. Then I'll bring you lunch." For a moment, I watch him as he lowers his head in resignation.

I feel sorry for the beaten, sweaty man who's tied up and all alone. How could this happen to the witty and caring Julian I thought I knew?

"I promise I'll make sure you're more comfortable as long as you promise you'll cooperate a little longer."

He doesn't look up but mumbles, "Okay."

Before I change my mind, I rush out of the garage and lean against the closed door, trying to process everything.

Knowing what I know now and seeing Julian like that, I feel queasy all over again. I vomit on the side of the garage, then take a few deep breaths to compose myself before returning to the house.

26. Three's a Crowd

E veryone remains silent while I explain what I learned from Julian. No one seems to know what to say. After a minute of silence, Paul's the first to speak.

"Something doesn't add up. Whoever NOEL sent to Theo's house was there to kill us. Not to capture us and bring us back. So, the question is, why capture you and not the rest of us?"

I shrug. "I'll try to find out more, but if we want him to cooperate, we need to make him more comfortable. No more beatings, and he gets all the food and water he needs. His wounds need to be cleaned and bandaged before they get infected. And we have to loosen the restraints." I can tell Theo wants to interrupt me by the way he opens his mouth. I hold up my finger. "Just enough to make him more comfortable. To make sure all goes according to plan, I will be the only one that talks with him."

Theo scoffs and shakes his head. If it were up to him, Julian would be dead. I ignore him and turn my attention to everyone else.

"James. Based on your ability, I assume you have some medical training?" I ask, and he nods. "Great. You will assist me with Julian's wounds. Go grab whatever supplies you can find and meet me in the garage." James immediately sets off for the task at hand. "Kat, I need you to get a fresh set of clothes that Julian can wear. Zeke and Paul. One of you fix a proper lunch for Julian, and the other needs to clean up around him. It's filthy in there. Also, give him a pillow and some blankets."

Zeke swears under his breath when he loses to Paul in rock, paper, scissors and has to be the one to clean up the filth. I turn away to begin my task, but Theo grabs my arm.

"What do you want me to do?" he asks.

I take a deep breath before turning to him. His expression is mixed with anger, discomfort, and a hint of pain. This is probably not easy for him, seeing me be kind to his enemy, the same enemy he had to watch me grow closer to, and there wasn't anything he could do about it. I place my hands in his. His eyes close at my touch.

"I need you to trust me." I hope he senses my sincerity. "I know this is difficult for you, but we need answers, and this is the only way to get them."

"Then, let me help," he pleads.

I shake my head. "Not until you cool down. He'll keep trying to get under your skin, and I don't think you're in the right mindset to be around him right now. Please, trust me."

"I'm afraid of what could happen if you're around him too much."

I don't have to ask what he means.

I cup the side of his face and look him in the eyes. "You have nothing to worry about. Whatever Julian and I had is over now. I want nothing more than to leave him in the past so we can start our future. Together."

His eyes light up with hope at the reassurance he needed. I raise up on my toes to give him a kiss. He wraps his arms around me, deepening it for a moment longer, before he gently pulls away.

"I trust you," he says. "I will step back and let you handle this. Remember that I'm one thought projection away if you need me." He kisses my forehead before walking away.

I meet the others at the garage. Each person holds supplies from the tasks I assigned. When we enter, Zeke's already sweeping the dirt around Julian, swearing under his breath. I walk over to Julian and kneel beside him.

"Hey," I say with a friendly smile.

Julian turns his attention from Zeke to me. "What's going on?"

"You know we can't let you go. We can't risk you telling NOEL where we are, but I can make it more bearable for you until we figure out what to do. We have lunch for you, clean clothes, and a blanket. We'll get you cleaned up and tend to your wounds. I know it's not ideal, but it's the best I can do right now."

"Why are you doing this? I betrayed you."

"I know. But you're still one of us, even if you aren't on our side."

Kat leaves the clean clothes next to me and returns to the house. I hope she goes to Theo. He shouldn't be alone, and they deserve to catch up.

Paul brings Julian his lunch. I untie his hands so he can eat properly. As Julian eats, Zeke finishes cleaning and stands next to Paul and James.

James's motionless demeanor shows he's indifferent about Julian's situation, whereas Paul and Zeke grimace that we aren't beating him to a pulp. I leave Julian's side to join them.

"I can clean and bandage the wounds, but I'm worried about infection," James tells me.

"How come?"

"He's filthy and staying in a filthy garage."

"What do you suggest?"

"A bath and somewhere cleaner."

With pleading eyes, I look at Paul. "No." He shakes his head. "Absolutely not."

"Isn't there a basement in the house?" I ask.

"Yes, but that's James's area. Plus, we can't risk him getting loose in the house and killing us all."

I turn my attention to James. "What is the risk of infection if he bathes but stays in the garage?"

"There's still a risk, but it should lessen the possibility, as long as we keep his wounds bandaged and cleaned."

"All right, see?" I say to Paul. "Perfect solution. We take him to the house to bathe and then we bring him back here."

I can tell the thought of untying Julian makes Paul uncomfortable, but he agrees.

I join Julian's side once he's finished eating and kneel next to him. "We're worried about you developing an infection in your wounds. You need to bathe before we can bandage them. We're going to untie you and take you to the house so you can take a bath. If you resist or try to run, they will hurt you, and I don't want that. Do you promise to cooperate?"

"Yeah, sure," he scoffs.

"I'm serious, Julian." I glare at him. "I'm trying to help you, but if you try anything stupid, they will bring you right back here and tie you up. Your wounds will get infected, and you could die. Is that what you want?"

He lowers his head and mutters, "No. I promise I'll cooperate."

Zeke and Paul take one of Julian's arms in a firm hold. Julian can barely stand, legs weak from sitting for days, unable to escape in his condition.

James and I lead the way to the house while the others follow. I need to warn Theo before we enter with Julian so he doesn't overreact.

Heads up. We're bringing Julian into the house to bathe.

Why?

James recommends it to reduce the risk of infection.

I hope he's not waiting by the door, ready to attack.

I enter first, provided he is. Theo stands in the middle of the room with his arms crossed across his chest. He doesn't react or speak, only observes. I head straight to the bathroom and start the water. When I feel I have the temperature right, I call Paul and Zeke to bring him in.

Theo follows directly behind them.

"Someone needs to stay with him to make sure he tries nothing stupid," Theo suggests.

Zeke and Paul exchange disgusted looks, neither of them wanting to be the one to watch another man bathe.

"Amelia can stay." Julian smirks.

"Over my dead body," Theo retorts.

"Something I think about often," Julian sneers.

Somehow, Theo remains calm.

"I'll stay with him." Theo smiles mischievously.

I don't trust Theo and Julian to be alone together. I'm afraid they will try to kill each other—which Theo will win, given Julian's current condition.

"We'll both stay." I give Theo a serious stare, showing him not to fight me on this.

Zeke and Paul help Julian sit on the edge of the tub before leaving the bathroom.

"Can I have some privacy while I get undressed?" Julian asks.

Immediately, I turn the other way.

Theo leans against the door with his arms crossed, glaring. "Not a chance. My eyes will be on you at all times." I stay facing the other way, waiting for Julian's snarky response, but it doesn't come. "Boxers stay on. Out of respect for Amelia."

Julian lets out a short, hard chuckle. "Not like she hasn't seen it before."

Theo tenses, then looks up quickly, shaking his head in disbelief.

I'm assuming that means Julian did not leave the boxers on. I hear water sloshing, followed by Julian's pained sigh.

"You can turn now," Julian says.

I look at Theo, and he nods. I turn and see the top half of him above the water. Red creases wrap around his arms, chest and back where the ropes cut into his skin. His wrists bear the same marks.

I look away quickly, not wanting to see the torture my friends caused to his body.

"Don't do that. I need you to keep your composure. I don't want you to feel sorry for me."

He uses my own words against me. I take a deep breath to compose myself.

"What the hell are you talking about?" Theo asks, irritated.

"Nothing." Julian shrugs. "It's an inside joke between Amelia and me."

Theo rolls his eyes.

I hand Julian a washcloth. He wets it first, then squirts soap into it and rubs it on his body. I look away to Theo.

Thank you for remaining calm. I know this is hard for you.

It's what you wanted. I'd do anything for you.

I smile at him and don't look at Julian again because I know it would upset Theo, and I won't give Julian that satisfaction.

When he's finished, I turn so he can dry off and dress. Once he's dressed, I call James to the bathroom to tend to his wounds. James disinfects the wounds and wraps them in bandages.

Theo and Paul hold on to his arms and lead him back to the garage. I follow to make sure everything goes smoothly. They tie him to the pole, leaving enough slack where it won't cut into his skin but tight enough that he won't be able to escape.

Once they're finished, we leave Julian alone again. Paul goes directly to the house, but Theo lingers behind.

He looks at me with concern, and I crash into him in a tight embrace. He wraps an arm around me, using the other to rub the back of my head.

"I'm so sorry," I say, trying to hold back tears.

"You don't have to apologize to me. You did nothing wrong."

"Yes, I do." I pull away. "Julian didn't use his ability on me. Not in that way. Everything I did with him was my choice."

"Is that what he told you?"

"Yes. And I know he was telling the truth."

"How do you know?"

"He told me the times he used his ability on me. Both times, I recall talking when I didn't want to. I didn't feel like that any other time."

Pain flashes in his eyes, but he shrugs it off. "It's okay. It's not like you knew you had another boyfriend. I knew there was a possibility you could be with someone else."

As he turns, I place my hand on his arm. "There's something else. The last time Julian tried to use his ability on me, I pushed him out of my head. When he tried to persuade me again, it didn't work."

Theo draws his brows together. "What do you mean?"

"I mean, his persuasion no longer works on me."

"I don't know how that's possible. You shouldn't be able to resist."

"That's what he said."

"I don't know, but I don't see it as an issue."

Back in the house, Paul sits at the table, concentrating on a laptop in front of him. Theo leads me to the table where we both take a seat on either side of Paul.

"I know that look," Theo says to Paul. "What are you searching for?"

"I'm hacking into Julian's phone and laptop. Now that we know he was in constant contact with NOEL, there must be something to find."

I raise my eyebrows at Theo to elaborate. "Paul's a skilled hacker and a technopath, so he can manipulate technology."

Paul taps away at the keyboard. "I didn't realize how useful my ability was until we escaped. I can go to any ATM and take out money or open up a bank account and transfer funds. That's how we're able to afford everything."

He pauses and looks at me. "Or make old, broken radios come to life." He chuckles.

"Ah, so you didn't actually fix the radio?" I ask.

"Of course I fixed it. Just not with my hands."

Paul continues typing. "I'm in." Theo and I wait in anticipation. "He was telling the truth. His mission was only to observe." Keys clicking, Paul shifts his eyes. "I found his messages to NOEL. He mentions being confronted by the target but not recognized . . . He says the target has befriended him . . . NOEL says to keep a safe distance. Hmph! Obviously, that didn't happen."

I roll my eyes. He didn't mean it viciously, but I don't need reminding that Julian and I were together.

"He never told NOEL you two had a romantic relationship. He claims he got his information from either observing you or talking briefly with you at your job."

That surprises me. Why withhold information from NOEL? Did he do it so he could continue to be near me?

"They tell him they're pulling him from the mission, but then, the next day, he tells them Amelia was attacked by a rogue agent named Mark."

Hearing Mark's name sends a shiver down my spine, but he can't hurt me anymore because Julian killed him.

I wonder how he did it? Did he make him suffer? Part of me hopes so.

"Dr. Sheffield tells him to take care of it. He reports back later that day, saying he eliminated the agent. Then later that day, he writes that he recognizes Amelia's neighbor to be Theodore Wilson. The next day, NOEL keeps him on the mission to observe. Almost a week later, NOEL instructs him to capture Amelia and bring her in. That's the last of the notes."

"He was telling us the truth," Theo says in amazement.

"Is there anything else?" I ask Paul.

"Probably. I'll keep digging."

"Let me know if you find anything." I stand from the table, swaying with the rush of sudden dizziness, and hold on to the back of the chair to steady myself. The lightheadedness recedes but leaves my head throbbing. It's only late afternoon, and I'm already exhausted from today's events. It feels like I've been awake for days.

I trudge up the stairs and head to Theo's bedroom. I close the door behind me and lean against it. Closing my eyes, I take a deep breath, wondering how I got here.

In the distance, Kat laughs, and for a moment, it sounds like Trish. Tears swim in my eyes as I think about my old life and how much I miss it. Missing Trish, tequila Tuesdays, and my job at the country club.

I used to wish I could remember the time before I had amnesia. Had I known it was like this, I would have appreciated the chance to live a boring life.

It makes sense why we went back to fight after we escaped. So we didn't have to live our lives running and hiding, to have a chance at a normal, boring life. But we'll never be normal because we're enhanced by NOEL's human experiments. Although I can't remember, I understand the old Amelia's determination to fight NOEL. Her drive rises inside of me, and I want nothing more than to take down the organization that held me captive and wiped my memories.

I push the thoughts aside and crawl under the blankets, too tired to make plans for NOEL's demise. My eyes barely close when someone knocks on the door.

"Yes?"

Theo sticks his head in. "It's me." He enters the room. "Sorry, I didn't mean to wake you."

"I wasn't asleep. You can come in." Theo closes the door and sits on the end of the bed. "What's going on?"

"Nothing. I wanted to check on you. You seemed upset downstairs."

I shake my head. "I'm exhausted, and I have a splitting headache. I barely slept last night, and it's already been a long day. I just need a nap."

Theo nods. "I'll leave you to it and make sure you're not disturbed."

When he turns to leave, I realize I want him to stay. *Will you lay with me until I fall asleep?*

He pauses before turning around, then lies next to me. I lay my head on his chest, and he wraps one arm around me. Within minutes, I'm asleep.

27. Enhancement Files

My eyes drift open. Dim lights shine through the blinds. I don't know if the sun is setting or rising, but I feel well rested.

Theo's deep breathing moves my head on his chest, and for a moment, I watch him sleep. For once, he looks peaceful. Gently, I run my fingers through the front of his hair, then kiss his cheek. He inhales deeply and smiles without opening his eyes. I lean in again and place a soft, long kiss on his lips. His hand fists through my hair while the other wraps around my waist, extending the length of the kiss.

"From now on, I only want to be woken this way." He places a soft, quick kiss on my lips, then pulls away, stretching his arms. "What time is it?"

"No idea." I wipe my eyes before getting off the bed. "We should check if Paul found anything else."

Voices of our friends echo from the kitchen. I rush down the stairs as Theo trails behind me. Now I can tell that it is nearly dusk and not dawn. I'm relieved we didn't sleep all night.

Paul sits in the same spot as before, except, this time, the laptop is closed, sitting next to him with a pile of papers on top. He glances at us when we approach. "Good, you're up. Wait till you hear what I found."

Theo and I sit while the rest gather around. My knee bounces beneath the table, and I hold my breath until he speaks.

"There was a file on NOEL's server marked classified, so of course I had to read it, but it was encrypted. I knew it had to be good because it took me fifteen minutes to break through." He pauses, and a beaming grin crosses his face. "Files on us. Every orphan they ever experimented on has a file." Everyone glances at each other in amazement.

"What's in the files?" I ask curiously.

"Case notes of the experiments they did on us." Shock silences everyone. "Oh, I almost forgot. I made copies of all our files. Here." He passes out stacks of papers to each person. "I have Julian's, too. Never know if it will be useful."

"Shit!" I exclaim. "I forgot about Julian. I was going to bring him dinner."

"It's okay, Amy," Kat says. "I brought him dinner. You needed your sleep." I give her a grateful smile.

With her calling me Amy again, we might have a shot to get back the friendship we once had.

I hesitate before looking at my papers. It has been difficult not remembering my life at NOEL. Everyone is concentrating on their files. I bow my head with my eyes closed, willing myself the courage to open them. After a moment of steady breathing, I open my eyes and read.

NOEL Forgotten

Name: Amelia Evans

DOB: August 22, 1999

Date: August 22, 2001

Phase one–Cognitive Enhancement

Notes: *Amelia's cognitive recognition is advanced beyond anything we have seen. We believe she has a photographic memory that was developed during gestation. For this reason, we are starting phase one of the enhancement process.*

Procedure: *Phase one will include administering the cognitive enhancement serum directly into the temporal, frontal and parietal lobes.*

Hypothesis: *Amelia is the youngest subject to receive phase one. We believe because of her advanced brain development, and her current age, she will exhibit higher results in intelligence testing than former subjects.*

Observations:

*Date: 2/22/2002 **Age:** 2 yrs. 6 mos.*

Amelia can engage in conversations with adults using full sentences with the correct enunciation of a typical eight-year-old. She can also read at a ten-year-old level, but she still has the attention span of a typical two-year-old. So far, her cognitive achievements have exceeded a rate higher than any other subject.

Date: *8/22/2002* ***Age:*** *3 yrs.*

Amelia's cognitive achievements continue to increase at a faster rate than the other subjects. Her attention span has lengthened to that of a six-year-old. She reads and speaks at a middle school level. We will continue to monitor her progress annually.

Date: *8/22/2003* ***Age:*** *4 yrs.*

The rate of increased cognitive achievement has leveled out. Amelia has shown a disinterest in studies and testing. It is hard to tell if the rate of acceleration has leveled because of the lack of effectiveness, or her free will as a four-year-old.

Date: *8/22/2004* ***Age:*** *5 yrs.*

There is no intellectual increase since the previous year. Amelia has the intellect of the other subjects but is the youngest among them. The other subjects do not want to engage in typical child play with someone younger than them. Amelia is exhibiting emotional distress from social differences. We worry it is affecting her potential. Our suggestion is to bring in more children closer to her age that she can socialize and interact with.

Date: *8/22/2005* ***Age:*** *6 yrs.*

Over the past year, Dr. Sheffield recruited ten new subjects that were closer to Amelia's age, ranging from five to eight years old. There has been a significant increase in her social and emotional state. The new subjects look to her as their leader. Her cognitive tests show a 1% increase from last year. We will monitor her progress again when she reaches ten years of age. We believe she is mentally ready to receive phase two of the enhancement process today. (See phase two notes for updates)

Date: *8/22/2009* **Age:** *10 yrs.*

Amelia's cognitive achievements have increased since her last test. Her intellectual state is at a college level. She has showed the most progress out of all the subjects. Her fullest potential is yet unknown. Amelia is ready to receive phase three of enhancement today. (See phase three notes for updates)

Date: *8/22/2014* **Age:** *15 yrs.*

Amelia's intellectual state continues to increase. Other subjects have exhibited full intellectual potential by the time they reach puberty. However, Amelia's intelligence has steadily increased 1% every year for the past five years, surpassing all other subjects. We suspect it is because of her photographic memory. She has developed some typical emotional distress that comes along with puberty, but it hasn't created a cause for concern at this time. Amelia has reached full physical growth and is ready to receive phase four of enhancement today. (See phase four notes for updates)

Date: *8/22/2019* **Age:** *20 yrs.*

Amelia has reached adulthood and has received all four phases of the enhancement process (See phase two, three, and four for updates). The increase in her intelligence rate has slowed by 0.5%. It's concerning that she still shows an increase in cognitive retainability because we don't know how much information the human brain can absorb without being damaged. We will continue to monitor her.

That's the end of the case notes for phase one. I can't believe they started experimenting on me the day I turned two. My hands clench at the thought that my friends were only brought in to be companions for me. I know NOEL didn't stop with only ten kids. They brought in more children whenever they could. Theo and Kat arriving two years after the first group is proof of that.

I glance around the table. Everyone's enthralled in their case notes. I flip to the next page and read the case notes for phase two.

Name: *Amelia Evans*

DOB: *August 22, 1999*

Date: *August 22, 2005*

Phase Two–Ability Enhancement

Notes: *Amelia's cognitive strengths and advancements make her a perfect candidate to* *receive phase two serum that will allow her to connect to another's mind and enable telepathy.*

Procedure: *Phase two will include administering the ability enhancement serum directly into the temporal and frontal lobes.*

Hypothesis: *Amelia will hear another human's thoughts. With concentration and practice, she should be able to control it over time.*

Observations:

Date: *9/22/2005* ***Age:*** *6 yrs. 1 mo.*

Amelia claims she has heard a constant hum since the day after the initial injection. She has yet to hear a clear thought of someone else.

Date: *10/22/2005* ***Age:*** *6 yrs. 2 mos.*

Amelia claims the hum is exceedingly loud and overwhelming. She has had a constant headache that cannot be subdued with pain medication. We believe she is hearing everyone's thoughts at once and cannot concentrate on one person's mind. We suggest isolating her and having her practice on one person at a time.

Date: *11/22/2005* ***Age:*** *6 yrs. 3 mos.*

Amelia spent two weeks in isolation. The first week she spent learning to shut out the noise. The second week, trying to connect to another's mind. Dr. Amanda Sheffield volunteered to be the test subject. After the second week, Amelia could shut out the thoughts of everyone and connect to Dr. Sheffield's mind; hearing her thoughts. She was released from isolation and has since connected to two other minds.

Date: *2/22/2006* **Age:** *6 yrs. 6 mos.*

Amelia can now control when and whose thoughts she connects to, as long as she has previously talked with the person. She can keep the connection open for ten seconds before it closes. She will continue to practice lengthening the time and connecting to unfamiliar people. We will record the updates on her scheduled testing date.

Date: *8/22/2009* **Age:** *10 yrs.*

Amelia has significantly improved with her telepathy. She can keep the connection open for five minutes. She has successfully made connections to humans she is unfamiliar with as long as they are within her sight. We believe she will hold it open longer with practice. In time, we will continually work toward her hearing distant people's thoughts as well.

Date: *8/22/2014* **Age:** *15 yrs.*

Amelia can keep the connection open for thirty minutes. She also can hear a person's thoughts without seeing them. However, this is only possible for her to do with the subjects she is emotionally close to and within close range. Maximum range recorded: Two miles.

Date: *8/22/2019* **Age:** *20 yrs.*

Amelia can keep the connection open as long as she chooses. Distance has increased to ten miles.

It doesn't say in my chart notes that I can project my thoughts. Theo had mentioned it was our secret, and I'm glad to know that it was.

The other two pages contain phase three and phase four notes. They are shorter than phases one and two. Phase three is called the *Speed Enhancement,* with observations for each month after they administered the serum, ending at the six-month mark. Notes continue on regular testing dates that record the increase of distance, speed, and endurance.

Phase four is called the *Strength Enhancement.* They recorded the same observation notes as phase three—once a month, then ending at the six-month mark but starting again on the regular testing date. They documented various strength tests—amount of weight I can lift in pounds, surfaces I can break through, and endurance performing the strength tasks.

I've experienced my strength enhancement, but I'm still not sure how to control it. Speed is something else entirely. I've been running in the park for three months, but I don't know how to tap into that part of me. However, according to my case notes, I wasn't very good at it because I only scored in the tenth percentile.

"I hated testing day," Zeke admits.

The rest nod in agreement.

I shrug. "I don't remember it. Was it that bad?"

"It was brutal. The doctors and scientists would hook you up to machines, scan, and poke you with needles. Then they made us do a series of tests that would last all day. As much as I hated my studies, I hated testing more."

"That sounds terrible." I glance over my files again and realize I don't know much about everyone else. "When did everyone else arrive? What abilities did they give you?"

My second question is more for Kat and Zeke.

Zeke speaks first. "I arrived when I was six, in two thousand four. My ability is super strength. Hence the giant muscles." He flexes his muscles.

"And yet, I still broke your fingers," I banter.

He lowers his head and mumbles, "You caught me off guard."

I stifle a laugh.

"James and I arrived in two thousand five," Paul states. "I was seven, he was five. You already know our abilities."

"Theo and I arrived together, obviously," Kat says. "That was in two thousand seven. I was eight, and he was ten. I have enhanced hearing and vision, which allows me to hear and see super far away, and I have night vision."

I glance at Kat's eyes and realize why they look different from the memory of her first day at NOEL. They didn't only inject a serum into her brain for her ability, like they did with me, but also altered her eyes and ears.

What other horrible things is NOEL capable of?

I shift in my chair and look away from Kat. "How many of us were there?"

"Our unit was the largest, with twenty-four. All the others have twelve," Paul says, like I should know what he means.

"Unit?"

"Right," he says. "You don't remember." He puts his file down as if to prepare himself. "They arranged us in units based on age groups. Think of it like advancing to the next grade in school, except we only have three grades—which we call stages—and we move up as a unit. The age range in a unit is usually three years from youngest to oldest. Once the oldest reaches the age limit, we move up together."

"What age do you move on to the next stage?"

"Ten and under is stage one. Stage two is eleven to seventeen. Once the oldest in the unit turns eighteen, they move on to stage three."

"How long do we stay in stage three?"

"No idea. There was only one other unit older than us. The oldest was twenty-five, and they were still in stage three when we escaped."

"Out of twenty-four in our unit, only seven of us escaped?"

Everyone is silent for a moment.

"There were twelve of us that tried to escape," Theo says, pain tattering his words. "Nine of us made it out successfully. NOEL killed the other three before they crossed the wall. Zeke and James took off on their own until Paul and Kat found them near Pittsburg a week later, but Molly and Brooke traveled south. Who knows where they ended up? You, Jackson, and I went back . . . but you remember that . . . and what happened next."

No one speaks for a moment, and out of respect for those they lost, I stay silent.

Theo breaks the silence.

"Were you able to find any information about why NOEL is doing experiments on children?"

Paul shakes his head. "Not yet. I'll do more digging tomorrow." He adds his files to the stack of papers on top of his laptop, then stands. "I'm exhausted."

"Paul?" I call out. "Can I see Julian's files?"

Paul shuffles through the papers and hands them to me. I nod a thank you, and he heads to bed.

Looking for something to eat, Theo rummages through the fridge. Kat, James, and Zeke exit after Paul, taking their files with them. I scan over Julian's files, while Theo reheats leftovers.

His files are arranged like mine. He arrived when he was five, on October 1, 2004—the same year they brought in ten new subjects with whom I could socialize. He received phase one on the day of his arrival, phase two a year later, phase three when he was ten, and phase four when he was sixteen. His test results regarding the phases were exceedingly well. It says he was having a hard time socializing with the others, so he spent a lot of time in the labs, helping the doctors and scientists. Nothing seems out of the ordinary, except Julian's files have an extra page than I do. A fifth page titled, *Quadripartite Booster–Administer Log*. The log list contains dates every two years following phase four.

I don't know how important this is or what it does.

"Theo?" He turns around from the microwave with raised eyebrows. "Do your files have a fifth page? It should say Quadripartite Booster."

"Uh . . . yeah. I think so."

"What is that?"

"It's like a booster shot."

"For what? What does it do?"

"Not sure. They said we needed to have it. If I had to guess, it's keeping the enhancements active." He removes the container from the microwave and walks back to the table.

"What happens if you don't get the booster?"

Theo sits across from me and opens the container lid and steam rolls out. "Hopefully, we go back to normal." He scoops a heaping portion of lasagna onto a plate and places it in front of me, then does the same for himself. He places a forkful into his mouth, then spits it out. "Careful, it's hot."

Why do Julian and Theo have records of a booster shot, and I don't? Maybe Paul forgot to give me mine? I take a bite of lasagna, hoping the food will melt away my concerns, but it seems like a piece of information is missing.

When the food is gone and dishes are done, Theo taps his fingertips on the table. "I know we napped earlier . . ." He swallows. "But do you want to go to bed?"

"Oh. Um . . . sure."

My heart quickens, and my palms clam up. We had spent three nights together in hotels. In separate beds, of course, but we shared the same bed only hours ago. I suppose my exhaustion had shut my mind off to intimacy, but now it's turning a nonstop wheel.

I stand from the table, and we stroll up the stairs. He eyes the bed, as if he's suffering an internal conflict at the sight of it.

I'm about to reach into his mind to listen in when he finally breaks the silence. "I can sleep on the couch again if you're not comfortable sharing a bed."

"No, it's okay. You can sleep in here."

Theo steps in and closes the door.

Upon shuffling through my backpack, I realize my clothes are dirty. "I have nothing clean to wear to bed."

"I can wake Kat and ask her for something of hers."

"No. It's fine. I'll sleep in this T-shirt. I'll need to take off the jean shorts, though."

Theo gulps and turns the other way. I remove the shorts and quickly get under the blankets. "You can look now."

He turns around, then looks at his own clothes. "Do you mind if I sleep in my boxers?"

"It's fine. I don't mind."

I close my eyes to give him privacy. After a moment, the light beneath my eyelids goes dark.

"Okay. I'm done."

I open my eyes to a dark room, and his silhouette saunters toward the bed. The mattress shifts under his weight. We both lay on our backs at opposite ends, staring at the ceiling. He seems anxious, and I'm curious if he's uneasy about sleeping in the same bed. His thoughts break the silence, and I can't help but listen.

She only remembered this morning. It's too soon. I need to wait until she is ready.

This morning feels like ages ago. The kiss we shared was passionate and primal. We wanted to take it further, but there were more pressing matters at hand.

As I lie here, memories I had earlier flood back to me, not just pictures in my mind but real ones. I remember everything about them. I remember the sounds, the scents, the *touch*. I remember the love that consumed me . . . *consumes* me.

Rolling toward him, I rest my head on his chest. He puts an arm around my shoulder, but he's tense. I trace his collarbone, down his chest, and circle the spot above his belly button. I remember, now, doing this before. His heart thumps fast against my ear. When I kiss up his collarbone to his neck, he inhales sharply.

I slide my leg across him and nestle myself onto his lap. His eyes stare into me, twinkling from the moonlight shining through the window. Taking his face in my hands, I lean in, and the sweet taste of his lips lingers on mine as we kiss. He grabs my hips, fingertips pressing slightly into my skin—the *touch*, I remember—gentle yet firm. His hands travel up my back, and he gently tugs my hair. When I pull away, the sound of my pounding heart mixes with our labored breaths. He stares at me, full of hunger, but I still sense his hesitancy.

"What do you want?" I whisper.

"You," he breathes. "I only want you."

"Then, have me."

Those three words were all he needed to hear. He sits up, meeting my body, then wraps his arms around me and collides his lips to mine.

28. The Power of Persuasion

I wake to soft kisses tracing my collar bone, and I let out a soft moan.

"Wake up, sleepyhead," Theo says.

"A girl could get used to waking up like this."

"Then, your wish is my command." He kisses my neck until he reaches my lips, then deepens the kiss, letting me know he's yearning for more. I pull him on top of me, letting him know I do, too. Our love-making last night was slow and gentle. Almost like the first time all over again. Full of nerves about rediscovering each other. But those nerves are gone, replaced with a palpable craving that intensifies the moment he thrusts into me. He's anything but slow or gentle, and it fuels my burning desire until my craving is satiated.

We lie there, sweaty, breathless, and too exhausted to speak, so I project my thoughts to Theo.

Wow! That's what I've been missing for the past five months?

You and me both.

Someone knocks on the door.

"Ugh!" Theo rolls his eyes. "What?"

Zeke shouts through the door. "Hope you saved some room for breakfast after you had your dessert. It'll be ready in five."

I pull the blankets up to my mouth to stifle a laugh.

"We'll be right there." He leans over and gives me a quick kiss. "I would stay in this bed all day with you. Just say the word." As if on cue, my stomach growls. His eyebrows raise. "On that thought, let's go eat." Still naked, he gets out of bed. I revel, gawking at him. Swaying his hips, he glances over at me with a smirk. "Enjoying the show?"

"Very much so."

"My offer still stands."

"As much as I would love to take you up on that, I need food."

Theo nods and dresses. I get out of bed and put on the clothes from yesterday.

Theo glances at me again while I dress. "We'll do laundry after breakfast." After dressing, he crosses the room and wraps an arm around my waist, growling into my ear and squeezing my right butt cheek. I yelp in surprise, then giggle. He places a long, hard kiss on my lips. "I'm so glad I got you back. And not for the sex." He plants a peck on my lips. "Although the sex is a great bonus."

As soon as I descend the stairs, the aroma of bacon and eggs makes my stomach rumble. We enter the kitchen right as Kat is dishing out the plates for breakfast. Theo and I take a seat at the table with the others. Kat places a plate in front of each of us—scrambled eggs, bacon, and toast. My mouth waters at the sight, and I don't hesitate to dig in.

Theo and I are the first to finish our breakfast. We stand together and wash our dishes. I scoop the remaining eggs and bacon onto a plate and stick a fresh piece of bread into the toaster.

"Going for seconds?" Theo asks me while drying off the plates.

"This is for Julian."

"Right." He places the clean dishes into the cupboard. "I'll go with you and then we'll do laundry." The toast pops up, I butter it quickly, and Theo and I head to the garage.

Julian stirs as we enter. He manages a smile when he sees me despite his swollen eye. "We brought you breakfast." Julian's smile fades when he looks at Theo.

Ignoring the exchange, I kneel beside Julian and untie his hands, then hold out the plate for him. He takes it with a grateful smile. "How are you feeling today?"

"Better now that you're here."

He's trying to flirt with me. I don't know if he's being genuine or trying to antagonize Theo. Either way, I refuse to react. Instead, I pretend to pick a piece of lint off my shoulder.

"We found something yesterday. Can you help us understand it?"

Julian scoops eggs into his mouth and talks between chewing. "I was wondering how long it would take Paul to go searching." He swallows, then grabs a bacon and waves it in the air. "So . . . what did he find?"

"Files on us. Notes of the experiments."

"And?" His tone is annoyed. "It's not like this is news."

"What do you know about the boosters?" I ask.

"That we get them every two years after phase four."

"What are they for? What happens if someone doesn't get their booster?"

"No idea."

His answer frustrates me. Theo thinks we will go back to normal, but there is a dreadful knot in my stomach whenever I think about it.

"I read your file," I say. Julian turns, his eyes cautious, as if I discovered something he didn't want me to know. "You spent a lot of time with the doctors and scientists. What were you doing?"

He exhales, and his shoulders relax. "Nothing, really. When I was younger, they let me watch them work. Sometimes, I would clean. The more time I spent in there, the more I started asking questions, and they started teaching me about the research."

"What did you learn?"

Julian eats another forkful of eggs before answering, "Science, obviously." I ignore the sarcastic remark and stare at him until he continues. "Learning science wasn't part of my training, but it fascinated me. I once asked Dr. Sheffield if I could switch and be in the same classes as James, but she said, 'You only need to learn what is necessary for your purpose.'" He raises his voice an octave, I assume, to sound like Dr. Sheffield.

"What does that mean?"

Julian sets his empty plate aside. "Our training and learning are solely based around our abilities. My ability is persuasion, so my classes were psychology, human interaction, expression, and stuff like that. My purpose was to learn how to read people, then get them to like me and persuade them to do whatever I want them to do."

"Why do we each have to have a purpose? What is the reason for enhancing us in the first place?"

Julian frowns as he shakes his head. He tries to adjust himself, but the ropes around his torso provide little movement. "I'm not sure. No one dared to question why."

"Didn't you ever wonder what they were doing with us? There must be a reason we are the way we are. It can't be for one giant science experiment."

"Like I said, I don't know."

From the look in Theo's eyes, I can tell he also doesn't believe Julian.

Things don't quite add up. NOEL kept us locked up, never letting us leave the facility, yet they sent Julian and Mark to monitor me. Why? He also didn't relay all the information to NOEL about our romantic relationship.

"Why did you lie to NOEL about us?"

It comes out in a whisper.

Julian looks into my eyes with pain, as if he's remembering our time together. "It was against the mission. Had they known the truth, they would have taken me off the case. I didn't want to leave you."

Compassion helped me get through to him before and may be the only way to get anything out of him. When I place my hand on top of his, his eyes soften. I don't have to look behind to know Theo's eyes burn into me. I don't want to upset him, but I know he'll understand the kind gesture is necessary. To my relief, he doesn't react.

"Why did they send you and Mark?" I ask. "I thought no one could leave."

"I volunteered because I'm the one that hated you all the most. They accepted because they knew I wouldn't be biased and could get the job done. They sent Mark with me for another set of eyes."

"Why do you hate us?"

Julian shifts his hatred-filled eyes to Theo, then back at me. "Remember that story I told you on our picnic about the bullies? You lot were the bullies."

My hand recoils from his. Would I have bullied Julian? It seems likely since I threatened Zeke and eventually followed through with it. There's still so much I don't know about my past. The more I learn, the less I want to know.

"Even me?" I ask.

"Not as bad as the guys, but . . . yes."

"How could you stand to be near me, then?"

"When I met you at Chubb's, you seemed different from the Amelia I'd known. At NOEL, you were focused, determined, and kind of cold-hearted to anyone that wasn't in your circle. Basically, you were a bitch."

"Watch it!" Theo steps closer.

I put my hand up to stop him. He exhales heavily and slams his palm against an old toolbox. "It's okay. I need to hear this." I look back at Julian. "Please continue."

"Like I said, you were a bitch. But when I met you as Jane, you were none of those things. You were carefree, optimistic, and happy. I hated Amelia from NOEL, but I liked Jane from Bridgeport."

Julian smiles and touches my cheek. I jerk back at his touch. His hand falls while he lowers his head in disappointment.

"I think that's enough. I'll have James come to change your bandages." Without waiting for his response, I rush out of the garage, while Theo stays to rebind Julian's hands.

***

Two hours later, Theo and I finish washing our laundry. Paul is so focused on his laptop that he doesn't notice when we enter. We head up the stairs to put away our clothes.

I hang mine in the closet as Theo loads the dresser. He's been silent since we left the garage, only exchanging words like "Can you pass the detergent?" and "The dryer's free."

"You've been awfully quiet since this morning. Everything okay?" I ask him casually, not able to take the silent tension anymore.

"Yup."

It's hard to read his tone. He acted this way at times on our journey here. I thought that, once I remembered us together, he would open up to me and not leave me in the dark anymore.

I hang the last shirt and turn to face him with my hands on my hips. "You're doing that thing I hate again."

"What thing am I doing?"

"That thing where you're lost in your own mind, and you won't talk to me about it. I get you did it before because I couldn't remember our relationship, but now I do, so you need to talk to me. I don't like it when you shut me out."

Theo sighs. "You're right. I'm sorry. It bugged me when Julian was comparing who you were then to who you are now."

"Well? Was he telling the truth?"

He glances sideways at me, then returns to folding his clothes and placing them neatly in the dresser drawer. "Yes and no. He was right that you were focused and determined, but I never thought of you as cold-hearted. And you definitely weren't a bitch."

"And now?"

"I watched you for five months. Yes, you were carefree, optimistic, and genuinely looked happy. But I saw you when he didn't. You were still as focused and determined as you were before. But you could have those good qualities because you didn't have the pain and burden of your memories."

I'm terrified of the answer of what I want to ask. I take one steadying breath before speaking.

"You loved me for who I was before, right?"

He looks at me in shock. "Of course. You know that. You remember us together. You're everything to me."

"What about now? Can you still love me, even though I'm not the same?"

I choke on the last word.

Theo immediately closes the distance between us and embraces me. "Of course I still love you. I will always love you. I love you as much as I did then. I'm sorry if I ever made you feel differently." Finally, I embrace him. He tilts my chin up, so I'm looking into his eyes. "You were, are, and always will be my entire world. No matter what. Never forget that."

He leans in and kisses my lips, long and soft, before pulling away and wiping the tears from my eyes. When I loosen my grip, he tightens his. He holds me a moment longer before letting go.

When we walk into the kitchen, Paul is in the same spot, barely acknowledging our presence as we rummage through the fridge for lunchmeat and cheese.

"Any luck finding anything else?" I ask him, making a turkey sandwich.

"Oh, I found something all right," Paul says. Something's different about him. His eyes look gleeful. "Blueprints to NOEL."

"What?" Theo exclaims. "And you're only now saying something?"

"Yeah, sorry. I've been trying to get into the other files, but one of them is password protected, and I'm afraid if I put the wrong password in too many times, it could erase the whole thing." Theo and I bring our sandwiches to the table. "Here are the blueprints." Paul slides the papers to us.

Sifting through the pile, I glance at each page. NOEL is huge. Five floors high with three wings—north, east, and west.

Familiarity creeps in. I've seen these before. It's hazy, but during hypnosis of my escape, I remember everything my past self had thought, and she racked through her photographic memory to see the blueprints. The memory was fleeting, not enough to remember the specifics but enough to know the sewer drain tunnel's location.

"I know it's not much, but it's more than we had before," Paul says.

"We could take them down," Theo says with a hopeful smile.

"We still have a long way to go. But yes, with the information I've found, and still have yet to find, plus with everyone together, we may have a chance."

"What else have you found?" I ask Paul.

"Nothing too significant. More records of the orphans." He glances at Theo. "Death records."

"Death records?" Theo's face falls. "Is Jackson's name on there?"

Paul pauses before answering. "That was the first name I looked for. There's no record of his death."

Theo slams his fist against the table, startling me. "Son of a bitch. That means he was reconditioned." Theo's eyes fill with pain and guilt.

"Hey." I place a hand on his arm to soothe him. "We don't know that for sure. Whatever happened to Jackson is not your fault. The three of us chose to go back."

Theo pulls away from me. "I need a minute." He storms out of the room.

Although it's better to give him space, I want to follow and console him.

My attention drifts back to Paul. "Did you find anything more about the booster?"

"Unfortunately, no. I tried to find information on the reconditioning unit and came up empty. It could be on the password-protected file I can't get into yet."

"I know I'm not a computer whiz, but can I see what it looks like?"

Paul turns the laptop toward me and clicks on the file he's been trying to open, a label containing numbers that make no sense to me, 152211419. "What do you think the numbers mean?"

"No idea. It's the only numbered file. It could be a code for something, but I'm not sure what."

My head cocks as I stare at the familiar sequence. I've seen them before, but I can't pinpoint where. Pushing the feeling aside, I give Paul a small smile. "Thank you! I'm going to bring Julian lunch. Let me know if you figure it out."

I throw together another sandwich for Julian. I'd prefer Theo to come with me, but he's still having his alone moment.

As I enter the garage, a grunt follows a *smack*. Zeke is tied to the pole, while Julian stands above him, punching him in the face. Neither of them has noticed I've entered, so I hide behind a cabinet to stay out of sight.

I'm no match for Julian in a fight. I could beat Mark easily, but that's only because Theo's telekinesis held him in place. The first thing I can think of is to project my thoughts to Theo.

Theo, help! Come to the garage now . . . quietly. Julian tied up Zeke and is beating him. Please hurry.

I'm coming.

Within thirty seconds, Theo arrives but not before Julian sludges Zeke three more times. Zeke groans with each strike, and Julian's face glows triumphantly. Theo enters the garage with perfect stealth and stands behind me. I think out to him.

What do we do?

I'll use my telekinesis to hold him back as long as I can. Paul is outside waiting for my signal. We'll grab him and tie him back up. Meanwhile, you untie Zeke.

I wait for Theo to make the first move.

Julian rears his fist to deliver another blow. Before he makes contact, Theo thrusts his hand out in front of him, and Julian's fist freezes inches away from Zeke's face.

Theo yells out to Paul while Julian struggles to fight through the telekinesis, but Theo's invisible hold is too strong. I run to Zeke and untie the ropes. Paul and Theo tackle Julian and tie his feet together and his hands behind his back. Zeke shakes himself out of the ropes. His eyes are dark and fierce, with shallow cuts on his lip.

"Are you okay?" I ask him with concern.

"Physically, yes," he says with spite. "Fucker used his ability and got me to untie him."

Theo throws Julian back against the pole and ties him tightly against it without saying a word—I think out of respect for me.

"What the hell, Julian?" I spit out at him. "I said as long as you cooperate, I will try to make things as comfortable as I can for you. You blew that."

"Amelia, please," he begs. "Please, let me go. You know I won't go back to NOEL. They'll recondition me for failing my mission. I'll run, and you'll never hear from me again."

"That's a risk we can't take."

"You can trust me." His voice changes to a smoothing tone, and he glances at all of us. "You all know you can trust me."

Shockingly, all the men in the room nod.

"We can trust you. We'll let you go."

Paul moves toward Julian.

I stand between him, putting my hand up to stop his advances.

"What the hell are you doing? We can't trust him."

Paul ignores my words and walks around me. When I see Julian's smug smile, I realize everyone is falling for his persuasion except me. All three walk toward Julian and slowly untie him. I project my thoughts to Theo, hoping it will break him out of the hold.

Theo. Listen to me. Julian is using his ability on you. You have to fight it.

Theo's expression turns to confusion as he realizes he's helping to untie Julian. His face strains when he pauses with his hands on the ropes, then he continues to untie him slower. Sweat beads off his forehead as he's trying to resist.

That's it. Keep fighting it. Listen to my voice. You do not trust Julian. You do not want to untie him.

It's as if Theo finally wakes up and comes to his senses. He acts quick and punches Julian, knocking him unconscious.

288

Paul and Zeke snap out of the hold.

"He fucking did it again, didn't he?" Zeke snarls.

"Tie him back up and let's get out of here before he comes to," Theo commands.

They tighten the ropes and put tape over his mouth before we return to the house.

Zeke goes straight to the bathroom to wash out his wounds while Paul, Theo, and I remain in the kitchen. Theo sits at the table, resting his head in his hands while I lean against the island.

Paul fills a glass with water from the faucet. He gulps it all before turning his attention to us. "I don't get it. He could've used his ability on me at any time to let him go. So, why now?"

I shrug. "Maybe he's sick of being tied up and beaten without knowing what's going to happen to him in the end."

Theo shakes his head. "No. That's not it. Any of us would have fought back from the beginning. There's got to be another reason."

We remain silent as we think of the likely reasons, but Kat's suspicions of me on the first night here ring loud in my head.

"He wanted to know where we are," I say. Paul and Theo look at me. "Why else would he let himself get dragged here and beaten? He needed to see where we are so he can tell NOEL."

Paul leans against the kitchen counter and shakes his head. "If he just wanted to see where we're hiding, he could've persuaded me to let him go before all the beatings."

Theo stands and looks directly at Paul. "Unless he's somehow in contact with NOEL and needed to stay until they show up."

Paul shakes his head. "How could he be in contact? I emptied his pockets. He has no phone or keys with him. I even left his watch behind, just in case."

I rack my photographic memory of all the conversations I had with Julian before coming here. On our dates, we talked about his fake job and traveling. We would lay in bed and talk about his childhood. But before he told me about being bullied, I traced his skin to the scar on his bicep, and he joked about being abducted by aliens.

My face falls at the realization. Paul must notice because he steps toward me with a questioning look.

"He has a tracker in his arm. I felt it when . . ." I glance at Theo and stop talking when I see his face contort.

"Fuck!" Paul rushes out of the room.

Theo lays a hand on my arm, but I can't force myself to look at him. Paul returns a moment later with James, holding a small bag, and they rush out of the house.

Theo and I run after them, but they're already in the garage when we catch up. We stand by a stack of boxes and watch James stand in front of Julian, eyeing him from head to toe.

"Left arm."

Paul grabs onto Julian's left arm, but he struggles beneath his grip, trying to scream through the tape. Then Julian stops and closes his eyes. Paul loosens his grip and steps away.

"Fuck, he's doing it again," Theo says.

"But his mouth is taped shut."

"He doesn't have to speak to use his ability. Just has to tap into their mind." Theo charges and punches Julian in the face. Julian's head jerks to the side, but he remains conscious. Theo draws his fist back again.

"Wait!" I yell, and Theo stops. "What are you doing?"

"Knocking him out, so we can take it out of his arm."

Julian's eye is still swollen shut, knuckles bloody from punching Zeke. A fresh trickle of blood seeps from his nose. He's been through enough, but I don't want to take something from him while he's unconscious.

"I'll do it."

Julian's eyes snap open, and he stares at me as Paul regains control of his body.

James is silent as he hands over the scalpel, then leaves. Theo and Paul look at me.

"I'm immune to his persuasion, and I'll be gentle. It has to be me."

Theo clenches his jaw but nods, and he and Paul leave the garage. Julian winces as I remove the tape from his lips, but he doesn't speak.

"How long till they get here?" I ask. Julian scrunches his lips and turns his head away. I untie his hands and hold on to them tight. "Julian, please."

Julian finally looks at me, his demeanor softening. He inhales deeply and squeezes my hands. "It's been three days since I've been here. If they're coming, they'll be here soon."

"Why?" is all I can manage to say.

Part of me hoped for Julian's redemption, but the other expected something like this.

"I don't want to die," he breathes.

"You're not going to die."

"I'm not stupid. Your friends are going to kill me eventually. I only stayed and endured everything to make sure you were all right."

"I am. But now I won't be if they come."

"Take it out." He squeezes my hands harder. "I don't want them to find you. Take it out and send it somewhere else. They'll track that instead."

Standing, I scoff. "Like I'm going to believe that."

Julian leans forward, but the restraints hold him back. "It's true. I'll prove it by letting you take the tracker out of my arm. But you have to keep it on the move far away from here so NOEL can track it. If you damage it, they'll think I'm dead and come for my body."

The scalpel weighs heavily in my hand. What other choice do I have? I sit next to Julian, and he holds his left arm out for me, closing his eyes. "It's not too deep. Should be able to pop it right out."

I grab his arm, my fingers tracing the jagged lines of the scar. The inch-long implant bulges beneath my fingertips, its cylindrical shape about the size of a grain of rice. Placing the scalpel against the top of the scar, I take a moment to steady my trembling hand before making a small incision.

Julian scrunches his face. Beneath the bleeding flesh is a sliver of hardware. I pinch his skin and squeeze. He groans, but I keep going until all of it is out. The black tracker rests in my palm, covered in Julian's blood. Closing my fingers around it, I wrap his wound with a bandage from James's bag, then rebind his wrists.

After walking toward the door, I turn back to Julian. "This better work."

He nods.

When I return to the house, Theo and Paul are waiting in the kitchen. I hand the tracker over to Paul and tell him what to do with it. Paul holds the tracker in his palm and closes his eyes. The tracker glows blue in his hand, and a moment later, he opens his eyes and says, "It's done. I used my ability to send the information to Texas. If they're tracking it, that's where they'll go."

I breathe a sigh of relief and lean into Theo, but Paul rubs his chin and narrows his eyes at us. "One more thing. How did Theo know to come to the garage? And how did you get him to resist Julian's persuasion?"

Theo and I exchange a look like he caught us committing a crime. Theo nods, and I know we are about to lose the secret that, so far, has just been his and mine.

29. Unique Brain

Paul shifts his eyes to Theo, then back at me, waiting for one of us to talk.

I take a deep breath. "I can project my thoughts into Theo's head. I got into his mind and told him to resist."

Paul's eyes widen. "You learned how to reverse engineer your telepathy. Do you have any idea how huge this is?" Paul grins. "We all thought there was a limit to our abilities, but you proved that's not the case."

"I don't know if it's like that with everyone. Besides, I'm only able to do it with Theo."

"Only because you haven't tried to do it with anyone else. I'm sure you could project your thoughts to anyone if you practiced."

Paul makes a good point. I never have tried to project to someone else. Part of me always wanted it to be our secret.

However, if we are to take down NOEL, it would be useful if I could communicate my thoughts with everyone— like a broadcast. Is that possible? If I think of it like Theo's analogy, I should be able to. I'm the radio, and they're the stations.

Kat, Zeke, and James walk into the room.

"Why do you look like you're up to no good?" Kat asks accusingly.

Paul breaks away and goes to Kat's side. "Amelia learned to advance her ability, and I think we can, too, if we practiced."

James holds up a finger and furrows his eyebrows. "We can't advance our abilities. There's a limit to them."

Paul's face lights up with excitement. "NOEL lied to us. We can." He looks at me. "Amelia, try on James."

Closing my eyes, I concentrate on James. I imagine my thoughts like a wire, stretching from my head and into his. When I'm confident I made the connection, I project into his mind.

Hi, James.

James jumps, clearly confused, and looks around. "I heard you in my head. How?"

"I'm able to project my thoughts into someone else's mind."

"No way!" Zeke shouts, reminding me of the guys at the bar attempting an impressive dance move who everyone cheers on. "Do me next."

"I think that's enough for now," Theo interjects. Zeke pouts like a child who was told they couldn't have ice cream for dinner. "For now, Paul, work on getting into those files." Paul nods, sits, and opens his laptop. "And no one is to go into the garage except Amelia. She's not affected by Julian's persuasion."

No one disagrees and carries on busying themselves with other things.

The only person who hasn't moved is James. He looks at me, moving his eyes from my toes to my head. He shakes his head with a perplexed expression, then repeats scans my body again, leaving me uncomfortable.

After eyeing me the second time, he notices I'm staring at him, yet he doesn't act embarrassed that I've caught him. He scopes the room to make sure no one else has noticed and raises a finger to his temple, tapping it twice.

I give him a confused look, and he does it again. A split second of panic rises in me when I realize he wants to have a silent conversation.

What is it? I relay to him, hoping my thought voice doesn't sound as worried as I feel.

We need to talk. Meet me in the basement in ten minutes. Try to act normal and come alone.

The urgency in his tone worries me more. He silently walks out of the kitchen and into the hallway that leads to the basement stairs.

How does he expect me to sneak away to meet him without Theo noticing? I'm not fond of the idea of keeping this from Theo, but I want to know what James has to say before I tell him anything.

Paul is deep in concentration on the laptop. Zeke has disappeared to who knows where. Theo and Kat are leaning against the kitchen counter and chatting. I walk over, rubbing my temples from a sudden oncoming headache.

I wrap an arm around Theo's, resting my head on his shoulder. They're laughing about something. For a moment, I watch them being happy as brother and sister. Moments like this don't happen often. At once, I know how to preoccupy them enough to not notice my absence.

"Hey, I have an idea," I say. They look at me, their face still lit up from laughter. "You two haven't had any sibling time together. Why don't you use this free time to catch up on the last five months?" I notice the hesitancy on Theo's face. "What if you teach Kat how to drive like you taught me?"

"He taught you how to drive?" Kat slaps the counter, then turns her attention back to Theo. "Well, now I want to learn. What do you say, big brother?"

Theo squints at me and sighs, and I give him an innocent smile. "Fine."

Kat's face beams with excitement. "Yes! I'll go get my shoes and be back in a minute."

He slides my hair behind my ear. "Will you be okay without me?" Resting his hand on my cheek, he stares into my eyes.

"I'll be fine." I give him a reassuring smile and draw an X over my heart.

He gives me a swift kiss on the lips. Kat returns, standing in the doorway, impatiently waiting for Theo.

"Go! Have quality time with your sister."

He stares at me a second longer before retreating.

As soon as the front door closes, I peek out the window and watch until they are out of sight. After one glance at Paul, I'm confident he is not paying attention to me. I exit the kitchen and make my way to the basement. The basement isn't a place I have explored yet. My heart hammers in my chest as I descend the stairs. As I step off the last stair, I feel like I've transported into a laboratory with rows of tables covered with beakers, vials filled with substances, and unfamiliar machines.

James sits at a desk, peering into the end of a microscope. I clear my throat to get his attention, his shoulders raising quickly at the sound. Swiveling in his chair, he notices me and stands, meeting me halfway.

"Thank you for meeting me." His tone is formal, as if we're having a business meeting.

When he doesn't continue, my anxiety rises again.

"You wanted to talk about something?"

"Oh, yes." He holds a finger in the air as if he got an idea. "When we were upstairs, I scanned you again." I had figured as much after noticing his eyes motioning my body from head to toe. He continues, "The first day you arrived here, I scanned you and recorded the results. After today's scan, your results have changed." I wait for him to elaborate. He ushers me to follow him to the desk with organized files stuffed with papers. "The memory wipe that courses through your brain is fading at a rapid rate."

"That's a good thing, right?"

"Yes, it is. Although, I expected it, since you've already started regaining your memories."

"Do you think once it's out of my system, I'll get all my memories back?"

"I believe so."

His urgent tone earlier made me to believe he had bad news, but I take this as good news.

"You had me worried for a minute there." I breathe a sigh of relief. "You could've said this in front of the group."

James's expression turns serious. "That's not the only thing I wanted to talk to you about. It's about your brain."

"Oh?" Feelings of worry creep back.

"It was hard to see your brain properly with the first scan because of the memory wipe. Now that it's wearing off, I see that your brain is unique."

"Unique how?"

James removes a sheet from the folder with a picture of a brain scan with four white dots throughout the brain.

"These dots represent the four enhancement phases. This one here"—he points to a dot—"is the cognitive enhancement. And this one"—he points to another dot—"is the ability enhancement." He pauses and looks at me.

"Why didn't any of this show up on my brain scans at the hospital?"

"Regular machines aren't equipped to show the enhancements. Only the machines at NOEL and my ability have the capability to see them." When I nod, he continues. "This is the size they're supposed to be, but yours are much larger. I think that means yours does not have a limit."

"I'm not sure I understand what you mean."

"I don't know how to explain it." He shakes his head and places the paper back in the folder. "Our enhancements are meant to have a limit because the human brain can only handle so much. It could explain your photographic memory, how you're able to project your thoughts, and why you're able to resist Julian's persuasion."

My files said as much when they wrote that my cognitive enhancement kept increasing after it should have leveled out. They didn't know why either, but I don't understand why he couldn't say this in front of everyone else.

Afraid to ask, I gulp. "What are you not telling me?"

"The memory wipe is reacting negatively on your brain. I don't know why. There are many factors to consider. Every time you regain a memory or advance your ability, the memory wipe wears off faster, but your brain is suffering the consequences. Have you been experiencing any dizziness, nausea, or headaches?"

I vomited after I found out about Julian, but I thought seeing him beaten is what made me nauseous. I also got lightheaded yesterday but played it off as exhaustion. Now the slight throbbing in my temples remains, and I realize that these aren't normal reactions. They're side effects.

"Yeah, but more so in the past few days. What's going to happen to me?"

James stares at me as if he doesn't want to say. He closes his eyes and takes a deep breath. "It seems your brain is deteriorating."

My breath leaves me in an instant, and I sit on his chair, gripping the armrests as if it will somehow save me.

James rests a reassuring hand on my arm, but I barely feel it. I look at him and see his mouth moving, but I can't hear him. Tears prick at my eyes, and I have the sudden urge to scream. I bite the inside of my cheek and try to inhale a breath that never comes.

James places his hands on the side of my face and forces me to look at him. His brown eyes stare into me, and for a moment, they glow to a dark amber before he pulls away and crosses the room. He comes back and holds a bottle of water to my lips. I'm reluctant at first, but I finally take a sip. He's silent while I catch my breath and process everything.

When I find my voice again, I ask, "Am I going to die?" James's silence and grim look give me the answer. "How long do I have?"

James shakes his head. "It's hard to say without running tests. At the rate I've seen it grow in the few days you've been here, I would guess you have . . . six months . . . maybe a year. That's all contingent on how often you regain a memory or use your ability. If both happen every day . . . maybe two months."

Two months? That's all I have? If I could remember my old life, I think it would flash before my eyes. Instead, the life I had hoped to live flares before me. A life of traveling the world. Of seeing the Statue of Liberty or the Eiffel tower or the Rome Colosseum or Stonehenge. I won't get to see any of it. Even if I weren't dying, traveling wouldn't be an option as long as NOEL stands. And two months is not enough time to take them down.

I want more. I need more. I certainly deserve more after everything I've been through.

I take a deep breath and concentrate on what matters most right now. And that is to help find a way to take NOEL down—even if I'm not there to watch it crumble.

"Can we keep this between us for now?" I ask.

"Of course."

I give him a curt nod and ascend the stairs.

Theo and Kat aren't back from their driving lesson yet, and Paul remains at the table in front of a laptop. I step outside, and the sun warms my skin as I fill my lungs with the refreshing summer air to help me focus. It's not as thick as the humidity-filled air in Bridgeport and that makes me feel homesick. Stepping off the porch, I walk into the woods. The breeze dances around me, sending the leaves into a flurry of sound, disrupted only by the twigs cracking beneath my feet. It's serene, but not enough to help me forget about my untimely demise, which makes me reflect on the past, when I had a normal life.

It seems like ages ago I was working at the country club with Trish.

Trish, oh how I miss her. What went through her mind when I was there one day and gone the next? Is she mad I haven't tried to contact her? It doesn't matter how well Paul cleaned up. She must have her own suspicions about Julian, Theo, and me mysteriously disappearing at the same time.

If only I could reach out to her and let her know I miss her and that I'm okay.

But I'm not okay. James just delivered news of my death sentence. This situation is what I would talk about in Dr. Wagner's sessions. I hate to think of it, but I miss him, too. If I could go back under hypnosis, there might be a solution buried deep in my mind.

I freeze in place as the realization dawns on me. The numbers on the encrypted file Paul can't get into looked familiar because I've seen them before, the numbers on the door with no handle in my hypnotic state. But what do they mean?

I run through the woods to get back to the house. Muscles in my legs heat up, and I'm running faster than I ever have. Surely, it must be my speed enhancement finally kicking in. Everything passes in a blur, but I avoid every fallen log and branch. My breathing remains steady, and I feel like I can run like this for hours without getting tired.

I reach the house within minutes, right as Theo and Kat pull into the driveway. My enhanced speed doesn't allow me to slow quickly enough, and I almost lose my balance as I reach the porch. Terror drops on Theo's face as he notices me. He exits the car before Kat puts it to a complete stop and rushes over to me.

"Everything's okay," I tell him.

"Then why were you running so fast?"

"I remembered something, and I need to tell Paul." I don't wait for him to respond, and I rush into the house. Theo follows. I don't bother with casual greetings. "One, five, two, two, one, one, four, one, nine." I blurt, startling Paul. I inhale and start again, slower this time. "The numbers on the password-protected file are one, five, two, two, one, one, four, one, nine. Is that right?"

Paul's expression remains nonplussed. "Yes."

Kat finally catches up to us and stands next to Theo. I turn my attention back to Paul. "I've seen those numbers before when I was in a hypnotic state. They were on a door, but I don't know what they mean."

No one speaks. They only stare at me. Either they're trying to process what I said, or they think I've lost it. Looking at each of them, I've deduced they think I've gone mad. Knowing I have to give them more to go on, I try again.

"What I'm saying is . . . I think I can figure out how to get into that file."

Finally, Paul breaks the silence. "How?"

I smirk as excitement rises in me. "Anyone know how to do hypnosis?"

Maybe I have gone mad.

30. A Clue Left Behind

E veryone gathers silently in the living room. James places a pendulum on the coffee table in front of me, almost an exact match to Dr. Wagner's.

"Are you ready?" James asks in a calm voice, but his face tells me he's worried.

I read his thoughts.

Forcing memories will surely speed up the process in your brain.
It's okay. This is important.

James tells everyone to be silent. They stand around the room, staring anxiously at me. I close my eyes and take a few deep breaths, then look at James and nod. He raises the one end of the silver metal balls and releases it, causing it to click against the other ball, raising the opposite end and repeating the process. My eyes follow the rising and falling of the balls, back and forth, back and forth. The click, clack, click, clack loosens my muscles.

In a low monotone, James tells me to relax and clear my mind. My body complies with his command. The room disappears, enclosing my vision into complete darkness.

Surrounding doors blink into existence. I notice the metal door with the numbers inscribed on the front within seconds, and it's as if a gravitational pull draws me toward it. Other doors blur and fade in my peripheral vision.

This is the one I'm meant to go through.

I brush the engraved numbers with my fingers, feeling the grooves of the precise cuts. It reads: 152211419, exactly as I remembered. The doorknob is still missing, and I'm not sure how to enter. I rub along the seams, hoping for a clue, and I realize there are no hinges. It doesn't swing open. It slides. There must be a way to open it.

I step back to examine it fully. A small horizontal slice resides on the right side of the doorframe. It's thin and about two inches wide. I don't need a key but a keycard like the ones from the motels Theo and I stayed in.

As I circle each door, I hope to find it somewhere sticking out in plain sight against the darkness of the abyss, but there's nothing.

I shove the cold metal with my hands, with my shoulder, with my back. Nothing happens. Taking a deep breath, I close my eyes and concentrate, trusting my enhanced body to bring the strength forward. Hoping the momentum of my body slamming against it will open it, I run toward the door. It should be painless, considering it's not real and only in my mind, but as my body makes contact, the force of my shoulder against the immobile object is the equivalent to what I imagine being hit by a truck feels like. Tears tingle my eyes, and I wonder if my arm is broken.

I hold on to my arm and kick the door in frustration, then sink against it. If I can't get it open, I've risked more damage to my brain for nothing. There must be a way inside, or else it wouldn't be here for me to explore. I have to think logically. If I were a keycard, where would I be? An idea occurs to me, and I bolt upright, fisting into the front pockets of my shorts. Nothing. Checking my back pockets, I find a thin, rectangular piece a plastic, and I jump for joy.

My hands shake with excitement as I fumble to get the card into the slot. Once I do, I pull the card out, and the door slides open, blinding me with a bright light. I step through the barrier.

Everything is white, and the room appears empty until my eyes adjust, and shapes emerge, which turn into objects, and I can tell it's a medical lab. Cabinets with glass doors are filled with vials, bins, gauze, and syringes. A counter appears against the adjacent wall, lined with a microscope and other scientific instruments that I wouldn't know what to do with. It reminds me of the lab James uses in the basement.

A desk with a computer pops into existence, and the center of the room takes focus. Three monitors appear around a bed, then an IV stand and, finally, a woman lying on the bed. I know it's me before her features fully appear.

Her eyes are closed, her breathing steady. An IV drip connects to the vein in her arm. A strange device sits against her hair with small circular disks protruding from the ends, resting at various parts around the head. I thought I'd be used to this by now, but it's still uncanny seeing myself from the outside looking in.

Another woman enters the room, and I jump, heart racing, until I realize she can't see me. She approaches Amelia's bedside, tablet in hand, white lab coat swaying behind her. The scent of coconut shampoo fans out from her chestnut-colored ponytail. She glances at the monitors, then taps the tablet.

Whoosh. The door slides open again. The click-clack against the floor draws my eyes to the emerald heels, then slowly upward to a matching-colored skirt suit, until they rest on the face of a woman. The clicks against the floor stop. Her eyes settle on the bed, and just for a moment, her lips set in a hard line. Her straight golden bob barely moves as she walks directly to the computer. She leans forward and types at the keyboard.

"Her vitals are stable, Dr. Sheffield," says the woman with the tablet.

So, this is Dr. Sheffield?

"Thank you, Rita. That will be all for now," Dr. Sheffield says, and Rita exits the room. Dr. Sheffield walks over to Amelia. She gently squeezes her hand, and I can feel it in my hand. She stares at Amelia's immobile body, eyes trailing from her face to their intertwined hands.

"Dammit, Amelia!" She whips her hand out of Amelia's. "What were you thinking? You could have died." She clears her throat and blinks back tears. "I blame that boyfriend of yours. I should have separated you two from the beginning." She huffs, then switches her attention to the monitor. "No matter. You won't remember him soon enough. I wish it didn't come to this, but I don't know what else to do. I only hope it bides me more time."

Dr. Sheffield pulls a syringe of blue liquid from the cabinet. She removes the cap, then holds it up, pressing on the plunger until a tiny amount escapes the tip. She inserts the needle into Amelia's temple.

I automatically touch my temple, feeling the needle pierce my skin. Dr. Sheffield administers the rest of the liquid into Amelia's brain. A rush of coolness disperses across my head. Dr. Sheffield disposes the syringe into a medical waste basket and exits the room without a glance. The door slides closed with a *whoosh*, then locks with a *click*.

Amelia's eyes shoot open. She hurriedly removes the head device and IV and hops off the table. She searches the cabinets, swearing under her breath when she doesn't find whatever she's looking for. Next, she goes to the computer, and I follow. She types on the keyboard while files on the monitor open and close. A distant noise comes from outside the room, and we both look toward the door. She turns her attention back to the computer, and I feel her panic when she can't find what she's looking for.

"A message. I need to leave a message," she says to herself. She opens a blank document on the computer and stares at it. I watch her look around the room quickly until her eyes rest on something against the far wall, and she smiles. "Yes! That's it."

My eyes follow the spot where she looked. A poster of the periodic table hangs on the wall.

She types numbers into the blank document. Her hands are moving too fast for me to register what she's typing. She moves the document into a new folder and labels it 152211419, then adds the encryption on it.

"Paul will realize the password is the file name in code." She quickly types letters and saves the file to a shared network.

The noise gets closer, as if it's right outside. Amelia grabs the tubing from the IV and presses herself flush against the wall.

The door slides open, and Rita enters. She gets halfway to the table before she realizes Amelia is no longer there, then stops her in her tracks with a confused look. Amelia jumps out and wraps the tubing around Rita's neck. Rita struggles, but Amelia doesn't let up. Rita, eventually, goes limp, and Amelia gently lowers her to the ground.

Amelia grabs Rita's keycard and inserts it into the door. It slides open, and she looks both ways before bolting. I run after her, but as I cross the threshold, I'm consumed in darkness, once again surrounded by doors. The door behind me disappears, fading out of existence.

My heart pounds from the adrenaline, but relief washes over me. Now that I've had the chance to witness it firsthand, I remember what the numbers mean. It's the A1Z26 code for my name—A. Evans. The password is in code, and I'm assuming it has to do with the periodic table of elements. Knowing this, we can uncover the message I left.

As much as I want to explore another door, I need to get back to the others and divulge my discovery. I've been in this hypnotic state for maybe thirty minutes, and I'm sure the others are getting worried.

I yell for James to pull me out, hoping my physical body is yelling out to him. The doors blink out of existence, and the darkness lightens. The center takes focus first as I see the pendulum swinging back and forth. Gradually, the room comes into my vision. At first, I see James sitting across from me. Then I see Theo's concerned face and then the others appear.

Once I'm fully back to consciousness, I look around at the confused faces of my friends.

"You didn't find it, did you?" Paul says with disappointment.

I smile. "I found it. Why would you think I didn't?"

"You were in there for like two minutes," Kat says. "How did you find it that fast?"

"I was in there for at least thirty minutes. At least, that's how it was for me."

"Time works differently in hypnosis," James says. "It's like dreaming. Dreams feel like hours, when, in reality, they're only a few minutes."

"What did you find out?" Paul asks.

"I'm the one that created the file. The numbers are in A1Z26 code for my name, and the password is the file name but in another code that I made from the inspiration of the periodic table of elements."

"No way! That's clever," Paul says with amazement. "What's in the file?"

"A coded message. At least now we can open it and know how to decipher what it says."

Paul rushes to the kitchen as the rest of us follow. I sit next to Paul. He opens the file and slides the laptop over for me to type in the password. I pause momentarily, not knowing what to put in.

The periodic table flashes in my head, and I instantly know each element with the symbol and atomic number. The first number is one, which represents the A in my name. One is the atomic number for Hydrogen and the symbol is H. The second number is five, which represents the E as the first letter of my last name. Five is the atomic number for Boron, the symbol B.

Going through the rest of the numbers as they represent my name, I discover the password must be HBTiHSiK. I type in the letters, taking extra caution, then press enter.

The file opens. Inside the file is only one document comprising six lines of a string of numbers that I know are in code.

"Can you print this page out?" I ask Paul. "It's in code and might take me a minute to decipher it."

Paul clicks the print button, and the printer spits out the document. He hands me the paper and a pencil.

Everyone gathers around. A stabbing pain radiates from the base of my skull to the top of my head, but I ignore it and look at the paper in front of me.

90 68 99

42 75

92 7 19 102 74 7

49 9 8

9 53 60

74 47 7 68

Assuming I used the same method with the periodic table, I know ninety is Thorium, sixty-eight is Erbium, and ninety-nine is Einsteinium. Their symbols put together spell out *T H E R E S*. Moving onto the second line, the message spells *M O R E*. Each line reveals another word. After a minute, I successfully decipher the first five lines. The message reads: *THERES MORE UNKNOWN INFO FIND . . .*

I decipher the last line. Everyone watches in silent anticipation. The first number, seventy-four is W then forty-seven is AG. I continue with this pattern.

I write the last two letters, and the word that appears in front of me causes me to push away from the table and rush to stand. My breaths come out in quick gasps. It can't be who I think it is. Surely, I must have deciphered it wrong? No, I know I did it correctly.

"Amelia?" Theo looks at me, concern prominent on his face. "What is it? Do you know what this means?"

I look at the message again, confirming that it reads:

THERES MORE UNKNOWN INFO FIND WAGNER.

"Wagner was my therapist in Bridgeport." It feels as if someone else is saying the words.

"It could mean someone else," Zeke suggests. "Wagner is a pretty common name. It could be anyone."

I consider Zeke's suggestion, but I think it's unlikely that it's a different Dr. Wagner. Why else would I whisper "Bridgeport" to Theo when he rescued me from the ditch?

"Paul, are there files on the staff at NOEL? Can you search for Dr. Wagner?"

Paul clicks away at the mouse, taking only a minute to find the file and search for Dr. Wagner. Once he finds it, he turns the laptop to me. In bold, capitalized print, it reads DR. PETER WAGNER and shows a picture of the man that I spent the last five months confiding in.

I stand and point at the screen. "That's him. That's my therapist."

"It says here that he left the program seventeen years ago," Paul states. "Do you think he's trustworthy?"

My head is reeling, and I don't know how to answer. I thought I knew Dr. Wagner, and I want to say that we can trust him, but he also lied to me from the beginning. However, I left this message for a reason.

"I don't know, but I think I have to talk to him. He must know something, or else I wouldn't leave that message. I'll try calling his office."

"It's too dangerous to discuss this over the phone," Paul urges. "Ask him to fly to Colorado, and we'll cover the cost." He hands me his burner phone, and I dial the number to his office, then stop before I press send.

"I don't know what to say. You never told me how you cleaned up. How am I supposed to explain my sudden disappearance?"

"Right." Paul snaps his fingers. "I packed some of yours and Julian's things along with your phones in case NOEL was tracking them. I sent them on a delivery truck that was going to Florida. But, before that, I sent texts to Trish and your boss saying you and Julian were going on a spur-of-the-moment vacation, and you weren't sure when you were going to return. But I didn't know about the therapist, so I didn't give him notice. But stick with the vacation story." I nod and finish dialing the number. "Oh, and pretend you're Jane, not Amelia."

After three rings, a woman answers.

"Good afternoon! Dr. Wagner's office. How can I help you?"

"Hello! I'm calling to speak with Dr. Wagner."

"He is about to have a session with a patient. Did you need to make an appointment?"

"No, I don't need an appointment, but it is urgent that I speak with Dr. Wagner. Can you tell him Jane Doe is on the phone and needs to speak to him? I think he'll want to take my call."

"Of course, please hold."

Soft music plays as the receptionist places me on hold. A minute later, the music stops, and Dr. Wagner's panicked voice comes on the other end.

"Jane? Is everything okay? You've missed your sessions, and I've been worried."

"Hi, Dr. Wagner. I'm sorry to have worried you. Everything is fine. I went on a spur-of-the-moment vacation to Florida."

"That's good to hear. I hope you are enjoying yourself."

"I am, thank you. But I really need someone to talk to."

"Yes, of course. When will you return? I can make an appointment for you first thing when you're back."

I glance at the others, then pace in the kitchen. "That's the thing. I'm not coming back. Can you come to me?"

"That's not how I typically do things," he replies. "If you tell me what area you're in, I can refer you to another therapist."

"Dr. Wagner, please." My voice lowers with desperation. "I need to talk to you in person. Only you. It's important. I can't say much over the phone about it, but it is crucial you fly out to me. Trust me when I say you will want to hear what I have to tell you."

"Jane? Are you okay?"

"No." I shake my head. "No, I'm not. But I think you are the only one that can help me. I remember things about my childhood. Where I grew up. Things only you can answer."

I hope my emphasis on the last sentence is enough to convince him.

He doesn't answer back right away, and I wonder if he's ended the call. Then, finally, he speaks. "Where do I need to go?"

His tone is clipped and determined, like a soldier receiving instructions.

"You will get a plane ticket sent to your email with a meeting time and place," I say with confidence, as if I'm his captain giving orders.

"Understood." He ends the call.

Paul finds a flight from Bridgeport to Colorado and sends the ticket to Dr. Wagner's email with instructions about a meeting place and time.

We'll meet two hours away from Blue River in three days. This gives us enough secrecy of our location in case he reports back to NOEL.

31. Compromised

The next morning, we gather around the dining table for breakfast. Kat makes Paul put the laptop away for the meal, but he scarfs pancakes into his mouth as if he hasn't eaten in days. He opens the laptop when he clears his plate from the table but not without a glare from Kat. He clicks the mouse and taps the keys while everyone else finishes our breakfast.

I help Kat clear the table and wash the dishes while the men make themselves scarce. It's the first time we've been alone together for more than a couple of minutes. Neither of us speaks while she washes, and I dry the dishes. Her body is tense, and she occasionally glances sideways at me.

Kat hands me a plate to dry, then strains her head toward the window. "Julian's awake."

I place the dish in the cupboard. "How do you know?"

"I can hear him rustling."

I freeze with my hand on the cupboard door. Can she hear everything? Has she been eavesdropping on my conversations with Julian? I take a deep breath and grab the next dish.

"Can you turn your ability on and off like the rest of us? Or do you hear everything all the time?"

"I can turn it on and off."

"And you just so happen to have it on now?"

Kat turns off the faucet and dries her hands. "I was listening for him to wake up so you can bring him breakfast." I scoff, and she turns to me. "Something wrong?"

"You turned on your ability so you could tell me when Julian is awake to bring him breakfast, which I was going to do after I finished helping you. It just seems you're still trying to get rid of me."

She sets the towel on the counter and inhales deeply. "You're right. I'm sorry. This is weird for me. We were best friends, and now it's like—"

"We're strangers?"

She nods. "I miss you, Amy. I don't want it to be weird between us."

I rest my hand on hers. "I can't remember everything, but I remember enough to know we wouldn't let a little mind wipe get in the way of our friendship."

Kat chuckles and squeezes my hand. I smile, but she stares at me as if she's looking right through me. Her face falls, and she squeezes my hand tighter.

"Kat?"

She shushes me by placing a finger to my lips, then looks out the kitchen window again. After a second, she rushes to the living room and peeks behind the curtains.

"What is it?" I whisper.

"I hear footsteps, but I don't see anything."

"Maybe it's just someone hiking in the woods."

She retreats from the window and closes her eyes. I stay silent as she leans her ear toward the front door. When she opens her eyes, she says, "I don't think it's hikers. We need to get the guys."

Without missing a beat, she dashes up the stairs while I peek out the window.

Cascading shadows spread across the lawn. The only movement comes from the tree branches swaying in the wind. A moment later, Kat returns with Paul, Theo, Zeke, and James. Theo pulls me away from the window to stand by the stairs.

"What do you hear, Kat?" Paul asks.

We stay silent as Kat closes her eyes. "Three . . . no, four people. They're in the woods. I can hear the branches breaking beneath their feet."

Paul looks at me next. "Can you try to listen to their thoughts?"

I stiffen. My enhancement files state that I can hear thoughts without seeing someone, but I haven't been able to do that since I've learned about my telepathy. Theo grabs my hand and gives it a reassuring squeeze. Taking a deep breath, I close my eyes. Hoping the idea of a visual will help, I picture four featureless bodies among the trees, ducking out of sight. The invisible wire branches out from my head and weaves through the leaves. I wait for a click that I have made a connection, but nothing comes. I open my eyes and shake my head.

"I can't hear anything."

"You wouldn't if they're reconditioned soldiers," James says.

Zeke steps forward, placing himself between the front door and us. "Are we just going to wait for them to barge in, or are we going to take these fuckers out?"

"We don't have weapons," Paul says.

"We don't need them. We have abilities. They don't."

"What do you mean, they don't have abilities?" I interject. "I thought they're like us, just without memories."

James answers, "Reconditioned soldiers have the ability marker, but they aren't able to use their abilities. I'm not sure why, but I'm guessing NOEL did something, so they can't use them."

I want to ask more questions, but Kat shuffles backward, dropping my curiosity. "They're getting closer."

Theo runs to the kitchen and comes back with knives, handing one to each of us. I hold the knife in front of me, but it shakes in my grip. Theo and Paul position themselves in front of Kat, James, and me. If NOEL soldiers are outside and barge in, we'll be ready. But will it be enough? Can the six of us take them down?

We stand silently at the ready. My heart pounds in my ears. Seconds tick by that feel like minutes.

Kat stands straighter and whispers, "They're on the porch."

Zeke steps back from the door at the same time it flies off the hinges and smashes into him.

I flinch backward as shards of wood break off. Two soldiers rush in. Theo and Paul are the first to charge them. Fists are thrown in a blur, and it's hard to make out who is hitting who.

Zeke chucks the broken door at the soldier running through the threshold and doesn't wait for the soldier to fall before he advances on him, crushing him beneath the door, delivering blow after blow. The fourth soldier marches toward Kat, James, and me. Kat and James rush forward, knives raised. James drives the knife toward the soldier's chest. The soldier knocks the knife out of James's hand, clattering it to the floor. Kat doesn't hesitate to plunge the blade of her knife into the soldier's armpit. The soldier inhales a sharp breath, holding it for a second, and when he exhales, blood sprays from his mouth. Kat dislodges the knife and moves on to help Paul. The soldier coughs twice before collapsing.

I stand, transfixed, staring at the dead body. His eyes are still open, blood trickling from his mouth, and a larger pool of blood from his armpit spreads outward onto the hardwood floor. When I look up, it's as if everything is moving in intervals of fast, then slow, then fast again, and I can't force myself to move, only watch.

James reaches for his knife, but Paul stumbles backward and accidentally kicks it under the couch. As James reaches for it, the soldier kicks him in the face, knocking him unconscious. The other soldier pinned under the door breaks free, leaps to his feet, and body slams Zeke into the glass coffee table. I scream as it shatters beneath him. The soldier stands, but Zeke lies, motionless.

I run to him and place my hands on the sides of his face. "Zeke?"

His chest moves up and down, and I breathe a sigh of relief. When I turn my attention back to the room, the soldier is now advancing on Kat.

"Kat, watch out!" I yell, but it's too late.

The soldier tackles her to the ground, disarming the knife from her hand. She's pinned, facedown, the soldier's knee pressing to her back. He produces a thin rope from his pocket and wraps it around her neck. She gasps and claws at the rope. With each passing second, her face reddens, her fight faltering.

The soldier's face shows no emotion. No joy, or empathy, or remorse. Only blank eyes.

The same eyes that flash in my mind. But in this memory, he wore a ski mask as he descended on me. I stood straight, ready to fight with my bare hands, and I wasn't afraid. When the memory disappears, Kat grabs at the rope one last time before her hand goes limp, and it snaps something within me. In two strides, I leap onto the soldier's back, press the blade to his neck, and slice. His grip on the rope loosens, and Kat falls to the floor. I toss his body aside just as Kat inhales a ragged breath.

"Are you okay?" I ask.

"Yeah." She coughs. "Go help the guys."

Paul and Theo have lured their soldiers into the kitchen. Theo uses his telekinesis to throw objects at one soldier, while Paul wrestles the other to the ground. His knife lays out of reach, but that doesn't deter him from striking the soldier. After three hits, the soldier stops fighting enough for Paul to wrap his hands around the soldier's head and twist.

The other soldier advances on Theo. Theo thrusts forward, halting the soldier in place with an invisible force. The soldier fights it, and Theo's face strains in concentration as the soldier moves forward an inch. "I can't hold him for long."

Paul rolls to the side, grabs the knife from the floor, and tosses it to Theo. "Here."

Theo catches it but loses his concentration, and the soldier breaks free from the telekinesis. He lunges forward, and Theo stumbles backward, slashing the knife in front of him and slicing into the soldier's arm. Still, the soldier perseveres. Paul shuffles to his feet and gets behind the soldier, pinning his arms behind him, and kicking the back of his knees, causing him to kneel. He struggles to hold the soldier in place until Theo thrusts his hand outward.

"Hurry, Theo!" Paul says. "Kill him!"

Confliction crosses Theo's face before he steps forward and rests the blade against the soldier's neck. "How did you find us?" Theo growls.

Anyone in the soldier's position would show some type of emotion, whether it's fear or courage, but the soldier stares straight ahead as if nothing has happened.

"What are you waiting for?" Paul shouts. "Do it now."

Theo bares his teeth, letting out a growl. The knife in his hand shakes with each pant of breath. Sweat drips off his forehead as he shakes his head from side to side, a physical sign of his internal thoughts. Theo's not a killer. He can't bring himself to do it, no matter how much the soldier deserves it.

I place my hand on his and guide it away from the soldier's throat. Knowing what I must do, I can't bear to look at Theo. I don't want to see the same shock and horror that crossed his face the last time I killed two NOEL soldiers.

Out of the corner of my eye, Theo turns away. I stare into the soldier's eyes before I plunge the knife into his heart. He inhales a sharp breath, but I don't remove my blade or look away. I watch the life drain from them.

32. On the Move

Everyone shuffles around, packing only the necessary items for our move. Now that NOEL knows where we are, we're no longer safe in Blue River. Paul cleans the blood as best he can, then he and Zeke pile the four bodies in the basement.

"We're just going to leave them here?" I ask.

"NOEL will cover their tracks," Paul says. "They'll send someone to get them soon."

"And where are we going?"

"I have another safe house in Woodland Park. It's less than two hours from here, and it's too close for comfort, but we should be good for a few days. That will at least give us enough time to talk to Wagner."

We leave the house with a backpack full of clothes. Paul, James, and Kat pile into Paul's car, while Zeke and I pile into Theo's.

Just as Theo turns the ignition over, I shout, "Stop!" He turns to me with a furrowed brow. "Julian."

He clenches his jaw. "We're leaving him here. NOEL will come for the bodies, and they'll take him with them."

"And what if they don't find him?"

Theo glances at Zeke, then back at me. "The tracker in his arm led to all of this. The fucker can rot in there for all I care."

I glare at him, and before he can put the car into gear, I jump out of the car. "If you want to go without him, then you'll have to go without me."

"Amelia, get in the car. We don't have time for this."

Crossing my arms, I give him a look of defiance. Theo stares at me as he taps the steering wheel with his thumb. He clenches his jaw. "Fine. But he's riding in the trunk."

An hour-and-a-half later, we drive down a dirt road, surrounded by trees on either side.

My breath catches in my throat when we pull into the driveway of our new safe house. It's much smaller than the house in Blue River, but it's beautiful. It looks like an oversized log cabin. It can't be seen from the road, and neighbors are nowhere in sight, so it offers the seclusion we need.

Zeke and Theo drag Julian out of the trunk and lead him to the garage. Just like the garage in Blue River, there's a metal post. They bind him against it. Once they're finished, Theo rests a hand on my arm and nods toward the door.

"Give me one sec," I say.

I watch them leave and turn to Julian.

"What the hell is going on?" he asks.

"Four NOEL soldiers came to the house and tried to kill us."

Julian's jaw drops. "But we took the tracker out. Did you send it somewhere or leave it at the house?"

"Paul used his ability to reroute it, but they must have already been on their way and figured it was a ploy."

He lowers his head. "I should've told you sooner."

I squint at him. "Isn't this what you wanted? For us to get caught?"

He shakes his head. "Maybe at first. Then I just wanted them to rescue me. Then . . ."

"Then what?"

"Then I realized I didn't want them to find you."

I furrow my eyebrows. "I don't understand."

Everything he's done, from coming to Bridgeport to dating me to persuading me for information, then drugging me, was all to bring me back to NOEL.

"Isn't it obvious?" He stares at me like I know what he's talking about. I shake my head, and he sighs. "Never mind."

Sitting next to him, I place my hand on his. "Tell me."

"I started this mission as revenge to get back at you and your friends for bullying me. Then everything changed in Bridgeport. You were nothing like you used to be, and . . ." His fingers brush against mine, but the restraints prevent him from fully holding my hand. "And I fell in love with you."

My heart skips a beat. Part of me wants to pull my hand away, and the other wants to hear him say it again.

"Julian I . . . I . . ."

"It's okay. I know you don't feel the same way. That doesn't change the fact that I want to keep you safe." He stares at me, eyes pleading to say something.

I want to say so much, but I can't find the words. He still stares at me while I wipe dust off my shorts.

"I have to go. I'll be back soon with food." I leave without waiting for his reply.

Back in the house, everyone tries to settle in after this morning's events, but everyone is on high alert. Every so often, Kat stops what she's doing to stand on the porch. She looks out through the forest and strains her ear toward the wind. After a few minutes, she gives up and comes back into the house.

I bring Julian some lunch, but I don't stay and make conversation. I still don't know how I feel about his love confession. Is he being truthful or deceitful?

After dinner, we all sit around the table with blank stares.

"What do we do now?" I ask.

Paul shakes his head. "We can't stay here long, but we meet with Dr. Wagner in two days. In the meantime, I'll start looking for another house."

"Those four soldiers almost took us out," Theo says. "Even though we knew they were there, we weren't prepared. We need to brush up on combat training."

Paul nods. "Training is not a bad idea. The neighbors can't see us from here, so we should be safe to do it out front."

Kat stares at the table, not making eye contact with anyone. A deep purple bruise lines her neck. Zeke's arms are covered in bandages from the shards of glass that cut his skin. I rest my palms on the table, digging my bloodstained fingertips into the surface.

"I want to kill them all." My voice is low and husky. Everyone looks at me like I've lost it. "All of them. All the reconditioned soldiers, Dr. Sheffield, and every scientist that held us down and experimented on us."

"How are we supposed to do that, Amy?" Kat asks.

"We train and prepare. We scope the grounds and find their weak spots. We can do it."

"There are almost a hundred reconditioned soldiers. Not to mention the dozens of doctors and scientist on the staff. Their security is top-notch and—"

"And we still escaped."

Kat sits up straighter in her chair. "And three of us died. Then you and Jackson were captured, and you had your memory wiped."

I slam my fist against the table. "Because we weren't prepared."

"We planned for a year. There just aren't enough of us to bring them down."

I lean back to take a few deep breaths. It does nothing to calm me. "They won't stop, Kat. They'll keep looking for us, and next time, we won't be so lucky to get away."

Kat opens her mouth to speak, but Paul raises a finger.

"Hold on a second." He looks at Kat with pleading eyes. "Just hear me out . . . When we escaped, we used whatever we could find within NOEL. We didn't have all the information available to us. Now that we're out, I can access their servers. There's so much more to learn. I think if we're smart about this, we can take them down. It will take a lot of planning, and we'll need to train, but I think it's worth a try."

Kat closes her eyes. "I don't want to live like this anymore." When she opens her eyes, she looks right at me. "I'm in. Let's take them down."

Zeke smiles and pumps his fist. "Now that's what I'm talking about. Let's show these fuckers what we're made of."

We erupt in laughter but stop when the doorbell rings.

I look at Theo, who looks at Paul. Everyone freezes, their faces a mix of panic and confusion. The doorbell rings again, followed by three knocks. I look around the room and realize no one wants to answer the door with fear that it might be more NOEL soldiers. I close my eyes to concentrate on listening to the mind of the person on the other side.

Please open the door, the voice says. It's a woman's voice but doesn't sound like Dr. Sheffield's. The person's tone is cautious, almost uncertain that they're knocking on the wrong door.

I stand and walk away.

"What are you doing?" Theo asks in a frantic tone.

"Answering the door," I say plainly.

"It could be NOEL."

"I doubt they'd ring the doorbell."

I ignore the hesitation between the others and open the front door. Two women stand before me. Both have beautiful black hair, but one wears hers cropped and the other long, spilling past her shoulders.

"Hello? May I help you?" I ask them.

"Amelia?"

The voice comes from a distance. The women in front of me suddenly vanish, and two identical women step out from behind a tree and walk toward me.

I freeze in place, not knowing if they mean any harm. Theo's chair clatters to the ground as he rushes toward me.

33. Strength in Numbers

Has forcing memories affected my brain, causing me to hallucinate? I could have sworn the women were just on the doorstep, but then they were behind a tree. How is that possible?

Theo joins my side, sees the women approaching, and steps out onto the front porch.

Are they a threat to us?

"Molly? Brooke? What are you doing here?" Theo greets with a smile.

Now it's clear to me that these women are not strangers at all, but they are our friends who had escaped with us from NOEL.

"I had a vision that led us here," says the cropped-haired lady.

Theo hugs each and leads them inside.

As the long-haired woman passes, she stops to embrace me tightly. "I've missed you."

I stand there awkwardly as her arms wrap around me. She pulls away, and I force a small smile. I don't know how to tell her I don't remember her.

Theo leads Molly and Brooke into the kitchen where the others are. "The gang's all here now!"

The women gather with the others, exchanging hugs and greetings. I notice with a twinge how much the others are more welcoming to them. I sit silently in an empty chair as I listen to their conversations, trying to piece it all together.

After our initial escape, Molly and Brooke had gone their own way. They made it to Louisiana, where they hid for weeks until they traveled west. They camped or found kind strangers who would take them in for a few nights. They never stayed in one spot for long. Every few weeks, they moved on to somewhere else.

"How did you end up here?" Paul asks.

"I followed a vision," says the cropped-haired lady.

"What does that mean?" I blurt.

Everyone stares in my direction, and the woman cocks her head and scrunches her eyebrows.

"Molly's ability is precognition," Theo says to me, then turns to Molly. "Amelia has amnesia. We had gone back to fight, and they captured her. She escaped but doesn't remember anything."

Molly places a hand on her chest. "I'm sorry. I didn't know." She looks away, clearly embarrassed.

I force a smile. "It's okay. I'm still learning it all and have lots of questions. How does your ability work? Do you see the future?"

She looks back at me and clears her throat. "Not exactly. It's more like an instinct. Sometimes, it's a strong feeling that I need to do something or be somewhere. Other times, a picture flashes in my head. They're never quite clear, and I don't always know what they mean."

"What led you here?"

"I saw the house in my head and felt a pull to go toward it. I didn't know why, or who would be here, but I'm glad I followed it."

I look at Brooke. "And you're some kind of illusionist?" I ask, hoping I wasn't hallucinating thirty minutes ago.

Brooke smiles. "That's exactly what I am. I wasn't sure if we were walking into a trap, so I conjured up an illusion of ourselves on the porch."

I thought, by now, I'd get used to the abilities, but it amazes me how different we all are. I don't like the idea that NOEL experimented on us to give us these abilities, but they're fascinating. Precognition and illusionist seem a lot more fun to use than listening inside someone's head.

Conversations erupt about their travels, the places they've been, and the world they got to see. All the things I had wished to do one day, but I was stuck in Bridgeport. Theo and I could have had that if we didn't come here. If destroying NOEL and curing my deteriorating brain wasn't so pressing, I'd convince Theo to leave with me in the morning so we could explore the world together.

"Now that you're here, we could use your help," Paul says.

"With what?" Brooke asks.

"We want to fight NOEL. Destroy them."

"How?" Molly asks.

"We're still working out the details, but we have more than we did before. If we all come together, we might stand a chance."

"Fighting them is suicide. Molly shakes her head. "I think you'll have to count us out."

"Babe." Brooke turns and grabs Molly's hand. "I love you, but I can't live like this anymore. I'm sick of running and constantly looking over my shoulder, wondering if today's the day NOEL finds us. Maybe your vision led us here, so we can fight."

Brooke's pleading eyes stare into Molly. Molly yanks her hand away, and the chair screeches against the floor as she stands.

Her body sways, and she holds on to the table to steady herself.

"Molly? Are you okay?" Kat asks.

Molly shakes her head and takes a deep breath. "I'm fine. Just tired from the travel."

"There's an office upstairs. We can make a bed for you and Brooke to sleep," Kat says. "I'll show you where it is."

The room is silent until they're both out of sight.

"She'll come around," Brooke says. "Either way, I'm fighting alongside you."

"Perfect. We'll need all the help we can get," Paul says.

For once, I feel like we have a chance. Our combined strengths, abilities, and skills may be enough to tear NOEL to the ground.

I just hope I'm around long enough to see it through.

34. Traitor's Club

On the grounds, near the back of the house, is a fenced-in space meant for horses, but, today, it's our training grounds.

Paul insisted we get an early start. We gather around while Paul preaches to us, but I don't hear a word because I see the way Theo's jaw clenches when he concentrates, and I flash back to last night.

I still feel the softness of his fingertips tracing the outline of my collarbone. The hardness of his abs pressed against my back. His breath against my ear as he moaned my name.

"Shouldn't we wait for Brooke and Molly?"

Zeke's voice pulls me out of my daydream.

"Molly isn't feeling well," Kat says. "And Brooke stayed behind to look after her."

Paul tells us to gather in a wide circle for one-on-one combat exercises. Although I can't remember, I assume this is how they did it at NOEL. Everyone watching and critiquing as two people fight in the center.

Theo leans in and whispers, "While I'm fighting Zeke, project into his mind. I'd like to give him a little payback."

I don't have to ask him to elaborate. The relevance is clear to me.

He and Zeke take the center. Theo winks at me as he enters the circle. Before the fight begins, I concentrate on making the reverse connection into Zeke's mind, being careful not to project any thoughts yet. They each take their stances. The whistle blows, and neither of them hesitates to make the first move.

For minutes, it's a whirl of thrown and blocked fists. Zeke lands a punch into Theo's shoulder, which doesn't seem to faze him. Theo counters with a kick to Zeke's thigh and misses as he moves out of the way. They bob in circles momentarily. Theo quickly looks in my direction and is about to strike, and it's time for me to make my move. There's a slight shift in his weight, and I project to Zeke.

Watch out for the right jab.

Zeke freezes in place, eyes wide with shock, as Theo delivers a jab to his eye, causing Zeke to stumble backward.

"What the fuck?" Zeke's tone isn't malicious but more so dumfounded. He takes a moment to gather his bearings. "That's not fair. Amelia caught me off guard by talking in my head!"

Theo chuckles. "Same thing happened to me. How else do you think you could give me this scar?" He touches his eyebrow. "Be glad I grazed you and didn't break the skin."

"Oh, yeah. So lucky. I'll only have a black eye later."

"At least it will take the attention away from that ugly mug of yours," Theo banters.

"Okay, guys. That's enough." Kat makes her way to the center. "Amy, be my partner?"

This shouldn't surprise me, yet a part of me thought I would start my training off slow, not jump right into a fight. Hesitantly, I say, "Sure." I join Kat in the center of the circle.

Surely, I'm going to lose this fight quickly and be embarrassed, but how else am I going to learn? Kat puts her fists up, ready to fight. I match her stance and try to calm my nerves by listening in on her thoughts.

She always could kick my ass, but I have the one-up on her now.

I can use telepathy to my advantage. The whistle puts me into focus.

Kat doesn't hesitate and charges first, throwing a right hook, which I dodge by a hair. She throws a left hook and hits me square in the jaw. Momentarily stunned, I wobble backward. A metallic taste fills my mouth, and I spit blood onto the ground. She smirks and takes a few steps back, waiting for me to make a move. The hit jolts rage inside of me. The same rage I felt when Mark attacked me. I charge, preparing to make my first move.

She always goes for the side kick.

Kat's thoughts ring loud and clear in my head. I didn't know my fighting tactics were predictable. I fake like I'm delivering a kick, and as she puts her arm out to block it, I ram my elbow into her arm and throw a right hook into her cheek, then deliver a turning kick to her gut.

She falls to the ground, gasping for air. Blood leaks from the side of her mouth. She's vulnerable, and I prepare to knee her in the face. Suddenly, I'm pulled back by an invisible force.

"Amelia. That's enough."

Theo's voice pulls me out of my rage.

Paul rushes to Kat's aid as I stand there in shock, realizing I could have severely hurt her without a second thought. It's as if my survival mode kicked in, as it did before. I couldn't think, only act. It's as if I was no longer in control of my body.

With Mark, my focus was to cause pain. He certainly deserved it, but I almost killed him. If it wasn't for Theo, I would have.

We were only training, with the intentions to get back into practice. Although I bled, the blow to my jaw didn't hurt. It was the remembrance of being hit and the taste of blood that sparked the anger inside me. At that moment, I didn't see Kat but a predator.

Kat clutches her side and coughs. I step toward her, but Paul puts a hand up to stop me. "Oh my gosh. Kat, I'm so sorry."

She flicks a dismissive wave. "I'll be fine."

Paul helps her to her feet. She stands and avoids making eye contact with me. Theo walks silently by my side, glancing at me for only a second, before going to his sister.

They walk away.

"No more training for today," Paul calls back to the rest of the group.

Each looks at me with a mixture of disgust and fear. Others disperse, but I'm the last person they want to see.

Alone, I stand there, and it's as if the world around me has gone completely silent. I fall to my knees with my head in my hands, trying to hold back tears. For several minutes, I sit there, and every time I close my eyes, I see Kat hunched over, gasping for breath.

What have I become? Or is this who I always was?

I mosey back to the house and enter through the back door.

Paul's laptop sits abandoned on the table. No one is lounging around in the living room, and the only sound comes from the upstairs shower. I grab two bagels, two bananas, two bottles of water, then quickly exit. I jog to the garage, hoping no one looks out the window and sees me. Julian's asleep, so I quietly set his breakfast next to him and sit on the floor across from him. I sit in silence, wondering about how I can make things right again.

I observe Julian as he sleeps. He's barely recognizable with the bruises and cuts all over his face and a black eye that's still swollen. Stubble lines his chin, hiding his dimple, and I find myself missing it.

Behind the marks of brutality is a handsome man. A man that took my breath away the first time I saw him at Chubb's—at least, I thought it was the first time. Did he leave someone behind when he left NOEL to find me? Surely someone had the hots for him.

Julian stirs and opens his eyes. He smiles the moment he sees me, and I can breathe steadily for the first time. "Come to watch me sleep?"

I shake my head. "I brought you breakfast."

He glances at the food, then back at me. "You could've dropped it and left."

Shrugging, I cross my arms, rubbing my scar. "They're not happy with me right now, so I thought I'd join the traitor's club."

"The traitor's club?" He chuckles. "I didn't realize I was part of a club. What did you do to get in?"

"I lost it during training and hurt Kat pretty badly." I look away, not wanting to see the same judgment on his face as the others. "I don't know what came over me. She got the first hit in, and I lost control."

"Don't beat yourself up over it. You reacted exactly how you were trained to."

I look at him. His expression isn't one of judgment, but one of understanding. "But I should've been able to control my temper. She hit me, and I turned into a different person. It happened with Mark and the NOEL soldiers."

"The one's from last night?"

"No. Different ones that attacked us on the way to Blue River. I killed them both without a second thought. It was like I wasn't in control of my body. It was the same after Kat hit me, but she's my friend, and I didn't know how to snap out of it."

"Because you forgot how. It's not your fault. They shouldn't be mad at you for that."

Not saying anything, I stare at him.

He doesn't show an ounce of shame or disgust, only compassion. Theo looked at me like he didn't know who I was.

"Well, they are, and I don't know how to make it right." I press my fingers into the rocks on the garage floor and hold back tears. When that doesn't work, I slide my hand back up to my scar.

"Is that why you're nervous? Because they're mad at you, and you don't know how to make it right?"

"I'm not nervous," I snap.

He raises his eyebrows and glares at me. "You have a nervous tell. You rub the scar on your arm."

I drop my hand. "I didn't realize it was obvious."

"I'm just observant." Julian's voice is soft, and he tries to reach out, but the restraints hold him back. He lets out a defeated sigh. "I hate seeing you like this and not being able to comfort you."

I scoot closer to him and put my hand in his.

He rubs the back of my hand with his thumb and stares into my eyes. I can't bring myself to look away, though I should. It feels wrong sharing this moment with him, like I'm betraying Theo. Quickly, I let go of his hand and look away.

"I wish you didn't have to be in this situation, but you left us no choice," I say.

"I know you think I'm the villain, but please believe me when I say that I thought I was being the hero."

"Heroes don't drug their girlfriends and hand them over to the bad guys."

"I know it seems that way, but I was actually trying to run away with you."

His answer shocks me. All this time, I thought he was betraying me.

"Why?"

"I told you my mission was to observe and report back. I wasn't supposed to be in direct contact with you. But since we were, I couldn't pass up the opportunity to gather more intel. What I didn't expect was to fall in love with you."

There's that word again—love. When he says it, it dances along his tongue and sings in my ears. If he keeps saying it, I might actually believe him.

"When they told me they wanted me to bring you back, I told them I would. I lied to them but had to act fast, otherwise they would send someone else to capture you. That was the reason behind my erratic behavior that day."

"You were my boyfriend." I place my hand on his again. "Why didn't you make up a lie about taking me on a vacation or something?"

He smiles when he looks at my hand on his. "I thought about that, but I didn't know if you'd agree. Plus, I'd have to make it seem like a vacation, which would mean you'd have your phone, and they would track us even if I got the tracker out of my arm." He flips his hand over, interlocking our fingers.

"So, your bright idea was to drug me and kidnap me?"

It wasn't funny at the time but looking back at it makes me chuckle.

Julian shrugs and chuckles with me. "Yeah, I guess so." He drops my hand and sighs. "I was trying to get you to safety. I gambled you would be angry once you woke up and probably hate me, but it was a risk I was willing to take. I would have explained everything and hoped you would understand and forgive me."

I wonder if I would have been understanding. Theo essentially did the same thing. He kidnapped me, and when I woke up, he had to explain everything, and I never once held it against him. Had it been Julian instead of Theo, I probably would have been just as understanding and forgiving.

Two men with the same good intentions of getting me to safety, yet I viewed them both differently after that day.

In my eyes, Julian was the villain, and Theo was the hero. Now I'm not so sure.

Both men lied to me from the moment I met them. They kept my identity a secret while I spent months trying to figure out who I was. However valid their reasons were, it still upsets me, but I can't deny the feelings I have for both. The love I have for Theo goes back years, and once I remembered, it resurfaced as if no time had passed.

I never admitted it, but I also love Julian. After everything he has done, I still love him. The love I have for Julian is different. He hated me and pursued me out of revenge but fell in love with me despite how terribly I had treated him when we were younger. He saw me for me, when I didn't have the corruption of my past standing in the way. I think he wanted me to keep my positive attitude because he once admired it. Now I realize I can forgive Julian as easily as I forgave Theo.

I grab his hand again. "I forgive you."

He exhales deeply, as if a weight has been lifted off his shoulders. He leans forward but is pulled back by the ropes.

"If I loosen your restraints, do you promise not to do anything stupid?"

He nods, and I untie his ropes, leaving only his legs bounded. He shakes his arms, then stretches.

"Thank you." He breathes with relief.

Raw flesh lines his arms where the ropes had ripped away old scabs.

"Let me clean those for you."

He shakes his head. "It's fine."

"Don't be ridiculous." I give him a serious look.

He nods and holds out his arms. I find a semi-clean rag in a desk drawer and use the water from my bottle to saturate it. I dab the wounds. He winces and hisses.

"Sorry." I pull the rag away, then continue with less pressure. He doesn't make another sound, but I see the pain behind his eyes. "There has to be a better way than keeping you tied up like this," I say, dabbing at his skin.

"You can let me go," he whispers.

I stop and look at him, expecting to see a mischievous grin but am surprised that his expression is pleading with a hint of pain.

"Julian, you know I can't do that."

"Why can't you?"

"You know why. We can't risk you going back to NOEL."

"I wouldn't put you in danger like that. Plus, I can't go back. They'll either kill me or recondition me."

He's telling the truth.

"Where would you go? You don't have money or a car, and your appearance will attract attention."

"I'll figure it out. I can be quite persuasive." He smirks and flutters his eyebrows.

He's told us everything he knew, and the only reason he's still held prisoner is because we were afraid he'll turn us in.

I'm the one who insisted we bring him here. Now that I know he won't go back to NOEL, I don't see a reason for him to still be here. I untie the ropes around his legs and toss them to the side.

"I'll check to see if the coast is clear, then you can go."

He stares at me in disbelief. "You're letting me go?"

"Yes. I believe you, and there's no reason for you to still be here." I jog to the door and peek out. No one in sight. "Wait here. I need to make sure they won't see you."

Julian hasn't moved from his spot since I untied him. He continues to stare at me with an incredulous expression. I exit the garage and run to the house. Still no one inside. I run back to the garage and find Julian in the same spot, but instead of sitting, he's standing.

"Okay. The coast is clear, but I don't know how much time you have, so you have to hurry." The words come out in a rush. He doesn't move, and I'm almost certain he didn't hear me. "Julian." I wave in front of his face. "Now's the time. Hurry."

He starts toward the door, and I follow. I rest my hand on the knob, about to turn it, before he lays his hand on top of mine.

"Come with me." A spark of hope flickers in his eyes.

"I can't. I have things to do here."

Julian places his hand on my cheek. I lean into it, closing my eyes. It feels like a lifetime ago when I last felt his touch.

Without thinking, I place my hand over his. His thumb skims over my bottom lip, and I exhale a long breath. His free hand wraps around, resting at the small of my back. He doesn't press me closer, but my body instinctively leans against his. We stare into each other's eyes as he leans his face closer to mine. My mind is telling me to pull away, but my lips part, and my chin raises toward him. In an instant, his lips gently find mine, and I kiss him back guiltlessly. He pulls away, leaving me breathless.

"I wanted to do that one last time," he whispers against my lips, then steps back. "I love you, Amelia. I always will."

"I love you, too."

The words come out breathlessly. This may be the last time I see him, and I want him to know the truth.

He rests his hand on the knob, pauses, then turns his head toward me. "Do you mean that?"

"Of course I do."

His hand drops, and he takes a deep breath. He turns around and walks back to the pole.

"What are you doing?" I ask.

"I'm not leaving here without you, so I'll continue to be your prisoner." He picks up the ropes and holds them out to me. "Go ahead. Tie me back up."

I shake my head. "I won't tie you back up. The others know I'm the only one allowed in here. Stay or go. It's your choice."

"I'm not going anywhere."

"Okay, then. I have to get back, but I'll be by later."

The house is quiet when I get back. When I peek in Theo's room, I find him asleep on the bed. Not once did he come looking for me when I failed to return.

Before the incident with Kat, he barely would let me out of his sight. He must be upset with me. I close the door without entering and head back downstairs. I grab a throw blanket and lie on the couch, waiting for sleep to take me.

***

Muffled voices wake me. Paul, Zeke, and Theo sit at the kitchen table. They stop talking when I enter. I try to ignore the silence and vacant stares and proceed to make a sandwich. I lay out two pieces of bread and spread peanut butter on one, jelly on the other. I stand at the counter and take a bite, determined to stay in the kitchen as I eat. They remain silent and won't look at me.

"Don't stop on my account." I stare at them, but they won't meet my eyes.

"We were discussing plans for tomorrow's visit with Dr. Wagner," Paul says.

I set my sandwich on a plate in anger. "You didn't think to include me in the conversation, since I'm the one that will be speaking to him?" They remain silent, which adds to my irritation. "You can save your breath because I'm going alone."

"The hell you are," Theo says in a raised voice, but he still won't look at me.

"Excuse me if I'd rather be alone half the day than spend it with people that will pretend like I'm not there."

"It could be dangerous." Theo glances at me, then looks away quickly.

"I can obviously take care of myself, not that it's any of your concern."

Theo winces, and I regret my choice of words but keep my composure. I don't wait for him to respond as I grab my plate and walk out the front door. I sit on the steps, taking bite after bite, trying to form a plan to see Dr. Wagner without them.

I won't be in danger. If Dr. Wagner wanted to harm me, he would have already done so. I stay on the porch, breathing in the fresh air. Theo doesn't join me to talk things out.

Tomorrow, I will meet with Dr. Wagner alone and, hopefully, get some answers.

35. Dr. Wagner

The house is dark and silent. I tiptoe through the kitchen, searching for the papers Paul printed out with the meeting instructions. Keys to both cars hang on a hook near the door. I grab them both, so they can't follow. Quietly, I gather food for my travels and extra to leave for Julian, then find a scrap sheet of paper to leave a note.

> Went to meet with Dr. Wagner. I've left food for
> Julian. No need to check on him. I promise I'll
> be safe, and I'll be in contact. See you soon.
> - Amelia

Pausing near the door, I check once again that I have everything I need, then put on my baseball hat and leave. Julian's asleep when I enter the garage. I set the food next to him, along with a note of where I'll be for the morning.

The engine turns over, and I hope it doesn't wake the others. I leave the headlights off while I drive away, only turning them on once I'm on the road.

I wait in a parking lot of a local park.

It was smart of Paul to choose a public place to meet. I don't think NOEL will strike in front of civilians. As I wait, I watch the groups of people interacting in the park. Families gather, playing, and laughing. Others play frisbee with their dogs, and children chase each other on the playground. It reminds me of the people I watched in the park on my runs. Back to when I was free to go where I pleased without worrying about hiding. I regret taking that freedom for granted. If only I knew then what I know now, I would have cherished it more.

Dr. Wagner walks across the field and sits on a bench.

Keeping my promise that I'll stay in touch, I reach out my thoughts to Theo. I have the strongest mental connection with him, and I hope it spans the distance.

At the park. I see Dr. Wagner. I'm going to approach him, and I'll update you after.

Silence. It didn't work. I'm too far away to project my thoughts.

I take a deep breath, praying I'm right that I'll be safe. If Theo can't hear me, they won't know if anything goes wrong. I step out of the car, and Theo's voice rings in my head. *Okay.*

I sigh with relief, but I'm annoyed he took a while to respond and only said one word.

Dr. Wagner looks around the park. He seems anxious, so I approach with caution.

I take in my surroundings in case he brought company. Nothing seems out of the ordinary, so I approach the bench and sit on the opposite end in silence.

"Jane. I'm relieved you're okay."

The relief in his voice tells me he means it, but the way he uses my alias bothers me.

"You don't have to pretend anymore. You can say my real name."

"I'm sorry." He shrugs. "Habit."

"Listen, I don't want to be here any longer than I have to, so let's skip the pleasantries and cut to the chase."

Lips set in a hard line, he shifts in his seat. "Fair enough. What do you want to know?"

"Tell me how you started working at NOEL."

He sighs and glances at a family walking by. Once they're out of earshot, he turns his attention to me. "I studied psychology in college. The way the human mind works fascinated me. It was there I met Amanda."

"Amanda Sheffield?"

"Yes. She studied neuroscience and physiology. We spent many hours together fantasizing about the capabilities humans could have. Once we graduated, we combined our expertise to continue researching. Her family was wealthy. She bought land and had a facility built. We used that facility for our research, and she hired the brightest doctors and scientists to help." He pauses and closes his eyes as if remembering that time.

"It was innocent at first, but after a while, she became obsessive. She was convinced that our fantasies could become a reality if we could experiment on human DNA. That's when she brought in human subjects. Those poor innocent people thought she was trying to help them. I believe she thought she was. But in the end . . ."

A baseball lands near our feet, and a small boy comes running over. Dr. Wagner picks it up and tosses it to the boy, then watches as he runs back to his dad.

"What happened to them?" I ask.

"They all died." He looks away. A glimpse of regret flashes in his eye, but he dismisses it and turns to me. "We started with terminal patients. We were their last hope to live, but their bodies were too weak for the enhancements." He clears his throat and blinks rapidly.

Is that a tear? Does talking about this upset him?

Good.

He should be upset. He was a part of NOEL. He helped start NOEL. Those deaths are on his hands.

"Then Amanda hypothesized the enhancements would work on those in outstanding physical health. The only issue was getting volunteers."

"Why?"

"Because healthy people do not need medical intervention. Plus, if we told them we have a drug that would make them faster and stronger, and then they died, it would draw too much attention to our work, which wasn't legal."

"Is that why you took orphan children? Because no one would notice if they died?"

"Yes and no. Experimenting on children happened by accident. Once Amanda realized children could withstand the enhancements, she sought orphans."

"How did Dr. Sheffield *accidentally* experiment on children?"

On the grass in front of us, a child trips on a rock and cries, and her mother comes running over.

Dr. Wagner takes a deep breath. "When Amanda was fifteen, she had a baby . . . a daughter. But I think the burden of motherhood stood in the way of her ambitions, so she gave her up for adoption. Twenty-three years ago, her daughter, Lia, found her. She was sixteen, her adoptive parents had just died, and she was three months pregnant.

She came to Amanda for help. Lia was her own flesh and blood, but she used the enhancements on her while she was pregnant. She wanted to see what the outcome would be."

I grip the edge of the bench, fingertips digging into the wood. "How can someone do that to their own daughter, not knowing what would happen?"

"I wish I knew what she was thinking. She kept Lia a secret from everyone at the facility. I found out by accident, and she asked me not to tell anyone."

"Did you ever tell anyone?"

"Not until this moment. I kept her secret, and it's pained me ever since that I never tried to stop her. I left the program five years later."

"What happened to her? Lia."

"Lia became severely ill two months after the first round of enhancements, and it put her baby in distress. That's when Amanda realized the first round of enhancements don't work after puberty. There was no way to reverse the effects, so she induced her into a medical coma and kept her alive long enough to give birth, so she could continue experimenting on the baby in the womb."

My jaw drops in horror. Does Dr. Sheffield have no regard for human life?

"Once Lia went into labor, Amanda delivered her baby via cesarean. Lia's body wasn't strong enough to handle the delivery, and she died two minutes after giving birth."

"And the baby?"

The child who was crying in the grass stands and walks away with her mother.

The sun is hot on my skin, and just for a minute, a breeze moves in that reminds me of Bridgeport. I lift my face to smell it before turning to Dr. Wagner.

"Don't you get it?" he asks. "Don't you get it yet?" Dread comes over me before I fully understand. He reaches forward and puts his hand on the bench near my leg. "That baby is you."

The realization hits me. It explains why I was there as a baby and why Dr. Sheffield wants me alive. She is my grandmother, and she killed my mother to make me how I am. The information is too much to handle, and I'm on the verge of hyperventilating.

Dr. Wagner places his hand on my back. "Breathe, Amelia. Deep breaths."

I take five deep breaths, and my body relaxes. "She got the idea of using children because I survived." I say to myself under my breath. The loathing I feel for my grandmother is unbearable. "Did I know about this? Is that why I escaped?"

Dr. Wagner shakes his head and shrugs.

"But I must have known something. Before my escape, I left a message to find you. You are the only other person who knew about my mother. That must be the reason, right?"

"I'm not sure. Amanda never mentioned you knowing."

Unable to breathe, I stare at him. "You still talk to her?"

Panic rises inside me as I look around the park, waiting for her to emerge. Is this all a trap?

Dr. Wagner places his hand on mine. "She doesn't know about this meeting. I never told her you were in Bridgeport. That's probably why it took her so long to send agents after you."

Relief washes over me. I can trust him. That must be why I sent myself that message.

"I have a couple more questions, if you don't mind answering," I say, and he nods for me to continue. "We found medical charts on all the subjects. They're all the same, except everyone has an extra page that I don't."

"Are you referring to the boosters?"

"Yeah. How did you know?"

"Because you're the only one that never needed them. Amanda suspected it was because Lia passed down some of her enhancement to you."

"What are they, exactly?"

"They're like any booster. They prolong the enhancements."

Hope swells inside me.

"So, if someone doesn't get a booster, they'll go back to normal?"

Theo hoped that's what it would do, but Dr. Wagner's grim face makes my hope vanish.

"No, Amelia. If one doesn't receive their booster as scheduled, they fall ill. Immediately, their body starts to shut down, and if they don't receive the booster within days, they'll die a painful death."

This information isn't good for the eight enhanced orphans in Woodland Park, Colorado. Without the boosters, they will die, and going back to NOEL is not an option.

"How can I get the boosters for my friends?"

My voice is full of desperation.

"You can't. They're at NOEL, and I don't think Amanda will hand them over willingly to escapees."

"Not even for her granddaughter?"

"She was willing to kill her own daughter for her experiment. What do you think?"

He makes a valid point. She would never hand them over. I will have to find another way to keep my friends alive.

"That's all the questions I have. Thank you for meeting me."

"Of course."

I stand and recede, but Dr. Wagner calls out, "Amelia." I turn to face him. "I know how determined you are, so whatever stupid thing you're thinking about doing, please be careful."

Once I'm safely inside the car, I project my thoughts to Theo.

I'm safe, like I said I would be. On my way back. See you soon.

Okay.

Theo's reply is just as short but more immediate.

I put the car into gear, and his voice rings in my head again.

Please drive carefully.

His thoughts make me smile.

Although he's angry with me, he still cares about my safety.

I hope that never changes.

36. Booster Effects

I walk into the house, prepared to tell them everything Dr. Wagner told me, but I'm struck with worried faces.

Molly rests on the couch, shivering underneath a blanket. Her dark complexion is paler, and she's sweaty and unresponsive. Brooke is by her side, holding her hand and dabbing a wet washcloth along her forehead.

Theo stands in the doorway, arms crossed, forehead creasing with concern.

"What's going on?" I whisper.

"Molly's super sick. James can't figure out why. We've never been sick. Not even with a common cold."

Molly looks frail, and I know why. As to not alarm the others, I project my thoughts to Theo.

I need to talk to you in private.

Now's not the time.

It's about Molly.

He finally looks at me. I keep my face serious, hoping he'll understand the urgency.

He leads us through the hallway, out of earshot. "What is it?"

"I think I know why Molly is sick. She needs her booster. Dr. Wagner told me about them. Without it, she'll die."

"Fuck."

His voice is elevated but low enough to not startle the others. Turning away, he rubs his hands through his hair before leaning his forehead against the wall. "How do we fix her?"

I don't know how to tell him we can't without the booster, that the process has already started. Within days, her body will shut down, and she will die a painful death.

All I can do is shake my head.

"There has to be a way."

His eyes fill with tears.

"I'm sorry, but we don't have the boosters to give her."

"I refuse to believe that. We'll figure out another way. James will figure out another way."

A single tear flows down his cheek, and he's having trouble getting the words out. He's mad at me, but he needs comforting. I embrace him, and to my surprise, he leans into my shoulder. "I thought we'd have more time."

"I know." I try to calm him by rubbing his back. "If only we found out sooner, we could've had more time to save her."

He shakes his head against my shoulder, then pulls away to meet my gaze. "I'm talking about us."

I furrow my brows. I don't know what he means about us having more time.

Panic rises inside me. Has he found out about my brain?

"August thirtieth," he says. "My next booster is due in a month and a half."

Air leaves my lungs, and I feel like I did when I accidentally stepped off that cliff. I didn't see his file, so I couldn't know the last time he received his booster. Six weeks is all I have left with him unless we figure out a way to get the boosters. I want to scream or cry or punch something, but I stand still and emotionless. I don't have time to feel the weight of it all but need to stay focused and figure out what to do next. It is my fault we're in this mess. Had I died at birth, none of this would have happened to them. Had I not been antisocial as a young child, Dr. Sheffield wouldn't have felt the need to bring in more children my age. They are all here because of me, so I need to be the one to fix it.

"I'm going to fix this if it's the last thing I do." I turn away, and Theo grabs my arm.

"What are you talking about? What are you going to do?"

"I don't know. I need space to think. I'll figure something out." I leave him standing in the hallway.

Everyone else is too focused on Molly to notice me walk out the door.

Pacing in front of the house, I take deep breaths to clear my mind. We could try breaking in to get the boosters, but the chances of success are slim to none. We still need more time to prepare for an attack. By the time we're ready, it will be too late for Theo, and I'll be damned if I let him die before he gets the chance to see NOEL crumble.

I pick up a rock, toss it in the air, and catch it as if it were a ball. Dr. Wagner doesn't think Dr. Sheffield will give me the booster. She killed her own daughter, after all. But he left when I was young. He wasn't there to see if she ever cared for me. I don't remember everything, but I remember how she looked in that last memory. She held my hand and looked remorseful. She might have cared for me, not in the way a grandmother should, but in the only way she could.

I toss the rock again, and as it lands in my hand, I know what I have to do. It's stupid, but I'm desperate. I close my eyes and think of her.

Dr. Sheffield? It's Amelia. If you can hear me, just think, and I'll be able to hear you.

Amelia? I'm relieved you're all right.

Through thought, I hear her tone. She tried to sound sincere but fell short.

Yeah, whatever. Listen, I need a favor . . . I need the boosters. My friends will die without them.

Yes, I know they will. I designed them that way.

I chuck the rock into the forest. It wasn't enough for her to experiment on us. She had to make sure she could control us, too. Even down to our life spans.

I get it. You're mad we escaped. I'm asking, as your granddaughter, to let me have the boosters to give to my friends. I can't lose them. Please?

I wait for her reply. Silence. Ten seconds go by. Then thirty. I want to scream out of frustration.

Fine. But I want something in return. I want you to come back. Then I'll give you what you want.

Unable to breathe, I freeze.

All of this, everything I've gone through, was to be free of NOEL, to be free of Dr. Sheffield.

I'll never go back.

Time's ticking, Amelia. Molly doesn't have much time left, and the others will shortly follow.

We'll find another way.

You might, but by then, it will be too late for Molly.

She's right. It will be too late for Molly, but maybe we can figure out another way to save the rest of us.

I won't come back.

Suit yourself. But my offer only stands for the next twenty-four hours, and Molly will be dead by then. But the question is, how much longer do you have? Have the headaches started? I can help you. I can fix it.

Did she do this to me? Was this her plan all along? To inject me with something to make my brain deteriorate so I'd have to rely on her to reverse it?

I was willing to die escaping. At least now, I'm surrounded by people that love me, and I'm free from you.

Always so stubborn, her thoughts growl, and I know it's not the response she was expecting.

I should have known reaching out to her would be useless. Searing pain stabs at the back of my eyes, and I break the connection. I slump against the porch, hunching over as bile rises to the back of my throat before I choke it down and sit on the front step, breathing in the summer air until it subsides. My symptoms have gotten worse. What if James was wrong, and I don't have months?

37. Searching for Answers

I walk back into the house and stand at Theo's side. "How is she doing?"

"Not good. James thinks he can recreate the booster if he has the formula, so Paul is searching NOEL servers again to see if he can find anything about it."

"Good. That's good." I inhale deeply, trying to push the headache away.

"Listen . . ." He tucks my hair behind my ear. "I'm sorry about before. I was mad about the Kat thing, but I'm not anymore."

"It's water under the bridge. There are more important things to worry about now."

Light from the kitchen shines incredibly bright, forcing my eyes closed. Tapping of computer keys rings in my ears as Paul searches through NOEL's files. Each keystroke sounds like nails on a chalkboard. Throbbing in my head intensifies, and I'm afraid if I don't get dark and quiet soon, it will consume me. I turn toward the stairs and Theo grabs my hand.

"Where are you going?" he asks.

"I need to lie down for a bit."

Theo follows, matching my slow pace. We enter the room, and I close the door behind us. It's enough to drown out the noise from downstairs. The light is off, but sunlight shines through the window. Rays scatter across the bed like a spotlight on a stage. I draw the curtains closed. It's still bright enough to see but dim enough to subside the pain.

As I sit on the bed, Theo leans against the dresser and eyes me warily. "Are you okay?"

I force a smile. "Yes, I'm fine. Just tired. Give me thirty minutes, and I'll be down."

He nods and exits the room.

As I lie in bed, I search my photographic memory for anything that could be useful, but without my memories, it's impossible to know if I had any knowledge about the boosters. Going under hypnosis again is too dangerous, and contacting my grandmother is pointless.

How could she think I would go back? I know I can't remember my time at NOEL, but I escaped not only once but twice. That's enough proof to know I wouldn't give myself up willingly. The biggest mystery is, why does she want me? It can't be because I'm her granddaughter. She killed her own daughter and tried to have me reconditioned. I can't believe she'd want me back just because we're blood related. There must be some ulterior motive at play.

Maybe I have something she wants. Maybe I took something when I escaped. If I did, I don't remember, and getting me back would be useless for her.

Even if I agreed, how could I trust she'd give me the boosters for my friends? With the little knowledge I have about her and NOEL, she can't be trusted.

The enhancement files scan in my head as I use my photographic memory to reread them. Nothing useful comes to mind. Then I go over Julian's files again, carefully paying attention to his booster log. There are only the dates administered, no formula details, but Julian's file said he spent a lot of time with the doctors and scientists. He told me he learned things from them but didn't give more information about the boosters when I had asked. Maybe he was holding back information. He may be the only chance we have to find out how to make it.

Without waiting for the headache to disappear, I rush down the stairs. Kat and Brooke remain by Molly's side, while Paul sits at the dining table, deep in concentration on his laptop. James, Theo, and Zeke are nowhere in sight.

I busy myself in the kitchen, preparing two sandwiches and fruit, then head directly to the garage. Julian rests against the pole, hands wrapped behind with rope. Panic sets in as I wonder who found him and tied him back up.

"Julian?"

His head tilts my way, and he breathes a sigh. "Oh, it's just you." He shimmies out of the rope. "I heard Theo and Zeke earlier and thought they might come in and check on me, so I did the best I could to make it look like I was still a prisoner."

The tightness in my chest releases. "Thank God. I thought someone tied you back up."

He removes the ropes around his legs and sets them next to the pole. "How was your visit with Dr. Wagner?"

I hadn't been able to tell the others about the meeting because of Molly, and while the others don't trust Julian, I do. I settle next to him and inhale.

He eats as I tell him everything. He listens without interruption as I explain the details of my newfound memories. Then I tell him everything I learned from Dr. Wagner, about Lia and Dr. Sheffield, and how I'm related to them.

His face grows somber when I explain about Lia's death. Then I tell him about the boosters and how Molly is sick because she didn't get hers.

"You worked a lot with the doctors and scientists," I say. "Is there anything they told you about the boosters? Like how to create them or what the formula is?"

"No. I'm sorry. I wish I could be more help."

I grab his hands and squeeze. "Just think. Maybe it was written somewhere, and you saw it by accident."

"It wasn't. I swear I saw nothing about the boosters."

"Dammit!" I yell out in frustration. Tears prick at my eyes.

Julian grabs my hand. "Paul is really good at what he does. I'm sure he'll find something. And if he doesn't, James is the smartest person I know. Even without the formula, I believe he'll find a way to recreate it."

"But then it might be too late for Molly."

Julian lowers his head, and I know he understands. It might take James weeks to figure it out and Molly only has days, if that. In a moment of silence, I twist the ropes in my hands.

Julian rubs his chin and speaks with caution. "This might sound crazy . . . but have you thought about contacting Dr. Sheffield? You're her granddaughter. She might help you."

Scoffing, I drop the ropes. "I tried that already. I projected to her as soon as I found out about Molly."

"Projected?"

Julian doesn't know about my projection ability.

"My ability works both ways. I can hear thoughts, but I can also project my thoughts into someone else."

"That's pretty cool, actually."

"Yeah, well . . ." I shrug. "I asked her."

"And she said no?"

Wondering if I should tell him about her terms, I go back to twist the loose ropes aimlessly. I could never tell the others I contacted her. They would be furious with me for reaching out. But I picture Kat's bloody face when I hit her, and Brooke's clear panic at Molly's illness. They'd gladly trade me in to save Molly but not without a fight from Theo.

"Not exactly," I say tentatively. "She said she would if I came back to NOEL."

"What did you say?"

"No. Obviously."

"But Molly—"

"I know!" I throw the ropes aside. "I know she'll die without the booster, but I won't go back."

I can't trust Dr. Sheffield to keep her word. For all I know, I'd come back only for her to not fulfill her side of the bargain. Or worse, she'd kill them all in front of me out of spite, a risk I'm not willing to take. If I did, Molly's life wouldn't be the only life lost. At least her death won't be in vain. Her death will push the others to find a way to replicate the formula. They'll have it readily available and can be free of NOEL forever. They'll have a chance at a normal life.

I shrug. "Sorry if that makes me sound like an asshole, but I escaped twice for a reason."

"What reason is that?"

"You know how it was there."

"Not really," he mumbles, scuffing his shoe on the dirt floor. "It was different for me. I liked being there."

His words sting, and I scoot several feet away from him. "How can you say that?"

"Because Dr. Sheffield saved me from a life of pain and misery. She made me better."

"What are you talking about?"

He sighs. "I lied to you before. My parents never took me to Disney World. They were high and drunk all the time. They were abusive toward me. When they overdosed, I bounced around from foster home to foster home until Dr. Sheffield rescued me and gave me a place to belong."

I can relate to feeling like you don't belong until you find something that feels like home. For me, that was Trish.

"Oh, Julian." I embrace him. "I had no idea."

"I know. And I'm sure you have your reasons. You don't need to explain them. Your word is enough for me."

I pull away when I hear Zeke's voice in the distance. "I should get going."

As I exit the garage, Theo and Zeke walk out of the forest.

Zeke goes toward the house, while Theo walks toward me.

"What were you two doing in the woods?" I ask.

"Just getting some fresh air and clearing our minds. Zeke's not doing so well with the news of Molly."

"Yeah, none of us are."

"What were you doing in the garage?"

"Bringing Julian some food."

I force a grin and hold on to Theo's hand, guiding him toward the house before he demands to check on Julian for himself.

38. From Bad to Worse

At first, there is darkness, yet I'm not afraid. The warmth and constant *thud-lump* lulls me into a steady stream of calmness. My lungs suck in liquid, but they breathe as if the air is pure.

Where am I?

Muffled voices shout in the distance, followed by the sound of tearing flesh. Blinding brightness pierces the sky. Something large wraps around the back of my neck and across my entire back, and I'm ejected from my safety.

Instantly, the warmth is sucked out from around me, and icy blasts freeze every part of my skin. Everything is a blur of meshed colors . The light is too bright; the sounds are too loud. Nothing is distinguishable. I don't know which way is up or which way is down, but the hold on me is strong yet gentle.

Forcefully, something shoots its way to the back of my throat, then up my nose, tearing the remains of my liquid breath away. A gust of air fills my lungs, and I let out a sob.

The sob is an echo, and it's not from a twenty-two-year-old woman. No.

It's the cry of a baby.

The muffled echo of a cry continues as a shape of colors come into view. The shape in a silhouette of a woman.

"You're both safe," she says.

The voice, though muffled, is recognizable. I've heard it twice in the past week. Once in a hypnotic state and the other in my thoughts. It belongs to the person I hate the most. The person I risked my life to get away from, and who I wish would suffer . . .

My grandmother.

With a gasp, I wake and bolt upright. A cold sweat drips from my forehead as I pant.

Theo startles awake. "What is it? What's the matter?" he asks, panic-stricken.

Hearing his voice relaxes me.

"I had a bad dream. I'm sorry I woke you." I smooth my pillow back down.

"It's okay. Was it a bad dream or was it a memory?"

Pressure builds behind my eyes. The dream was more than a nightmare. It was a memory. But of what?

"I'm not sure," I say.

"Want to tell me about it?"

"It's hard to explain. It's not like the other memories. Usually, I'm on the outside looking in. This one was through my eyes. It was hard to tell exactly what was going on, because everything was blurry and muffled, but I think I saw my birth."

"How is that possible?"

"I don't know? Maybe because of my photographic memory."

Pressure builds in my head to a throbbing pulse. I don't want Theo to notice, so I place my feet on the floor, determined to rush to the bathroom.

As I stand, the room spins, a tingling radiates from my neck up to my head, then everything goes black.

"Amelia!" Theo shouts. "Help! Someone help!"

I try to tell him I'm all right, but my words cannot escape my throat. Even though I can't see him, I can hear him. I try to move, but it's as if I'm frozen in place.

Footsteps approach into the room. "Put her on the bed," James says.

I feel Theo's arms wrap around me, and I'm lifted in the air and set gently on something soft. Pinpricks crawl from my limbs to the center of my body. My eyes flutter open, and I can see again.

"What happened?" I'm relieved my voice works.

Theo brushes the hair from my face. "You fainted."

"I'm fine. I just got light-headed from standing up too fast," I say to ease the worry in his eyes.

"I want to check you out just in case," James adds. "Please give us a moment," he says to Theo.

Theo kisses my forehead and exits the room. James closes the door and comes to my bedside, eyeing me from head to toe.

"No injuries from the fall, so that's good."

"See?" I smile. "Like I said. I'm fine."

"No, you're not," he says grimly.

I know better than to lie to James. He's the only one who knows about my condition, and by his tone, it's gotten worse.

"Just tell me."

It comes out in a whisper.

"Your prognosis has changed from months to weeks. Your symptoms are only going to get worse from here on out. Maybe it's time you tell them."

I dig my hands into the sheets. "No. They have enough to worry about with Molly. I can't add to that."

"I won't go against what you decide. But, Amelia, the progression has changed in a matter of days. Tomorrow, it may go from weeks to days and then from days to hours."

"I understand. Thanks, James."

He turns to leave and pauses with his hand on the doorknob. "Can I give you one word of advice? If you have any wrongs, set them right. Don't leave anything unsaid. You never know when it's going to be too late."

With that, he leaves.

***

The house is eerily quiet. Brooke and Kat stay by Molly's side while Paul and James comb through every piece of knowledge they have. Zeke has made himself scarce, taking walks in the forest or chopping wood with his bare hands. His super strength makes it easy, but his skin isn't tough enough to withstand the repeated contact against bark, splitting his knuckles that bleed to where he has to keep bandaging them. Theo tries talking with him, but the news about the boosters has turned his usual joking demeanor upside down.

Theo distracts himself by cleaning the house and checking to see if Kat or Brooke need anything. He's brought them water, tea, food, and extra blankets.

I heat leftover pizza and visit Julian in the garage. He bounces an old tennis ball against the wall and catches it repeatedly.

"Hey you!" I call as I enter.

He drops the ball and strides across the garage to meet me. He takes the plate from my hands and sits on a bed of blankets, leaving an open spot next to him. I sit in silence as he eats, rubbing the scar across my bicep.

"What's wrong?" he asks.

"Nothing."

He raises an eyebrow. "You're rubbing your scar again. Something's bothering you."

Dropping my hand in my lap, I stare straight ahead at a broken desk. There are things he and I need to discuss, but I'm not sure how to say them or where to start. "We still haven't decided what to do with you yet."

"I figured. Especially with everything that's going on with Molly right now. It's okay. I'm in no rush to die."

He says it as a joke, but the mention of him dying forms a lump in my throat. I don't know how much time I have left on this earth, but the moment I'm gone, they'll kill him.

"You need to leave. Tonight," I say.

After setting his plate aside, he turns toward me. "I already told you I'm not leaving here without you."

"That's no longer an option. They'll kill you when . . . *if* anything happens to me."

"Nothing's going to happen to you."

Tears swim in my eyes.

"There's something you need to know." I turn toward him and grab his hands for comfort.

It all comes out in a rush. Every last bit of it. About what James saw on my scan and how it's deteriorating my brain. I tell him that my symptoms have gotten worse and that my prognosis has changed from months to weeks, but that can change at any moment.

"You see?" I squeeze his hands. "I don't know how much longer I have left. You need to leave tonight before it's too late."

Julian shakes his head rapidly. "No." He drops his hands from my grip and paces the garage. "This can't be true. Maybe James was wrong?" He looks at me for confirmation, but I can't give him any. "There must be something James can do."

"There isn't. I'm going to die, and it will be soon."

He pulls me tight to his chest, grabbing at the back of my shirt. His heart beats rapidly beneath my ear. A tear falls from his eye and onto my cheek and he chokes out, "I don't want to lose you."

"I know. I don't want to lose anyone, but it is what it is."

He releases my shirt and finds the sides of my face, pulling me closer to his. He doesn't ask or search my eyes for permission as he crashes his lips to mine. It's fierce and sudden but completely welcome. My lips part, and our tongues swim together. It's not a kiss of passion or longing or to spark desire. It's devastating and messy as tears stream down our faces. It's a kiss to say goodbye.

He pulls apart, keeping his hands on my cheeks, resting his forehead against mine. "I love you." His breath ghosts along my lips.

"I love you, too."

He leans away to look at me again but keeps his hands on my cheeks, as if he can't pull away.

"Tonight, when I bring dinner, I'll also bring you some supplies for your travels. Some clean bandages and clothes, money, food, and water. After everyone goes to bed, you sneak out and go."

He nods. I wipe my tears and compose myself. I don't look back as I exit the garage, but his sniffling and quiet sobs echo through me. I have to hold my breath before I lose control and run back to him.

I spend most of the afternoon sneaking supplies for Julian's escape. Thankfully, everyone is too preoccupied to notice.

Upon returning downstairs, I notice they've made some changes with Molly. She's now hooked up to a heart monitor and IV drip. The monitor beeps at an abnormally slow rate. Her once-vibrant skin is dull aside from the darkened circles around her eyes. Her breaths are shallow, and I know it won't be much longer now.

I sneak past, backpack full of supplies slung over my shoulder, and jog to the garage.

Julian waits inside, sitting against the wall, knees up and head lowered.

"Everything you'll need is inside. I'll project to you when it's safe to leave." I plop the backpack next to him.

"I don't want to do this," he says without looking up.

"I know. But you have to."

"They might recondition me for failing the mission."

It hadn't occurred to me he would go back to NOEL, but of course, he must. He'll need the booster eventually, and NOEL is the only place to get it. Otherwise, he won't survive and letting him go to save him would be for nothing.

"But you'll be alive," I say.

"Alive and soulless," he scoffs.

Nothing I say will make it easier for him to leave. I hate what might become of him, but I can't let him die at the hands of my friends. Knowing he'll survive—no matter what state of mind he'll be in—gives me a bit of comfort.

"Goodbye, Julian." I turn away.

If I don't leave now, my selfishness wins.

Brooke sleeps at Molly's side, nested in the recliner. Zeke's the first to turn in for the night, the others shortly after, with Theo and me the last to go upstairs.

He lies in the bed next to me as I pretend to be asleep. Within minutes, his breathing steadies, and I know he's out. Even though it may cause a side effect, I reach out to Julian.

It's time. Everyone's asleep. You can go without being seen.

Goodbye, Amelia.

Be safe, Julian.

Pressure forms around my temples, seeping its way to my forehead. Taking deep, long breaths, I exhale through the pain, hoping it doesn't progress into something worse. I concentrate only on breathing and counting.

Inhale—one, two, three, four.

Exhale—one, two, three, four.

Over and over, I count, in and out. Eventually, the pain recedes, the pressure lifts, and I fall asleep.

39. Downward Spiral

Sunlight peeks through the curtains. Theo's snoring softly next to me. For a moment, I watch him, memorizing every line, freckle, scar, and feature to his face. I must have studied his face a thousand times before, but it's as if I'm truly seeing it for the first time.

My days are limited, and when the time comes, I want to picture every moment we've shared, every moment I can remember. Even though I can't remember the specifics, I saw how our love has transpired in the flashes of memories. All the feelings I've ever had for him resurfaced, and I know how true and real our love for one another is, even if my heart is divided.

It's not fair to him, keeping him in the dark, but I don't want my final days to be spent with him worrying over me. I want to spend them with him, fully and completely, surrounded by love and happiness. But that's a pipe dream, because, downstairs, Molly is dying. But right now, I can cherish this moment and hold on to it a little longer.

Theo stirs awake, inhaling a yawn and stretching an arm out. He peeks through one eye. "Watching me sleep?"

"Yeah." I giggle. "You looked so peaceful. I didn't want to wake you."

He moans and pulls me into his arms, kissing the top of my head. My head rests perfectly in the crook of his neck.

Two light knocks echo from the door before Kat peeks inside, pushing her way through as she sees we're awake. Her face is grim.

"Molly's getting worse. You should come downstairs."

Theo and I rush down the stairs to the living room.

Brooke pats Molly's head with a wet washcloth, while the others stand idly by. Molly's body trembles with shivers, but her clothes are soaked with sweat.

"We can't get her fever to go down," Kat says.

Theo's head whips around the room. "Where the fuck is James?"

"Right here," James calls, jogging through the hall.

Brooke screams as Molly's body convulses and vomit dribbles out of her mouth.

James pushes his way through and turns her on her side, head facing down. Vomit drops to the floor. He thumps her back to help release anything that may be stuck in her throat. The convulses subside, and Molly lets out a faint breath.

"We need to keep her on her side so she doesn't aspirate on her own vomit," James says.

We wait and watch as Molly fades by the minute. Her breaths are slow and shallow. Brooke continues to dab her forehead with a washcloth. It does nothing to help, but I think it calms her to try. Is that how it's going to be for me when the effects of my brain take over? Theo by my side, uselessly wiping my forehead while I convulse and vomit on myself?

"She's stable for now," James says.

Theo pulls him aside into the hall, with me following. "How are you coming along with the booster?"

James shakes his head. "Paul can't find anything on NOEL servers, and I don't know anything about it to recreate it."

"Dammit!" Theo mutters. "So, that's it, then? Molly's going to die, and we're all screwed."

"I'm not giving up." James gives Theo a tight-lipped smile and walks away.

A lump forms in my throat, and it takes every bit of strength I have to not collapse under the guilty pressure. I could have saved her if I had given myself up.

Did I make the right choice?

Pushing my thoughts aside—and to keep up appearances—I prepare breakfast for Julian.

When I enter the dark and empty garage, my heart sinks. A part of me hoped to see Julian to pretend our world isn't collapsing in on itself. But he's gone, and all that's left is reality.

I set the bagel and banana upon the broken desk while I gather and fold the blankets and pillow. The more I erase the remnants of Julian, the more I think about him. I breathe out a soft wish for his safe return and good will to meet him at NOEL.

Like Trish, I'll never see him again, but at least I had the chance to say goodbye this time.

Will they recondition him, or will they spare him? If spared, will he find love again? The jealous part of me hopes not. The part of me that cares for Julian hopes he finds a life worth meaning, a life worth living, and a life with love. It pains me too much to think otherwise.

Everyone goes about the day on autopilot. No conversations or laughter. Plates of food sit untouched around the table. To keep up with my secret, I prepare a plate of food—for the third time today—and head to the garage.

Three full meals sit atop the broken desk, gathering flies. I'll have to remember to bring a garbage bag tomorrow to discard of the food before it attracts mice.

When I return to the house, the sun has dipped below the horizon. The lights have been turned on in the living room and kitchen. Everyone gathers around Molly, while James checks her vitals.

"It won't be long now," he says. "You should say your goodbyes."

Brooke steps forward first. She leans close to Molly, holding her hand and whispering in her ear. As she steps away, Molly convulses. Brooke steps forward with a scream of anguish, but Kat holds her back. Vomit trickles from Molly's mouth again, and then she stills, not breathing.

James rushes toward her, placing two fingers on her neck, and turns her on her back and delivers chest compressions.

Brooke cries into Kat's shoulder, and I'm paralyzed. There's nothing I can do except watch her die.

Is this my fault? I had the chance to save her, and I didn't.

Minutes feel like hours.

James continues with the chest compressions and checks her pulse occasionally. Finally, he lets out a relieved sigh and steps back. "Her heart's beating again."

"Is she in pain?" Brooke blurts.

James shakes his head. "I don't know."

Brooke forces her way out of Kat's grip and stumbles toward me, grabbing my shoulders. "You can see if she's in pain."

I shake my head.

"You can tap into her mind. See what she's thinking. Please?"

James shoots a warning glance at me. If I project into her mind, I'll experience side effects and speed up the brain deterioration, but I can't tell anyone that. Nodding, I step forward, placing my hand in Molly's.

The smart thing to do is pretend to connect to her mind and say she's not in pain, but if she is, and I have a way of preventing it, I can't, in good conscience, lie.

I close my eyes and concentrate, connecting to her mind. Molly's thoughts are a tangle of shouts and whispers, but every thought is a jumble of words that make no sense.

Pressure builds behind my eyelids, spreading its way to my temples, then outward to my entire skull. I collapse to my knees, screaming out in pain, clutching the sides of my head. A flow of blood seeps from my nose.

Theo's hands are on me in an instant. "Amelia!" he shouts in a panic.

I break the connection, hoping it reduces the pain, but it intensifies. I can't hold back my screams of pain, so I concentrate on breathing.

Inhale—one, two, three, four.

Exhale—one, two, three, four.

Throbbing pulses through my head as if it's about to explode.

Inhale—one, two, three, four.

Exhale—one, two, three, four.

My screams halt, but the throbbing remains. Blood drips from my nose onto the carpet. My stomach twists into knots, bile rising to my throat. I choke it back down, but then another wave of searing pain creeps its way into my head, burning upon throbbing, and I wail out again.

"James, do something," Theo yells, his grip tightening on my arms.

"There's nothing I can do," James says.

"What's wrong with her?"

"She's—"

"No!" I manage to shout through the pain. Forcing my head up, I stare at James, pleading with him to keep quiet. He shakes his head.

"Her cognitive and ability markers are larger than normal, and it's reacting negatively with the memory wipe. It's as if her brain is trying to fight it off but with very dire consequences."

"What are you saying?" Theo asks.

James glances at me, and he doesn't want to say it, but he will if I don't.

"I'm dying," I say.

Theo's head whips toward me, and his hands tighten on my arms. His eyes, full of disbelief and confusion, search mine. "No," he murmurs. "No, you're not. Please tell me you're lying. That this is just some sick joke."

Kat steps forward. "Hey guys? Is it just me or—"

Theo ignores her while he searches my face. "Amelia, please tell me this isn't true."

"Do you guys hear that?" Kat interjects. She steps closer to the window.

"Hear what?" Paul asks, and, finally, Theo breaks his attention and looks at Paul.

"Footsteps," Kat says when she's almost at the window. Before anyone can question her further, the door bursts open, and six NOEL soldiers rush inside.

40. Broken Trust

In an instant, Theo's on his feet, pushing his way toward the soldiers. Zeke and Paul fight two at a time, while Theo fights the other two. I try to get to my feet to help, but the moment I stand, the pain comes back, forcing me back down, and all I can do is watch as all hell breaks loose.

James and Brooke hover over Molly, protecting her body with theirs. Kat joins in, fighting with one soldier. Everything is a blur of movement—arms and legs swinging, fists against fists, objects being thrown. It's hard to tell which side is winning.

Zeke wrestles with a soldier in the kitchen and tosses him in the air. The soldier lands on the dining table, breaking it in half. Zeke moves on to the next soldier, but the fallen one quickly recovers, advancing on Zeke.

I try to scream out to warn him, but the soldier moves faster than my mouth can form the words. In one quick move, the soldier wraps a thick black device around Zeke's wrists. Zeke pulls at the restraints, but they don't budge. The soldier kicks him in the back of the knees, forcing him to buckle, and presses the barrel of a gun to his head. Zeke stops resisting, watching with wide eyes as the others fight.

Paul and Kat tag team another set of soldiers. Their blows do little to affect them, and within seconds, they're on their knees with the strange handcuffs around their wrists. The soldiers keep them kneeling with a tight grip.

Theo's the only one left fighting. Brooke hovers over Molly, crying into her shoulder, while James watches everything unfold in horror. Why isn't he fighting back?

Theo uses his telekinesis to smash a lamp over a soldier's head. He sways from the sudden impact but shakes it off quickly and continues on toward Theo. A pointed, triangle shaped shard of ceramic skids across the floor, landing directly in front of me. I grab it to use as a weapon if I can get to my feet. I try to push myself up, but it's as if a weight is holding me down. Even the smallest of movement drains the little energy I have left. All I can do is watch and pray Theo takes the soldiers out.

The soldier makes his way to Theo, striking him twice, once in the ribs, then across the jaw. Theo stumbles backward and bumps into another soldier who grabs his hands. Theo struggles against the soldier's grip, trying to break free, but the soldier forces him to his knees and locks his hands into the same type of handcuffs. Another soldier kicks Theo in the stomach. Theo hunches over with a groan, gasping for air.

The remaining two soldiers rush in on Brooke and James. They don't fight back and willingly allow the soldiers to cuff them. Six soldiers on six of my friends as they kneel, handcuffed, held down. Only the incapacitated, Molly and me, remain free.

Heels clinking against wood forces my attention toward the broken front door. Dr. Sheffield crosses the threshold in a navy skirt suit and nude pumps. She glances around at

388

each of my friends as they pant and sway, restrained and held at the mercy of soldiers. Her eyes rest upon me, a smug smile spreading across her lips.

"Amelia." She nods.

"How did you find us?" I growl.

"With a little help." She glances over her shoulder, out into the night. "Julian? How about you come say hello?"

The breath leaves my lungs at the mention of his name.

Julian steps forward next to Dr. Sheffield, standing tall, staring straight ahead and wearing all black. An emotionless, soulless killer. Reconditioned. Cuts and bruises still line his face, but he's freshly showered, and his face has been groomed to show off a bare chin.

"How did you get out?" Paul shouts.

The soldier rams the end of the gun to the back of Paul's head.

"Amelia let me go yesterday." He glances my way.

His eyes aren't void of emotion, and I can tell he's not reconditioned. He's fulfilling his mission. I'm a fool to have trusted him.

Theo's breathing hitches, and he bares his teeth. He tries to get up, but the soldier forces him back to his knees.

"If you're trying to use your ability on me, it won't work," Julian says. "Those are ability-blocking cuffs."

I force myself to stand, hiding the shard behind my back, and I sway from the dizziness. Julian steps forward, outstretching his arms to catch me, and I slap them away.

"I trusted you," I snap.

Julian's eyes lower to the floor, and he returns to Dr. Sheffield's side.

"Amelia, don't be so dramatic," Dr. Sheffield says. "Julian did what was right. Now, you're coming with me."

"I'm not going anywhere with you."

Dr. Sheffield reaches into her breast pocket and produces a syringe filled with an opaque liquid. "This is the booster. From the looks of Molly, she doesn't have much time left. I can give this to her right now to save her life. But I'll only do so if you come with me."

Theo shakes his head as if to tell me not to trust her.

I stand straighter and more defiantly. "I won't go."

"Very well." She points at the soldier holding Theo. "Shoot him."

The soldier's finger inches its way toward the trigger. Theo looks me directly in the eye and mouths "I love you." Theo's eyes close shut as the soldier's finger lands on the trigger.

"Wait!" I scream. Dr. Sheffield holds a hand up, and the soldier stops. I keep my face as serious as I can muster. "Give Molly the booster. Let my friends go, and I'll come with you."

"Your time for negotiation is well past due."

I only have a moment to think everything through. If I go with her, all she has to say is one word, and they'll all be dead. How am I to trust she won't have them killed the moment I agree? She doesn't care about their lives, but she does care about mine. I'm the one she wants alive. If my life hangs in the balance of saving my friends, how can she refuse but to let me have my way?

"If you kill them, I'll never go back with you."

"Or I can kill them anyway and drag you back. It will be easy. You're in no shape to fight. They will die. You will come back. It's no longer in your hands."

"But you're wrong." I put the ceramic shard against my throat, scraping my skin. "You want me alive."

Dr. Sheffield's eyes widen, and she steps forward.

In one quick move, I slice the side of my throat. Blood pours out of the wound and onto my shoulder.

"No!" Dr. Sheffield screams and rushes forward before I can finish the job.

I hold the pointed end of the shard toward her. "Don't come any closer."

"Okay." She holds up her hands. "I have to apply pressure before you lose too much blood."

"Or I can just bleed out, and you won't get me back."

Panic fills Dr. Sheffield's eyes. She looks at Molly, then back at me. "I'll give Molly the booster and let your friends go. Her words are calm, as if she's talking to a lunatic. "You have my word they won't be harmed."

I hold my free hand against the wound, applying pressure. Dizziness creeps in, and I push it away. "I can't trust you. Give it to her now. I need to make sure it works."

Dr. Sheffield goes to Molly's side and injects the liquid directly into the vein on the inside of her arm. Within seconds, Molly's quick, labored breathing steadies. The grayish color of her skin fades to normal, and her eyes flutter. The heart monitor beeps at a steady rate, and her vitals start returning to normal.

"See? It worked," Dr. Sheffield says. "She'll wake in about an hour."

"And the formula? James needs it to replicate."

She slowly produces another syringe from her pocket, filled with the same opaque liquid and sets it next to Molly. "He can analyze the liquid from this one."

Now it's my turn to make an impossible choice. I don't trust her, but if I stay and try to fight, we'll all die. But, if she keeps her word, and I go, I only risk my own life, but then I still lose them all.

It's not such an impossible decision. In my eyes, the choices are simple. Fight and everyone dies. Or go and only I might die.

The decision is simple. I must go.

"Let my friends go, and I'll come with you."

"No!" Theo screams, fighting against the restraints.

The soldier points the gun at his head again.

I hold up my hands and look Theo in the eyes. "I'll be okay. I promise." With my finger, I trace an X over my heart.

Theo stops fighting and slumps on his knees.

I look at Dr. Sheffield. "Let them go, and I promise I'll go with you."

I notice a glance between Julian and Dr. Sheffield a second too late. Dr. Sheffield draws herself up to full height, which, in her heels, is almost taller than the soldiers. "Code yellow."

Julian removes a small device from his pocket and presses down on the red button. All six of my friends slump forward to the ground.

"No!" I scream. I rush toward my friends, but Julian's hands wrap around my torso, pulling me back. I claw and kick, but my weakened state doesn't do any damage, and I watch my friends recede as I'm dragged out of the house and thrown into the back of an SUV.

41. Return to NOEL

Julian holds me down in the back of the car, binding my hands and feet with rope.

"What did you do to them?" I yell over his shoulder to Dr. Sheffield.

"The cuffs injected them with a minor sedative. They'll wake in an hour. I couldn't risk letting them go and attacking me."

"You gave me your word."

"And I'm keeping it by letting them live. Now hold still, so I can tend to your wound."

Julian holds me in place as Dr. Sheffield cleans and stitches up the gash on my neck. I hate her hands on me, but I hold still enough to let her work.

All I can imagine is Theo's face and determination when he wakes up.

"They'll come for me."

"Then, they will be killed on sight."

"Which is why you have to let me warn them. Let me write a letter to tell them not to come for me. Please?"

Dr. Sheffield nods at Julian, and he removes a pen and notebook from his pants pocket. "What do you want me to write?"

I shake my head. "It has to be in my handwriting. Otherwise, they won't believe it."

Dr. Sheffield finishes the last stitch and places a bandage over my neck. She nods to Julian.

He removes the rope from my hands and gives me the pen and notepad.

I know things didn't go according to plan, but you're alive and now you have the booster to create more. Now no one has to die. Don't come for me. I'll be okay. If you come, you'll be killed, and my sacrifice would be for nothing. I'm sorry I didn't have the chance to say goodbye. Be well and be safe.

Amelia

I hand the notebook and pen back to Julian without meeting his gaze. He rebinds my hands behind my back with rope before tearing the sheet out of the notebook and folding it in half.

"I'll leave this inside where they can find it," Julian says as he returns to the house.

A moment later, he sits in the driver's seat, and Dr. Sheffield sits in the passenger seat. One of the reconditioned soldiers sits next to me in the back, while the others gather in a different SUV. The engine turns over, and I watch the house recede as we pull away.

I use the ride to the airport to reflect. How is it I went from plain Jane from Bridgeport to enhanced Amelia from NOEL in a matter of weeks?

I spent my entire life wishing to escape for a normal life, only to have a normal life wishing to escape for adventure.

If I knew this was the adventure that was waiting for me, I would have wished differently.

The SUV turns onto a road leading to an airfield with a private jet. Julian escorts me inside the jet, leading me to the front seat. He reties my hands to the armrests and sits in the seat next to me. Dr. Sheffield sits in the back row, a guard to her side and another in front of her.

Engines roar to life, and I realize I've never flown before. My hand yanks at the restraint as my instinct to rub my scar takes over, but I won't get the comfort I need. My breathing hitches, and Julian places his hand on top of mine.

"Don't fucking touch me," I growl, and he recoils.

My body presses against the seat as the jet jolts forward. I can feel the ascent, and my knuckles turn white from clutching the armrests. Finally, the jet levels out, and it feels as if we're not moving at all. I look out the window and see the tiny lit town below. If I were under different circumstances, I might actually enjoy it.

"Please let me explain," Julian whispers.

"What is there to explain? I trusted you, and you, once again, betrayed me. Fool me twice, shame on me. Right?"

Julian glances behind him. I follow his gaze to Dr. Sheffield, who is staring out the window. Julian turns back to me. "I didn't betray you."

I scoff and roll my eyes. "You brought the enemy to my doorstep."

"To save you."

I glare at him. "Did it ever occur to you I didn't want to be saved? I was willing to die when I escaped, and I was willing to die, as long as I never had to go back to NOEL.

Yet, here we are. On our way back to the place I hate the most."

"I'm sorry," he murmurs. "But I couldn't lose you."

"You lost me the moment you told her where I was."

Julian is silent for the rest of the plane ride.

***

Three-and-a-half hours later, we land at a private airport. When we exit the jet, there are two black SUVs waiting. Five soldiers jump into one while the rest of us enter the other.

"I know it's late, but we have a lot to discuss once we return," Dr. Sheffield says to me.

It's a short fifteen-minute ride to NOEL headquarters. Once we turn off the main road and onto a road hidden by woods, it's a straight shot until we reach the tall stone wall, a barrier to keep the outside world out and everyone else in. It looks exactly like my memory.

The barrier opens onto a path leading to the inside grounds. In the distance stands the building where I spent my life being manipulated, controlled, and experimented on.

We drive down the long path until we reach the guarded front doors. Julian unties my feet so I can walk and escorts me inside the building. The front entrance looks like a main lobby that splits into three wings—one straight ahead and one on either side.

"Please escort Mr. Thomas to room fourteen east."

Dr. Sheffield instructs the soldier, and they head on their way. She turns to another soldier. "Let the chief know we're back and Julian is ready for him."

The chief? But I thought Dr. Sheffield ran NOEL. Who is the chief and what does he want with Julian?

The soldier gives a curt nod, then proceeds in the opposite direction, leaving me alone with her. "Come, follow me." She walks straight, and I follow.

We walk down the hallway until we arrive at an elevator. Dr. Sheffield inserts a keycard then presses the Call button. As we wait, I look around and the blueprints flash in my mind.

Julian went to the east wing, the soldier to the west wing, and we're at the elevator that leads beyond to the north wing.

The elevator dings, and the doors slide open. We enter, and Dr. Sheffield inserts the keycard once again and presses the button labeled 5N. I note the nine other buttons. One through five by themselves, and one through five but with an N. After reading the blueprints, I assume the N stands for north.

The doors close, and the elevator ascends. It doesn't surprise me there's a lack of elevator music, but it makes the ride up eerily awkward.

Behind us, the doors open to a long hallway. Each door we pass, I hope to get a glance at what's inside, but they're all steel doors with a metal plate engraved with numbers, just like the one from the memory when I escaped. I wonder if there are people behind these doors receiving the memory wipe and being reconditioned just as they tried to do to me. I don't dare ask this soon. In time, I will find out.

We reach the end of the hallway, and Dr. Sheffield uses her keycard once again to open the wooden door. She gestures me inside, and the lights turn on without the flick of a switch. A mahogany desk sits in the center of the room with two chairs in front. Three bookshelves line one wall, and windows line the other, displaying a view of the grounds behind the building. From here, I can see how far the barrier wall extends. It seems to go on for miles with endless woods behind that.

"Please, have a seat," she instructs. She sits across from me and folds her hands, resting them on the desk.

"Are you going to keep me tied up the entire time I'm here?" I ask.

"That depends on your cooperation."

"So, I'm a prisoner?"

"I don't wish to keep you this way, but you didn't leave me with many options."

"Says the person who injected me with the memory wipe that's killing me."

Dr. Sheffield adjusts in her seat. "That wasn't my intention. Your reaction to the memory wipe is different from everyone else's."

"So I've been told. Right now, I should be a soulless monster, right?" I raise an eyebrow.

"Interesting choice of words. But, no. I gave you the memory wipe to save you."

"From what?"

"You were dying before you escaped. The memory wipe was my attempt to slow it down enough until I could find a cure."

I blink. How could I have been dying before? No, she must be wrong. James had been very clear that this was because of the memory wipe. Unless he was wrong.

"Did you find a cure?"

"Possibly. It's all in theory. I won't know if it will work until I try."

"You're going to experiment on me again? Great." I roll my eyes.

"This could save your life."

"Or end it."

"What do you have to lose at this point? You're already dying. Why not let me try?"

"What do I get out of it?"

Dr. Sheffield shoots me a pointed glare. She taps her pen calmly on the desk. "You'll survive."

She says it as if she's doing me a favor.

"I thought I made it pretty clear that I don't care about surviving."

She glances at her hands as if she hopes to find patience in them. "I won't pursue your friends as long as you let me try."

I know better than to trust her completely, but she gave Molly the booster and let my friends live. If I don't let her try, I'll die anyway, and I won't be able to protect them.

"Fine. I'll let you try."

Dr. Sheffield leads us back into the hall and onto the elevator. She presses the button for the second floor. I know there's a chance I might not survive whatever procedure she plans on doing to me, and I can't let my last words to Theo be in a letter. Even though I know it might kill me, I try to connect to his mind.

Theo?

Amelia? Are you okay?

I'm fine. But I don't have long.

Pressure forms behind my eyes, and I breathe through it, hoping I can withstand it long enough to finish my message.

I meant what I said in the letter. Don't come for me. You'll be killed. As long as you stay away, you're all free. They won't come for you. Once Dr. Sheffield saves me, I'll reach out. I'll gather as much information as I can on the inside and relay it to you. From there, we can form a plan to fight back and take them down once and for all.

Pressure builds to a burning sensation throughout my head. Blood drips onto the front of my shirt. Black dots seep in my vision, and I know I only have seconds.

Theo, I love you.

The burn intensifies, as if my hair is on fire.

I love you, Amelia.

The world around me spins in my vision. I try to brace onto the elevator wall, but I tumble downward, and the world goes dark.

Acknowledgments

Writing NOEL Forgotten has been an adventure from the start. It took two years to get to this point, but I finally did it. NOEL Forgotten was a small idea I had for a book when I was in my early twenties. It wasn't until my early thirties I decided to put that idea on paper. And now that it's officially published, I have many people to thank.

My son, Owen, you may not realize you helped at all, but fulfilling my dreams of becoming an author is because of you, and the reason I dedicated my first book to you.

My parents, Lisa and Kevin, thank you for always supporting me through all the ridiculous ideas I've had growing up. You taught me to dream big and never give up. And an extra thank you to my mom for being one of my beta readers and finding all the plot holes I missed. Your feedback and suggestions helped transform my book into a better story.

Thank you to my siblings, KJ, Sarah, and Andrew, for always being hard on me. Your "tough love" made me strong and gave me the courage to write. Even if it's not a success, I have the backbone to be okay with that. Plus, you three have always been my biggest supporters and push me to do better.

To Lindsay Connolly, my best friend and biggest cheerleader throughout this entire process. You were there from the first day I started writing and never left my side. Thank you for the long hours you spent listening to me as I figured out the details, the plot, and the characters. Your positivity and encouragement gave me motivation to keep going.

This book wouldn't be anything without the early feedback from my beta readers: Stephanie Martin, Cheryl Eisbrenner, Donna Olzak, and Lisa Hanson. The four of you read that first draft and told me it was good, which was the encouragement I needed to hear to continue with the process.

Feedback and encouragement aren't enough to put a worthy piece of literature into the world. Because of that, I have to thank my editors for their expertise. Thank you to my developmental editor, Dana Boyer, for finding all the issues in my story and giving me ways to fix it. Because of you, I am a better writer. Thank you to Samantha Pico for the copy/line edits and interior formatting. The way you transformed my sentences left me speechless. My book was good before it fell into your hands, but now it's magnificent.

I am completely awe-stricken by the love and support I received during this journey. It takes a village, and I'm so happy you are all part of my team.

About The Author

Nicole Y Hanson is the debut author of NOEL Forgotten and proud owner of White Door Press. Nicole lives in Hazel Park, Michigan with her son and adorable tri-colored Aussie. She developed a passion for writing as a teenager and pursued that passion as an adult. Her love has always been for the romance genre, but she also enjoys the mysterious and impossible elements of science fiction. Nicole writes in her spare time while working full time as a purchasing administrator and attending college to earn a bachelor's degree. Aside from her busy schedule, Nicole likes to spend time with her family, play board games, and dabble in escape rooms and murder mystery games.

You can learn more about Nicole at
www.nicoleyhanson.com
tiktok.com/@nicolehansonauthor
instagram.com/nicoleyhanson
facebook.com/nicoleyhansonwrites